W9-BIL-573

The Goss Women

Other fiction by R. V. Cassill

DOCTOR COBB'S GAME

LA VIE PASSIONNEE OF RODNEY BUCKTHORNE

THE HAPPY MARRIAGE AND OTHER STORIES

THE FATHER AND OTHER STORIES

THE PRESIDENT

PRETTY LESLIE

CLEM ANDERSON

XV X III

THE EAGLE ON THE COIN

The Goss Women

R. V. Cassill

Doubleday & Company, Inc.
Garden City, New York

1974

Grateful acknowledgment is given for
permission to reprint the following:

Three lines from "Turning" which
appeared in Reiner Maria Rilke's *Selected
Works,* Vol. 2, Poetry Copyright ©
Hogarth Press Ltd., 1960. All rights reserved.
Reprinted by permission of New Directions
Publishing Corporation.

Two lines from "The Man with the Blue
Guitar" Copyright 1936 by Wallace
Stevens and renewed 1964 by Elsie Stevens
and Holly Stevens from The Collected
Poems of Wallace Stevens. Reprinted by
permission of Alfred A. Knopf, Inc.

ISBN: 0-385-07553-7
Library of Congress Catalog Card Number
73–83619
Copyright © 1974 by R. V. Cassill
All Rights Reserved
Printed in the United States of America
First Edition

for Kathie, Vera and Kay
and certain others. . . .

Contents

Book I	The girls in the garden	1
Book II	Collision	81
Book III	Flight	147
Book IV	Trial	345
Book V	Mortality	403

Work of sight is achieved,
now for some heart-work
on all those pictures, those prisoned creatures within you!

Turning by R. M. Rilke

. . . the experience of beauty is a product of *the sense of im-
minent instinctual danger controlled down to the finest hairline*
. . . the problem of beauty is to *endure* it, rather than to
understand it.

Art and Mythology: A General Theory
George Devereux

The Goss Women

Book I

The girls in the garden

Chapter 1

"Ordinary things show up in extraordinary dimensions when one lives this close to an artist of Goss's stature," Susan Vail would write. "I can't explain to you how this happens." In this letter to her agent she did not even explain the episode that prompted her remark. Perhaps her agent would not have thought it was as "ordinary" as she insisted.

She had been on her way between the tennis court and the rose garden of the Trebbel estate. She had just lost a set to Fiona Trebbel. At the older woman's suggestion they had ambled down toward the rose garden to look for Goss, who was painting there this afternoon. When the two of them turned past the hedge into the garden, Susan saw the girls posing. In this environment that should have passed as an ordinary spectacle. But something played a trick on Susan's eyes.

Caught without warning or a chance to blink, her gaze identified the nakedness of the three girls as part of a fable. They looked like figures escaped from a museum to the freedom of this ocean light and a natural setting among roses and white urns. They didn't look human, she would remember when she gathered her wits. In their immobile pose she saw colors like fired enamel, not girlish skin. The hedge behind them was green as the depths of an imaginary sea.

A sudden, singing thrill of terror passed through her, like the vibration of a fiddle string in her blood. A purely instinctive alarm. Her foot was momentarily frozen in place as if her flesh knew before she did that she was trespassing. For that first instant of surprise, intuition warned her she had come upon the enactment of a legend that was supposed to have been screened from mortal eyes for thousands of years.

A legend of dangerously naked immortals who wake a sleeping boy to demand from him an impossible judgment of their beauty. . . .

And then—because the girl in the center of this voluptuous composition was her daughter Tamisan—Susan's breath popped in a small explosion of laughter. The panic of surprise at seeing Tamisan's breasts, belly and quaint pale shape of pubic hair exposed in this fabulous transformation gave way quickly to a milder anxiety. Susan was simply afraid she would say or do something awkward before she was fully recovered from her confusion.

Beside her Fiona Trebbel said, "I thought you'd been told. Jason arranged for his father to paint them here this afternoon." Apparently Susan's face and sudden halt had communicated her consternation to the older woman, and there was no neat way to disclaim it. So Susan merely shook her head and grinned as gamely as she had when Fiona beat her at tennis.

"She's more beautiful than I'd realized," Fiona said. In her slow, pondering voice Susan heard some echo of the dread that had flashed to her own unguarded consciousness. As if a lifetime among artists had taught Fiona to be wary of any excess of beauty; as if the revelation here in the garden of her Long Island estate might be a glimpse of fate.

Then, both dangling the rackets they had carried from their game on the courts beyond the mansion, the women went down together into the garden, among the younger artists of the neighborhood who were painting with Dean Goss this afternoon.

Bern Whitestar and Miriam Barnstone were the only two of the artists, besides Dean Goss himself, whom Susan recognized among those at work here and there around the posing girls. Bern and Miriam were seated comfortably cross-legged in the grass with sketchbooks open on their knees. Across the garden a melon-shaped man with his hair in a pigtail was attacking a small canvas set on a light easel. A black man with a Van Gogh straw hat was on his knees over a prostrate drawing board, backgrounded by one of Fiona's finest rosebushes. The sheer intentness of concentration on their work admonished Susan to keep the poise of Tamisan's Mama come to approve classroom activities in which her child was participating. How many of these nine or ten toilers bowed over their work had their tongues stuck out between their teeth like kindergarteners?

With towels of red, cinnamon and cerulean dropped at their feet, Jean Simons and Janis Ward stood on either side of Tamisan in a languor amounting almost to boredom. Neither of the others had a stitch or a ribbon more to cover her nakedness than Tamisan. Their elbows and pert buttocks were as sharply silhouetted against the roses and greenery and twinkles of sand through the dark green hedge as Tamisan's. Why did her daughter look so naked when the other two merely looked as if they had no clothes on?

She's *doing something* the other two aren't, Susan's anxiety hissed.

. . . but the blessed child was making no motion that even suggested conscious awareness. She stood there jutting her veal-colored nipples, wrapped around the loins with an untanned girdle of delicious white, dangling her arms like unbaited fishing lines. She gave no sign she had been aware of her mother's arrival with Fiona. Still . . . she projected the look of someone being looked at. There was defiance and sly mockery in the very lines and colors of her body, whether she twitched them or not.

So when Jason Goss came over, stepping delicately and courteously among the sketchers, Susan said, "I'm glad she's your responsibility, friend, not mine." She was still grinning, to show the facetiousness of her remark. Yet Jason took it seriously.

"We looked for you, Susan. I told Tamisan she mustn't unless you thought it was all right."

"I was playing tennis with Fiona."

"I didn't think to look for you on the court," he said with that sweet, deferential note of concern that was his specialty—another slightly false note in these bizarre circumstances, Susan thought.

But she was determined to play her role smoothly. She put

a nonchalant arm around Jason's shoulders. "Heavens. Tamisan hasn't asked for permission for anything at all since puberty. Why now? Oh, it's lovely, Jason. A garden's lovelier with naked girls. Why not show it off if you've got it?" Her words were facile enough to suit her, but even she heard the faintly hysterical pitch of her voice and Jason, who had a musician's ear, paid more attention to tone than the sense of her protest. "Jason, just tell me honestly whose harebrained notion it was and I'll settle down to enjoy it too. I'll bring out my Crayolas and pitch in with the gang."

Jason would never lie to her. But he could be slippery to soothe her feelings. So instead of explaining first the presence of the outsiders he said, "I've known since last winter I truly wanted a painting of her by my father. Just as she is now. She looks like the whole summer, doesn't she?"

Ah yes . . . Tamisan's skin shimmered like the blaze of July on fields whitening for harvest. No honest eye could deny that much, but . . .

He tossed his own fair head blithely and went on, "Well, it's a freak idea, but we don't have to take it seriously. I don't think Dad is. He hasn't painted much in watercolor since he was a young man, and he's doing it now for a busman's holiday. I think Janis may have thought of it first. Then I picked up the idea. Seemed like fun. It's my fault and . . ."

In the midst of his cajolery, Susan at last took a good look across the greensward at the old painter.

Dean Goss didn't look like a man making a joke. He didn't look like a man at all to her sun-struck eyes, which went right on with their mischievous teasing of her literal mind. Just as the posing girls had first flashed on her vision as strangers, not quite human, the old giant seemed to be here in disguise. Like a bull or a lion, she thought, who's rented himself a human skin for the occasion, so he can pass as one of us. As if he had always fooled her before when she had watched him in his studio or at the mansion, but could not fool her here in the light that crackled back and forth between ocean and sky. "Your father looks pretty animated for a man on holiday," she murmured to Jason. And that comment also merely approximated the truth that came sizzling into her eyes. The animation of the painter was not visible at first in gymnastic flourishes with his brush. She saw him lolling at ease in his white canvas chair while his eyes held on the posing girls, but again she was reminded of the almost careless slouch of a great animal stalking. She shivered and said, "But it looks like he's having fun."

Susan was a guest on the estate this summer because she was working on a book about Dean Goss. She was the observer, the note taker, the mouse in the corner of Dean Goss's present life, she kept telling herself, and it should be part of her role to keep the record of this happening along with all the other protean aspects he chose to let her glimpse. It was untidily unprofessional to let herself be distracted by worries about Tamisan's exposure.

There sat the master, at the blue edge of shadow cast by his studio wall. His watercolor easel was poised on spidery legs in the grass before him, looking like a cute little antique piano, its varnish sparkling. He was wearing unusually gaudy Bermuda shorts and dirty sneakers. His sunburned arms and close-cropped head twitched busily and almost menacingly as he painted. A pair of steel-rimmed spectacles perched on his nose. The famous roan-colored beard—part of his projected image for forty years—jabbed and stabbed the air with electric fervor.

His left hand, holding a fat watercolor brush, scraped down from top to bottom of his paper as if he were shaving an enormous soap bubble. How sexy that combination of muscular strength and infinite care! At the end of each majestic stroke he leaped in his chair with such pure and childish delight at what he had done that any Mama would be stirred to pat his head and tell him what a creative boy he was. . . . How touching the combination of authority and naïveté!

Jason said, "I didn't think it out sufficiently, Susan. I don't suppose it truly was ever a *plan*. It was a notion that snowballed. Janis Ward and Tamisan and I were in a bar near Southampton last night and met Bern Whitestar with some of his friends. So! By that time we were tickled by the possibility.

Bern said he'd like to get in on it. This morning after I got Dad to agree, I called some of the others."

"Fine," Susan said. "Your father will make something extraordinary out of it."

"He always does," Jason agreed. "I'm glad you don't mind too much."

"I'm"—Susan shivered—"I'm sure it's the sincerest form of flattery for Tamisan."

Young Jason's eyes were as guileless as the afternoon sky. "Only, now that it's happening, I wish the others weren't here painting and posing—so there'd be nobody but our girl in his picture." He was concerned and reasonable and meant only what he said. Why then, for just an enormous fraction of a second, should Susan think he was referring to some invisible *others*—antique demons and satyrs spying from amid the roses and leafy shrubs? *Others* who snickered goatishly as they watched?

Later Susan would suppose she had been jolted to find her daughter posing so casually right out in the open because it seemed to put a strain on Fiona's tolerance and hospitality. To be sure, Fiona as well as Dean Goss knew that Tamisan and Jason had been sleeping together since last winter. Fiona knew that for the past several weeks of summer the kids had been roaming the whole country in the green Toyota Jason bought for their adventuring. "I rejoice that they feel so footloose," Fiona said.

When the Toyota with eight thousand recent miles clocked on its speedometer rolled into the drive of the Trebbel estate (called North Atlantic) five days before, Fiona was calmly pleased that the birds had come home to roost for a while before they flew off again. Nevertheless, knowing that they were on their way here, she had put another bed in Susan's room in the guesthouse. For Tamisan. Of course Fiona had not blinked an eye when this courteous preparation was ignored and Tamisan went to sleep each night with Jason in his room in the mansion. Fiona was not a blinker. Susan thought the dear woman would be drawn and quartered before she admitted the slightest prudishness, except in her own conduct.

Susan had heard her ask what Jason and Tamisan had done in their wandering around the various states as far west as Montana.

"Druid things," Tamisan said.

"I see!" Fiona said, cocking her head in expectation of more enlightenment. When no other specifics were forthcoming, she said, "Druid things! How nice"—as if she had been satisfactorily answered.

But Tamisan's freaky dismissal of the older woman's interest had sounded intentionally offensive to Susan. Had sounded, as a matter of fact, as if Tamisan meant to imply indecent exposures on the Mississippi, lewdness on the shores of the Great Lakes, orgasms fired like rockets against the bastions of the Republic. If there was to be an American Revolution, Tamisan might be counted among the first to fuck for it.

Susan was convinced as well that it had been Tamisan, not Jason, who asked Janis Ward to visit them here. Of course Fiona had welcomed Janis too—"I understand you are one of Tamisan's teachers at Hunter, Mrs. Ward. So important for teachers to be *friends* with their students . . ." Though Susan did not much like Janis, she had no precise grounds for criticism (except that her breasts tended to dangle infirmly, as she noted now).

Yet these tokens of discord had grated on Susan since her daughter showed up, marring her contentment with her own position in the household. In late May she had been invited to spend the whole summer at North Atlantic, if she wished, while she worked on her book about Dean Goss. She was to have a room in the guesthouse. She had access to the Goss archives and the collection of his paintings in the mansion. She spent some part of nearly every day with the painter in his studio. She kept a flow of her dialogues with him going into one or another of her color-coded notebooks. And the weeks had thus far flowed on in sparkling calm.

When asked how her book about the artist was progressing, she said, "Just fine." When asked what aspect of his life or work she was going to focus on she said, "I don't know yet." For once in her hectic life as a writer, she was in no hurry to shape up her material and hurry it to market.

"I keep my head down," she confided to her friendly editor, Hal Robinson. "No one imagines I'm his intellectual equal, so I try to be Goss's favorite jester. Dream interpreter. Fortune-teller. Each time I go to the studio I take him a goody from the *I Ching*. The other morning it was 'Bring news of danger to the king.' He said—ho-ho—that, lacking talent, he needed a bit of danger to keep him in working trim."

She had, she told herself, been prepared for the life at North Atlantic by her forty-one years of barely interrupted disappointments and crises. The servants here seemed like the servants of a good cause. Goss and his patroness Fiona Trebbel were the "working rich" as distinct from the idle or debauched rich and the crooked rich, whom she would have had to despise on political principle. The company that came in the hope or expectation of a visit with Goss was mostly good company. Even the few Susan didn't like had nicer complexions and thinner ankles on these enchanting premises. When the unpredictable old painter holed up in his studio or sneaked away to sail or swim without a word for the admirers who had come hoping to see him, she helped entertain the sort of people who were as good for her soul as for her ego. It was even a bit miraculous how much she liked herself amid the people she liked this summer. For the summer she had even suspended her perpetual and well-grounded worries about Tamisan.

The situation had been, thus far, idyllic—and it was Susan's nature to suspect that all perfection is fragile. "Good luck scares me," she had blurted to Fiona earlier this afternoon when good luck had put her two games ahead in their tennis match. And then she had gone on to lose. Fiona had no malice whatever. She collected points methodically, evenly, without haste, as habitual winners do. Fiona, who measured everyone around her with such placid strictness, would hardly fail to register the false pretenses involved in Tamisan's display. She'll know, Susan thought, how brazen it is for Tamisan to show off the goods in front of Jason's father.

She heard the melancholy exhalation of Jason's breath, almost a sigh. She saw he was squinting through narrowed eyes, as painters do to resolve a scene to its fundamentals. "It's a moment that shouldn't end," he said.

"It's already a work of art," she agreed, squinting herself, hearing the faint grind of her back molars. "Why bother to paint it?"

"Yes! It's all here, isn't it? Nothing *has* to come afterward. All complete!"

In this shorthand definition of beauty, Susan heard his father speaking through him. They were so much alike in spite of appearances, the burly old man and the rather fragile boy, young enough to be his grandson. And there was some comfort, also, in supposing that Dean Goss was taking the same positive pleasure in what now came to his eye.

They shared an uncanny shrewdness of perception. Yet Jason's knowing gaze was tempered by love and an evidently endless charity.

Her only child stood naked to Dean Goss's eye, a human and female shape of no more erotic interest to him than the shapes he was putting on his watercolor paper. Probably less. But—she couldn't help thinking—what he sees when he looks up at us is *everything*.

In Tamisan's case that was just too damn much.

from Susan Vail's red notebook:

Tamisan was still a cute, crooked twelve-year-old when she announced "I want to become a legend." There was no reason I should take that as an ominous prophecy. Until proved wrong I was entitled to think she had in mind something in the style of the legendary Maggie Goss, Jason's mother—whose loving memory seems to color all Goss attitudes and conversation. One of the queens who died young and fair . . . Hence deathless.

At thirteen Tamisan took the fancy that she and I were "adventuresses." Becky Sharp and her sharpie mother, I suppose.

That merged over into her conviction that we were some of the "beautiful people"—belonging to a bargain-counter jet set. I lived with lovers instead of husbands. We tootled around the poverty fringes of the Mediterranean. Morocco. Ibiza. And one grim year in an Irish bog while I wrote the novel that paid for straightening her teeth and sending her off to get deflowered at a high-priced girls' school. Ergo, we were beautiful people, in her wishful accounting. "We are the working poor," I told her. She seemed to believe this was merely our disguise, our *cover,* as they say in intelligence circles. She has her father's beauty and his gambler's disregard for the laws of probability.

Which is now and then lucky for me. If she hadn't turned up in Jason's bed, there would have been no introduction for me to Dean Goss. Etc., etc. Once again my errant girl, the mistake of my youth, turns out to be my pioneer sent into the big world.

Until she was sixteen I thought I understood (with pain) why boys in her school never seemed to be much interested in her. I believed it was because of her size—Tamisan is taller than Hersh; she could break Billy over her knee; the teeter-totter didn't work out well between her and Patrick; with her longer legs she is able to torment him with jolts that snap his head back and forth until he sasses her and runs off from the threat of her fist.

Ah, vain illusion. Like so many other maternal illusions bitterly abandoned. It was because her endowments caught the eyes of older men.

Which endowments? Not those we propagandized for in *Calendar* magazine. Something far less scrutable to Mama's eye than boobs and butt. Some disposition rarer than the fact she began to menstruate at eleven. Not her physical self, then, but perhaps an attitude toward her physical self that signals *en clair* to lechers beyond their thirty-fifth year, though men are deaf to it before. An attitude toward her (admittedly) abnormally long nipples? "Mama, they are like the wolf that fed us."

Embarrassment. "I suppose they are like sucking a real prick."
(I gleaned this from eavesdropping on a phone conversation
with Debbie Holland. Vanity?)

She *wants* to be honest. Hell, she thirsts and gasps for honesty, as her Mama did before her. It is plainly the clear honesty
in Jason that has her anchored now in love. But . . .

If she were only body, no problem. If she were a bodiless
spirit or intelligence, no problem either. It is the incongruity
of the two that has plagued her into self-deception and deceit
that tormented me again and again and again and . . . Like
that ghastly time when I questioned her to find out if she and
Bob F, with whom I was living then, had ever . . . Well, of
course they hadn't, actually. But it took Bob's involuntary testimony as well as his angered protestations to make me sure.
Then it was even worse to feel that Tamisan had deliberately
laid a trail and a trap of doubts for me to stumble into.

"Mama Dear, I've mastered the politics of the easy lay. Leave
me alone or I'll end up a mental case."

I don't even remember for sure how old she was when she
made this declaration of independence. It was after her first
year in school in New Hampshire. After I had concluded that
her defloration had been accomplished and endorsed by the
male faculty there. Mama Dear chose not to be shocked. You
think I'll weep, no, I'll not weep. This heart shall crack into a
hundred thousand flaws or ere I'll weep. Etc. Etc.

from Susan Vail's green notebook:

DEAN GOSS: For art, intoxication and sobriety are both required;
for serious work, both at the same time.

DEAN GOSS: One form persuades another to come out of the
woods and show itself. Some are so wild and secret by nature
it's almost sacrilege to lure them into the open.

DEAN GOSS (to Vincent Costello): Paint the face! Don't neglect
the face—but make it the face of the body. Its true character
comes into it from the body.

13

from Susan Vail's red notebook:

"Every canvas of mine is a gambling table," Dean Goss said the first time I drove out from New York to his studio at North Atlantic to offer myself. "I can't win much when I don't take chances. I might lose everything if I got stupid."

In the middle of the painting on his easel that day there was the lumped-in figure of a woman. In sanguine. Below her there was a straight line of little fishes. Scarlet. Swimming in what might be called the sky was a whale that was bigger than all of them though it took up fewer square inches on the canvas.

The good old flirt offered to let me paint on it if I saw something he had neglected. I declined.

"So," he said, "if you mean to do another book about me, I hope you will take it on as a gamble. There may not be anything left to write about me. Only a little something at the end. Make a little book that goes for the jugular," he recommended, adding another of the little fish at the bottom of his picture. "Who would the book be for? For the ladies? For students? You didn't tell me who was your publisher." (I had told him. He forgets things with the selectivity of genius.)

"For you," I said.

"For me? Hmmmmm. Well . . . For *me,* yes," he said. He glowered cheerily as if he knew very well that all three of his sons—Godwin, Vidal and even Jason—had advised me separately to approach him through his vanity. (None of them had put it in *quite* those words.) "Another book would certainly give me a parting look at myself." (They warned me he was apt to go melancholy about his lonely old age.) "That would certainly be useful to me."

His gaze drifts away and returns with startling speed. He comes at you like a shark on the verge of retirement, indolently rolling to bite. You don't see the agitation in the water until suddenly you see the rows of teeth in close perspective. You don't feel the bite until you see blood in the water which is probably yours. You note how Dean Goss's trademark steel-rimmed spectacles glitter before you know he has seen right through you and is inwardly laughing and crying at what he saw.

He offered again to let me take up one of his many paint-brushes. This time I added a yummy dab of pink paint where it didn't seem to hurt anything.

The next time I saw him, he told me he had destroyed that particular canvas. So my labor was lost. "I destroy lots," he said. "You can't win all the time."

But he agreed to let me hang around and do the book because I am the mother of Jason's girl. "Marvelous girl," D.G. says of Tamisan, making her sound like an educational experience that befits Jason more than college would. "Just what Jason needed."

As Tamisan never ceases to remind me, everything in the art world and publishing is done through connections. Personal contacts. She hooked a last chance for me to redeem myself from *Calendar* and the lady readers by bringing Jason to bed. He arranged for interviews with his brothers Godwin and Vidal as well as with Dean Goss. Then, when I had the nod from all of them, the publisher almost ditched me.

A heart surgeon, an astronaut, the richest man in the world, the alleged mistress of Dwight David Eisenhower . . . "If you're going into non-fiction, why not someone like Howard Hughes, darling?" said Hal Robinson in March. Hal has been not only my editor but my brotherly supporter at Finley, Schreiber, and McGrew since they did my first novel fifteen years ago. Bless his good intentions, he has fluttered the nice reviews of my novels vigorously around the town, trying to smuggle me over among Established Authors. He wangled me my job at *Calendar* magazine, at which I am all too good and clever.

"What's left in Goss for you, Susan?" Hal said that day at lunch. I was not an art critic. I said that Dean Goss even trusted me to work on one of his canvases. Hal ignored that. He said there were already enough Goss books in print. The

Retrospective Catalogue of 1961 and *The Body's Eye,* which the old boy had written himself in collaboration with his wife and Fiona Trebbel, were still selling moderately in quality paperback. There was the Haupt-Eisinger biography for scholars. New monographs were in preparation at Yale and the U. of Chicago presses. Hal said, "I know the way you work too well to think you want to rehash the old art wars and sensations where Goss figured twenty, thirty, even forty years ago."

I thought he was trying to bait me into going for the jugular with melodrama. I played my next card by reminding him how much of that there had been over the years. The painter burns off his hand for the sake of a crazy mistress. Marries the teen-age daughter of actor Gregory Niles after the outraged parent pursues them from Paris to Athens. Cohabits with a rich, eccentric old maid in a gaudy Long Island mansion. . . . Forgive me, all you fine, serious, precious real people!

No dice. Hal had been programed for squashing my idea before they let him out of the morning editorial meeting to come and feed me. "You *could* work Goss up as the mad artist," he agreed, "but that's not your best vein. Anyway, the sensations would have been topical twenty years ago, not now. Goss has been good too long. He's been taken up into the heavens." If I had a compulsion to write about artists in spite of my ignorance of them, couldn't I at least infiltrate Andy Warhol, Roy Lichtenstein or Simon Polva?

I said I had never heard of Simon Polva—a lame argument, since Hal's business as editor is to know what bandwagons are being gilded and hitched up for next year's parade. America will hear of Simon Polva, but not from me.

The trouble was, I had made the proposal without figuring a good selling angle. As Hal saw it, I should be too professional by this time to start from only the circumstance that my daughter had made friends with Dean Goss's son. From there—thinking he had successfully aborted my book—he demanded that I have another drink and tell him all about Tamisan.

Being out of sorts from silly opposition, I said, "Well, at least she has stopped fucking older men because of Jason Goss."

That shook poor Hal. He's been in New York twice as long as I. If there's any perversion, vice or corrupt combination of dong and twat he hasn't heard of and learned to take for granted, it's hard for me to imagine. But with all that, he is sentimental about my sentimentalities. He cares about me and mine. Patting his lips with a napkin, he took my hand and murmured, "Susan, you mustn't bad-mouth her. You don't need to say things like that . . . not to Hal."

I began to cry—from nerves and pure exasperation, nothing else—nothing else unless it was pure relief that what I'd said about Tamisan was the hard kernel of truth. She had been constant and really in love almost since she turned nineteen. For three good months now.

I said, "Jason Goss is a *Wunderkind* and wise and subtle beyond his years. Talking to him is what convinced me I could do a real book about his father, and you have to give me three thousand dollars' advance on the book, which you know to be only chicken feed, so make it five thousand, because I've got to have the summer off from doing *Calendar* pieces or lose the few brains I have left. Hal, save my life. . . ."

Right on, Susan. The best bargaining tactic for a woman in business is to fly to pieces right in their faces.

It worked. I do not overwhelm. Never have. But when I'm in earnest I can always get a foot in the door. On the spot, before my cheeks were dry, I had Prince Hal's personal commitment that Finley, Schreiber, and McGrew would pop. "Four thousand," Hal said. I must remember I still owed them part of an unearned advance on each of my novels. I must remember that Hal would have to persuade Alvin McGrew himself that my irrational whim was not an irrational whim. Why should Alvin McGrew care that my life was a bore and Tamisan a worry for which I deserved workman's compensation?

Tamisan thought I should have held out for five. "You always settle for peanuts, Mama Dear." She does not exactly have me pegged as a loser. She has merely concluded that because

17

I am a Midwestern preacher's daughter I have a permanent handicap in dealing with the power brokers of the arts and the literary establishment. "It's okay to be a preacher's daughter," she concedes. She reasons that such origins made me indifferent to merely mortal laws and hence what she used to call "an adventuress." She merely thinks I wasted my freedom from convention on losers like Bob, Bob and Tom. And she suspects—as I do too, on sober second thought—that accepting a miserly advance will put me at a psychological disadvantage in writing about anyone as used to money, fame and power as the Gosses. They are in art the way Kennedys are in politics. Vidal and Godwin, Dean Goss's sons by his first marriage, have obviously climbed the ladder their father built for them. Vidal, who has long been operating out of Paris, is celebrated for the visual beauty of his films. It is more than a slogan to say he inherited his father's eye. Godwin's career is less visible. As painter, theoretician and by now an international taste maker, he tips the scales that weigh the new fashions and theories. There were no humble origins for Dean Goss either. At the turn of the century his father, Henry Hayden Goss, was the most respected muralist in the country. A bit of a fancy Dan, I conclude. Why should they take me on except as a charity case?

Because they love to work with unpromising materials, that's why. Because they're artists and relax better on their thrones than money men.

Because I'm not really a basket case, and they see something through my useful disguises of preacher's daughter and worried Mama, I like to believe. Not one of the Gosses, including Jason, has read any of my novels and I don't go to them waving my credits. But as my subtle and barbarous Tamisan said once, "I am very good at being a woman."

Obviously Jason had briefed Vidal about me before I got to his hotel suite. He was in New York for a week to raise money—"That's a large part of what a film maker does if he wants to be even moderately independent of the big boys. I am

tired of it—who isn't tired of it now? I ought to take a year off
and retreat to a hermit cell like Jason. For meditation."

I remarked that the taste for solitude is a matter of temperament. And note here that it is probably not a taste that Vidal
shares with his young half brother. As we talked a couple of
slick and shimmery Italian girls—his traveling companions, I
took them to be—twinkled back and forth between the back
rooms of the suite. Vidal is a polished public charmer, more
conveniently handsome than his father in spite of receding hair.
With none of Jason's baby-faced delicacy.

"Who feeds Jason? The ravens feed him, to be sure," Vidal
said. "I should have known better than to worry about him as
I did all this year past. You may know it was arranged for him
to come to Paris and work with me—or do as he pleased; one
doesn't pressure Jason; I do understand that—and I still don't
know why he backed out. Though he leads me to believe that
the spirits he communes with predicted he would meet your
charming daughter if he prepared himself by vigil and fasting."

My Tamisan was among the ravens who had fed him, I said
demurely. It relieved me to find or infer that here was one more
suave cocksman of middle years who knew her only by idealized
report from Jason.

"She can hardly be a raven," he said, in compliment to my
perennial charms, visible even in the low profile I affect. "But
. . . but . . . but . . . *Will* you have one more martini with
me? Luciana, will you fill us?" One of the beauties Tamisan's
age came condescendingly out from her preparations for the
evening—came damp from the bathroom steam—and made us
another drink. "But . . . but . . . but . . . you're here to get
perspective on the virile dean of the declining Goss clan. I
must warn you, Susan . . ."

One characteristic Vidal emphatically shares with his unworldly half brother is an undiminished fascination with the
Papa. Vidal is ironic and sometimes rueful but hardly less absorbed. He kept me on and on that evening—not for my charms,

19

to be sure, but because I was so warm a listener to his Dean Goss anecdotes. (The restless girls kept coming and going as background for his recital, like the women in the poem, no doubt talking of Michelangelo.) He gave me both a brotherly warning to "keep a distance from the old elephant" and encouragement to "find out really what makes him go on ticking."

"I'm a storyteller too, Susan, and I've given up imagining there is a single Dean Goss story. Every day is a new lifetime with him. Several stories going on at the same time, appearing and disappearing like brooks among boulders. He can't keep track of them himself. It's no use hoping he'll be candid—there's too much going on there for him to find reliable language for it. He doesn't mean to lie . . ."

I said the Haupt-Eisinger biography seemed truthful and coherent as far as the facts went.

"But dull, dull, dull—and therefore the most cunning falsehood he could issue as smoke screen; the ink a squid shoots out to blind whatever wants to eat him up. I don't mean to blacken Father's character. Not at all, not at all, but I always warn my friends . . . Do you know Zach Sandler?"

Everyone's heard of Sandler; not being of the Establishment, I couldn't claim he had ever asked me to his house.

"I see him only once a year any more. But yesterday at lunch I had to warn him. He's turned up in South America a couple of Dean Goss paintings of the early fifties that just might be forgeries. Even if they're not, I had to warn Sandler, they're not a safe investment. A year or two ago the Behn Gallery—have you met Bruce Behn yet?—sold three canvases to the Armitages in San Francisco. Well, *I* know that Father painted them. Bruce, who has been his dealer for thirty years, knew they were authentic. But when Father saw them in the Armitages' house, on the spot he repudiated them. Not his. Fake, said he. It made a considerable row and ended with Bruce having to buy the things back from the Armitages and take a considerable loss."

However comfortably Vidal laughed at this anecdote, while he was telling it I recalled that more than thirty years ago Dean Goss had deserted him, his mother and brother to go with another woman. That ancient wound, no doubt long forgiven and healed over and repudiated in its turn, might still be twinging under Vidal's maturity as he made a joke of the repudiated paintings. "Possibly he didn't like the Armitages' furniture," I said.

"It wasn't that. He didn't like the Dean Goss who painted them. I tell you he can be enough different people in any given day so he can afford to deny those different selves that offend his whim. And Sandler can afford to lose a few thousand gambling on his finds—though he doesn't like to. The Behn Gallery can afford it too."

As no one doubts. The newspapers reported that two Goss paintings brought over three hundred thousand last winter in Dallas.

I mentioned that and Vidal said he had been with his father in Osaka when they heard of the sale. They were in the Far East on a cultural exchange set up by Senator Burke and the State Department. Vidal said, "In theory I was tagging along to make a documentary film of Father paying back his oriental influences. He set foot on the sacred soil and declaimed, 'Hokusai, we have returned.' Something like that. You'll see some of my footage at North Atlantic. Fiona Trebbel is piling up all the mementos— I'm afraid my film isn't much more than that—for her eventual museum. Mostly my film shows Father floating in sampans on mystic lakes under nice mountains or being served in geisha houses. Fragments. Impressions. Flickering flicks. I tell you I've given up all hope of doing a connected story of the artist as artist. There *isn't* any. Tips of the iceberg. He shows tips of the iceberg and up to a point we believe there's one big single chunk down under the surface that connects them all. But there isn't, is there?"

Well, the entertaining anecdotes he had to offer me were the tip tip tip of any iceberg that might or might not be all in one chunk. I left Vidal with his girls and rode home thinking I damn well wanted more than to be another collector of anecdotes or Dean Goss aphorisms, either. Vidal was, I see, most helpful. He made me determined to see an artist who was all put together down where it counts.

21

Determined . . .

But I am a preacher's daughter who was taught long ago to be satisfied with what she gets . . . or can snitch . . . or can wangle . . . or can parlay . . . or abscond . . . or even stitch together from the discards of the mighty.

Godwin Goss is supposed to be the family strategist and reputation planner of the family Mafia, though Dean Goss is still the reigning patriarch. Godwin is consultant for the Behn Gallery and foundations, dealers and collectors from Hong Kong to Vienna. He started a career as a painter, using actual canvas and brushes like the peasantry. Years ago he moved from that into pure cerebration. Now he only plays chess, takes care of his exquisite fingernails and coin collection, expressing his relation to common humanity through impeccable tailoring.

Tamisan, convinced that I had somehow bungled my chance to get magic secrets in my interview with Vidal, insisted that she come along to Godwin's place. And why didn't Jason take her to inspect his siblings? "Mama Dear, you should know Jason doesn't communicate with people by *visiting*."

We found the living room of Godwin's apartment as barren and gleaming white as a laboratory. Not a single picture on the walls. Tamisan, who made it to his bathroom under cover of our lofty talk, said later, "Mama Dear, I don't think he lives in that apartment." Yet cool, jesuitical and reserved as he is now in his mid-forties, Godwin did not at all condescend to my amateur ignorance of painting or the vast intrigues of the art world. He welcomed my enthusiasm at least. My qualms grew from finding him so overwhelmingly eloquent on the subject of his father. Surely, he could say all that needs to be said about Dean Goss, and I should merely transcribe with tape recorder and typewriter.

Godwin said: "It's agreed that what he accomplished in his fourteen years with Maggie [wife Margaret, Jason's mother] are the summation of American painting in the century. You know the critical tag line: he took the very personal, almost autobiographical and daily, intimate minutiae of his life as husband

and father and made something connected with the myths and all the art styles of the museums. Very good. As a general description it can't be argued. Now . . . at a certain point an artist stops competing with his contemporaries; then he begins to define and secure his rank among the masters of all periods."

He took some time to make the comparison between the Rodin-Balzac project (that elaborate complex of paintings, sculpture and prints that Dean Goss has been busy with since Maggie's death) and Joyce's "work in progress" that became *Finnegans Wake.* "For an artist with such an extensive *oeuvre* already complete, the remaining task is to find the end, just as drama requires its obligatory scene and resolution. . . ."

He speaks, easily enough, of his father as "one of the rulers of the age."

On our way home from Godwin's apartment in the seventies, I found Tamisan twitchy with excitement. All that royal talk blew her mind, she didn't mind confiding. "I *love* people who know how things are done. You know, the behind-the-scene deal. I can see how he persuaded those Dallas freaks to lay out three hundred thou for those old paintings." After a minute's meditation she said, "But I certainly wouldn't want to touch Godwin."

I felt it unlikely she would be invited to do so. "I marvel that I raised a daughter with such a simple standard of human worth."

"Mama Dear, you'd be surprised what you can learn from skin contact."

I asked what she might have learned from contacting Jason's. What did he want for his father, as an artist or as a man?

"I dunno, Mama. And if he hasn't told me he won't tell anyone. Probably nothing except make Jason's mother come to life again. Some little old miracle like that to show people who he really is."

I pondered her answer and concluded that I wanted to see a miracle too.

23

from Susan Vail's blue notebook:

Goss lives now on a storybook estate on Long Island. The mansion is a gaudy example of nineteenth-century conspicuous consumption, built by the Duncan family in the 1890s. It came to its present owner, Fiona Trebbel, by inheritance from her father Henry.

Henry Trebbel in his prime was a Wall Street speculator who got his start in a copper strike in Montana. During the twenties he picked up the estate—called North Atlantic from the time of the Duncans—from a corporate partner whom he had deceived and bankrupted. The charm of the mansion and grounds is attributable either to the Duncans or to Fiona Trebbel. She redecorated and restored it to be a retreat, a spot for Dean Goss to work in his later years and, after his death, a museum. The Goss archives and memorabilia are, by now, in good order in the North Atlantic library. Fiona, with various assistants and the co-operation of the Behn Gallery, has listed the whereabouts of most of the major works of his lifetime (though she estimates there may be over eight thousand items that should be on record, she has fewer than seven thousand accounted for). Her memory, business judgment, and simple respect for fact are, by their mutual admission, better than his. It is her methodical devotion that provides at least an external unity to the protean life.

She was his student nearly four decades ago when he taught at a progressive college in California. She has been not only an enraptured disciple to the astonishing man ever since, but an aggressive patroness as well. His success has been hers by proxy. She invested in him instead of oil wells and they are both richer for that.

Fiona is a woman of chaste habits and speech. In her girlhood she set out to be an artist in simple, sheer rebellion against her father's disdain for the arts. It is her consummate revenge to have placed Dean Goss's present studio at that spot on the North Atlantic grounds where Henry Trebbel used to gun down live pigeons flung into the air by his servants. After she met Dean Goss she never expected any public career for herself. She found her destiny as Dean Goss's patroness.

When her rich father died in the mid-thirties, Dean Goss was already a name to reckon with. He had outstripped his father's reputation as watercolorist and muralist, was separating from the pack in American art, already one of the front runners. He had painted murals in a union hall in Detroit and in the library of a Western university. He had painted controversial portraits of John L. Lewis, Henry Wallace and Ethel Barrymore. His illustrations for Whitman and Melville were setting a new vogue for illustrated editions of American classics. A painting of Christ talking to workingmen had won second prize in the Carnegie International and was purchased for the permanent collection of the Whitney Museum. He was known in Europe. The art circles of Paris and London were conceding him stature as the most forceful American painter since Winslow Homer. His watercolors of the California coast, done in his early twenties, were being bought up by those collectors too timid for his later political subjects. He was already famous then by the ordinary standards applied to young American artists, and he might well have gone on to become rich when the Depression was over and the art boom followed World War II.

Those prospects were stunningly upgraded when Henry Trebbel died in the arms of a groom who was trying to keep him from delivering a second kick to the head of the man who trained his filly Brandywine. With the Trebbel fortune at her disposal, Fiona tripled all the bets on the career and genius of Dean Goss. She began to buy his early paintings from collectors at prices that made news. She put together a retrospective show (Goss was thirty-five then) that toured the European capitals before it was brought back to New York on the flood tide of critical acclaim that, some said, Fiona had coldly purchased in Rome, Paris and Antwerp from corruptible journalists and critics.

All these years it has been said, by friends, well-wishers and enemies, that Fiona Trebbel was not merely investing in his career. Wasn't it evident that she was buying the man she wanted for herself? There were those who remembered what an adoring student she had been in his classes at college and later in the Art Students' League. She might be plain. Nobody supposed she could be any competition for charmers like his two wives or his onetime mistress Eileen Forbes. But money! Loyalty, money and unmatched patience have their rewards too.

There are those who believe she has claimed him since his second wife, Jason's mother, died. "I was up for grabs," he says. "It was worse than that," Jason, in his turn, commented to me. "No one could reach him but Fiona. I was no help. She brought him here."

Fiona reclaimed the North Atlantic mansion that year. She brought the painter and his fourteen-year-old son here for recovery.

"Maybe you can call them a couple," Jason once said to me. "How they handle their finances I'll bet not even they could tell you. My father's very rich now, too, so it isn't at all a matter of who supports whom. But there was never any romance or anything close to that. Am I sure? Yes, I'm sure. There's just always been Fiona. My mother accepted it. I accepted. There isn't any name for what they are in each other's lives. You'll have to take what you see at face value."

Sometimes it occurs to me that Fiona's role in the Goss establishment is that of a nun—a very worldly nun, to be sure, though strict in her devotion to the service of a man she never quite thinks of as mortal. The sort of a nun that Pan might have in his service, the old goat god himself.

Chapter 2

"I never promised you a girl like Tamisan," Janis Ward had once said to Jason Goss. "I only promised to get you laid."

It would have been presumptuous of her to promise a girl "like" this one, because Janis had to admit she never had the same view of what Tamisan was from one occasion to the next.

This afternoon when Janis and Tamisan and Jean Simons were posing among the flowers, Janis felt very strongly that she wasn't even seeing the same body she had seen the one other time she and the younger girl had been naked together. That, of course, had been an occasion lit by dim interior lights. Tamisan looked different in the sun. A flawless skin deserves to be seen in a light that would expose flaws. Here Tamisan looked like a figure carved from perfect stone. That other time she had looked like a gorgeous tramp.

"I promised and she laid you and that ends my responsibility for both of you," Janis had said to Jason.

Of course it had not ended her fascination with them or her pride in bringing them together. There were times, even, in the past months when she had told herself that she had saved both of them by her efforts—saved Jason from a loneliness that made her shudder and saved Tamisan from squandering herself in bloodcurdling recklessness. She was Tamisan's teacher, after all —if her methods of "reaching" her student were, to put it mildly, irregular, the ends in this case seemed to justify the means.

"Of course I was lonely," Jason said when Janis claimed a little credit for her management. "How do you know it wasn't my choice to be?"

"Aren't you happier now? With Tamisan?"

"Happier," he admitted. "Are you sure I'm supposed to be happy?"

That was such a typically teen-age contrariness, she refused to admit he had actually said it. At eighteen Jason was anything but typical. At fourteen he had been a fully formed artist. A cellist. Janis' former husband (first-rate violinist; shabby marital partner) had claimed the boy was the finest natural talent he had ever come near. That it was a tragedy Jason had given up playing when he could already have begun a brilliant career.

He had given it up, in any case, in the aftermath of his mother's tragic death. He had finished prep school but made it clear he was not going on to college. He had cut away from his prep school friends and most older friends from the time his mother was alive, explaining often that he meant to go to Paris and work with his half brother Vidal, making films or something on that order.

The year that Janis got to know him best—and to mother him in his loneliness—he had chosen to live in a long-unused and unfurnished studio still owned by his father near Canal Street in Manhattan.

From September through the winter months Janis had him to dinner in her apartment on an average of once a week. It was much rarer for him to let her come for a visit in the unchanging emptiness of the studio, furnished with little more than a mattress on the floor and the appliances needed to cook for himself. "You haven't even got a tape recorder, or a radio or your cello for company," Janis said with big sister sorrow. "We've got to dig you up a girl who'll bring you out into the street, among people."

"Is everyone afraid I'll run queer?" he asked with the gentle irony he used to fend off all but the most insistent interference with his life. (He simply fled from heavy-handed meddling.) "Can everyone tell but me? Vidal practically hijacked me to Paris the last time I said I wasn't ready to go yet. My own family! It must be the way I look. Maggie was determined to get me laid, she said, that last time we took off for Paris."

"If your mother thought so, then my duty's plain," Janis insisted.

"Do you have a candidate?"

"I have students," Janis said. It was not, probably, a brilliant proposal. But then, she was not as well acquainted in New York as Jason. This was her second year in the city. She was a very junior instructor at Hunter.

"Herd some of them past me," Jason said. "I'll do my best by one or more." His agreement on this was as quick as on most things—and she trusted it as little, understanding it was a fencer's tactic designed to disarm any interference with him, preferably without needing to counterattack. "I thought you were going to offer yourself," he said.

"Oh no!" She was genuinely startled and later dismayed by this twist. Her feeling for Jason was too close to adoration to permit any sexual wishes. It would have seemed to her too much like incest.

"Oh, Jason, not me," she said with a laugh that was genuinely humble. She thought he was physically beautiful—just a trifle plump for his skeleton and muscular development, but ripe and sweet as a peach mellowed by the sun. He was cleaner than she had ever imagined sex could be. It would destroy her to touch him or invite his touch. She felt that. And even in those times when it seemed to her, in her loneliness, that she needed to get laid quicker than he, she denied any desire for him. "Someone younger than I," she said in a cool and sisterly manner. In the manner she used to keep her students at arm's length. "A girl a lot better than I. Or else lots worse," she said deliberately.

"Worse!" Jason laughed. "You may have to find me the worst girl in New York to make me perform. But truly I've been laid. I'm not a virgin and I'm not even gay, if you need to know the facts of the case."

"That one," she said to Jason at a party in Zach Sandler's house. "The girl over there beyond the piano."

Jason would remember that he first saw his love, looking lonely, bored and sullen, amid a crowd of older people. All he thought of her in that first glimpse was that her face might have

been painted in the melancholy style that was his father's trademark when he was a young man—something of the 1920s,
though the girl was wearing jeans and the kind of pendant she
must have found in a head shop.

"Is she better or worse?" he asked.

"I don't know," Janis said. "I think she's a champion liar.
I think she lives in a world of make-believe. She handed me a
paper about all the literary suicides—Hemingway, Harry Crosby,
Sylvia Plath, Virginia Woolf, Vachel Lindsay—you know—and
when I spoke to her first about it she announced that her father
had committed suicide and her mother had died in an asylum
after years of alcoholism. It turned out not to be at all true. She
told me solemnly she wanted to 'live the full criminal life.' All
she's waiting for is her mother's permission, I suppose."

Tamisan Vail looked as if she was waiting for something. And
Jason said, "Well, she doesn't have to make believe she's
pretty." He would never quite be sure whether it was that look
of waiting or the girl's beauty that penetrated his mind like a
fishhook.

As things turned out, he got no chance to meet her that evening. There were people at Sandler's party who wanted to show
their friendship for Dean Goss's son. There were artists, writers,
critics who came to Sandler's parties to see and be seen.
Sandler himself was an old friend of Jason's half brother Vidal
and had been asked by Vidal to see that Jason was amused
through the winter. There was Harry Dasher, the music critic
for the *Marat Review,* who had known Jason and his mother in
past years. He caught Jason soon after his arrival. "Delighted
you're with us again, my boy." Dasher's eye was blank when he
was introduced to Janis. With deft callousness he led Jason away
to meet the people who counted in this crowd and for most of
the evening Janis was left to find her own way.

She minded this much less than Jason would have thought.
She accepted the fact that she would hardly have got inside the
door of this East Side brownstone except by coming with Jason.
There was even a sort of snobbish satisfaction for her in moving
unknown among this crowd, picking out the celebrities. Jason
had hardly moved off with Dasher when she heard a bearded

critic baying, "Tarzan of the Apes! Tarzan of the Apes! Surely he is closer to the American phylum than Huckleberry Finn. . . ." It was this audacious, authoritative nonsense that she had come to hear and smile over. With a stiff drink in her hand she drifted about enjoying it.

Among a number of beards she knew by reputation, she recognized the host. Sandler was a dark-eyed, round little man with a perpetual sadness in his smile. ("Vidal says he's a rug salesman at heart," Jason had said lightly. "Still, Vidal thinks he's an oracle who always knows what the next art fads will be. He's supposed to be very generous to young artists, Vidal says.") She admitted to herself she was not quite sure what Sandler's New York reputation consisted of. Probably he was known for knowing people on the way up, for giving parties like this one. The principle around which they were organized seemed to be that Jackie and Ari might come in again unexpectedly—as they actually had one night in '67. Or Norman might stalk in to say something belligerent. Or Gloria. Shirley, Irwin, Philip, William, George, Diana, Barbara, Betty or Dwight. At any moment one or all of them might dash in from the autumn night. It was not only Tamisan Vail who conveyed the impression that she was waiting for even more glamorous figures to appear. Janis, who had no artistic career to advance in such a milieu, could smile at the pecking order where the rest were jockeying for surprise or advantage. An outsider, nothing could conceivably scratch at her insecurities—except the fact that she had spotted one of her students here ahead of her. So, itching only mildly with any emotion beyond curiosity, she had woven through the mine fields of intellectual conversation to confront Tamisan.

Jovially she said, "The company you keep! So this is why you can't make it wide awake to an eleven-thirty class." At close range she noted for the first time how much taller than she the girl was. When she had talked to her before, it had been in her office at school. Neither in her office nor in class had she quite comprehended how stony and emotionless that nineteen-year-old face could be, even while the eyes were absolutely clear, measuring and alert.

31

"Oh," Tamisan said. Her stare came from fifty miles away. Not defiant. Not questioning why her teacher Mrs. Ward had suddenly materialized among birds with fancier plumage. Merely out of range, like big artillery.

"Is it part of the criminal life?" Janis asked with a laugh that was still reasonably steady. In the stony non-response of the girl's stare she felt she had to hold fast to the gaiety that teachers suppose will relax their students. "I'm delighted to find you at a Sandler party, but . . . is it to bomb or blackmail? Diana Coors is in the other room wearing diamonds that ought to be worth your while."

True enough. By this time women with jewels and men in evening clothes were coming in after the theater. The Upper Bohemian mixture was approaching its normal balance of wealth and talent.

"Oh," Tamisan said. "Why I'm here?"

"Never mind," Janis laughed. "I'm glad to find one person I know so I won't be entirely out of my depth. I'm glad to see *you*. Your paper about the suicides has stayed in my mind like a dream, and we really must talk more about it sometime. I'll have you to my apartment one time for dinner. Yes, and there's a boy I'd like you to meet, as well. Someone intelligent enough to keep you interested."

"The paper was stupid."

"Not at all!" Janis said. "I thought it was brilliant in spots. To tell the truth, I've been abashed that I discussed it with you so . . . pedantically. After all, suicide is a subject for visionaries, not statisticians, and . . . Have you gone into any of the further readings I suggested?"

She ended out of breath, feeling that if the girl was not beaming pure derision at her it was because she was totally stoned. The voice of a hoarse river god interrupted from nearby: "Noam may locate it in the language, but I locate it in anality, do you see?"

Janis twinkled at this startling news, reached for her student's hand and said, "We'll never hear such gold-plated blather in class, will we?"

"Oh," Tamisan said. "You want to know what I'm doing at

Sandler's party. Oh. I fuck Sandler. It's his night. . . . My night.
. . . Something like that."

Her stare did not waver. Her expression admitted nothing beyond the fact she had recited. Certainly it did not strain to emphasize that the level words were the perfect putdown for all
adult authority that might attempt to claim her or even inhibit
what she was waiting to enact. Let no teacher approach her teach-
erly!

"Not better or worse either," Janis said to Jason, feeding him
her best goulash in her tidy little apartment. "At least I could
never judge her because the more I hear from her the more I
get confused between her lies and the truth."

"You've been feeding her too," Jason said. "You've been
mother-henning her too, because I'm not enough for you to
watch and pray over and feed."

"Yes, I brought her here to dinner and tried to get her to come
tonight. Because she fascinates me. As soon as she gave up the
story that her mother was an alcoholic and a loony, she told me
her mother was a novelist. I thought that was more of the same
make-believe. Or lies. I don't know why I even bothered to check
it out in the library. But that was true. Have you heard of Susan
Vail?"

"No."

"She's a respected but obviously not a popular novelist. After
I got the names straight I realized I'd been reading her columns
in *Calendar* magazine for years as I sat under the hair dryer.
She's made her living—and that ungrateful girl's—by hack work
all these years. Tamisan admits now her story about her father's
suicide *was* plagiarized from the facts about Harry Crosby. The
truth behind it all is merely that the girl is a bastard. Born out of
wedlock, I mean. Hence, understandably, comes her fantasy
about her father's suicide."

"How do you know she's a bastard?"

Janis' motherly-sisterly happiness in serving hot goulash on a
cold night expanded another notch as she laughed. "I don't," she
said. "How could I? But the more she lies the more I'm deter-

mined to find out what really makes her go. One time she'll seem hard and cold as ice. She's said some very cruel and belittling things about her mother. She's a girl, if she came in to rob my candy store—living her criminal life—I'd say, 'There's the till. Help yourself,' and step carefully out of her way. But the night she was here . . ."

"Eating your magic goulash," Jason said, gobbling away like the healthiest Boy Scout in America.

"Stroganoff. The night she was here she had me practically in tears telling me about her mother's sweetness and heroism and talent. . . . Oh, and she told me a little bit about how her mother took care of her in Africa years ago when she came down with ringworm all over her legs and face and hands. The man her mother was supporting and living with then—some pseudo artist type—was off somewhere balling *both* the Arab boys and American college girls. There's nothing can make a little girl hate herself like ringworm. And her good mother kept salving her and bathing her and telling her Bob whatshisname was really a fine fellow. . . . It was truly touching, Jason, though it sounds so itchy . . . so out of keeping with the fine skin she has now. Her teeth are so perfect and even. And her figure! But why I like her so much in spite of her lies is"—Janis waved her napkin around in the candlelight in search of words to fit the enthusiasm in her mind—"is her . . ."

"Purity," Jason said.

Janis nearly choked at the idea. "Jason, if I can believe her at all, she's balled an absolute record number of men since she was fourteen. And I have a theory about that too. She's really out trying to get revenge, and not just for herself, but for all the cruddy things men did to her mother. Women can think that way. And it's so sad. Who really gets hurt by all this revenging? She does. And her mother, for whose sake she took arms in the first place." The improbable complications of being a woman in New York sobered Janis' mood and she said, "Ah, the crooked girl is probably lying about the men too, so what's the use of any of my theories?"

Jason seemed to be listening to music. Somewhere between the candle flames above her dining table and their reflection dancing on the windowpane of her miniature apartment there seemed to be another presence with them. Orphan, criminal, outsider, avenger, alien . . . woman.

"My father says . . ." he began slowly.

"Your eyes get so big and solemn when you say 'My father'!"

". . . it's always better to believe what someone tells you even if she is probably lying because . . ."

"Because the truth is never good enough."

"No," Jason said. "No, if he didn't want the truth he would have laid down and died long ago when we all hurt him so much. He says the truth *behind* what they intend to be true or what they intend to be lies is the only thing worth finding out."

"If your father thinks like that, it ought to be good enough for us, oughtn't it?" Janis said—awed more than it was safe to admit by what she had heard in both his tone and his words.

She was not foolish enough to suppose his eyes had grown so luminous merely because he recalled a wisdom of his father's. He had been struck by some coincidence between that wisdom and the fragmentary sketch of a girl she had offered to his imagination. She had been given a glimpse of how he might fall in love. She was glad that, even if she had mentioned the men Tamisan had admitted, she had not mentioned any names or told him what Tamisan said that night at Zach Sandler's.

The girl ahead of her on the subway steps, wearing jeans and an utterly decrepit fur coat, thong sandals and no socks in spite of the cold of the afternoon, was Tamisan.

"Lucky I ran into you," Janis said, breathless from the hurry to catch up. "I'm going to have spaghetti with Jason Goss, who lives down past the Village in his father's old studio. Want to come along around seven?"

"He's the one you have the reproductions of," Tamisan said —not really confusing the artist with his son. "Wow, I'd like to. I've got to study tonight, actually, or they'll bomb me out of Human Studies." She grimaced at the prospect.

Janis resented the grimace particularly, because she did not believe the excuse. She went home through a fuzzy, early snowstorm nursing resentments that her well-meant attempt had been so ineffectual. She was so vexed that she postponed her evening with Jason. She reconsidered whether she could, or wanted to, bother his life by introducing the girl.

Her anger was still smoldering the next evening when Tamisan called with a debonair invitation of her own.

"Janis? Hi, Teach. Working hard? Would you like to run over to Zach Sandler's for a few minutes?"

"I . . ." Janis was close to slamming the phone back in its cradle . . . and slamming the crooked little devil back into hers. "I thought you had committed yourself to study."

"Yeah. I can only spare maybe an hour. . . . I know you don't approve of Sandler and his phonies. Well . . . they're not phonies altogether. Anyway, Sandler really *is* a freak and you only saw him at a big party."

"I don't think I need to see him at closer range to understand him," Janis said frostily, using her Ph.D. for its full worth to emphasize her distaste.

"I know you don't," the girl soothed. "I'd just as soon not go over there alone."

"Must you go? Aren't you *free* to refuse?" It was a release of joy for Janis Ward to be in a position to express herself so severely.

Tamisan ignored it. "You may not know the way Zach collects things. He collects people, but . . . all kinds of nutty things. Junk dealer, I call him. Shall we just call him an asshole dilettante and let it go? *Eh*-nyway. He's into records. Books. Magazines. You name it. He doesn't need the money but he'll sell anything. Avant-garde stuff . . . you name it. What he says he's got hold of now is a 'youth prayer' that some cat put on tape and Zach is wondering whether to issue it as a record. So I, Tamisan Vail, youth representative, get elected to try it out on. He wants my reactions. It's undoubtedly pure crap, Janis. And if I did like it that would probably mean it wouldn't sell ten copies to the other freaks. But if you're free and want to go over with me to listen to it . . ."

"It sounds utterly revolting."

"Yes!" Tamisan said. Her laugh was pure and sweet as the summoning tinkle of a crystal bell. "You can't tell, Janis. My grandfather was a preacher. Mama says I'll outwit her by converting back to fundamentalism. It might be tonight. Want to come and make bets? You can't tell."

Janis did not remember agreeing. Her resentment at Tamisan was not even faintly appeased by the girl's incoherent persuasions. She was so distressed that she mixed herself a small pitcher of martinis after the call, though it was her principle never to drink martinis after dinner.

Two hours later she was sitting on a campy bearskin rug in front of the whirling spindles of Zach Sandler's tape recorder. Another pitcher of martinis, considerately mixed especially for her since Tamisan was not drinking and Sandler preferred Camparis, was near her hand. The faintly Texan voice of an agonized boy was coming from the speakers.

I feel like an asshole, Jesus, but Mummy and Daddy are always dumping on me for tripping with the kids, while they sit around swilling their cocktails and highballs and flipping out on their prescriptions. . . .

"Say it, little brother," Zach Sandler chortled. He reached across the rug to refill Janis' martini glass. His long lashes fluttered in amusement over the fathomless darkness of his large brown eyes. "We thank thee, youth, for any reminder whatsoever, don't we, Mrs. Ward?" He was sitting just beyond the edge of the bearskin, under a voracious-looking potted tree. His upstairs study was full of potted trees. The walls were mostly decorated with tomb rubbings and the signed photos of writers and show people. A candle the size of a mortar flickered and smoked beside them in the stage-lighted dimness of the room.

Tamisan was sitting on the back of a couch above the two older people, her denim-clad knees spread athletically, her bare feet resting on the cushions.

. . . popping all their pills from the medicine cabinet. Sometimes life seems like a real bummer, Jesus, but I know it was the same thing for you. . . . The high priests and old Caiaphas

37

really dumped on you, Jesus, like unto what we call the Establishment does unto us kids. . . . We like to get together and have a little fun and make a little music, Jesus, and sometimes, maybe, there's a black kid we like and want to share the stash with, Jesus. . . .

Tamisan's voice broke in, lovely in its glee. "Go back, go back. Turn it way back, Zach," she commanded. "Run it back to where he says, 'Jesus, thou art the consciousness-raising most,' host."

"Perhaps Mrs. Ward . . ."

"Oh, I'm enjoying every blasphemous syllable of it," Janis said. "In my sorority we always talked about having a black mass and never got around to it." Enjoying it or not, she was at least relaxed beyond her usual condition. She was relieved to note that both Tamisan and Sandler seemed to share the pitch of her amusement at this outrageous garbage. "There's nothing like sacrilege to set the old pulses hammering."

"You were in a *sorority?*" Tamisan asked with glib surprise, just short of contempt.

"Not actually . . . only for two years until I caught on," Janis said.

Sandler, who seemed to be obeying Tamisan's command to return the tape to an earlier passage, said, "You have no precision in your recall, Miss Vail. You misquoted. I know exactly what you mean, though." The hissing tape ran back above his pudgy hands like a mechanical snake being charmed back into its infinite coil. Solicitously, while he rewound it, he wondered if this might not be the moment to get Tamisan a mild libation. "To wet your lips, at least. To share with you the wine of our communion."

"I told you we'd only be here a little while. I really have to get home and do my Human Studies or they'll exterminate me."

"I would mix you a cup appropriate for a schoolgirl," he promised.

Tamisan said, "I'll do on my natural high tonight, Gruesome."

"Zach, you're not actually going to add to the national corruption by marketing this thing in record form, are you?" Janis laughed.

He cocked a thick, undulant eyebrow at her. It writhed in expressive amusement like the twirled end of a mustache in a costume play. "Oh my! Oh my! What a wicked deed that would be!"

"Tamisan said . . . at least she suggested . . . perhaps I misunderstood."

"Miss Vail has traduced me yet again. What shall we do with the young, who pervert all our kind intentions toward them and give us a bad character? Miss Vail, unfaithful servant, thou shalt have thy consciousness raised by having thy girlish quim birched if thou continuest thy sportful lies to the unsuspecting. No, no, no, no, Mrs. Ward!" He put his hand on Janis' knee only to persuade her how she had been deceived through no fault or intention of his. "For the record, be it understood that I merely dabble in the record business. I dabble, dabble, dabble."

"Toil and trabble," Tamisan put in sweetly.

"I dabble in dabbling. I am not a serious competitor in commerce. I keep the death watch."

"You keep what?" Janis was not sure her brain had arranged his words in rational slots.

"Keeps fetuses in bottles of formaldehyde. Dead bird feathers," Tamisan said.

"The 'death watch.' You've lied again, schoolgirl," Sandler said, replying genially to both of them. "I thought, Mrs. Ward, that the term 'death watch' had common currency. Haven't I read it even in the columns of the good gray *Times?* You know —the 'death watch philosophers'? Those who understand there is no hope on this dimming, cooling planet."

"Yes," she remembered. "Yes, I've heard the term."

"I dabble in 'the waters of the end,' " Sandler said. "That's a melancholy phrase of D. H. Lawrence's—with a nasty *double-entendre* I shall not expound while your innocent student might overhear. I hear the lapping of the waters of the end, though I send forth no ships of death, not I." His sorrow, welling from the deeps of his eyes, was as genuine as it was transient. "But whatever my philosophic despair, I deny that I am a polluter.

No ecofreak—not the most puritan!—could fault me. I'll burn this tape on the spot if it offends you, Mrs. Ward, rather than have you suspect me of pandering youth to its misleaders."

"Yes, burn," Tamisan said, from somewhere out of sight.

"I selected this tape only for our delectation and amusement this unhallowed night," Sandler said. "I'm sorry you missed your black mass in college, Janis." The darkness of his eyes mirrored something in her soul. For the first time since her arrival she felt a twinge of unease. He distracted her from it by saying, "I'm sorry for anyone who has missed anything. I won't cheat. You'll see."

As if to prove his generosity by giving Tamisan what she had requested, his fingers flicked the switches of the tape recorder again. The unctuous, wailing, boyish voice returned, enveloping them.

Jesus, I know you had a body just like mine and you had, probably, impure thoughts, what they call impure thoughts, about a chick you thought was groovy, maybe, the way I have and like most kids and girls too, whatever they say, and is it impure if we groove on each other, her and me? Do we have to wait until the high and mighty elders say some words before our young bodies . . .

The dark eyes were measuring her as he poured her stemmed glass full again. They had all three quieted down from the hilarity they shared as the silly prayer had begun. But they had shared it and they shared, without disagreements, the mood of its aftermath.

With almost professorial authority Sandler was saying, "Mrs. Ward, there really is little left to elevate our spirits but camp—raised to whatever power we can raise it to. Where are the *Naked Lunches* of yesteryear? The frontiers of art are behind us. And Beckett is the bore of our forefathers. And Gênet went out in the sticks to the colleges ten years ago, to the amazement of drama teachers and faculty wives. So we're left here in the desiccation of New York among our own amusements, aren't we, Janis? And such elders as you and I have gone back to booze after the pharmacopoeia was emptied for the kids and the kiddy games ceased to beguile. We have to amuse ourselves with the invention of new games, for, after all, the primary definition of the artist, the fundamental one, is this! The artist is the man who amuses himself. The fox, Miss Vail! I heard you rummaging. Did you find our fox?"

It came sailing through the dim air to land between them— a moth-eaten fox neckpiece, bought at some secondhand store or Salvation Army retail center.

It landed red and limp on the campy bearskin. Sandler picked it up and put it around his neck. The fox head was cocked in his right hand. The little black eyes and eroded black muzzle twinkled as he swayed it back and forth in an imitation of the movements of life.

. . . and when we're living on the land, Jesus, trying to not do harm to Thy planet Earth, raising the most nourishing foods and maybe a little grass of our own to have fun with, because worship isn't all just being sober all the time, is it, Jesus . . . ?

Janis felt her body shuddering with laughter that no longer had anything to do with mirth. It was hard to tell what was funniest, the tape, Sandler's play with the moth-eaten fox, or the destruction of all the preconceptions she had brought to Sandler's place—the ideas of herself as guardian, guide or teacher for anyone.

Sandler was teaching her. He said, "I sought a way through in the drug fads, art fads, youth fads. I knew Leary. I used to believe we would emerge beyond drugs. Beyond! I thought there was such a thing as a natural high, as Tamisan calls it. There should be no need for LSD to make one acutely, painfully sensitive to the minutiae of experience. For example, the feeling of fur on fur." Slowly, illustratively, he smeared the fur of the fox through the bearskin by Janis' knee. "The millions of hairs touching, mingling, sliding against each other, each against each, like the cells touching each other in every animate thing in the universe. LSD gives some such perceptions, as you know."

"I don't know," Janis said humbly.

"It does. It should have taught us the path to such perceptions. Then we could have dispensed with it. *There* is the beauty of the last great dream.

41

"Come, let me show you something." He got languidly to his feet and reached down his hand to help her rise. She did not feel particularly drunk from the martinis as she got up.

"Look! You may think Miss Vail is asleep," he said good-naturedly. Tamisan was again seated on the couch with her head resting back and her eyes closed. "You may believe that there is some such mystical bullshit as what she labels a natural high. Her natural sensibilities liberated! There's no such thing, we know now. The simple truth is that she's pretending. Playing. That's all."

Then he said, "Watch!"

His pudgy hand reached out and his thumb with a square-cut, well-manicured nail pressed on the girl's eyelid and rolled it back.

Janis would remember this as the most indecent exposure she had ever witnessed. She might have been alarmed if she had seen the white of the eyeball, the eye rolled back in unconsciousness from actual narcosis. It would have strengthened her if she had seen then the hard and haughtily defiant stare she had encountered the night of the party when the tall child shocked her by saying, "I fuck Zach."

What broke her was to see exposed an eye that was only vague, cowed, feminine and idiotically submissive. It was the eye of a race sickened by boredom. An eye that had surrendered imagination and even fear, so it could not begin to conceive of shame. To see it so emptied of self-esteem was like slipping into nightmare.

The eyelid fell mechanically when it was released. In a minute Janis felt the pudgy, non-insistent hands of their host settle on the waistband of her skirt. Fingers dabbled the swampy softness of her abdomen.

"Now we'll take away your dignity," Sandler murmured into the damp hair on her neck. "We're going to set you free." She let her head flop in dumb acquiescence, feeling her dignity, the dignity of being female, already surrendered by what she had seen when he peeled back Tamisan's eyelid, as if her student had guided her into a community of defeat. She felt betrayed, and the hot sweetness of being captive to another will flowed through her like the secretion of her glands.

Fingers hitched her skirt up to her waist. A finger intruded into her navel without the urgency of desire—curious, probing, derisive. The hand of a meat inspector examining a carcass. Yet no caress had ever excited her more.

Against the delicious betrayal from within and without she began to babble, as if her voice alone could preserve the self which had fled the body without a fight. "Tamisan, I've had plans for you. You must meet—ooooh! don't! yes, yes!—meet Jason Goss. Take *his* dignity. Jason's epicene. No, ineffable. No, heroic! A marvelous boy for you and a true friend, dear." It surprised her a little that her voice sounded so drunken, as if it too was dissolving in the fluid of pure lust. Her pants were down around her thighs. Fingers were stretching her open with a curiosity at the same time infantile and professional, as if a nasty make-believe of childhood doctor play was luring her down and away from all the rigidities learned in adult life. As if even her bones were becoming flexible as an infant's.

And yet her voice went on babbling against this disintegration of her self. She talked while the fingers stretched and prodded and the nudging of his chest forced her to crouch with knees apart. "How silly me not 'member phrase 'dead watch.' They cer'nly do allatime. Or d'you say 'death wash'? Encountered it freakly onna prinna page, only hearing it loud make it seem unfamiliar. Ooooh, yes, yes, yes! There's such a breach 'tween one's own reading and the idiom suitable for class discussion. Watch, Death, watch! Hoooo-ooooh!"

A knee that must be Sandler's was pounding an insistent rhythm against her frenzied crotch.

"Ask!" a whisper commanded.

"Do," she pleaded. "More." The knee became motionless and she squatted more to bump herself against its cloth. She was, at least, glad Tamisan's eyes were closed again.

"Oh well," she said. She really wouldn't mind if the hands that peeled off her dignity went on to loosen every snap and fastener of her clothing and let it drop on the silly bearskin.

What high camp to stand there naked like a movie siren of the twenties, doing whatever the Lost Generation thought of doing!

His hands did no such service. She and Tamisan undressed Sandler.

Sometime—it must have been close to morning—Janis was lying alone on the bearskin in front of the silent tape recorder.

"Here is the fox," a quietly amused male voice said.

It came sailing through the dark over her, escaped from all proportion and scale so that it might have been a sea monster swimming between her and the breathable air somewhere far up above. It landed furry on her naked breasts.

"Play with it," the voice said.

She played with it, not even wondering why he had ever felt repugnance at the uses of her own hands.

Now, standing naked in the North Atlantic garden with Tamisan and Jean Simons, Janis could feel smugly enough that she had been forgiven for the ugliness of that night at Sandler's. It was past. It was, perhaps, a necessary part of the past that had moved on to this lovely and happy time where they showed their bodies freely to the sky and to the eyes of the artist without remorse. All *is* well that ends well. You'd *better* believe that or run screaming in front of the most convenient traffic or subway train.

The young lovers . . . had they not found each other after all?

With the benign sun warm on her eyelids as she stood between the other girls, she glanced lazily at Tamisan. There was a body to rejoice the eye of man or woman either. Whose? Tamisan's and Jason's. For the last several months they had shared it in love. The future was open to them. They were young, rich and free.

She looked for Jason. He was smiling at her as if he shared all her secrets and agreed with her that they were not worth remembering since everything had turned out so well. Whose gentleness was in that smile? Tamisan's and Jason's. She had not been wrong, after all, in imagining she could find him the right girl to open the shell of his loneliness.

And who else had escaped damnation on that night of the black mass?

She had.

She had wakened the next day remembering that her face had been held down over the little hole that leads from the ordinary world into hell. She had seen the writhing and had smelled the stinks.

She had crouched all the next day in her own bed in terror, fighting not to wake up and remember. She did not really wake until after four in the afternoon, when the students from her last class of the day would be already leaving the classroom in resentful bewilderment at her non-appearance.

She saw that the light of the winter afternoon was fading in her apartment. The screen of her television glowed a baleful gray-yellow. The vacant screen seemed to be watching. She imagined that at the other end of the circuit were studio technicians, newscasters and entertainers gathered in derisive expectation that she would put on an obscene display for them. She meant never to rise. She would keep the covers pulled to her chin until that spying stopped. She had looked into hell and gone mad.

Before full dark the phone rang. She reached from under the covers merely to stop the intolerable accusation of its ringing. She might have put it back without speaking if she had not heard the tone of pleading concern that came piping from it. "Oh, please answer. Are you all right? Please answer."

"I'm all right, Tamisan."

"When you didn't come to class today . . ."

"I was hung over. I'm all right."

"I didn't expect anything like that to happen. Truly, I didn't think it could with you along. I mean . . . he's evil. Truly, truly evil, and I guess I'd kill myself if you weren't all right."

"I'll be okay when I have a drink and a shower." As soon as she promised this, Janis believed it.

It took no very elaborate analysis to convince her that, once again, Tamisan was lying. Of course she and Sandler would have had at least a tacit understanding that Janis was fair game for their sport. But now such lies were positively medicinal. They made Janis feel less at the mercy of all the lies she had told herself to sustain her role as a woman who must make her way alone. How many foolish and unnecessary assumptions she had made about what she would never do. . . .

Now she had done some of them and survived. By the time she had toweled herself dry she could face her own reflection in the steamed bathroom mirror and raise her glass of gin in a rueful toast to its chastised smile. Now she could permit herself certain memories of what had been done the night before—now that they were behind her, they were not too gruesome to think about.

But for three months she managed to suppress most of her memories of what had happened that night. After three months she remembered they had taught her a great deal. At least they took away some fears about her body and other bodies that had menaced her all her life and had probably spoiled her marriage.

A year ago she would have been too anxious and uptight to enjoy posing like this, thinking like this, luxuriating in the kiss of the sun on her breasts, knowing that those who watched her saw her taking pleasure.

She heard old Dean Goss yell, "Take a break. Take a break, girls. Relax. You're not slave labor."

She picked up her cinnamon-colored towel and fastened it around her hips with a careless tuck. She ambled over the grass to see the great man's painting.

"It's not as good as what I saw," he teased as she stood nodding in appreciation of his watercolor.

"It's got . . . it's got . . . it's got . . ."

"What?" he inquired anxiously, as if he absolutely had to have her opinion.

"Purity," she said.

He laughed like a cynical old grandfather, but she insisted that was precisely what she saw in the three figures he had painted.

"At least your picture's given us back our female dignity," she told him in all earnestness.

"That there dignity of yours ain't so easy to lose as someone mighta told you," he drawled, and went on working.

from Susan Vail's red notebook:

The only secret she didn't need to keep from me, Tamisan kept best. She'd forsaken all others—thank God—for Jason two months before I knew he existed. I first laid eyes on him one glorious March day as she and I were coming out of Bloomingdale's. We talked to him on the sidewalk only long enough for me to realize he wasn't a classmate of hers.

"Nifty boy," I said to her as we walked on. Suddenly we were swinging along arm in arm, grinning at each other. "Isn't he beautiful?" she said. "He looks a lot like me." And I had to agree he looked like her plumpish twin as they'd stood there with me for five minutes on Lexington with the fresh cold smell of the Atlantic making our nostrils flare. His smile coaxed her to smile. They were twins in sympathy as well as looks. It was as if they shared a secret they might tell me if I were very, very good.

"We need a cup of hot chocolate," Tamisan said smugly. So I knew she was ready for confession. At last, I guessed, she had a confession rosy enough to offer instead of all the rough ones she's never made.

"Jason Goss is just as good as he looks," my darling said as she dabbed the froth of chocolate and cream from her unspoiled mouth. "He's accepted me. Just as I am, without one plea." Tamisan knows all the old hymns and can sing them to her own guitar accompaniment. She needed to say no more to pronounce him divine. "You couldn't help noticing his little frown?"

I was unwilling to admit any imperfection in him. My hair has been curled too often by drawing inferences about her other escapades. "The sun was awfully bright. He was squinting," I said.

"No. His frown is his sign. It never quite goes away. I peek while we're kissing. I *know* what it means." She shivered virginally and said, "Do I understand Jason? Karrumph! The way he curls his pinkie, even." She reached across the table to grab my hand, her thumb exploring the inside of my palm in a way that made me remember her at three. She said, "That frown is his way of asking, 'Are you all right?' He's so concerned for the people he cares about. His father mostly and me next."

"What's wrong with his father?"

"Oh, you'll hear about that. Soul trouble. But we're going to take care of that for him. But, about Jason, the bartender in this bar we meet sometimes always calls him Naz."

"That's not a very nice name," I said. It was phonetically unfit for the beauty who was, however temporarily, distracting my overgrown lovebird from dirty old men.

"It's an abbreviation for 'the Nazarene' and I think it's funny without being too funny. Everyone catches on that Jason is on a holiness trip, especially my teacher, Mrs. Ward, whose apartment we're often at when we're not at Jason's studio meditating."

"Meditating? Med . . . ? You . . . do what?"

"Of course we do other things too, Mama."

Then we boohooed together for a minute until I got hold of myself and demanded to know what her paragon was into besides the drug traffic, white slavery and sniping at the fuzz with high-powered rifles. *Meditation* sounded so lewd—or at least unfamiliar to my old ears—that my suspicions of her generation went out of control.

"We only smoke hash now and then and it's very pure," she swore. "I play my guitar some. . . . He used to play the cello. Mrs. Ward says he was a musical prodigy. He could be a professional if he wanted to be. He has too much sense to go to college. He meditates people instead."

"That sounds legal, at least."

"The reason he's living alone in this enormous, bare studio is to meditate his father. The trouble his father has is getting old and just being superficially great instead of fundamentally great like he was when Jason's mother was alive."

"Poor old fellow," I said, so swollen with the privilege of feeling sorry for Dean Goss I couldn't swallow my chocolate.

"Don't you think rich and great people have troubles too?" she demanded.

"I have not thought about that enough," I said humbly.

"We meditate you, too."

"I'm surprised there is time left over."

"The way you might fit in."

I weighed my fundamental merits: a simple heart, an inclination to idolatry, the grace I would bring to wealthy widowhood. "I could replace Jason's mother."

I was given to understand that was a *superficial* concern. "Jason's brother fixes his father up with *women*. He has all of *that* he can handle at his age. You're a writer. Everybody should do what he can do best."

So it appears that my book—even my wish to do it—was foreseen and probably plotted in their druidical meditations in that studio where all but the ghost of Dean Goss's youth has long since vacated.

Chapter 3

When Dean Goss yelled to the posing girls to remind them they were not slave labor, Tamisan picked up the cerulean towel. With that much covering, she shuffled across the grass to her mother. "Hi. Surprised to see me?"

"Delighted," Susan said. "Surprised, too. You're so much . . . taller than Jean Simons. I hadn't realized."

Tamisan snorted. "It didn't seem like such a freaky idea when we planned it. Too late to change my mind now."

"It's *not* a freaky idea," Susan said briskly. The familiar unbalance between her and Tamisan was showing up. The girl wanted her posing to seem an act of defiance. It put her off to find her mother taking it calmly. "It's a historic thing to be painted by Dean Goss."

Her daughter blew a soft but blatant raspberry. "Where's that rat Jason? I'm going to make him strip off too, now that he got me into this." She flipped her hair and turned to spot Jason coming through the group of sketchers, bringing Bern Whitestar to introduce him to Susan. Whitestar was a sculptor who had a house and studio near Southampton. Not far. The model Jean Simons worked for him three afternoons a week, when she was not needed by Dean Goss.

"I met you at the opening of your show at the Ferris Gallery last year," Susan said.

Whitestar looked apologetically puzzled. Susan laughed. "Why should you remember? There was such a mob of admirers."

In the casual, lovely setting of the garden, he seemed much handsomer than she recalled. His skin was brown as walnut stain. His slender brown arms and legs were corded with sinew, and his prematurely gray hair was curled in tight, faunish ringlets. His Spanish-Jewish face was sharp as a wedge. His eyes were yellowed hazel.

"Susan's last novel was *The Monkey Tree*," Jason said. Then he yelled, "Stop it!" Tamisan had grabbed the buckle of his belt and was trying to steal his shorts.

"You promised!"

Laughing and fending her away, Jason said, "I'm too exposed already. If I let them see you they can guess everything about me." Nothing was settled by their wrestling except that Tamisan's towel fell from her. Whitestar retrieved it and helped her fasten it again with a tuck. He seemed to forget, in the process, how Susan had been introduced to him and asked if she were a painter or a sculptor or what.

"I wrote *The Monkey Tree*. It's pure autobiography describing how I was raped by an ape and gave birth to this monster." She was really very hot with anger, for that minute. What she felt was not at all motherly. She had seen Tamisan's horseplay distract a fine man's attention from her. Now she had to stand by grinning while Whitestar opened his sketch book to show Tamisan the drawings he had made of her.

"I'm not *that* boxy," Tamisan said, flipping the pages of pencil drawings quickly. "Why just me? There are three of us posing."

Whitestar laughed indulgently. "I draw Jean Simons day after day. She's got what we like to call 'a strong figure' . . ."

"Big boobs," Tamisan said, nodding like the appreciative student she would never be, making her own, more refined breasts nod their intellectual appreciation of his explanation. "More muscle in the leg."

Whitestar said, "No, you're not that boxy, sweetheart. I'm a sculptor, so I make you all into cubes and spheres."

"Is *that* what you do to us?" Tamisan said, with sultry mocking. And her mother came within an ace of slapping her. Her mother devoutly wished Jason was the type to use a whip on his women.

"You're okay, Tami," Whitestar said. "You can work for me any time. Come over to my studio with Jean and I'll draw you both."

"Please don't call me Tami."

Susan said, "Well, she wouldn't take typing in school and everything else is beyond her, so I guess she has to go as a menial."

"I'll come sweep out your studio. I don't like posing," Tamisan said. "It's kind of sluttish, isn't it, Mama?"

Whitestar felt the tensions and retired to a milder line. He said to Jason, "Your dad looks happy as a clam. I didn't know he painted in watercolors any more."

"That was my idea too," Jason said, as earnestly as if he had not even seen Tamisan's flirtations. "When I was little I liked to see him do watercolors more than anything. Maybe because they can be finished in a sitting. They catch a minute of light that's marvelous and never comes again. . . ."

"You know he was first famous as a watercolorist," Susan said, as if she had proprietary rights on explaining Dean Goss to the world. He was her subject. She had done her homework on him. She had no bare tits to reclaim attention from her daughter, but in the warm confusion of the moment she could offer a mind to the competition.

"I've seen some from the twenties, of course," Whitestar said. "Yes, his reputation could stand on them if there weren't all the other, later things." And as his inner eye recalled paintings of Dean Goss, his attention went away from both Susan and her daughter. He seemed to be counting the artists still scattered around the garden—Ken Mandelstam, Baird Holman, George Vendler, Willi Poletski, Miriam Barnstone and her brother and half a dozen others of promise or accomplishment. "The truth is, Jason, that you had a very generous idea when you arranged this. All of us will be telling the story for years. 'Once upon a time, on a summer day you wouldn't believe, I sat in a garden painting three goddesses with Dean Goss himself . . .'"

"Goddesses!" Tamisan snorted. Her eyes went hard with contempt at such corny flattery and she hitched the towel tighter around her loins.

"Three goddesses," Whitestar insisted. "Look! It's precisely like the Judgment of Paris, when they appeared on the mountain in front of that boy Paris and told him he had to choose between them. Isn't that what you had in mind when you planned this, Jason?"

"That's not exactly the point," Jason said, frowning his polite and delicate frown. But whatever he was preparing to answer was interrupted by a call from Janis Ward.

"The boss says it's time to do our bit."

The red, the cinnamon, and the cerulean towels were dropped in the grass again. The hypothetical goddesses were at work once more.

The point, Jason thought. The point of this . . .

The point for him was standing behind his father at work. He stood there watching the rich, absorbent paper take the colors. He felt the old, marveling serenity he had felt at five or ten when he watched his father paint. *He is making things be all right. He is making them new.*

And his mother—more beautiful than any merely naked female shape could be—said, "Daddy makes worlds for us." He and his mother, both children watching with breathless anxiety, as if they might die unless the painter's hand made a world secure enough for them to lay down their heads and sleep.

The wash flowed on the paper. A flood of virginal color like that which must have colored Eden before the spots of flowers and apples and the stringy vines and the animal shapes were stroked in by the Creator.

His mother had been fresh and beautiful as that wash of color before the color began to define any shape of breast or torso or leg of the posing girls. Pure matrix of green, foretelling the shapes of girls to emerge, the way the new green of springtime prophesies the coming of a love that is altogether uncomplicated by the smears and complications that have gone before. The evening star is called Venus because it lays such washes of prophetic light down the cliffs of darkness. The light, the color are not the shape of love but that all-powerful promise from which the shapes and finally the names will inevitably emerge.

Breathless again, he stood behind his father's easel waiting for the shape of Tamisan Vail to become distinct—as the winter before he had waited for someone real to emerge from the sketchy suggestions Janis gave him.

In the candlelight over Janis' dinner table he had glimpsed some outline of impassioned and indomitable movement. Orphan, criminal, outsider, avenger, alien, woman. An Amazon smile of teeth bared in a hopeless and everlasting war.

There had been absolutely nothing soft, nothing gentle in that image where his love began. The necessary gentleness was in him—all that is usually called feminine—waiting to be claimed, mated, matched when Tamisan came to his father's abandoned studio and their erotic life changed from dream to a larger dream.

The first night Janis brought her there to meet him, the girl's question at the door was, "May I take my shoes off?" And he had answered, "Watch out then, you might get splinters."

Well, Tamisan liked to go barefoot and that was all the explanation required by people like Janis Ward, who saw only part of what was happening under her nose. Let Janis suppose the rest was make-believe to pass the time before her young friends got down to the real thing.

Certainly Janis had not said outright that she was bringing the girl to lay Jason. It did not need to be said. Tamisan had appeared that evening wearing a dress instead of her uniform jeans. It was, for Janis, a sign of readiness to begin something new. An abandonment of her defiant militancy.

What both the younger two recognized as Tamisan kicked off her shoes was that she was entering a shrine. "Why is it so empty except for you?" she asked Jason. Without waiting for an answer she went barefooted to explore that emptiness with obvious delight, declaring it a shrine by her ecstatic movement. They could decide later whom the shrine was dedicated to. She entered it as if it had been intended for her, as if Jason's lonely vigil had been a devotion she was now ready to claim. She moved away from them with the exhilaration of a skydiver giving herself to the freedom of falling. At the far end of the barnlike emptiness she twirled like a Degas dancer finding the

55

balance point in the limitless inward space of the painter's vision. Jason saw her claiming her place among those rare and stranger creatures of the inner eye his father had painted before he was born. Had painted here, between these walls. Those his father had caught on canvas were as dead as moths pinned in rows in a collector's box. The ones that had not been painted were still alive here. He had never been so sure of their existence as now, when they seemed to cluster around the barefoot girl and welcome her as one of them.

Tamisan came gloating back to the one corner that was furnished with Jason's mattress on the floor, his table and hot plates. "I've been here before," she told them.

"*Déjà vu,*" Janis said, but she was on the outside of a conversation already more profound than any sexual embrace she could have foreseen.

"What do you do here?" Tamisan demanded.

"I sleep a lot. Someone said that sleeping is the prime act of genius. I'm learning to sleep."

"Kierkegaard," Tamisan said, flopping on his mattress. "I'm not a genius. I'm just a walking gifted-child syndrome." She took the glass of wine he offered. It was sacramental when she put it to her lips.

He said, "I didn't know why I came to live here when I came. Now I know pretty well. With people I had to pretend to be whole. I needed this time to make myself whole." He blushed a little at the arrogance of claiming he had succeeded. "Not yet. I don't have the energy to waste on the human side of my life."

"I waste all mine," Tamisan said. "I'm paranoid of having any left over, because if I did I'd get in real trouble."

"It's good to be in trouble," he thought. "I came here to make things worse. I have to go past people to get outside my experience. I'm trying to get rid of what I learned at school. They said I was learning to get along with others. In fact I was getting too good at putting up stones in a wall that would shut me off—really shut me off—forever. I'm afraid that's what my father has done. I know my father was in trouble when he used to be in this place. Those were his bad years, and everything seemed to get smoother and more open for him ever since. But he thrived best on his trouble."

"Isn't he happy any more?" Tamisan's eyes were wide at the notion anyone as ancient and famous as Dean Goss might be unhappy.

Plainly this was the king of riddles for Jason and he tried to meet it with his queer, slow humility. "He's probably happy. With a man like that, who's smart enough to tell? Except himself. And he won't or can't any more. *That's* what is wrong and what I wish I could help him with by what I learn here. The real person has gone out of sight. It disappeared behind his work."

"That's the ideal," Janis said. "To slip out of nature like that." She could cite poems as well as critical opinion to bolster this view. "A man becoming immortal in his work."

Quietly but fiercely they both sided against her. Jason had thought it out. Tamisan didn't need to think about it. They refused whatever had a shell on it or a screen around it. How wrong, wrong, wrong for anyone vital to be smothered under his own creations! They made Dean Goss's paintings sound like the polution of an industrial society, cluttering the world.

"You're putting me on," Janis said—not for the last time that evening. But, truly, whatever they were doing they were doing with each other. Not quite ignoring her but outdistancing her from the beginning as they slid so easily into an intimacy she could not have foreseen.

"The beauty of my father isn't in what he does. That's only the rabbit tracks. The beauty is, he could always renew himself. That's why he's great. I know when he worked here there was a terrible crisis in his life. I don't know the history. I don't need to. I'm here to feel it. Invite it to happen to me. Think my way close to the secret. The renewal is the secret worth having. Letting himself sink, sink, sink so he can rise. It's what I want to contemplate. I don't want to see his things hanging in museums."

That was Jason's lead-off. Tamison's dazzled responses raced after his ecstatic surmises. It was like watching two long pennants stream out and ripple in the same wind as she seized the instant intimacy he offered. As if they had seen when they saw that they looked alike that there was an inner resemblance they needn't wait to claim. "An artist ought to go out like a kamikaze," she thought. "That's where my mother got stuck. From here on she'll shrivel up and die instead of opening up and dying at the right time."

"I don't want him ever to die, but . . ."

"I don't either. I know. How else can you talk about the way they ought to live?"

Suddenly they were parents together, worried about their reluctant children, wishing to shake them into haste enough to outrun the specter of age coming up behind them. Wanting language to warn their elders not to miss the one and only chance to be on time at the real feast of life.

"It's not that I want him childish," Jason said.

"Ridiculous!" Tamisan agreed.

"But isn't there always a child part that ought to be kept alive? With my mother we were like three children when we were best. I think he knew then the adult part, and money and fame and being a name, was mostly fraud. Before that is when it's best, I believe."

"That's when it's tolerable at all. Mama's life isn't like her at all. She gives in to it because she thinks that sets me an example. Oh, God! That's what killed things between us, watching her give in, give in. She uses me as an excuse and that's what made everything go topsy-turvy. But your father is rich and that's different."

Jason would not argue that the circumstances were not immensely different. It was a subtler sort of stagnation that terrified him. "He let himself become public property. He's still very much alive. Full of vinegar. But acting his life, not living it."

"We know that but we can't say it to them," Tamisan said. "Can't tell them to grab it while it's all ahead of them."

Janis said, "If you talk like this to them, it's no wonder they can't comprehend. You're utterly unintelligible."

Without stressing their superiority, they admitted they were unintelligible to her. Admitted how much more so they must be to their parents. And yet the overtones of what they said to each other must be translatable. There had to be some correspondences between the language that spelled out the good life and that which spelled out the life of desire.

"Janis thinks I'm a death freak because I wrote a paper about suicide," Tamisan said.

"Well, it sticks in my mind," Janis said wryly.

"Which only meant great people ought to live like suicides could. Not held back by anything. Then they'd be their best."

Jason said, "I've got a little list in my brain of the times my father ought to have killed himself and it's the same as when he was the greatest man."

"Yes!" Tamisan said.

"Don't do it while I'm on the premises, if that's your heartfelt conviction," Janis said. "I hate death."

"You have to be worthy to kill yourself," Jason said. "That seems very clear to me. It would take the greatest of all artists to make it right."

Tamisan said, "Yes, yes, yes, Janis. Jason, I know a death freak, but he's not worthy. I think about death but I never know what to do."

"If it was just *doing* things, I ought to go burn myself at the U.N. to protest the war and all the lies they're going to keep on telling," Jason said, frowning.

"Anybody should," Tamisan said. "Why don't you?" It was her way of declaring that she found him worthy.

"It's not that I'm afraid."

"Hush then," Janis ordered. "It's indecent to talk about such things unless you utterly mean what you say."

"We shouldn't talk at all unless we utterly mean it," Tamisan thought. But the challenge drove them to change the subject. In their humiliation, she and Jason agreed that only the dead truly deserved to talk about suicide.

They were not going to kill themselves—or even kiss—that night. But it would seem to them and to Janis later that something had happened that was on the same scale as one or the other. Some tangling of wings high in the air. A dalliance of

59

eagles. An invisible coupling that would not be more intense or better expressed when they lay together in a naked embrace while their sweat softened and crusted again to their rhythmic ardor.

They were putting her on. Putting each other on. Exchanging those mystic vestments of the body, the rituals of acceptance that always precede a coupling that is going to be inescapable.

"We were hot that night," each of them would say to Janis later. And she would answer, deadpan, "Yes, I could tell." And she would ask, as a friend, a practical and tolerant friend, "Why didn't you go after it? I was only waiting for a signal to take my coat and go."

And both would say, "We were *too* hot. We might have spoiled it before it really began."

It was going to be later than anyone else would suppose before they had any "grown-up sex." They touched with that ardor of children which they wanted renewed in their parents. He gave Tamisan property rights to all the invisible and intangible things hoarded and guarded by him in the emptiness of this abandoned studio. He let her through the gate into a world that was purely imaginary for her and yet beyond the imagination because the trees and flowers in it seemed to be watched by other eyes than hers. It was the world he had set out to reclaim when his mother died.

"My father and I went different ways after that. I lost my way of being with him. He was much older than I. Older than Maggie, too, of course, but since he was like her father too, he could be my super father. It wasn't a matter of being proud of him. We didn't ever think of that. He gave me a coat of many colors. A childhood so big I still can't even see to the edges of it. There's still so much room in it. We didn't use it all up before it was gone."

"You want him to come back there and play with you," Tamisan teased. She was not trying to stop this grave and gay revelation. She was angling for more.

"Yes!" he said. "You can make fun if you want . . ."

"Oh no. You're hiding away so no one can make fun of what's honest and that's what I want to do."

"I know it can't literally be. Still, I'm sure of this: everything that can be imagined properly can be translated—the way you transpose in music from one key to another—into ways to live."

"Can even dying be transposed into a way to live?" Janis asked.

"I don't know," he said with perfect humility. "I haven't got that far yet. But I'm working on it. I want to wait here until I'm renewed the way my father was. Then I'll go out of here like a storm."

Certainly his face was aglow with the hunger and fervor of life as he plotted to transpose the glamors of a dead time onto a future that was still just as lifeless. "I've got to get out by going back, back, back." It was in his retreat that the girl's passion moved in time with his.

From his skimpy bookshelves he pulled out photograph albums. All that remained of the years that had gone without being used up. A black and white map of the places and faces of the great good time. Nassau. Sardinia. Big Sur. Manhattan. Rome. Deauville. Aix. "Actually we didn't move around that much. I'm a city boy. We were mostly here in New York. But we *could* be wherever my father wanted to work."

For him the great good place had been a farm in Pennsylvania where his father painted in the remodeled barn many summers while his young wife sported like a sister with her growing son. As he offered the pages of this idyll, the series seemed to begin with a keynote photo of Maggie Goss as a naked girl, shy and strong, climbing into a shadowy grove beside the river, dragging her infant by one stretched arm. "That's where we built the boathouse later," he said, his trembling voice building it again. But Tamisan saw something else. "Imagine having knockers like that in your mouth," she crowed. "Talk about being spoiled!"

Jason said, "My father thought the main thing about breast feeding wasn't the quality of the milk but having something nice to squeeze in your hand while you feed."

"Did he try it too?"

"You can be sure he did," Jason agreed, delighted to be prompted with something he hadn't thought of yet. "He was never content to miss anything. But it wouldn't do to ask him now. You have to get at the real truth by meditating, don't you? I know he did. Yes, I know that *now,* thank you." There was too much more for him to pause just yet for the proposed meditation on suckling. It seemed something he would turn over and weave into the fabric of the rediscovered past at his leisure.

"Here," he said, turning a page, "Maggie's riding the horse we called Boss. You can't see me. I'm somewhere back in the clover field—coming around the wall she's just jumped—on my Shetland pony. And here . . . in this one Dad and Maggie are on the Rue St. Honoré. She's still only seventeen. Would you believe that? They got married when she was seventeen. That was Dad's last major scandal. She kept him busy at home, I do believe. My grandfather Niles raised hell on two continents because Dad was so much older and had presumably seduced the precious girl, though he says who ever knows which does it to whom? And Maggie seduced everyone. Not all the way. But everywhere you went you could see them turning like compass needles toward her. . . ."

Something in this celebration moved Tamisan to mutter, "I'm only nineteen."

He wanted her to know that the farm in Pennsylvania was bigger than the world the pictures showed. "From the window of my room, when the light changed over the river and the fields, the hills seemed to be moved from place to place. Like chess pieces moving by themselves. It was like watching Creation."

As they closed the album she said, "So why aren't you back on the farm instead of in this bare place?"

He had meditated on the answer too long to stumble over his reply. "Because if I was there I would see it had changed. From here it doesn't change. It's the same reason I had for giving up my cello. For a while it was my way to get to hear music, to know what it was. Now the cello, or records, only get in my way. The real music isn't sound, I think."

"That's in a poem by Wallace Stevens, that idea," Tamisan said. " 'Is it the blackbird's whistle . . . or the silence just after?' "

It didn't matter if an old artist named Stevens had written that poem. It was theirs. It was written for them. They were in the silence that followed the writing of poems, the playing of music, the painting of pictures.

When, at the end of that night, the three of them came down the broad steps from the studio and he had found them a cab on the nearest avenue, she said, shivering in the early morning cold, "Will you take me back to your farm sometime?"

It was plain that he would have liked to promise. He would have liked to promise something as impossible as taking her back to the lost summers of his childhood. But the impossibility made him stammer, and he even bungled his invitation to her to come again. "Come if you feel like it."

"When?"

"I don't care."

With a sad snort she said, "I'm noisy and you like silence."

Full of confused ecstasy, he muttered, "That's true."

"If I came back it would spoil what was good tonight," she said.

He missed the chance to deny it. He even said, "That's true, too." But then—betrayed by words, betrayed by the sad truth of reality—he suddenly pulled a key from his pocket, put it in her palm and forced her fingers closed around it. "It's my door key. Use it whenever you want."

"I won't," she said. "I'll just keep it for a souvenir."

Now, this afternoon, in the sun near the ocean, Jason felt memories of that night dissolve and flow into older memories as he watched his father painting. Watching the picture emerge gave no illusion that he and his father might escape from where time had brought them. No—but it woke a reverie in which the deep sympathies he had once shared easily with his father came back to confirm the wonders they could never express in common speech. A reverie so soothing that he could not help

resentment at its interruptions. It was another of those times—
the series going back forever—that ought not to end but go on
everlastingly embalmed in the atmosphere of the day, since
neither paint nor any other medium was quite adequate to preserve its essence.

It was a resentment he seemed to share silently with his father
each time there was a break in the posing and the girls moved
back into the faithless commonplaces of their characters and
names.

This time when the pose broke, Herb Treibaum and Baird
Holman got up from the grass and came over respectfully to
see the progress of Dean Goss's watercolor.

*They always come to him to make him be Dean Goss instead
of my father.* No blame to them for that. It was natural and good.
Why did the natural and good always have to nudge out other
things natural and good?

"Mmmmmmm. Mmmmmmmm!" Herb Treibaum said. "That
patch of green there. Mmmmmmm. The violet. Uhhhhhh." Nothing is more expressive than the noises of painters faced with a
painting. And I love that too, Jason thought, but . . . "Do you
put the burden of statement *there* on the negative space? Thee,
ah . . . yuh. Yuh, yuh, yuh."

"I'd better!" Dean Goss laughed. "Negative space, how I
love thee. Three twats in a negative space."

"Great title!" Holman said. "Negative space descending a
staircase. . . . That yellow. Is it New Gamboge?"

"It is, it is. Lovely stuff," Dean Goss said. "Do you ever get
the feeling the painting is already there, inside the tube? Three
twats in a tube."

"We seem to agree that the *mmmmmm* . . . ladies have to
be somewhere," Treibaum said. "If we knew just where they
ought to be, we'd know how to get back to figurative painting.
There's got to be a way back to the figure, don't you think so,
Mr. Goss?"

"We must feel our way back," Goss said. "What you suggest
is very interesting. The ladies have got to be somewhere in the
painting. They're necessary in the process. Yes, yes, yes. Without the twat, no painting at all. You young fellows should tell

me where our lost Aphrodite is hiding in your work. In the veins of the body? In the painter's hand? In the tubes of color? In negative space?"

"You've put her back in her visible body," Treibaum said with a handsome jerk of his thumb at the watercolor paper.

"Don't flatter me," Dean Goss said. "She's not as easy to find as that. I feel she's among us, though."

"In the left or right testicle?" Holman laughed.

"I used to believe that," Goss said. "Well, we pay tribute anyway, though she hides from us. We know we can't get back to the figure the easy way, so we go on doing our best."

In a minute Goss was talking to the younger men about the brush he was using. "The Chinese knew that using only a single brush will unify the work. My father now, my father, you know the good old fellow came within an ace of being president of the American Watercolor Society. Claimed it was only politics that kept him out. Nevertheless in his lifetime I'd say he accumulated at least three hundred watercolor brushes. All sizes. All hairs. All degrees of stiffness. Fat ones to hold lots of wash. Skinny stiff ones. Some that would droop over like a wilted flower. If he saw me now, trying to make do with only one brush, he'd see all his prophecies of my decadent future confirmed. But the Chinese would see him as a decadent and so it goes. We try to find our place. . . ."

It was clear to Jason that the younger men were listening for more than technical tips or anecdotes from his father. They liked the banter. They strained to hear the fervor it masked, just as they were all straining to see the female image they bantered about manifest itself *either* in the girls posing *or* on the paper or canvas they were using.

We're all in this together and that is good, Jason thought. He felt no jealousy in thinking the others were his father's sons as well as he. But . . .

"Watercolor's a devilish medium," his father was saying. "That's why I gave it up long ago. I couldn't match its trickery. There are no mistakes in a good watercolor painting. My father told me that. 'Don't make mistakes,' he said. Ha! Of course we'll make mistakes. But then! You have to reclaim them.

65

You have to make the mistakes part of your own design. Make them intentional after they've happened. That's the great challenge. But it's too hard for me. Too hard. It's only amusement for me now. A little play, with pretty girls to ogle. That's enough."

And it's what he deserves, Jason thought, to be turned loose to play. To be respected and at ease. But still, the little insect of resentment and frustration buzzed in his head.

"You want him to come back there and play with you," Tamisan had teased. And that was it, just as sure as it was impossible. He wanted his father to come back again, again, and always to reclaim the oldest mistakes, losses, tragedies, glories in his life and once again make something new of them all. He wanted to see the master trick of renewal done once more.

So I'll know that what I'm doing with my life is possible at least, Jason thought. That what I've supposed about Tamisan and me isn't the worst mistake I could possibly make.

He had been in love with Tamisan before he knew her and had made every possible mistake with her and every mistake about her.

He had wanted her. He had not wanted her to interrupt his loneliness any more than he wanted to take her back down to the Pennsylvania farm to see the deep pool in the river where he and his mother had bathed in erotic innocence. He did not suppose he had anything to give her. He was doing nothing that could be shared. The emotions he might have concentrated exclusively on her were less troublesome when they were left to spread at their own whim through the silence of his solitude.

"Didn't you even think of telephoning?" she would demand —after that mistake had been reclaimed and made all right.

"No," he had admitted. He might have admitted he had not even been ashamed of this lethargy until it was too late to do anything about it. He was already settling into the habit of thinking she was someone he had loved once upon a time when she called him.

The first call accomplished nothing practical. She said, "I've been thinking about all the freak things you said that night. You've already had your whole life. I've already had mine and it was lousy." It was her way of renouncing the men who had always found her willing if not eager.

The next call from her was equally cryptic and brief.

"Girls," she asked. "Are you seeing any?"

"Not lately. I haven't even seen Janis since you were here."

"Then you do need something."

"I suppose I do. I like people."

"Then why don't you *need* them?"

"I don't need them close. *Alles ist weit.*"

"Teach me German," she pleaded.

She called a third time. "You're right about not needing human beings. You and I don't need them. But don't we need each other?"

"I thought we did. I thought you were going to bring your guitar and sing to me."

"That's why I haven't come," she said. "I'm no good. My voice is all right, but I can't play. Not really. I do it to *inflict* myself on people who deserve punishment. I thought you could teach me just to sit still with my guitar and not make a sound."

On that pleading hint, he offered to take her to the Metropolitan Museum to see the collections of antique and exotic musical instruments. It was the quietest date she had ever had. They stood together in front of a tall glass case containing fourteenth-century horns from Hungary. Great loops of slender tubing against a red velvet background, the metal richly patinaed with time, the tubes flaring to bells as homely and awesome as cooking utensils.

Tamisan's finger traced the elfin geometry of the instruments protected by the glass. She said, "You always teach me things. I see what you mean about hearing music when no one is really playing. You don't really have to touch. You don't really have to hear. . . . But what if I shut my eyes and couldn't even see?" She was completely earnest in expecting an important answer from him. "Do you think lots about death?"

67

"Not by itself. It's always *part* of my thoughts about anything. It's like the velvet background behind those horns. It's always visible behind things and makes them stand out brighter."

That pleased her and made her brave enough to admit, "It comes and goes with me. When it comes—whoosh! It's very big for me. Whenever I think about death I masturbate," she said in a low, thrilling voice.

Then she felt she had been too brave. He went dead silent at her confession, seeming to be unaware of her presence. He turned to walk away from the displayed instruments as if he were alone. She followed, a little angry at herself, angry at him for giving her the confidence to make a fool of herself.

They were out of the museum and walking in the park when he said in a voice that was like a loud whisper, "It could be a sacrament."

"What?"

"Masturbation. It's not such a simple thing as everyone makes out."

"The argument against it is it makes you anti-social," she said, not only relieved that he had been heavily meditating rather than shocked, but glad to feel that her secret had mirrored or echoed what he would otherwise never have yielded to her. "Do you, a lot?" she asked.

"Sometimes lots," he said. "Sometimes not for weeks. Emptiness—like the emptiness in the studio—makes me hot. I come in from the streets sometimes and the emptiness is like . . . is like . . . is like . . . not a woman, but . . ."

He seemed to be speaking from that emptiness, in a voice without the volume of ordinary conversation—as if he were speaking to himself, yet anxious that she should overhear him.

"You *have* to worship it," she said.

"It is a *kind* of worship," he answered, with the totally vulnerable frankness that made her weak with sympathy.

"It's better than a woman," she guessed.

"What's better?"

"That emptiness where there . . . where there . . ."

"Where there *could be* a woman," he finished.

"Where there could be the perfect woman."

"Only there isn't," he said. His frown deepened, as if an invisible fingernail might be making a track across the skin of his forehead. "Except . . . I don't *know* that I'm alone when I do it. Sometimes I literally don't believe I am."

"Who's with you?" she asked, half breathless with jealousy.

"I don't know. I couldn't say. Truly."

"Is it pictures or someone you've actually known? I've never had a boy who'd tell me anything about it. And men lie when they say they're reminiscing and make it something to laugh about. Always."

"It isn't pictures. Not magazine pictures. It isn't fantasies either. It's as close as I can come to clairvoyance. I know the women are there . . . that is, I don't know, but they are anyway."

"Sort of," she agreed encouragingly.

"But I don't see them, either, or touch them. It's beyond that."

"Is it your father's women? The ones that would have been there in the studio with him before you were born?"

He started to blush but smiled instead. "You're mighty smart."

"Only about some things," she said smugly, very pleased with both of them. Their dialogue had been of an intensity that changed their awareness of their surroundings. They had made the wintry park and the black trees stirring against the harsh sky into a fearful garden where they went on tiptoe like Hansel and Gretel afraid of the witch.

They were afraid—and yet they had dared expose their tenderest and most secret honesties to this biting weather. Their daring burned like a coal in the wind.

She said, with the gravity of a princess climbing the steps of a scaffold, "I suppose I do that better than anything I do. Masturbate. God! What if that's true?"

He saw her mouth try to smile. Try . . . and the smile was there, self-mocking, melancholy, even deathly, but somehow indelible. As if the wintry day itself had managed the smile of its bitter certainty.

"I always knew I'd be the champion of something there can't

be a champion of," she said, with a voice that thrilled him like the north wind in its attempt to joke.

Burned by her crazy gallantry, he wanted to embrace her and shelter her. He did nothing of the sort. They trudged on, their faces reddened with the cold.

But it was as if he held her now. . . . They had both been thrown down from a terribly high place, spinning downward past the beasts of space and darkness, lost beyond gravity itself, and yet locked each to each in a despair so fine it was like joy.

She was breathless and red-faced once when she met him in a midtown ice cream parlor.

"Why'd you run? It doesn't matter to me if you're late," he told her.

"I saw a man coming toward me down the street."

"Did he chase you?"

"He didn't even get close enough to see me. I was scared to meet him again. I ran all the way here."

It had never occurred to him that any man could frighten her. "I thought you got along all right with men."

She snorted coarsely, near tears. "I suppose Janis told you I'm the easiest lay in town."

"She only said . . ."

"Okay. I've screwed a bushel. Men! Zey say, 'Do zees, do zat, do ze ozzer sing.' So I did."

"Did you like it?"

"They liked it, so I got to liking it. I didn't like them. It's a good thing you like silence, because if I ever started to talk I'd really gross you out."

"That's silly."

"Ho! I told you I masturbated and you held that against me. I'm too dirty a girl for you to love, Jason."

"No!" he said. "What you've done with men couldn't bother me."

"*Nothing* can stir you up," she said, suddenly veering off into sulkiness, pretending to be at the end of her rope because she could not rouse his jealousy.

That wasn't the point either. What had touched him was that she might be frightened by a human being, any human being. He had lazily thought of her as going her way, doing as she pleased, impervious to hurt. He did not want to own her, but he wanted to shelter her, to let her know she had a place of safety with him if he could offer nothing else. So he reminded her he had given her a key to his studio. "I thought you liked being there. If you want to come and read . . . Whatever you need to do without being bothered. Come any time, whether I'm there or not."

Confronted with such frustrating innocence, she said, "You're a total freak."

He liked that better than being considered a threatening male. "I'm Dean Goss's son," he said. "It's only natural my personality displays the tension of polarities that produces either geniuses or freaks."

"Wow!" she said. "We can both teach each other something."

She felt then that he had meant to trap her by giving her the key. She was incapable of believing that his cunning was less than hers. He was foreign to everything she had yet encountered —therefore, his designs must be incredibly sinister. Therefore alluring.

"I was very paranoid of you," she told him later. She was tempted by sheer and sometimes breathless curiosity about his schemes for her before she learned that he had none. He despised plans. "I don't think about the future," he said, grimacing with distaste. He was patient with the present only because it was still connected to the beloved past.

She used his key because she could not resist traps. Sometimes she had liked the traps men set for her more than the bait. But the door opened for her this time on simple shelter and quiet. On peace that stimulated her more wildly than two men at a time ever had. Jason was attentive to her coming and going, but he asked nothing. He was as undemanding and unassertive as her own image moving in a mirror. Once she climbed the long flight of stairs and opened the door to find him sleeping like a cherub. She sat watching him for an hour. If her face could ever be that *blessed-looking* she would want to die instead of waking.

Once she came in and found he was not there. She went to sleep on his bed while she waited. When she woke he had still not come in but she felt he had been there with her. The emptiness of the studio no longer seemed an emptiness at all. There seemed to be an unmeasurable tonnage pressing down on the skylight as if it might be buried under an avalanche. But something shouldered it invisibly from within, a nameless tranquil force that baffled her . . . and made her hot.

They both would have admitted their conversation was trivial when she visited. They never talked about art, politics, sex, ideas. He told her about *things*. If he had been walking before she got there, he would likely have stopped to read the labels on bottles in a drugstore display window. Or he had walked across the bridge to Brooklyn Heights. What he had marveled at was that the gulls were flying *under his feet*. Did anyone but him stop to count the cables on the bridge to see if there were as many on one side as on the other? He had counted seventy-four ships in the river or visible in the harbor beyond the Battery. The number seventy-four seemed to impress him as much as anything he could remember to tell her about the farm where the shifting daylight on the hills had made him think of Creation. She listened in awe. She wanted seventy-four ships of her own. . . .

He came in one February afternoon to find her ahead of him. All that was different from other days, he thought, was that she was wearing his jeans, his sweat shirt and boots. The jeans, at least, were identical with her own. But as soon as she heard his key in the lock, she had risen to meet him, growing taller like the image in a mirror heightening as he walked to meet it. She paused when he paused and it seemed to him the expression of surrender on her face was exactly what his must be. Her tongue wet her lips and she tried to say something.

They both nodded when he tried to say, *Help me. Please.*

Their fingertips met in a delicate frenzy and they stood holding each other off that way in an emptiness that would have collapsed like a vacuum unless they were strong enough to fill it with breath.

"I don't want to be me," she said. "I want your life. Please!"

They had never yet kissed and they did not kiss then.

"I want it when you were a little boy and happy," she said. "Fuck it into me."

He put his hands on the belt he had fastened only yesterday around his own waist and undid the buckle. He unfastened the catch. His hand slid down the smooth, twitching curve of her belly—and down and down, encountering no crisp shield of hair but incurving smoothness and warmth and that curled edge where the skin becomes a surface more alive and sweetly moist.

"Look, too," she said. The jeans fell around her ankles and she threw up her arm to hide her face. "I was like this," she said with echoing melancholy.

Her smoothly shaved mound was pale as the ghost of the innocence she wanted him to take.

The discoveries of touch were sheer surprise. It was as if someone had hit him a great painless blow in the back, driving out his breath and bewildering the nerves that moved involuntarily to recover it. To find this proudly passionate woman's body offering him the hairless orifice of a child was like uncovering an unexpected mutilation, sacrifice and transformation that changed him too. It was a shock that invaded him to the deepest roots of erotic memory, flinging him back into those shadow years when the idea of *girl* was still not distinguished from the disturbing rumors of pleasure and fear that pulsed in the hardening of his little cock.

It broke the shell of manhood he had been trying to escape in meditations. It freed him for a startled moment from the image of his own body and when he knelt, now, to look at what his astonished fingers had found, he knelt unself-conscious as a child awed into forgetfulness of his own body. The pale smoothness of her pubic curves stretched in his vision like a moon-yellowed snowhill bending to an indistinct horizon. He laid the curve of his cheek against it as if it might cool the quick fever that made him weak.

"Gift," she said. "Don't laugh at me."

He could not have laughed or thought either until she knelt facing him and began to peel his clothes down. And then his thought seemed to be forming again, not from the present, but from a simpler, worshiping self that had been dead within him and was reclaiming its life where it had left off. She found his cock and cherished it in both her hands as a child might stroke an unfeathered bird, reassuring it. Trembling herself, as if any wrong move might panic the wild and alien sweetness they had found together, she rolled back and brought him into her quickly as he came.

The flood of his own juice around him kept him going. He could no more stop now than he could have paused in mid-air at the height of a jump. He thought he was trying to escape but the motion of withdrawal brought him forward again against the polished, shaven smoothness. Her arms and legs bound him and enforced the rhythm until it was his own. The limits that separated one sense from another were melted away and, with them, whatever it is that perceives the distinction of one body from another. He was no more in her than she was in him and what they exchanged were the virginities they had been afraid to yield or even admit before.

They knew that as they clung together. And knew the fear of it as they finally relaxed apart. They had shared a transgression. Their own thudding hearts would have murdered them if they had gone any farther. If they tried to turn back now they would be tracked down for their blasphemies. They had been initiated into a strangeness that was merely opened to them by the pleasures of the senses. They belonged to *it,* if they did not yet belong to each other.

"I was only the *organ* of whatever you were fucking," she said wonderingly. It sounded no stranger than what they had known together. In fact, not strange enough to match it, so he said, "Yes," only because he was afraid not to be affirmative.

"It was what you wanted," he said.

"I wanted it all right. I didn't know what it was I wanted until it was happening. Now I wish I hadn't tricked you."

"Shaving?"

"Am I too crazy? I thought it would be a sign to you. I could've got a tattoo. 'I love Jason.' "

"We were waiting for the right sign," he said.

"Signs come from heaven or hell or the beyond."

He agreed gravely. "But they come through the imagination of artists."

"We're not."

"With each other we are. We give signs that come through us."

"Like through electric wires," she mocked. "Like babies come through women. Somebody's got to make them up in the first place. Who makes up what we know?"

He only shook his head. "We have to believe in signs wherever they come from."

Sometimes they believed in them. From the weirdness of that February day it seemed to them they had been given the means to decipher all the mysterious things that separated them, even the mysterious differences of their bodily formations. On which they meditated. They were children of the mysteries now. Artists . . . *if* they could communicate to anyone else at all what they supposed they were on the verge of grasping for themselves.

They were the ruling cryptologists of the universe—as long as they shut themselves in from it. Until May came, neither wanted out. They were not literally in isolation in the studio. Tamisan's mother, who was wrong but no fool, believed her daughter was "leveling off" and supposed Jason might be.

They walked the streets. Tamisan did as well as ever in her classes at Hunter. All outside was foreign to them, simply, while

75

they celebrated the mysteries opened by the symbolism of their erotic adventures, in which she was the inevitable leader. He had seemed to her an almost bodiless reflection of herself, of what she ought to have been. He had seemed not to need his body to be himself. She found ways to claim it for her own. His gentle, supple sensibilities kept her in awe. His body was her bride.

She courted it. She dominated it. He was the one who went down on his back on the mattress, while she peeled their clothes away and mounted him. She enticed him with foreplay, twisted him, posed him, rode him, roughed him sweetly, tongued him with fierce hungry jabs of the tongue past the point of protest, pounded him under the cannonade of her hips—and promised, "I'll teach you everything." It was as if she could not be satisfied until she had re-enacted, on his assenting flesh, all that had been lustfully performed on hers. As if she had gone as a spy into all the other beds merely to learn what his gentleness permitted her to perform in rioting, dominant ecstasy. It was his orgasms that kept her marveling and fierce. The fine, rosy bow of his cock and the faintly plump smoothness of his almost virgin body that focused her need to possess and multiplied her awe.

"I'll take you." Her cry.

She took him—rosy, more dewy, more like a child after nourishment as he softened to her striving over him.

He said, "You give me so much. I want you to have yours."

"I *get* mine. Can't you tell? Don't you know anything, about women? Don't you want me to teach you everything? Isn't that what I'm for?"

"Yes. I do. Yes."

"May I have him in my hand again? Gently? He knows me, him. He's mine. See, I'll hold him in both hands. I found him in the bulrushes. Don't laugh. See. He's so hard. He's so strong. He's not tired. He wants to be mine. Look, look, look. How he swells. Like a lady slipper. Lady slippers are like the cock of a god. So red! May I now? May I? May I?"

Yes.

"Mine! Mine! Mine!" Her greed flowered into peace fit for their solitude, as he gave.

"You're making me a girl," he meditated.

"You know better than that."

She was holding him motionless in the beauty of his puberty. She was taking from him the signs of a wonder that he alone had witnessed when his life dawned.

"What have I done to you?" she wept. "I've made us both queer. If we ever go out of this place the dogs will all bark at us."

"We'll come out. You made me whole. Together we're one person, at least."

He trusted her to lead him out of his isolation in his father's studio, from the vacated years that had been his peace.

"We'll buy a car and drive everywhere."

Hopefully they had gone out together to look for the America that had to be there. In their new green Toyota they tried to sneak up on what had hidden itself. They thought they knew how to see it now, after what they had broken into. "We'll see it like druids," they promised each other, not knowing what else they were fit to be called.

And had they seen it on some early morning drive after they had slept under a bridge in the Valley of the Kaw? From high bridges or behind the morning's dark blue shapes in mountain country?

Not yet. Not yet. Almost.

The curious lavender blue of afternoon sky above the ocean was in Dean Goss's watercolor. It hovered above the three female figures like a blessing. The big brush seemed hesitant now, as if searching for the last few definitive strokes to finish with. As if the meaning and culmination of the work could not be summoned from anything reported by the eye but had to be invoked out of thin air.

The visible was not enough. . . .

"Damn!" Dean Goss said, loud enough for everyone around

him to be startled. His massive, bearded face crumpled in a
smile of embarrassment, as if he had been caught in some fool-
ishness of senility. He plopped the watercolor brush into its can
of water and leaned back in his chair. "I told you, Jason. I
can't bring it off any more. I *saw* something. It was there. Now
I muddled it and made a pile of crap."

"It never goes away, Dad. You can still do it. I can see it."
Jason offered his father the face of a believing child.

"Did you get a glimpse, even if I muddied it up afterward?"

"I saw it. I think it's what you saw."

"If you saw it and I saw it—then who cares if anyone else sees
it?" Dean Goss asked. No one could either recover or deny what
had passed between them while he was painting. Father and
son had seen an ancient simplicity—had seen that this image
on the paper might have been a wall decoration from the temple
of priestesses who ruled before Aphrodite was born.

"You don't have to butter up my vanity, Jason. But you
can rub my neck if you want to. It gets stiff when I work so
hard." As Jason began to knead the big muscles of his shoulders, he went on mumbling. "It's not so bad? Will it do? They
won't make fun of me? Jason, I don't trust anyone's opinion
except yours."

"It makes up for everything," Jason said.

"At least you can go over to look at what he has painted,"
Susan said to her daughter.

The hurricane color of anger clouded Tamisan's eyes. Her
lips twitched with a curl of pride and she shook her head. She
gathered her robe from a stone bench at the side of the garden
and went on with the maddening tread of a martyr.

"Oh, for God's sake," Susan said. "I thought all this was your
own idea, yours and Jason's."

"Maybe I was wrong again."

"Darling, if you're not interested in his painting it will seem
to everyone . . . Were you just showing off the bod?"

"Well . . . that's a fact, Mama!" Tamisan said mournfully,

and hurried to catch up with Janis, who was headed for the guesthouse.

"What everything will *seem* to everyone! Fuck, shit," she said to Janis. "Jason and I were doing all right until we came here. Everyone here knows what I am. I'm just someone to blow their precious boy and keep him in mental health. I should never have gone out there and let 'em see what he's getting."

"You said they treated you wonderfully. You know you love Jason."

"I do," Tamisan said. "And, sure, they treat me better than I deserve. Who cares? It's what they *think*. Janis, please stay tonight, at least. There'll be something for everyone. People are coming. Senator Burke's coming, even. You told the class he was your candidate for President."

"He was very good on the Vietnam war," Janis said. "And of course I'd love to meet him." She patted Tamisan's arm. "It wasn't planned that way."

"You mean even Jason didn't ask you to stay over? That's what I mean about this place. They're too cool for me. I wish you were staying with me. I'll blow it. I know I'll blow it."

Janis was not impressed. "They all like you. It's not an uptight establishment."

"Oh, it's a real commune! That's it. Everyone's easy but me. I made Mama nervous today. I don't want to blow things for her."

Janis went on fixing her hair. "You looked pretty relaxed."

"I can fool all of the people some of the time," Tamisan said, "but it's always easier to fake among fakes. I'm very paranoid of honest people. Don't they think it's funny I show my ass to Jason's father?"

"They wouldn't laugh at you."

"I don't mean me. I won't have them laughing at Jason."

Book II

Collision

Chapter 4

Dean Goss's mood that evening was as far from laughter as it was from tears.

"No one gets home free, Marian," he said, snapping his red suspenders, "so when I rounded third base I headed for the dugout and the showers." He squinted at his old friends Senator Burke and Burke's wife Marian over the diamond-bright surface of his martini. "I've quit. Let life get along by itself!"

"Absurd!" Marian said.

"I believe you might say I was tagged somewhere in the wide-open spaces between second and third," Stan Burke said, leveling his martini also at eye level like a little horizontal mirror. Senator Burke had lost in the last elections, and what had gone down in the 20,000-vote margin of his defeat was heard by implication in their conversation now. The decision of the voters was his permission to voice the pessimism that had been building in thirty years of public life. He had been one of the first national figures to take a stand against the Vietnam war. When opposition to the war became popular, he was unforgiven for having been ahead of the majority.

"Both of you are talking absurdities and I don't think either is sincere," Marian Burke said vehemently. "Everyone remembers that you spoke up for decency," she admonished her husband.

"That will be long remembered and little noted," he said in a tone void of irony. "We live among generations who have long memories and castrated attention spans. Do you suppose, Dean, that the end will come with a collapse of the attention span to zero?" He smiled into the mirroring martini in his hand—Socrates studying his countenance for vanities in the reflecting surface of hemlock like an adolescent counting his pimples. Unlike Socrates, Stanford Burke was still a very hand-some man, his white head still sleek with senatorial barbering.

"Both of you are at the peak of your lives," Marian said with thrilling sternness. Politicians might lapse to pessimism or even cynicism and despair, Dean Goss noted, but politicians' wives never gave up their clutch on the flag. And yet, he thought with an old, familiar awe, it's not political politics we're hearing from her. It's the politics of being a woman, of never con-ceding that the end *could* come to decency or hope or beauty either.

And that inability to despair made women nuisances, as well as making them indispensable. Marian had kept her good looks into her late sixties not by cosmetics, exercise and diet alone but by sheer conviction, he supposed, that without beauty she too would be vulnerable to the flaws in the social order. Her white hair matched Stan's, but her face was not betrayed by that faintest suggestion of a mortician's make-up job that preserved the Senator's image from his fighting days.

"I've never seen you looking spunkier. Fiona says your new work is—ah!—out of this world," she said.

"It's true that I get prettier," Dean Goss confessed, preening his red galluses again.

"She says that Jason's got himself a splendid girl whom we'll meet this evening. I'm . . ."

"Relieved?" Goss asked.

She admitted it. "It's been five years, Dean, since we saw him that time in Paris." *That time* was the disastrous week when the first signs of Maggie's terminal illness appeared and drove her and the boy prematurely home to America. "It was a terrible blow to him at a vulnerable time in his life."

Goss shrugged. "There'll never be any other kind of times for Jason. If there were any use worrying about him, that's what I'd worry about, not just his loss of Maggie."

"They were so close. You said . . . I remember Jason tell-ing me you'd entrusted Maggie to him for that trip. He was so grave in thinking he'd failed his responsibility, though of course he had no way of knowing then how badly it would turn out back here."

"Close? Incestuous," Goss said. For a minute he closed his eyes—but only to give the Burkes time to realize it was his brutal joke to speak of incest in the relation between young Maggie and her son. "Marian, I'm relieved, Fiona is relieved, the Goss family is grateful to almighty God that Jason has got the sort of girl he's lucked into. Into? I use the word advisedly. Miss Vail is what they call a pure sex object. The American Dream. Pure unadulterated pewtang. God send us all such good luck!"

"You're as mean as ever, Dean," Marian Burke said. "You make her sound . . ."

"Like the 'Battle Hymn of the Republic,'" Stan Burke said. "If you'll refill my glass—thanks, Dean—I shall drink to her sight unseen." He raised his glass with gaiety, saluting gaiety, however brutally it had to be wrung out of the brutality of life. "*After* I've seen her I shall no doubt want to run for office again."

"For *her* office," Dean Goss said. He wiped a tear of laughter from his cheek with his good hand.

"Giggling!" Marian Burke said with mock savagery. "How vile you both are! When you're unmasked, neither of you is better than the stereotype dirty old man. Talk about the detachment of the artist . . . !"

"You never heard me mention it," Goss said.

"I always prefer to take my mask off when I assume *that* office," the Senator said. His thin, powerful shoulders quaked again as he fought to hide his mirth. "Ah, darling, you're right. The best thing in life is to remember what keeps the comedy on the boards."

"In your case, what kept it on the office carpet. That, I understood, was why the voters blew the whistle on you, Stan."

Marian waved her hand in stern protest. "Mean as ever! Oh, Dean, it's been such a long rough time since we've had you to keep us stirred up. We came expecting . . ."

"Sentimentalities," Dean Goss said. "And we've got plenty of those for you sweet old ladies, Beauty. Fiona keeps them neatly filed with the rest of the goods. Everything's in order now. As for my new painting being 'out of this world'—Fiona's exactly right about that, too. You can always trust Fiona's word. It's not abstract stuff in the popular sense of the term. You can recognize faces, bellies. Maybe minds, souls. It's not abstract—but the stuff is my retirement plan. A last effort at self-conquest. Putting the life of the artist in universal terms so for once it won't be confused by Goss's hot flashes. You'll see."

"We came to see that too," Marian said.

"You won't like it. It's all masquerade, like my red suspenders."

"We will!" Marian insisted, and Goss gritted his teeth at her. If she had decided so firmly in advance to "appreciate" his work, then she had squandered her last chance at true communication with him, the chance that his work might repeat the communion of their vanished lives in the stern, cold and appropriate terms of their old age.

He said, "I don't want anyone to like what I'm doing now. I don't want it to be ingratiating, even to me. I want all emotion to hibernate in it. I've gone into the long hibernation, bit by bit, since Maggie died. 's true! I'll let my public image live my life for me while I doze here among the things I made. I work. The last refuge. I won't run for office again, either."

"I don't believe it," Marian Burke said. "You're luckier than Stan, don't you see?"

"Because art doesn't have to speak for decency," Goss agreed. He watched the feminine calculations make their barely visible traces on Marian's fine-boned face. Many profound and painful histories had been touched on in the short conversation since their arrival. And though she might, indeed, have come to sip again at what he labeled sentimentalities, she wanted no real wounds opened.

Deftly skimming the surfaces, drawing the right smile from her arsenal, she said, " 'Pewtang.' I remember that's one of the bits of American slang that Maggie liked to use. You taught her."

"I brung her down."

"You taught her how to 'live high on the hawg,' darling."

"It was an unfair characterization of Jason's young lady, to return to that subject," said Goss, speaking through yet another of his quick-change masks. "On his authority I have it that they go in for 'heavy spiritual raps.' The new American slang and thank God Maggie didn't live to hear too much of it. However, it is not my responsibility to be just or fair to Miss Vail except when I paint her—as I did this afternoon. I paid my tribute then."

"The responsibility is Jason's," Stan Burke said dreamily. He saluted again with his empty glass. "Long may he retain his seat in that august body!"

"You haven't even seen her yet," Marian scoffed.

Gravely her husband replied, "You might say I *have*. Never underestimate the genius of Dean Goss for projecting vivid—may I say *burning?*—images upon the mind's eye of his tottering cronies. Images to make us all repent the name of decency. Shall we have one more before we join the others?"

They were savoring their icy drinks in what had been the billiard room in North Atlantic's sportier days. Against the gaudy marble paneling of these walls Fiona's father had racked up his cues and made his avaricious bets on a simpler game. Now it was used as a hideaway parlor. It was a favorite place for Goss, especially at an hour like this when the evening light gave it an air of Venetian glamor. Its windows looked out on the east lawn where the other guests had been gathering since six. The glimpse of ocean beyond might have been the Adriatic seen from a window of the Doge's palace.

The exoticism of the light reminded Goss of his voyages and he mentioned the tour of the Far East he had made under the auspices of the State Department. "I've not yet properly thanked you for that favor, Stan."

"The State Department was eager to get you. The favor was to them. Was it good?"

"Lovely. It pampered my senses." Then Goss reconsidered. "It reminded me my traveling days are over. I get more mileage out of my imagination now. From my work." In his imagination that streak of blue beyond the window became the Adriatic, a majestic trough opening down toward the white-gold islands off the Greek shore—god-infested tangles of laurel and olive trees, fit habitation for the girls he had painted in the afternoon.

He said, "You know Vidal was along with me in Japan. He's got me on film. Fiona will show some of it tonight for whoever wants to see. The man with the funny beard in the film will be *me*. But when I first saw it I knew *I* was someone else. Ever get that feeling? Watch it! You'll see me dance like a dancing bear among all them geishas. *I* don't dance any more."

And even as he described his trick of detachment he was performing it—going away from them behind his smoke screen of small talk.

He might like the Burkes as much as he had in Maggie's time. As a matter of fact, he did. He liked them, but they did not hold his attention as they had then. Stan had a point about attention spans.

These two people had once been instrumental in giving Maggie to him. They had, at least, introduced him to her father, the British actor Sir Gregory Niles. They had connived—wasn't that the right word?—when he outraged the Britisher by eloping with his daughter. Maggie was only seventeen then, and of course did not know her own mind until he showed it to her. But her wild, wide eyes had, from the first, recognized the prospects of adventure in a life with him. The Burkes, bless them, had soothed old Niles enough to keep him from legal action, if they had no more active part in the girl's capture. They had a proprietary interest in her and a deeper fascination because she was younger than their daughters but married to a man their age. And if Maggie was their special enthusiasm, they had been hers. She had loved America with that peculiar British romanticism and staunchness that had got it going in the first place. Until she died she had cheerily believed America could be saved if men like Senator Burke could get a grip on its runaway powers. In his last successful campaign she had politicked for him in his home state, using for that good cause her famous father's name and a reclaimed British accent rather than her famous husband's name and raunchy Americanisms he had taught her. "Winning for me," Stan Burke said, "because the good farm and small-town folk remembered how her father had stood up to the dark-skinned tribes without the law in so many of his movies."

"Good fun," Maggie said, excusing herself for the charade in which the ghost of English imperialism helped smuggle a left-leaning Senator past the suspicions of the common men he hoped to speak for.

Good fun and good games in Maggie's day. And no detachment separating his life from his work, but that happiness was only one of the alternative good seasons for an artist, and he had slipped over into another. Without minimizing his love for Maggie or the first savagery of his bereavement, he knew well enough now that being her widower had its consoling advantages. Terrible to say that this was so—but then most of the granite truths of his life were terrible to say. It was a good thing he was a painter and not a writer. In painting, the terror of stark forms was compensated for by the beauty of materials. The senses were appeased for the unbearable cruelty of truth abstracted into words.

He would not say to the Burkes that Maggie had died at the right time, though he had settled with himself that it was so. She had been mercilessly surprised in her thirty-first year to learn her illness was terminal. She had died with a multitude of plans and yearnings unfulfilled. But the great determination of her life was to be a beautiful wife and beautiful mother to Jason as she had been a beautiful daughter to the windbag Englishman from whom he stole her. Her death made no sense except as a capstone on that pyramid of beauties, and, as that, his artist's heart accepted it. If he had been religious he would have felt that now she was safe in heaven. He was not religious, so he merely felt that she was safe, her life a masterpiece that might have been degraded by another touch.

And so, too, he was saved by the inexplicable timeliness of her departure. It freed him from his major obligations to keep art squared with life. Real detachment for the artist was to mount beyond the rim of tragedy and find that the long climb ended in a plateau. There he gazed around like a visitor to the penal colony of the world, not an inmate. He had earned that time of life when he could look at the shape and colors of horror like old Monet attending his water lilies at the end, with a joy that no longer had anything to do with hope.

Sure enough, he was luckier than Stanford Burke; the Senator would never be able to separate the onrushing ghastliness of history from his own sense of personal failure for failing to avert it. When you let go your hold on the string, the world went up like a red balloon, getting prettier and prettier as it flew away.

"Let's go out and see who's here," he said. "If Jason's girl does not look as advertised, then you're old enough for retirement, Stan."

They had lingered inside just a bit too long to catch up with Jason and Tamisan then. Miriam Barnstone and Jacob Ellmann noted the Senator coming down the mansion steps with Goss and moved to claim their attention.

Altogether there must have been nearly fifty people around the white-sheathed buffet tables on the green east lawn. More? Sixty? Fiona would know. She arranged things like that. She would also know why they were all here, Goss thought, though at the moment he did not. As he introduced the Burkes to Jake Ellmann, it came to him he would like to ignore them all and trot down to his studio for another brief go at the watercolor he had painted this afternoon. He had not staked very much on it. Painting it had been a diversion. But, as he felt now, he had come to the verge of some revelation that resisted him while he worked. Using his thumb and a little spit, he might make the dumb thing speak. A touch of cadmium violet . . . ?

"I've been your fan since you clobbered Rusk on the televised hearings of the Foreign Relations Committee," Miriam said.

"My finest hour?" the Senator mocked gently. It suited him to be in the group on the lawn and take a dominant place in it. He had an extraordinary profile and eyelids that made you think of a caged hawk. The Undefeated. The natural leader of a government in exile. And Jake Ellmann was responding to that charisma and other things when he said enthusiastically,

"Nothing is lost, even if the war goes on. I was telling you, Miriam . . ."

"At least we got Lyndon out," she said.

"'What though the field be lost?' Well, it's a privilege at last to shake your hand. Do you know Henry Lewis, Senator? Henry, this is Mrs. Burke," Jake said.

In the midst of introductions Goss saw that his son and the girl had wandered off by themselves down the darkening slope of the lawn—and the devious man was just as glad to watch them from a distance. The truth was that he was feeling very reverent about them as a pair and would not want to see them ruffled in the midst of this cocktail chatter. He might not be satisfied with the painting he had made in the afternoon, but something of importance had begun to clarify while he was working there in the garden. He had felt that Jason and he were on the verge of ending the mysterious estrangement that had lain on both of them since Maggie died.

Watching him work, Jason had said, "It makes up for everything." A cryptic statement. A message in a baffling code. But any sign that came from Jason's depths was going to be hard to decipher. So hard, Goss thought, that he had better trust his eye with the task instead of the analytical mind, or speech either. Trust the visible, said the voice of the demon who had guided him all his life. Nothing could have been more persuasive to him than to see his fragile, manly boy keeping pace with the gliding girl.

"She's sweet enough from this distance, anyhow," he said to Marian Burke. Tamisan was wearing a dress for once. A white caftan that swirled down to her bare feet. She had a flimsy scarf around the shoulders he had painted so reverently.

Watching over the heads of the guests as the boy and girl drifted into the watercolor wash of shadow coming in from the sea, he admitted there are evenings one has surely visited before, like mournful parks with deserted bandstands and sculpture amid the trees, with caped policemen coming in pairs to lock the iron gates while nursemaids scurry, clucking to children reluctant to go home. He saw Jason and the girl glide together against the indigo background of trees at the end of the lawn, saw them cling and separate. "She's what he needs for the time being anyhow," he said to Marian. "It may not last. Why should it? I wouldn't want him to keep her after he's sucked the honey out."

For that moment, the boy and girl figures he was watching were anonymous, reminding him of no one at all, because he was trying to remember what it was that lay so patiently in that ambush of shadow behind them.

"Stop it!" Marian laughed. "It's terrible to say that."

Lions, he thought. Lions in the shadow. There was always a lion waiting belly down, its claws patiently sheathed, black lips closed over its heavy teeth, trusting time and patience as no boy or girl ever dared trust them, as it waited to pounce.

"Aw now, Marian, don't tell me you just now findin' out what a monster I am," he said. He felt himself turning into a monster of envy—not envying his son the honey flesh of that girl, but perhaps just the danger she represented. Surely his artist's eye was good enough to see how sinister the lines of her pelvis and breast were—the primal threat of beauty to his gentle son.

And right along with the envy flowed a contradictory impulse to safeguard the boy, since it was out of the question to warn him. As long as Jason was vulnerable, it was mere delusion for his father to dream of detachment.

It was comfortable to take his pose of resignation. To declare to old friends he had headed for the showers. To tell himself he had let go the string by which he had kept his dangerous beauties tethered. That Maggie was safe.

That part of Maggie which lived in Jason was not safe, for he was born to be an artist in his turn. It was too late to whistle him back away from the girl who had led him down the lawn. Too late to tell him, Son, there are decent ways to live. There are ways to sit and admire beauty without pursuing her right up to the edge where the world drops off beneath your feet. . . .

Tamisan had come down the lawn slithering her bare toes through the grass as though they were a bunch of minnows she was chasing. She said, "I wish this place was mine and I had been Fiona. Been rich. If I was, do you know what I'd have been here? A flapper."

Jason said, "Not if you were Fiona, you wouldn't."

"A 1920s flapper with a great big Rolls-Royce. A green one."

Jason agreed that it ought to be green. Hand in hand they passed the Milles fountain—a touch of Fiona's. She had commissioned it in the thirties when North Atlantic was to be leased by a Catholic seminary for girls and she had supposed she was leaving it for good.

"I'd make it growl when I drove out of here and I'd keep it full of boys with flat straw hats and bow ties and hip flasks."

"And run over peasants."

"Not if they were careful," Tamisan said. She did not really want to break bones and draw blood if the way she felt could be expressed without human sacrifices. She simply had not quit feeling naked when she quit posing three hours earlier. She did not feel clothed by her dress—but only felt that the old goofs at Fiona's party were too blind to notice she had come among them naked.

She felt she had gone to sleep standing in the sun with Janis and Jean. She had learned some things, she thought, that can only be learned asleep. While they all painted her, she had felt dangerous, as if the arrowhead shape of hair in her crotch might really be sharp-edged and risky to touch. From time to time she had noted the twinkle of Dean Goss's steel-rimmed glasses. She had supposed they were two little mirrors reflecting the image of her thoughts.

Now, looking back up the lawn toward the group around the white tables by the mansion, she could again make out the flash of his glasses.

"Jason?" She filled her mouth with wine from the glass she had carried away from the tables. When she pulled his head over for a kiss, she let the wine gush from her mouth into his.

Overhead there were three planes waiting for their turns to descend toward Kennedy Airport. They looked ghostly and pure as soaring swans with the sun slanting up beneath them.

Her white scarf fell from her shoulders as she and Jason

kissed. Stooping to retrieve it and regaining her full height, she felt the drag of her belly and breasts like the weight of an animal mounting her. She tossed the scarf in the air, tossed it as the fountain tossed its glossy spray into the thickening twilight.

"Why were they too dumb to ask Janis to stay?" she demanded. "It would have made her feel like a big shot to meet the Senator."

"I could have arranged it."

"It's not your fault. Why are they so afraid of anyone young?"

At dinner after full dark had moved the party inside, she and Jason were seated at a small table with an art historian and his wife. When Fiona filled her dining room, she almost never lined up her guests at the grand banquet table taken over from the former unfortunate owners. Most of the gaudy formalities were replaced with contemporary and genial comforts. Her dining room looked more like a first-class restaurant than a holdover from the Gilded Age.

Nevertheless, Fiona had planned the seating from her guest list conservatively. It miffed Tamisan that her mother got a place at the table with Bern Whitestar, who seemed lively and was certainly handsome, while she and Jason had to be stuck with the Stricklands. Strickland, also, was a handsome devil, no doubt a real hero to his students and a flashing actor in the classroom. Tamisan knew the type. She was bored with the type and had even stopped wondering why such handsome academic devils always turned out to have small, cautious, dimly pretty and fragile-looking wives.

"That is really—'The Surrender'?" Mrs. Strickland asked as they took their seats and she saw the enormous painting over the fireplace. "I've seen it so often in reproduction. My!"

Her husband was more urbane. He was not going to expose himself by comment on a Dean Goss canvas in the old man's own house. He would have preferred to talk about the mantel and the "era of American taste" it represented. But his wife was here to pay tribute.

She said, "In the right-hand corner of the painting. Those are lances, aren't they? Surely they echo . . . I mean intentionally echo, not borrow . . . the lances in Velasquez' 'Surrender at Breda'?"

Strickland was watching her mouth with an indulgent smile. It seemed to amuse him that intelligible syllables could come from such a prim orifice.

He said, "As all sophomore art history majors know, my love, that's precisely Dean Goss's genius. He's taken the vital signals from the art of all cultures and synthesized them in a peculiarly American way, a contemporary mode. Landslides of the past and the remote into an American idiom! He doesn't borrow. He steals. That's the difference between a great artist and one of our novelty-mongers that journalism inflates for a season."

With a sense of having been squirted on but not penetrated, Tamisan realized he was addressing her as well as his wife with his condescension. He wouldn't dare pick on Jason.

"It's a big painting," Jason said. "I suppose it's better than wallpaper." He spoke so mildly and diffidently, the Stricklands didn't catch the scorn in his words for a moment. Then Mrs. Strickland giggled obligingly.

"Well, it's a hoax," Jason said.

Strickland stopped rubbing Tamisan's leg and cocked his ear to listen. "Hoax?" he chuckled. Surely Jason was putting him on.

"Everything he's done—nearly all of it—since my mother died has been a hoax."

"In what sense of the word?" Strickland wanted to know.

"A hoax isn't a genuine thing, is it?" Jason asked, so earnestly that his voice quavered.

"I can assure you 'The Surrender' is taken altogether seriously. Not merely by promoters in the art world. I've seen a doctoral dissertation by a chap at the University of Bonn which traces the sources of the elements in the composition through all the phases of change your father explored before it was finally achieved. There are, fortunately, photo records of its evolution. There was a loose-leaf notebook of sketches and

95

comment to supplement the photos. Pity that hasn't been published yet."

"I've seen the stuff. He has all the apparatus working," Jason said, looking dazed, bewildered, very childish.

Why doesn't he let it go? Tamisan thought. She wanted to stop him. Why should he give them blood when they asked for shit? But then . . . why was he Jason? Jason gives blood, she thought, as she concentrated on not listening.

"It's a hoax because it doesn't go on with the story," Jason told them.

"But Dean Goss is not a literary painter!"

Jason's response sounded like the lies of a bad student trying to weasel out of a mistake. "There was a story in what he did when my mother was alive. . . ."

"Ah. That was his *manière magnifique!* But there's agreement that the Rodin-Balzac things represent an intellectual advance, however difficult to decode. . . ."

"Godwin makes such elaborate codes for all of it!" Jason said. "That's hoax too. My father's an old magician tinkering with his apparatus when it won't produce anything but illusions."

"That's clever."

Jason despised cleverness. He had stumbled into saying something clever, and he went on trying to climb out of it. " 'The Surrender' started out to be about the death of my mother and why he didn't go with her. I know. I was with him. It was the first winter we came out here, before he built his gadgety studio. It was painted in the music room, right down the hall. We were all in pieces about her dying. We had to grab at what straws there were. His painting for him. The painting started . . . it was his insanity."

"Insanity . . . figuratively speaking," Strickland said.

"No. Really speaking. I never could understand what figurative language is. For artists a thing is so or not so, that's all. I said we were all in pieces. There were times when it was all up to Fiona whether or not to turn us over to the men in white suits. But, with a man like my father, you don't consult doctors. That painting started out as a battle for survival."

"And he won!" Mrs. Strickland chirped.

That wasn't what Jason had meant to convey. Not at all. But he paused rather than embarrass the woman.

And now they would misinterpret his silence, Tamisan fumed. She didn't know just what he was driving at either, but it seemed to her completely unjust when Jason, who adored his father, appeared to attack him while people who cared nothing about the *man* defended him because he was an artist.

Mrs. Strickland had returned to her contemplation of the picture, as if somewhere on its surface a light might flash on saying either TRUE or FALSE. "It's impossible to say what art means," she offered. She held the delicate white meat of her lobster on a fork poised halfway to her mouth.

"Not if you know," Jason said with so much surface humility that the Stricklands heard nothing else.

"I know your feeling," Strickland said in an undertaker's voice. He was the man of the academic world consoling overwrought youth. From his experience he understood why a student-age boy was impelled to utter such absurdities.

Tamisan could stand no more. Abruptly she rose to leave the table.

"Don't you feel well?" Mrs. Strickland asked. She got no answer.

It tamed her feelings to be in Jason's room, among his things. Here on the second floor of the mansion Tamisan's fury at Strickland subsided to manageable proportions. So he was a turd and a phony. . . . She was proud of her restraint in not calling him those names at the dinner table.

It always tamed her to have Jason's personal world around her. While they were shacked up in the studio in town, it had been her practice to ransack his laundry bag for unwashed clothes of his to wear when she had to go out to classes or home to her mother's place. All spring she had hardly gone anywhere else without him.

This room was a place Fiona Trebbel kept up for him with the same meticulous care she showed in housing his father's paintings and archives. Probably it was artificial—a cross between a museum and a playhouse. Jason hadn't often spent time here. But with the old lady's care it was made to seem the armory and citadel of a boy's life. There were bows and hunting arrows on the wall. A telescope on a tripod. A framed target with five nearly invisible punctures of .22 bullets in the bull's-eye. There was a cabinet of toy soldiers—the regiment of Sambre et Meuse. A prep school banner. A framed letter from Senator McCarthy, who had heard Jason play his cello back in his prodigy days and wanted the boy to know how deeply he was moved. A photo of Jason just two years ago looking very much like a young Cuban guerrilla in the jungle, holding up by one ear the head of a very dead cougar in the wilds of Yucatan. A dozen lithographs and paintings by Dean Goss, Fiona Trebbel and Godwin Goss. Posters advertising Vidal Goss's films. A reproduction of Watteau's "Embarkation for Cythera." Photographs of his mother and his grandfather Niles. One of Maggie Niles as a child when she had been given a bit part in a film in which her father starred.

Here were the signs of his rich life which she had only heard about before they drove in here a few days ago. When he first brought her into it she had felt the envy a tomboy feels for the legitimate first baseman of a team she will never be asked to join. After balling a few times in this bed (and they were in the habit of getting his rocks off two or three times a day) she quit envying him this, too, because she felt it was hers as much as his. There was nothing of her own here except her blue guitar. Her own clothes were down in her mother's room in the guest-house. There was also a bed for her down there—some sort of proper make-believe that Jason said they needn't bother with.

Here she was going to forget about every Strickland there was in the world. Try to recapture the way she had felt on the lawn with her mouth full of wine when she seemed to stand tiptoe before mysteries as tantalizing as crime to her outlaw heart.

It damn well would have helped her forget if Jason had come up with her. The guitar was a poor substitute for his prick to play

with on a night like this. It was beautiful to look at and fit to
her own shapes.

You wish you had one of your own, don't you, doll? Zach
Sandler said to her.

Mmmmmmm!

*Where would you stick it, doll? Come on, who'd you put it
in? In Janis? In her mouth?*

No one.

You'd keep it all to yourself, wouldn't you, doll?

Mmmmmmmm!

Why did it have to be a man as wicked, vile, evil, perverted
and coldhearted as Sandler who understood so well what it was
like for her to be a girl? But the damn truth of it happened to
be that he would have understood her mixed feelings right now
much better than Jason, whom she loved. For a few unpleasant
minutes she had to admit she missed old Sandler after all these
months. And would cut his throat if he happened to be where
she could get at him.

She sat cross-legged on the bed with her blue guitar cradled
between her upraised knees. She would just sing the saddest
song she knew until Jason came back to her.

Her thumb swept the strings. It was supposed to be a
D-minor chord but it was . . . it was shocking as the jangle of
a burglar alarm.

What the sweet fucking Christ had she expected?

It *was* a burglar alarm, and she was the burglar who had set
it off.

If she even touched those strings again the fuzz would rush
in and catch her . . . *up to her old tricks.*

And then she knew why she had got so upset this afternoon before the posing was finished.

She had stood there naked before all those people with their
silly pencils and paintbrushes and the sneaky bastards had made
her . . . *visible.* . . .

When that freaky thought really landed on her, she knew that
the guitar wasn't going to be any help to her until Jason came

and she certainly couldn't masturbate in the glaring light that was coming into her mind.

So she rolled a joint of their very druid marijuana and puffed as if her life depended on it.

Like the signs of the zodiac, grass could go twelve crucially distinct ways for her. For instance, it might turn out the light and let her be a very dirty girl.

This hit zoomed in from a different corner of the sky. It made her wise and good. It made her able to consider all the implications of having been made visible.

She had—take this argument point by point, please—stripped off her clothes for men plenty of times. But always before this afternoon, as soon as she got down to the buff, she *blinded* them. They went blind and started putting their cocks in one hole or another. They never saw her. They jabbed and shot their juice and left her invisible as a burglar in a dark house with nobody home. She had always been able to count on that.

Point two: If Dean Goss or somebody had made her visible this afternoon, then she had better open her own eyes and take a look at what she saw. Otherwise, give up right here and now.

Point three: (Score this one for Mama Dear, who had always been trying to say it, in somewhat different words.) Whenever Tamisan Vail met a challenge, she had gone down on her back to handle it. Whenever she was afraid, she had spread her legs to wrestle that fear away. She was terribly afraid of death so she tickled her cunt to persuade it to leave her alone.

Dean Goss's shining spectacles had frightened her this afternoon—so she'd flirted disgustingly with old Whitestar and embarrassed her mother by grabbing for Jason's pants.

At dinner she'd been frightened by Strickland. (He was still a pompous academic bore, but that wasn't what she had responded to. She had been frightened by his learning.)

Dear Gaaawwd . . . she might take Strickland on too, if she got to feeling invisible again. She began to remember the teachers she'd balled instead of reading the books they assigned. That list wasn't so long, and it ended with Janis on that evil, wicked night at Sandler's place.

The list of "smart people" was considerably longer and it

didn't exactly end with Zach Sandler. He was more in the middle, like one of the boxes on an organizational chart that shows the managerial lines, since he'd "farmed her out" to so many of his friends. Some farmer.

But the truth was that not one of them had intended anything evil or wicked, though evil had been done. With the same momentary honesty that made her admit that, she saw that she was not responsible for the evil either. What book was she supposed to look in to tell her where the evil had come from?

It had to be in her fears, she decided in that little time of stalwart honesty before Jason would come up to her. Out of her fears the evil came, and with just this much boost from the drug, she was no longer afraid—not even afraid of having wasted the time she might have spent *learning* instead of trying to pull even with smart and older people in other ways.

She had run away rather than face Zach Sandler on the street that time she was going to meet Jason. What could he have done to her then in broad daylight with people passing? He wouldn't even have mocked her for going to meet a boy in an ice cream parlor. It was only that she would have felt mocked by his knowing eyes if the encounter had taken place.

So much for honesty. It cheered her up and made her feel charitable toward Janis and Sandler and a lot of other people whose names didn't need to be listed. It comforted her. It led her to patience in waiting for Jason, and in her patience she went so far as to search out a very big, fat book on art history from one of Jason's bookshelves.

"Improve the time," she heard her Mama saying cheerily. "You have everything going for you."

The book happened to open to the pages devoted to Puvis de Chavannes. She didn't much care for the fellow's paintings. But she was fascinated with his name. What did his friends call him? And how did you pronounce it? Pew-viss? Pu-vee? Poovuss? How would she feel about her escapades if the name Puvis was on the list of intellectuals she had balled?

"You have a wondrous mind," Mama said.

Oh, Mama, if you only knew!

After all, the book put her to sleep before Jason came to the room. When she woke, she knew it must be very late. There was a smell of ocean in the room and a smell of morning, though the moonlight was still the only illumination. She saw Jason beside her with his face in his pillow. Moonlight gilded the line of his back and shoulder.

"Jason?" she whispered, knowing he was not asleep in the same way she knew the night was mostly past. "I had an icky dream," she said.

"You too? What was yours?"

"Part was people kept shining lights on me. The rest was that maniac Strickland. I was back in school and he was lecturing me like I was the stupidest one in class."

"Strickland means well. I know you didn't like him but he means well."

"Everybody does," she agreed cautiously, realizing Jason was troubled, feeling the rhythm of it in his breathing, his tight, burrowing wriggles against the mattress. "I wish I'd stayed at dinner to help you fend them off. I guess I failed you again." She put her arm over his back and sidled her hip against his. She dragged a breast delicately back and forth against his ribs. "Want to?"

"All right," he whispered. He rolled over to let her seeking hands explore his abdomen and trace the soft contours of his genitals. But it was no good. She knew he was only letting her play with him for her own peace of mind. She would not let him nourish her from his weakness.

"What happened?" Her question froze Jason.

"Strickland was very decent about it. They all were," he said.

"About what?" She was fully alarmed now and sat up. She left her hand lying on him, but only to promise he could depend on her.

"Strickland wanted to see the studio, naturally. In the mix-up he came along with Dad and the Burkes and me while Fiona showed the movie to the rest."

"Mix-up?"

"Strickland was really eloquent. That's why we stayed down there so late. He celebrated you. That is, he took off on the painting Dad did of you this afternoon. He related it to other paintings of nudes outdoors—like Manet's 'Déjeuner sur l'herbe' and Giorgione's 'Concert champêtre.' Manet was recovering Giorgione's dream—and Goss was reheating Manet's dream, and it all goes very far back, because Giorgione had re-created his group from antiquity, in true Renaissance fashion. From very, very far. . . . And what this apostolic succession of great painters was doing was keeping alive your myth. You came from far away. I always knew that."

"Stop! Stop! Please just tell me what went wrong, can't you?" It was the steadiness of his quiet voice she was trying to break through. He was not near tears. She knew he went far away from tears when bad things challenged. But her hand on his chest felt the trouble he was trying to disguise. The shape of grief within him was like a trout easing away when she reached into the water for it. But the direct appeal to share grief did not work with him as an appeal to share joy would have. So she said, "I wish I'd heard Strickland. Did it interest your father?"

"He wasn't there. He'd gone to bed."

"And left you to . . ."

His sigh was a sound she might have made. "Oh, we'd had a fight. Dad and I. I don't know how ugly it *looked,* but it shouldn't have happened in front of the Burkes. I stayed with them and Strickland as long as I did to . . . to make it seem trivial. To pass it off as one of the old man's eccentricities if I could."

"Was it bad? *That* bad?"

Now at last his voice quavered as he said, "I didn't want Dad to sound ugly to them. I wanted them to see his best side. I . . ." She could feel something leap within him, like the trout in panic thrusting past hands too clumsy to grip it. But at least she could gather his head in her arms and rock him against her.

Presently she said, "If you quarreled about the painting . . . was it about me posing?"

"I guess it started about you and your mother. He said something cruel about Susan first, then you."

"Oh, my God." The burglar alarm was sounding in her mind again. "I *knew* we shouldn't be sleeping together while we're here."

"It isn't that. And the Burkes didn't hear what he said about Susan. That was only said to me." Jason's low voice faded to nothing, then swelled with unguarded pain. "He damages himself by his cruelty. He's done it too much. He's denying everything sweet and good. That's why I had to fight him."

"I thought Mama knew how to handle him."

"If she'd been with us it might not have happened. Who knows? She'd gone off with Bern Whitestar, though."

"Whitestar? Him?"

"There's no reason she shouldn't have. I told Dad that. She has every right to come and go as she pleases. She's not Dad's servant. 'This isn't a jail or a dormitory,' I said to him."

"Mama fucks like a mink," Tamisan said. "I want it to be *over* that there should be cocks and cunts at all."

"You don't know why she left with Bern or what . . ."

"I *know*," Tamisan said with fury. "I know that woman." Now her breath was coming in noisy bursts, real little dragon pants of outrage and rebellion. "But your damn father has no right to turn on *you* because of . . . That's not fair and I'm going to straighten him out on a few things."

In a single explosive movement she stood upright on the bed, stepped over Jason, and sprang toward the door. She had already turned the knob when he caught her.

He held her wrists with surprising strength, forcing out of her the chaos of pure fury that had made her spring, displaying for once an authority of force she would not have thought him capable of. He had never kept her from acting out her impulses.

After a minute he laughed. "You're going to him like *this?* At this hour?"

It was only then that she remembered her nakedness. Honestly her anger had split the layers of her mind, but as they settled back together again she giggled.

"I guess you could convince him of anything if you went to him this way," Jason said, maintaining his grip on her wrists.

"I'll put something on. I know *exactly* what he's got to be told about how you care for him." She meant she was afraid she would forget or lose courage to speak if she waited. "I'll put something on. My robe's here somewhere."

"No, no, no, no, no, no," Jason said. It was impossible for her to be sure whether his voice sounded amused or hurt. "Don't ever say anything to him that I've told you. It doesn't matter. It will straighten out. It's nothing. It's blown over already."

"Well, we've got to do something."

"Can't we sleep? All right, let's run down and swim."

So, naked as they were, they tiptoed down the carpeted corridor, down the marble steps of the grand stairway, onto the moon-dappled lawn where they began to sprint. Across the rose garden, over the moon-colored sand, flinging their defenseless nakedness into the limitless cold of the sea.

As its chill radiance burst up around her thighs in explosive splashes, Tamisan thought: I'm going to have it out with that old bastard anyhow. I am, and damn soon. Now I have the right to talk to him straight.

Dean Goss had seen her naked in the afternoon. That gave her all the rights she needed.

from Susan Vail's blue notebook:

Let me try to put down in my own words the sense of the Rodin-Balzac project—which often sounds more like the name of a law firm or a brokerage than anything an artist ought to be up to.

Rodin (sculptor) gets obsessed with Balzac (writer). Sculptor makes many studies of big-bellied writer—*not* portraits in the conventional sense, but an attempt to show the essence of the imaginative effort in a three-dimensional form. A pose, a presence. In the attempt, the two personalities blend. So what is achieved is as much a revelation of Rodin as of his subject. A self-portrait *as* the portrait of another artist working in another medium.

So—add one more layer of complication. As soon as the imagination of Rodin has wrapped Balzac in a visible, tactile form, the imagination of the viewer begins to wrap *all that* in other visible and tactile forms. Art is a new skin around art.

It grows out from Rodin and Balzac. They are not his only subjects—presuming he *has* subject matter in any conventional sense. The things he has done within the series also include his adaptations from others he has incorporated in his ancestry— Titian, Van Gogh, Velasquez, Poussin, Cézanne.

"My thefts, my forgeries," he calls the drawings, prints, paintings in which he transposes from these people into his own idiom. "Susan, I'm painting myself right out of life." At the end, he says, he will vanish one day into the paint or be found covered with plaster or clay.

"I even forge myself," he says. And all this vaguely troubles him, though he is proud of it too. "It's right. It is what I want. It is bloodless . . . good, there has been too much blood in the painting. I'll save what I have left for the good life. I still have the appetite of a poor man, though I seem to have all this money. . . ."

It flatters him when I say, "This isn't a studio you've built here. It's a theater." Reference to the constant change of scenery as well as to the human actors he often assembles or permits to come in while he is working.

There are several sliding panels inside the building, large ones ingeniously hung from girders at the roof level. On one of them now he has a blown-up photo reproduction of a Chinese scroll— a calligraphic poem more than thirty feet long.

Whatever other stimuli, sketches, memorandums he pins up around him, there is always, nearby, the little Cézanne that Fiona bought for him long ago. However, as he points out, it is not exactly a Cézanne any more than his Rodin-Balzac or

Titian figures are his. It is Cézanne's little adaptation of Titian's very big "Entombment."

"I'm one of a long line of thieves and forgers," he says. "What do you make of that, Fortune Cookie?"

"I'm plugging along, Boss. I'll figure it out." I see at least that the little Cézanne is his touchstone, though no painting presently visible repeats anything recognizable from it. Alongside it now he has pinned a photo of the door of Cézanne's studio on the Chemin des Lauves in Aix. He has printed a quote from a letter by Cézanne to Cézanne's son:

NERVOUS SYSTEM VERY MUCH WEAKENED, NOTHING BUT PAINTING IN OIL CAN KEEP ME GOING.

That may be so. There's not the slightest sign of it. He seems tough as an old bull. Swims like one. Goes out jogging as if he were in training for a title fight.

The cast of characters in his theater-studio in the last month has been limited but heavily exploited. Fiona, the models, his assistant George Vendler, who makes prints, and now me. Plus such walk-ons as Richard Luellen, bringing the first bound copy of his collected poems (dedicated to D.G.) and the wife of Senator Burke.

I love George Vendler. Chiefly he maintains the print shop in the basement of the studio. Calls himself the "junior troll"— and earns the epithet among the wondrous machinery of the presses, the confusion of acid stinks and paper smells in his room. I run to George in the basement grotto when the Big Troll scares me, mystifies me, seems on the verge of biting my nose for stupidity. George and I are the eldest-children-of-the-studio, psyching out Papa.

Papa keeps his juices flowing by picking fusses with each of us, even with Fiona. The fusses are minor discharges of spite and thunder, but enough to keep a flickering, changing emotional play snapping around D.G.'s head all the time.

He tries to catch Jean Simons lying. He worries Vendler about the "importance" of what he is doing. ("George, this whole Rodin-Balzac project is a dead end and you know it. You let me blunder on for three years. *Three of my last years!* Do you think I'll live forever?")

"The place had *better* be a theater," he says. "If the studio jumps, the paintings and the sculpture jump. Paintings always look like the room they were painted in, did you know that?"

As a matter of fact, the whole immense interior of his very expensive studio—"my tax lawyer did most of the designing," he says—reminds me of the drama building at a progressive little college. There is the painting room, probably a hundred feet long. Divisible into various labyrinths by the movable panels. There is a hoist built into the floor to raise and lower oversize canvases. (None in progress at the moment. None even as large as "The Surrender." But he was delighted as a boy to run the machinery for me.) On this floor there is an office with a couch in it where he sometimes flings him down to rest and where the models change clothes.

At an angle to the painting studio is the sculpture room, almost as big, and the woodworking shop. Lots of stock for stretchers and framing there. The rolls of canvas are stored overhead.

The array of plaster and metal-lath figures in the sculpture room should be included in the cast of theatrical characters. What difference does flesh and blood make in here? No use listing the menagerie of terra-cotta heads, single plaster figures, groups of more or less humanoid constructions wired up in constantly changing states of incompletion. A child's sandbox kind of room . . . A place where he "thinks Rodin-Balzac thoughts" and slings plaster, sometimes with Vendler helping. I was told that the ceramists Hawkins and Gras have got their hands in for him too in the years this has been going on.

In there are things which I'd marry if they asked me. A little terra-cotta urn, for example, a softened cube that has been knocked out of square, with Balzac profiles incised on each surface. I can never figure out what makes these profiles add up to a single head, realer than real, any more than I can learn to whistle that passage in Beethoven's Piano Sonata No. 29 in B flat Major, which I first heard playing on the hi-fi here.

Or the metal and plaster mock-up, big as playground sculpture, of fat Balzac. The fatness is a huge emptiness, a *hungriness* in the artist's belly, a kind of male womb. . . .

There is almost always music in the studio. Either D.G.'s stereo upstairs or Vendler's in the basement. And now in the summer, fresh flowers in many corners. One day I saw an armful of great coral and yellow gladioluses in a wastebasket.

Not discarded. Just in excess.

A play of casual, construction-worker comedy flickering among the magnitudes:

Jean Simons perched, very bored and very naked, on a tarpaulin-covered crate in the sculpture studio, reading her latest, treasured issue of *Rolling Stone*. D.G. and Vendler have been half the morning throwing plaster on a Giacommetti-like group of figures that will stand for Rodin's "Burgers of Calais." D.G. is stripped to the waist. Little beads of plaster have accumulated in his chest hairs, like a garden of dead *muguets*. Something good has jelled in him as he marches around to squint at what they have changed by adding and pulling—or sawing—off plaster.

He turns to Jean and chants the bawdy limerick:

> "While Titian was mixing rose madder
> His model crouched on a ladder.
> Her position to Titian
> Suggested coition,
> So he stopped mixing madder and had her."

"Right on, Dean," she says. Turns a page.

"Flip us the beaver, honey."

"Why, *Mis*-ter Goss!"

He likes me to read aloud to him.

His reasons: 1 "I don't like to ruin my eyes with print. I like to look at ideas the way I look at skin or flowers."

2 Eileen Forbes was a poet. (He has hardly mentioned his women to me. Do I remind him of Eileen, who was the crazy one among them?) He himself "dabbled with writing" back in his years with Eileen. Might have turned into a writer if he had not burned his hand, thus making typing too difficult. (I set this down as he said it to me, deadpan.)

3 Words—quite apart from the ideas they may convey—are an important part of "the mix." As music is. "The mix" is him.

4 Words that he has read—and almost knows by heart—are different each time he hears them. This came out while I was reading him Rilke's essay on Rodin. At all the good parts he would say, "Yes, yes, yes. Susan, *pay attention* to that." And of course the words change for me as he emphasizes them in this way.

There has been much dwelling, between us, on the relation between Rilke (the writer) and Rodin (the sculptor). It fascinates D.G. that the young poet should have attached himself to the old artist and enlarged his own art by absorbing from the other.

Sometimes I've glimpsed in D.G. a fatherly wish that I should be growing both braver and smarter by spending time with him, and I find it awkwardly hard to reassure him that, oh yes, indeed, I am.

I'm your Rilke, sir.

And, on the other hand, he feeds on me. He tries to catch Jean Simons in lies and he badgers me for details about my small career in writing and publishing to keep his mind bending back toward our friend Balzac as well as Rilke. What a buzz goes on, spoken or unspoken. He milks me like I haven't been milked since I breastfed hungry Tamisan. He wants me excited —as he wants Jean on the edge of orgasm, I suppose. (Why else

badger her for the secrets she wants to keep from him by lying?
Oh, I recognize that game.)

And there was the grotesque episode of his demanding to see
my body. . . .

We had been talking about Rilke as a writer. I was showing
off my acquaintance with his poetry. D.G. shook his head in
a sort of angry bafflement. *"That's* nothing I can work with,"
he said. "There's no such thing as a writer without a body. The
voice has to be the body's voice. 'In the body life was greater,
more cruel and more restless.' Rilke said that and the words
are pretty. You read them to me *prettily.* I work with another
kind of image. I have to see the body the words come from."

I was, yes, a little shaken when I understood what he was
proposing. But Susan is not coy. Susan has a game little grin
when confronted with the unexpected. I nodded, laid down my
book, and started for the office where the girls undress when
they're scheduled to model. The unexpectedness of it had sexed
me up tremendously. Talk about "a sudden blow . . ."!

"No," he said with a frightening calm. "If you undress in
there you'll come back out hiding something. What you'll have
to show won't be a *writer's* body."

He wanted me to strip right there and then in front of him.
If I had been a child I would have cried. I hadn't the guts to
do it, and I knew he hadn't really wanted to see my body but
only the level of my courage about the body. And he'd seen
it. I felt as bad as if I'd broken that little terra cotta that I
love so much.

"Damn foolish of me to suggest . . . ," he said.

No. It was wise of him to suggest what he had, and in a
cruel way, kind. D.G. had given me the chance to make
words solid. To talk to him as an equal. For a minute there
had been a chink in the wall of years that separated us. A
chance. I booted it.

I spent the next hour assuring him that I knew *perfectly* what
he'd meant. (Ah, if only I hadn't.) But the only effect of my
explanations was to give him one of his rare, severe headaches,

so he had to pull the shades in his little office and lie down. Of course we continue to talk. I learn.

A few nights after I refused to let him see my writer's body I had a dream. I was a little girl wearing a boy's overalls. I was running up a hill through very green, very tall, very thick grass. My legs stung dreadfully. My father had whipped me with a green willow switch. I kept bawling, "I'll be good. I'll be good."

When I woke I remembered it had really happened like that once, with my father. Once I whipped Tamisan, also, and never again.

Chapter 5

The guests had been leaving the dining room when Dean Goss dropped his hand on Jason's shoulder and fondly nuzzled his cheek with his beard. "Help!" he said. "The Burkes are dear friends. I expose my secret heart to them, but I've done it all through dinner."

"You want me to get rid of them?"

"Nothing crooked! I want help talking to them. Get Susan. Bring Tamisan. The Burkes seem to feel I promised to take them to the studio to show them what I'm up to. We'll all go down together and I can shut up. I don't want to stay up late." As a matter of simple truth, he didn't want to go to the studio at all unless he could go alone. It had come to him in the middle of dinner that he was not *easy*, not satisfied, with the watercolor he had painted. Its afterimage lay undigested in his mind. Left to himself, he might have gone down and dabbed at it. Put it to the question. Washed some of it off and repainted it. Or lolled in front of it comforted by vanity if it looked better than he remembered.

But Jason had said, "I don't think Susan's here."

"Sure she is. I saw her at the corner table with young Whitestar." He did not mean to sound condescending about Whitestar. He did not mean to take any attitude at all, though his eye had somehow linked Susan and the sculptor as parts of a handsome composition.

"I think they may have gone. I'll come with you."

"Go look for Susan. She loves to talk. She and the Burkes ought to get to know each other better."

Jason, dutifully, had gone to look in the music room where most of the party was gathered to see Vidal's film. He must also have gone outside to check the veranda and driveway. When he came back he said with a note of apology for bringing unwelcome news, "Well, I think they've driven off. Bern's car's gone."

There was a sudden flash in Dean Goss's mind that should have been mere disappointment but which turned quickly enough to anger. *The bitch was always hanging around except when he needed her.* It was unfair. How pleasant to be unfair. And what a pleasure it would be to haul gabby Susan away into the dark and hush her as Whitestar probably was about to do. "Ah, never mind," he said, trying not to let Jason read his disappointment. "But I'm on edge tonight. I'll get bored and be offensive. Bring your girl along then. You can strip her off again if we need entertainment."

Surely the boy might have let that minuscule slur pass. What was eating him and what was so flammable under his gentle and sober smile?

Jason shrugged. "I think she's sleeping. She went up to our room an hour ago."

Then—with all his teeth bared in what Jason of all people should have recognized as a smile, with only a *slight* growl in his voice, a growl that could have been accepted as a chuckle —Dean Goss said, "Ah. It looks like both the Vail floozies find us uninteresting here."

"You don't have to be childish about it," Jason said. "You don't have to call them names when . . ."

"When I don't know what I'm talking about? All right."

"I'll ask Mr. Strickland to come with us," Jason said meekly. "He's eloquent. He'd be disappointed not to get inside the studio."

The point, Dean Goss might think, was only that he and Jason had no tolerance of each other. They paid no attention to each other's skin. With what fine needles they probed each other, exposing not only sensitivities but strangely knotted hostilities.

I said nothing that would have offended anyone else. I was annoyed for a minute, but I would have let it pass. Could have. He makes everything out of nothing. . . .

But then the whispers in Dean Goss's skull told him the uncomfortable truth he had been wrestling all his life. The artist *is* the one who makes much out of what appears to be nothing. There are always snakes and lions hidden behind the curtain of the skin. The artist and the paranoiac are alike in knowing that. Jason had to be treated as both artist and son.

So we are going to scrape at each other while people who can turn their sensitivities on and off go scampering away to the pleasures of the night. . . .

Certainly there was no reason for him and Jason to be angry at each other. Reason or not, the anger had been set alight and the small sparks caught where they could.

Let it be said that Dean Goss behaved ungraciously to all four of those who went with him to the studio. Surely he was sulking. And to know that he *was* being childish, when Jason had accused him of that, was an unfairness that again compounded his bad humor.

Let it be said that it was mean and rude of him to flip off the light switch in the sculpture studio while Marian Burke was listening avidly to Strickland yak about the derivation of forms and the ideogrammatic *Gestalten* of the pieces in the Rodin-Balzac *oeuvre*. Let Strickland go home and write a book about it on his own time. Let Marian take it to bed with her to read.

But who would claim it was his fault that Marian had banged her elbow against something sharp after he snapped the lights off and waited for them to creep out? No blood had been drawn. No work in progress had been knocked to the floor and broken. Dean Goss had gone out of his way to sympathize with Marian's little pink bruise. No one could say he hadn't, and no one had better. Now he had a beginning headache to justify any response he might make to accusations from without or within.

They were out in the big room to look at paintings before Jason brought his father's shapeless petulance back to focus on himself.

Marian Burke—count on her to have a neat assortment of motives for being here—had let out the fact that she was hoping that a museum in her home state might be in a position to add to its Goss collection. She was, in a word, a shopper, though it must be understood she was not the one who would make the decision.

"Looking for bargains?" Dean Goss asked her.

"Looking for what's new," she said meekly enough. "New branches from the old tree. You've changed so much in your work and yet remained yourself. I'm looking for your response to the present."

"You want to see if I've produced *novelties*. Something kookier than the young people who make the news now. I'm not responsible for all that disorder."

It came to him in a gust of dismay that she wanted to be able to tell her committee that Dean Goss was still in the avant garde, that he had a new *twist* for the season like a fashion designer. No, that was unfair to Marian. The truth was that the politician's wife knew what would be expected of her when she reported back to her anonymous associates. *They* would have to be assured that the artist was a nimble dancer, so unfettered that he was already far up the road of the future. No one seemed ready to grant that art, by its nature, had to linger back and gather up the pieces while the world whisked on its merry way. It was not just Susan Vail who dashed off into the night when life whistled at her to hurry. No one had the patience to hold the slow necessary pace with him.

But then, while he sulked in such thoughts of martyrdom, Marian caught sight of the watercolor done that afternoon. She began to praise its "freshness." As if it might be just the commodity she could endorse to the home-state folks. "At the same time it's monumental, for something so small. So . . . evocative. It has a smell, hasn't it, Jason? In your painting of Bandol Harbor that Maggie gave us I can smell the palms, Dean. Still smell them."

Jason's face was aglow as he nodded to her enthusiasm.

"A souvenir! A doodle," Dean Goss sneered.

"It's not so straightforward as it seems at first glance," Strickland said. "Levels of meaning are fractured by the distortions.

And yet I call it magical that it could seem so innocent. Oh yes."

"The smell of sex!" Dean Goss boomed. "I think I'm going mad. I work patiently. I work *devotedly* for years, but what you like is a soufflé I whipped up while I was half asleep in the sun. Of course, if you like it, Marian, it's yours. Take it and hang it in your boudoir. Bedroom art. But I wouldn't sign it. Don't tell anyone I painted it, hear?" He was laughing heartily. In truth, for the moment, he disliked the little picture intensely. "There are paintings in the racks to be seen, but if you'd rather sniff these three violets . . ."

The flush in Jason's cheeks brightened. His voice was urgently low. "It's not what you say, Dad. Marian only means this picture's . . . well, less cerebral than what we saw in the sculpture studio."

"I agree. Brainless."

"You have more than one side."

"I even have a side that can be humiliated," Goss said in a tone he should not have used with Jason except when the two were utterly alone together.

"I . . . I don't see . . . No one meant to do anything but praise you," Jason said. "But if you feel free to call people floozies who are utterly loyal to you and aren't your servants . . . you can't afford to have so thin a skin yourself, that's all."

"Bimbo! Tart! Floozy!" His loudness stunned them all.

"Dad! Let's knock this off, should we?" Jason turned to Marian Burke and said, "He offered the painting to you. Take him up on it. Take it home with you tonight. You're right . . . it does have a smell of afternoon about it. And it's a side of him that's better than . . ."

"Than what, Jason?" his father said with an angry laugh. "Don't mumble. Speak up. Finish your sentence."

"Than what you're showing now! I asked you to quit it. Don't quarrel. If you want me to get some paintings down from the racks I'll be glad to. Maybe Mr. Strickland will help. Will you, sir?"

"I thought *you* wanted the little doodle for a souvenir of your beast," Dean Goss said to his son. "But then, if it only smells like *afternoon* and doesn't have the smell of *pussy* about it . . ."

"What paintings do you want us to bring from the racks?" Jason said. His whole lithe body went taut as his father walked to him and spread his arms in bewildered pleading. "Don't touch me. Just tell me what you want brought out and I'll get it."

"Ah, get what you want. Or nothing. I don't care."

Walking very stiffly and carefully, the boy went with Strickland around one of the sliding partitions to the alcove storage room where works in progress were stored.

Marian put her arm around Dean Goss's weary shoulders. "Oh, Dean. You must not. Don't snap at Jason. Shall we go?"

"I didn't snap at him."

"We'll leave and you can make it up."

"I won't utter another word. Want some brandy? Stan? We'll settle down now and you can see how the old boy passes his time. I still do serious work, you know."

"You're tired," Marian said.

"I am not tired!"

He was very tired and that was when Jason hit him. The very first canvas he picked out to show was a disgrace his father had meant to destroy long ago. An enormous blob. A great big signboard of his failure. It was something he had—wisely—given up on before he painted "The Surrender." It was not just the sign of his grief at that time. It represented, in all ways, his abandonment to grief. And if the others couldn't see it, he and Jason knew what it meant. They had walked the slippery places together. He had come through, survived at least. Had meant to offer and share his survival with Jason. Now, in his high-keyed state, it seemed to him Jason was intentionally shaming him for having survived with as much intact as he had.

On the canvas there was a giant, ambiguous figure of a woman. Not defined. Merely sketched in a brutal diagonal up the height of the canvas. The whole thing was muddy in color except for the body. That was the torso of a bloody, flayed, immaculate animal, peeled and hanging in ambiguous space like Rembrandt's ox.

"Powerful," Marian Burke said. Trust women always to find something polite to say.

"I suppose I deserve this. Confronted with my horror show. Do me the kindness to think it's unfinished," Dean Goss said. The confrontation was only between Jason and himself. They were the only ones who could know it would have been worse yet if it were to be carried further. It was a horrible painting that had started out to be a confession of how he had wasted all the women in his life. Bluebeard's apology for what he couldn't help; the artist as butcher. The wild scream of his grief and inadequacy. If the others would never know that, Jason did. And now that both thin skins were punctured, his father thought, He has been challenging me since he came back. He didn't parade his naked floozy for nothing.

"I've had enough," he said with a chortling laugh. "Jason can take over for me. He can show off my failures as well or better than I. So, if you'll excuse me, dear Marian, dear Stan, Mr. Strickland—a pleasure to have you with us—I'll toddle off and get my beauty sleep. Sweet dreams."

Yet all he needed was to walk on the beach for a little by himself before he slept. Outside his studio everything was all right. The ocean was minding its own business. The graves did not open. Jason and he were going to be all right. They were going to live their not quite normal lives because there are ways to distinguish between the sensibility of the paranoiac and that of the artist.

Once the practice of art had cost him the better part of the hand he needed for it. Always, before and after that, the exposure required by art sandpapered his skin—but also toughened it. Art made life unendurable—and in turn made it endurable.

Jason, of all people, knew best where to wound him. Of all people, he himself knew best how to grow new tissue over the wound.

It took no more than his short amble from the studio to the

mansion to tranquilize his nerves after the clash with Jason. He soon fell asleep as straightforwardly as a child. He slept in the fortress of his surrender to the world and to passing time. He had no great wishes any more—only to stay steady.

And his steadfastness might not have been torn to shreds if a trivial coincidence had not wakened him to watch his best-loved son and the wild girl go romping to the beach for their swim.

Chapter 6

The moon was far in the west when Bern Whitestar brought Susan back to the gate of the Trebbel estate.

"No, don't drive in," she said. "Let me out here and I'll sneak across to the guesthouse."

"Feeling guilty?"

"Not overwhelmingly. Good night, darling." She kissed him richly before she got out of the car and started to cross the lawn. She took off her shoes to enjoy the tickle of grass through her stockings. Delicious. Every part of her body felt delicious.

That sheer sense of well-being made it easy to admit her guilts. She was doubly guilty, thank you. Guilty for slipping away from this wondrous place for a sex rendezvous. Guilty for not going through with what she had probably promised by going home with Bern Whitestar to look at his sculpture.

His wife Gloria was in Europe for the week. The good man surely needed something to store up against the drab impact of her return. He needed the basic reassurance she had doled out to a number of men she could not remember liking as well as she liked him. But what she had given him was, in essence, a monologue.

I'm a real tease, she thought. For a woman of forty-one it is among the nicest thoughts to savor as she steals back to her room through the summer night.

Almost certainly she *would* have gone to bed with him, but just before she finished admiring one of his big constructions of rosewood and walnut, the sweet man asked, "Tamisan. Is that a family name? Is it Scotch?" And both their idling erotic impulses got sidetracked at that point. With a drink in her hand, she sat on an uncarved stump of applewood and told him.

"Can't you accept it as pseudo Hebrew? My father was a preacher—you better believe it—and I was trying for an Old Testament sound. I made it out of my frustrations at getting trapped in pregnancy before I'd escaped from the Midwest. A girl with a name like Tamisan would *have* to split from the Midwest, I figured, and head for the capitals of glamor, naturally dragging Mama along as she glided temptingly back and forth in front of Nice and Cannes, yachting in the blue Mediterranean."

"She does glide temptingly," Bern said, finding himself a place on the studio floor to sit—probably not yet giving up his search for the right moment to pounce or fondle. Probably recalling how Tamisan had looked in the sun—to keep his resolve firm.

"While I was pregnant with her I sun-bathed nude in the tall grass behind our cabin—our shabby little tourist cabin—on the Missouri River, so that when I was delivered the nurses couldn't believe my over-all tan. Nature worshiper, Nurse Carlson called me. Sun lover. Child of the earth. Wild flower. She couldn't have been more wrong. My nest in the grass above the cutbank of the highway was my escape from the damn nature that got me in my fix in the first place. Also my escape from that tourist cabin I shared—more or less—with my one and only short-time husband, Christopher Vail.

"I believed then that you only had one crucial mistake allowed to you in each lifetime and that I had already made it. It was Christopher, not I, who was the talented one, you know. He was a *writer*. A blond gypsy with pale seafarer's eyes—like Tamisan's. He had won the Hopwood Award for fiction while he was in college. And how's this for glamor? He'd been an honest-to-God stick man in Reno and Las Vegas. All the rascal wanted was to get back out there and get the material to finish his novel.

"All that kept him from going was the fertile womb of Susan Snerr. I, sir, was born a Snerr, and now you've just been shown *the* most sensitive part of my anatomy. Yes, you may put some more ice in my drink, thank you.

"A girl who grows up with a name like Snerr is apt to name her child something even gaudier than Tamisan, wouldn't you think? For that matter, she might achieve conception by a pure act of will, for the sake of changing that Snerr to Vail, though we do not forget the Snerrs were good and godly people, yes, they were.

"My mistake? It was not just that I 'let him'—as we still said back in those douche-bag days before the contraceptive revolution. And it was not even to forget the damn douche bag on the one and only weekend Christopher and I ever spent in a St. Louis hotel. He had 'protection.' Protection! What's become of that innocent vocabulary of my college days? He had one dozen rubbers for that occasion in a cellophane-sealed box, like an uncut deck of cards. My gambling man! He let me roll them on to make sure there was no trick. I *loved* the smell of rubbers and all the things they were called—'cuntrums' one of my farmer uncles called them, and someday maybe I'll write about that, too.

"Oh, the mistake. . . . You know, Bern, my mistake was to suppose that because I idolized him I could hold onto him once he'd done the right thing by me and given us our right and proper names. His mistake was to think that those silly little rubber crowns I fitted him with could protect him against my idolatry. If ever a child was born of wishful thinking, you met her this afternoon.

"So . . . there I lay fat in my nest of grass that got whiter through the summer as I browned all over, hatching my enormous egg, and paying no attention at all to nature except for the big sky that served as a screen for me to project my fantasies about Christopher—*so* much better than living with the bum.

"He didn't intentionally give up the novel he was working on, even though my untimely pregnancy slowed him up for a while and obliged him to work as editor on a shoppers' weekly in St. Louis until he saw his way clear to taking us with him on his travels among the show girls and the gunmen of the sin capitals.

"Alas, I'll admit what had happened. I had already taken it

over on those days I was up there daydreaming. Talk about
prenatal influences! I would lie there watching him at the green
tables with his rake, indolent but quick as a cat. His whitish-
blue eyes never missing a move of the play but never failing to
measure the character of the gamblers who came and went
from his table, either. I'd lie there naming the women who
came to his table and to the shack he shared in the desert with
a dark Spaniard named Gutierrez. Alice, Pauline, Martha . . .
To this day I can remember that in my first, unwritten version
of this novel Martha had been a high school science teacher
before she went into the racket and had pubic hair like the fuzz
on a dandelion and waked Gutierrez with her yelling when
Christopher put it to her in those desert nights—which he had
altogether stopped doing to me."

"I suppose you intimidated him a bit," Bern said.

"Worse than that. Be warned about us Vail women, sir. I'll
tell you. One night in the early fall just before Tamisan was
born I woke up in that single-room cabin aware that my
Christopher had, at last, come home from putting the newspaper—or someone or something—to bed. He was oozing around
like a beautiful, sleepy animal, shedding jacket and shirt and
undershirt on the floor and furniture. At last, naked except
for his red, white and blue shorts, he yawned and stretched in
front of the refrigerator.

"I supposed he had a yen for a midnight snack. He opened
the refrigerator door and both light and frosty steam silhouetted
him. With a sigh of total bliss, backhanded—with his little finger
arched to an *exquisite* tension—he began to urinate on the pack-
aged meat I had bought for his dinner and the leftovers of my
salad.

"I just yelled, 'Christopher!' "

Bern Whitestar put his hands over his ears and flinched.
"The poor bastard."

"Yes! I could still weep when I think what that hideous
sound must have done to his delicate little pink brain. He gave
one pitiable cough of surprise and ran out to sleep in the car.

"If I had been the woman I was even five years later, I would have been able to go out to him that night, chuckle about it and cuddle up with him in the Chevy until dawn. One knows that kind of thing, looking backward. That's the sadness of it, because when I *was* five years older Chris and I were four years divorced. He was in Hollywood—the managing editor of a shoppers' weekly there. And I had written *his* novel about the gay, gallant, doomed young stick man at a Las Vegas casino.

"I took his novel over the way I had to take over other things in our eleven-month marriage—arranging time payments at the grocery store where Chris said he had paid up our bills each month, finding where to get a used magneto for his motorcycle so we could get it in shape to resell, giving him an enema when he was convinced he had either appendicitis or cancer of the bowel, borrowing money from my father's pastoral salary when Chris believed the St. Loo mafiosos were going to kill him or maim him for an unpaid gambling debt . . ."

"Ah," Bern said. "Now I know how novels are born."

"I thought I was telling you how Tamisan got born. It's not quite the same thing. Novels aren't quite as big as that enormous head coming out of you. I watched it and should have been warned right then. . . . Never mind. Dean Goss says that a work of art comes into being when some anarchic dream with a will of its own collides with our consciousness of the present moment." She closed her eyes and felt it happening right there and then—with no harm done, since Bern made no move to approach her and seemed content, now, to wait for Gloria.

"What's colliding up at the Goss shop?"

"It's all so smooth. . . . Fiona keeps it all oiled. I'm beginning to feel like a fraud who will never deliver a book again. I read and read. I look and look. Talk to the old man. There's too much to get around. The life is so enormous. So much has been written already."

"There's always a way for a lady to encompass an artist."

"I didn't come out here to lay him. Do you want me to write 'How I Laid Dean Goss and Found . . .'?"

"I'll buy it. What fascinates me is his burned, maimed hand. I know that's been written about. Poorly. We know it was over his troubles with women."

"He only jokes about it," Susan said. "I didn't come out here to tamper with his sanity, either. If he wants to tell me something new . . . I don't know if I'd publish it."

Bern scoffed lightly. "You parade your daughter in front of him and say you're not tampering with his sanity? Or mine?"

"She is disturbing," Susan admitted. "She won't be here long. She and Jason are birds. They're free. They'll fly on their way."

No. She would not enter on her books any guilt at all for her conduct of the evening. If she had exploited a captive audience to readjust her own legend of Tamisan's origin, Bern had got his evening's worth of her best female offerings.

Yet, lying untouched in her bed, she wondered just where she had warned him off from making an approach. To be sure, it must have been when she told him about Christopher and the refrigerator. He had been too wise to risk the trap that finished her one and only husband.

Warned not to come closer, not to touch, he had finished off their evening telling her what he labeled "apocryphal" stories about Dean Goss and his women. Gleanings from the locker room of art.

"You've seen him. You know how intensely he paints. Who else winds his whole soul up like that except to fuck? His models seem to understand what he's doing. Cleveland Armour used to paint with him when he was married to gorgeous Maggie and presumably not lacking for anything. Cleveland swears that more than once he's looked on while a model got off her couch and skipped over to kneel down and blow him where he stood. I'll only say this: once I boffed a model who'd come here from working for him, and I swear she had just been screwed and she swore he hadn't done a thing but lay up paint on his canvas. Eerie. . . ."

Yes, she supposed. Bern got what he wanted in telling her such tales, as she was fulfilled in telling hers.

It was a night when many dreams and daydreams collided at North Atlantic, under the placid moon.

from Susan Vail's green notebook:

DEAN GOSS: A work of art happens when there is a collision between the violent anarchy of a dream and the structure of a conscious present too rigid to accommodate it. The prescription seems also to fit revolution or crime.

from Susan Vail's blue notebook:

DEAN GOSS: I take my stand like a deer hunter at the point where the invisible and the visible come into collision. I am where they collide.

from Susan Vail's red notebook:

He stood there with the garden hose in his hand, tearing up the flower bed with the jet of water. "COLLISION!" he bellowed at me. I understood I was going to be hanged for a lamb instead of the sheep I might have grabbed.

Chapter 7

He had seen them race across the moonlit lawn headed for the sea, his son and Tamisan. He *happened* to see them because an aging man's prostate forces him to pee at romantic hours. He had looked out his bathroom window after he turned off the light.

The sight of them galloping bare-assed from the mansion gave him no ideas for a picture. They looked like something that had already been done—maybe by a Romantic painter a century or more ago. They looked like a pair of garden statues escaped from their pedestals as they scampered toward the beach. As Adam and Eve may have looked when they departed paradise at a dead run.

He did not even envy them their youth as he watched and then shook the drops from his drowsing cock. There was just enough erotic romanticism in the spectacle they made to turn his thoughts to girls he had known when he was Jason's age, his high school and college loves. How good they had been to him, how good for him! It was astonishing how fresh his memories were of patches of their skin and textures of their bobbed hair. How much erotic fervor they had pumped into him, even those—or especially those—who slapped his hands away when he tried to reach their garters! Long ago he had ceased to care or remember how many of them—how few to tell the truth—he had actually laid. He had other ways of ravishing them. His sense carried away a booty that fed his imagination forever after. He was one of those pirates of the eye who looted what all the splendid girls never seemed to miss.

The weight of his body, as he stretched it again on his bed, seemed good to him—best in repose. He could feel it lying there like a good piece of sculpture with a few chips and extremities lost but essentially solid and permanent. He had learned how to trust this feel of his body and its essential integrity. And in this trust he went back to sleep dreaming that he was Dean Goss, the best American painter of his century, still at the height of his powers, venerated by art historians and dealers, attended by women. He had become his own monument. What he had been born to do was already accomplished.

From this dream he fell into another.

A cheerful, girlish voice was calling, "Package for you, sir." There were two packages and they had come to him from Paris. Mummies wrapped identically for safety in shipment by air. The voice that spoke from the wrappings of one made a cruel and clumsy joke: "Maggie's in that one." It was Jason's voice. He had merely been hiding in the wrappings of the mummy on the right. He sat up and the swathings fell away. He began to unwrap the other mummy. Yard after yard of dusty cloth was unwound in his hands. "Don't worry," Jason said. "She's in there somewhere."

He had brought his mother home from Paris. "Don't worry just because she's dead."

Dean Goss was not worried. He was only terrified that Maggie had become so small. The mummy was all wrappings—miles of wrappings that fell around him and Jason like the coils of dead snakes—and what was left was only shoebox size.

"Don't worry!"

For the wrappings contained something after all: one dried and graying wing of a sea gull, something cast away and washed up in the litter left by tourists and the senseless natural traffic of the ocean.

"It makes up for everything," Jason said. He began to gnaw on the dried gray feathers. His father snatched the wing out of his mouth. He woke from that horror and it vanished. He slept again and the dream threatened to come back.

An hour past sunrise he was jogging on the black-top road a mile east of the Trebbel estate. He wasn't jogging for his health, though his doctor had advised him, "From now on you have to keep *trying,* Mr. Goss. There aren't any gifts after sixty-five, only what we earn the hard way." It seemed to him he was running for his life.

He was not fleeing any ghostly pursuers. They could not nail him in his dreams, however they might scare him and chatter behind him.

He was running—not exactly jogging now but up on his toes, exhilarated by the heavy pump of muscles in his old legs—because from the sheer misery of the dream something new and tantalizing had begun to flicker.

Cobalt and ultramarine, with a little bleeding of Prussian green near the beach. Pure cerulean flowing. He glimpsed the sea across the marshes behind Dinty's Clam Bar. An argosy of midget clouds, dangerous and bright as assault boats on D-Day. How would he know what all this meant until he began to paint?

On the homeward leg of his trot, he passed three cars left over from the Mulligans' party, a frayed army blanket spread and abandoned at the edge of the Congregational cemetery behind the church, and two hairy children in jeans with their blanket rolls flung down in the weeds of the roadside ditch.

These all meant something, too, as the morning colors did, and it filled him with rich melancholy that he dared not pause to find out what they meant. He was hurrying toward his studio —in that deliciously postponed haste that was half the secret of all art. In sheer physical exertion he had put off the poisoned *feeling* of his dream and that was step one in the process. When he went to shower, his breath seemed sweet as a child's. He ate a hearty breakfast.

After breakfast he was in the garden, watering plants and midsummer blossoms with the hose. The dream that had assaulted him like the beginning of illness still might spoil his morning. It had not spoiled *the* morning. He adjusted the brass nozzle. He felt the changing pulse of water under the massive insulation of rubber. He saw the concentrated jet of water burst through a bed of bachelor buttons like the rockets from a strafing plane. He watched it uproot a yellow gladiolus. How gratifying to destroy and make new things visible! That had been his life as a painter. He had torn apart the simple loveliness of surfaces and recombined the forms and colors. He had not worked from nature. He had worked with nature. He saw himself now in this garden as if he were the demon of his century, blasting apart Monet's bourgeois garden at Giverney to steal the colors and make new gardens from them.

And it was just in this pendular moment that Susan Vail came past on her way to breakfast in the mansion. From somewhere behind his left shoulder he heard her pleasant voice joking, "Without you this place would fall to rack and ruin. Now I know you do the gardener's work too."

That made him mad at her all over again. She did not seem to understand that he was most urgently on his way to the studio, that he was already at work. What was he doing if he was not tinkering a balance between mindless fears and mindless joys? And the straying little bitch was probably standing there grinning and making some easy Freudian interpretation of his doing pee-pee with the hose. . . . In the night when he needed her she deserted him and now wanted to snoop on him with her notebook again.

Ha. He drew a half circle around her shoes with an angry stream of water—just to show her she was not forgiven. "Collision!" he shouted.

She looked taken aback, but not much. And that was all right, since he was not very angry with her, now that he was beginning to get his interior universe in balance.

He said, "A woman once accused me of having to prove my manhood over and over again because I was unsure of it. Damn right! That's what we all have to do. Some can. Some can't. If you have any silly psychological insights about what you have just observed, please enter them in your notebook, madame."

He turned his back on her and went on having fun tearing up the flowers with the hose.

Now the curve of water from his hand seemed to carve—almost by accident—the white flank of a running figure. It looked like the ass of Tamisan Vail running through the dark with his son . . . or a mare's flank from a Delacroix painting.

Both. Neither.

There was nothing to be seen if he stared. The suggested images were gluing themselves together in his head. Tamisan. The all too human horseflesh of the Romantic vision, the female forever fleeing into the perilous darkness. His young wife pounded into the grave by the grinding of lust on her soft parts. A mare with a lion clinging to her flanks in some voracious parody of sexual coupling. A furious overlapping of colors . . .

Then, only one more thing was needed to get him ready. He had to imagine himself in the empty interior of the studio that waited for him not two hundred yards away—that comfortable and luxurious structure that he would daily make over into an arena where he must strangle monsters with his bare hands.

He wiped out all recollection of last night's visitors. He saw the emptiness of the warehouse-sized room with its tall windows on the north. The three big easels and the panels hanging from their overhead rails. The varnished tables and cupboards. The panel covered with road maps, photos of himself. Reproductions of Braque, Corot, Picasso and a photograph of Renoir's standing figure, "Le Triomphe de l'amour."

There was his touchstone Cézanne. The worktable on which he would lay out his paints and the postcard reproductions of Delacroix's horses and lions. And the treasury of materials— a fortune in paint and canvas. Brushes wide as his hand, with handles as thick as the hose he had been using on Fiona's garden. The record player and the records he had left out yesterday. The needle poised on a wrist of aluminum, delicate as a Chinese painter's brush about to trace a reed against a foggy marsh.

All the machinery needed to make Dean Goss function.

On one of the easels he imagined now, there was the painting Jason had brought out last night. That oversized, uncompleted, never-to-be-completed image of grief and chaos where he had vented his helplessness in the time after Maggie's death.

That image of a woman who had ceased to be Maggie and would have no identity except what she got from his battered hands. He had to finish it now. Not as *therapy* . . . ridiculous word. It was the task laid on the man because he had chosen to be an artist. Jason, after all, had called him back to it.

In his mind as he left the garden the imagined studio was empty. He walked toward its emptiness with flexed shoulders. He went as if on parade across the lawn under the towering pines. There were seven gulls in the immense clarity over the treetops. Two red kites feinted at each other above the motel farther down the beach. He didn't see them.

He imagined himself entering the imagined studio. Grunting and cursing the clumsiness of his bad hand, he cranked and dragged the easel and the painting to the place in the light he needed. He circled away from it, shaking his head in disgust at the mistakes he had left on the canvas as evidence for all his inquisitors.

Only now, as he spread his paint on the marble square of his palette, he lost the sense that this was an imaginary building and he a bodiless figure projected by some hidden movie projector.

Growling, he threw himself on the woman with a stripe of searing green.

Now it was coming as it had in his great years. The sense of being only a tunnel through which living water flowed from an underground source. Or being at the tiller of a boat, making nothing happen himself, but balancing with his will and desire the shapeless forces of the wind, the water and the tool-like shape of the sail and the weight of the hull.

Form and meaning came at the same time. Or, rather, it had to be put in the plural—forms and meanings. So very many of them that he felt like Horatio at the bridge, fighting off whole armies of *possible* paintings that were trying to crowd onto his canvas. He was destroying them as he had, quickly enough, destroyed the appearance of the woman who had occupied the canvas for four years. *She* was gone within minutes of his starting to work. She disappeared, dissolved under the colors of flowers and spruce and the shaded corner of the lawn he had sprayed with the hose. Now the representation was not of a flayed and mutilated goddess, but a fecund and fecundating bearer of fruits and ferns—with flanks as ample and simple in their curve as the parabolic arch of water from the hose. A mare's flanks in their powerful, loose modeling.

He was making something so different he should have started on a new canvas, he told himself cheerily when he had been working for an hour. But the truth was he always preferred to start anew on something already begun—painting over it, re-structuring it with charcoal and added paint, washing and scraping away with Zip-Strip to get back down to bare canvas when he had to. Most of all and most important, letting the very process of destruction become part of the rhythm of creation.

There was no haste or frenzy in the way he was working. He could feel the big rhythms of his body matching pace with the progress of the painting. All of it was as easy and reassuring as his jogging on the road five hours ago. After all, it was going to come fast. He was already beginning to develop a surface on the painting. Or else, of its own intention, a surface was developing, the way thick soup will begin to skin over as it chills.

From the pocket of his smock he pulled a small round mirror. With his back to the canvas he held the mirror in his cupped left hand to study the painting in its miniature depths. It said hello. There was someone there. A presence ready to parley with him.

He wiped his hands clean of paint, fitted a cigarette into his filtered holder, put Beethoven's Piano Sonata No. 29 in B flat Major on the stereo and sat down to rejoice.

As soon as he sat down, he thought, *Mirror*. He had liked what he saw in the tiny mirror at least as much as what he had got down on the canvas. What he had seen in the mirror had to be put in too.

It was just past noon when Fiona came in. She found him settling a second canvas, a new one of the same majestic size,

135

on an easel dragged up beside the one he had been working on. A cigarette was glowing to furnace heat precariously near his beard.

"Godwin and Bruce have arrived," she told him. "Did you forget they were coming to lunch today?"

He had to rescue his beard from the fire before he could remember that Godwin was his son and that Bruce Behn was his dealer. When he did remember, he began to sulk. He kicked the rollers of the second easel so the two canvases sat next to each other at a very slight angle, like the pages of a book fallen open to an often-read passage.

"See?" he crowed. "This won't amount to anything, but it has got me going. It's the woman and her mirror. The mirror of Venus. Narcissus and his mirror. Forget about the sex, I know Narcissus was a boy." He attached a square of charcoal to the end of a bamboo stick, pranced back and aimed the stick at the upper right corner of the blank canvas. "Women are never real to themselves except when reflected!" Abruptly he charged. They both heard the teeth of the canvas disintegrate the charcoal as he swept a large, tilted oval onto it and placed a head atop the two-by-four neck to mirror the female head on the older canvas. "They'll have to be shown together at exactly this angle, Fiona. Where the hell has Susan been all morning? She's usually right under my armpit when I *don't* need her."

"She's entertaining Bruce and Godwin on the balcony. They're having martinis. There's an extraordinarily beautiful view of the sea today. I suppose we'll lunch there."

"The one morning I needed someone here to talk to!" he complained. "Vendler's off somewhere ogling tourists on the beaches. Susan's entertaining men—which she seems to specialize at. Well, she missed everything this morning. By now she could have got at least one book out of me. I had bad dreams all night. Now I've converted them into . . . If she'd been here with her tape recorder, I could have talked the whole process out and we could let her go home."

He put a duster on another bamboo stick and erased his first tries with the charcoal. He drew another head, somewhat larger, and in profile rather than full face. Fiona sat in the director's chair where he had rested so little all morning. She had very bright, very thick lipstick this morning. It had a startling effect on her massive face. He stared at the freckles on her arms as if noting them for the first time. Freckles on top of freckles. And that was fair enough, because just now he had eyes inside his eyes and they were missing nothing.

She said, "Susan has the idea you're not pleased with her. I've spent most of the morning talking to her and Jason. He's hurt and repentant about last night. He didn't mean to embarrass you while the Burkes were here."

"Explain to them both I'm a boor. Sometimes I can be hurt too."

"Sssssh! They could hardly miss that fact." This was as close as Fiona usually got to chiding him. It was enough. All the minor, present annoyances had been absorbed in the painting hours ago, absorbed much easier than the bad dreams, naturally.

"I'll tell you," he said to the one woman who didn't have to be tricked to do his bidding. "Couldn't Godwin and Bruce come back tomorrow?"

Fiona had apparently weighed all this before, arranging all she could before she brought it to him, as she read and sorted his mail and disposed of most of it. "Godwin can stay, but Bruce can't, so they both may drive back again this evening. It's rather important. Bruce wants some sort of statement from you for the people at the Metropolitan. He's confident they've bought the idea of another retrospective for your seventieth birthday. They'll want to know early. Whether there's anything new and major . . ."

Onto his marble palette Dean Goss was scraping out the contents of a can of cobalt violet. "There'll be nothing new if I don't have any peace to work," he said pettishly. "Of course at this rate I may finish this afternoon. It may all go sour on me. In a couple of hours I may discover my great mistake and quit, but . . . Fiona, tell them I wish I could be free to sit in the sun on the balcony and drink yellow wine . . . What's for lunch?"

"Trout."

"But if they'll only let me get this out of my system and then come back next week. Or in September. . . . Can you explain to them?"

Of course she would explain. Explanations were easy, just as real statements and real communication were infinitely hard. Explanations were the cushions on which the nitroglycerin of essential truth in its fragile bottles had to be transported across the spaces of the social world. He did not despise them. In fact he was desperate for more, calling out for help as he juggled his nitroglycerin barehanded.

"Explain to Susan," he said, with an angry frustration laced with pity, "that she might as well pack her bags and go. I tried to teach her you've got to *swing*. If you're a foolish virgin, you've got to be there when the bridegroom cometh. If you're a hunter, you've got to be there when the buck comes out of the woods. If . . ."

"Those are her very words," Fiona said placidly, without irony.

He glared at her nevertheless—and resented Susan for learning, from him or from life, such cardinal principles, but not learning them well enough or soon enough to be with him in his need. "Words, words, words," he grumbled. "She's full of them."

"Shall I ask her to come down after lunch?"

"No!" he roared in pain. "Well . . . No!" He had to punish Susan for her failures, and he had no time to fool with explanations of the subtle complexities that made her miss what she probably thought she had seized. He flapped his arms in frustration. "I don't like the idea of her gossiping with Godwin and Bruce, either. You know. Susan's a bit of a . . . She's the sort of woman that . . . She rouses suspicions. I never had anything but generous, intellectual relations with her. Fatherly feelings. But she'll give them the idea there's something more going on."

"I never heard anything so ridiculous in my life," Fiona said. And went out to manage his needs as fully and as beautifully as she always did.

He was very hungry but his mouth was foul from too many cigarettes. He had taken one or two bites of the cold trout Fiona sent down for his lunch. He had sipped the wine the others were enjoying while he sweated himself like a man trying to fight his way out of a mine disaster. The trout tasted like pure tar and nicotine. The wine, instead of its distinguished French label, should have borne a warning from the Surgeon General's office that it might be hazardous to health.

He supposed it was probably past five in the afternoon. If he had not somehow mislaid his watch he might have known it was nearer seven.

On the canvases he had made images of women worthy to sit in front of. He was worthy to sit in front of them—and never mind that Susan Vail would never write down in her book how many fearful and tragic things had been compounded into these images.

He was very tired, but he was sitting there well in charge of his life when Tamisan came in demurely and solemnly to talk to him.

"Isn't it about time for you to quit?" she said cheerily.

"I have quit, sister." He turned, stupid and dazed, to invite her to sit in the chair beside him and gaze upon what he had wrought. He saw she was wearing hip-huggers and a red bandanna brassière. Her skin looked glazed by sun and water. Her almost white hair was damp at the tips. "Good afternoon at the beach?" he asked.

His heavy head turned back to contemplate his women again. He was wondering how they would look hung next to Titian's "Pardo Venus." A difference of techniques, of course. A difference of composition. What did that matter? What did it matter that what he had flung up there on canvas was only one day's work? . . . Only one lifetime's work, he thought. Hell, he wouldn't hang them up there for competition, but only to see if, as he worked, he had been *right* about women. If the tragedy and the joy he had felt were all the truth.

Tamisan's big hips made a cozy, slapping sound as she took her seat in the chair next to his. Frowning her own best imitation of Jason's frown, she said, "I think it's time we had a good old heart-to-heart."

"You bet," he said. He wanted her to know it was nice to have her company at the end of his enormous day. It was like sitting with his favorite granddaughter Monica, Vidal's youngest child.

"We've been *acquainted* quite a while now," she said. She was gathering breath and nerve to utter some important, girlish observation, he noted. Yes, they had been acquainted. Once or twice in the spring he had visited Jason at the old studio. He had had very little curiosity about her beyond what his eyes could tell him.

Then she said, "Now that you've painted me, I can talk to you."

It was a trick. The voice he heard saying this was the clear emphatic voice that had summoned him to his bad dream of the night before, calling, "Package for you, sir."

It was not much of a trick. Only a bit of mischief that fatigue played with his nerves. Of course he was well enough acquainted with her voice so his dreaming mind could appropriate its tone to tease him in his defenseless sleep. It was one thing to be tricked and bewitched in a dream. In his wakefulness Dean Goss was not that easy to catch. He thought of the "Pardo Venus" again. Of the stag being torn by dogs behind those magnificent foreground figures of the kneeling satyr digging his goatish toes in as he gets ready to mount the willing goddess. *The sound of horns and hunting that will bring Actaeon to Diana in the spring* . . . The marvel of Titian's painting was that he had modernized the old device of continuous narrative. He had made a painting that was at the same time static, monumental and a developing drama of youthful gaiety turning into thunderous lust. A drama in which the separate acts were defined by spatial sequences on the canvas. Now, Goss thought, how would it work if he linked the two separate figures of *his* diptych with a horizontal pattern beneath, a pattern of continuous narrative in the idiom of a modern comic strip?

". . . not at all frightened of you any more," the girl was saying. "So I'm going to be very frank."

"Frank about what?"

"Why Jason and I are so *worried* about you. That's the main thing. Why you aren't *living up* to what we think you could do. I haven't seen all that many of your paintings and I don't know that much about art. I barely know who Puvis de Chavannes is. But what I've seen of your recent work is *good*. Jason thinks the watercolor you did of me is at least *alive*." She bobbed her head impatiently at his huge canvases in front of them. "These may not move me as much as some things younger people are doing now, but . . ."

He wanted to be very kind to her. But she ought to go away *now* without having to be ordered out. Maybe if he concentrated harder on the "Pardo Venus"—projecting it in his memory, doodling a quick sketch of its formal organization—the child would get her heart-to-heart over with quickly and let him go bathe. If Godwin and Bruce Behn were still hanging around he wanted a drink with them. Suddenly he felt a desperate longing for the sophisticated talk of older people.

She said, "You'll probably laugh, too, about our meditations. We don't pretend to be experts in astrology or reading Tarot and *I Ching,* but we do that too. It's kind of a mysticism of the body. . . . Well, of *love,*" she amended thoughtfully. And now her voice was so throaty she sounded like Titian's Venus cooing to that shaggy satyr. "So even if you don't know much about me, I know just about everything about you. Not just what Jason told me, but what we learned in our *meditations.*"

For just an instant he visualized them meditating on the mattress in that other studio. Now in continuous narration, the big knees of the goddess fell apart and the satyr sprang!

She said, "Just because you're old you don't *have* to believe you're finished as an artist."

"I suppose not," he said dryly. In the morning he would get

George Vendler to help him scrub off the face of the figure on the left-hand canvas. It wasn't right, and it wouldn't stand over-painting.

"We *scrutinize* as well as meditate," she said with a touch of desperation at her failure to claim his full attention. "What do you think Jason was doing all winter in that old abandoned studio of yours if he wasn't trying to *scrutinize* you?"

"Scrutinizing you."

"Screwing me," she corrected calmly, "but even that was him trying to see back into the part of your life when you were al-most as young as he is. His way of knowing about the women you knew then.

"The essence of it is," she went on with her terrifying cer-tainty, "is that, well, we are *young* and we're awfully *committed* though it may not look like it and we don't do any peace march-ing or burning ourselves at the U.N. But that's what our being together means. We're serious." She gulped a bit because he did not seem to be listening to her. She went on out of sheer mo-mentum. "We're so sure of ourselves we want to share with you what we have. That's what Jason means by *religious* and he's taught me. I understood. You ought to listen. I'll save some of this until you're not so tired if you want, but . . . You've got so caught up in being famous and having everyone flatter you and bow to you . . . like Mama, whom you've scared to death so she hardly peeps in your presence. . . . Jason and I want you to get back to being as serious about your life as we are."

"Serious?" he asked in genuine astonishment.

If she had blundered in her choice of words, she was unaware of it. "Well, as Jason told that art historian last night, every-thing you've done since 'The Surrender' has been a hoax."

"Hoax?" He bobbed his head as if, at last, he had begun to see how determined this attack was.

"Your painting doesn't speak any more. You don't show yourself to Jason in what you're willing to do now. You threw in your towel—not that I'm such a great judge of what you may be doing here." With a casual shoulder she pointed at his labors of this long day.

The shocks had been coming too fast for him to say which

stung him into reaction. But now he rose out of his chair like a big strange animal climbing so fast from its cave that he seemed to tower over her at an unbelievable height.

She got up too. Frightened he would squash her in her chair unless she was in a position to run. She lifted a hand to protect her face. "No!" she squeaked. "Maybe I can't express myself well, but . . ."

"Get out!" he thundered. "Don't try to tell me about Jason, you fucking idiot!"

She stood rigid then. Her eyes were closed, her arms now hanging limp at her sides, in a pose that both understood. If he slapped her face she would not duck. Her lower lip was caught savagely under her upper teeth. An uncontrolled flow of tears ran down her cheeks and dribbled on the slopes of her breasts.

He could feel the negative force of her submission, like the suck of a spent breaker swirling sand from under his feet as it spills back from the beach. It was the tug of a tide running warm, an overwhelming sweetness of summer going that could lure a man to let go and drown.

"Here then," he said with marveling tenderness. "Tell me. Tell me what you and Jason think. Yes, I'll listen to it all. Tell me about you and Jason in that other studio." He put out his mutilated hand and felt it watered with the hot moisture of her cheek. "I want to get to know you, love."

She crouched against him, as much in shame as anything else. Her brash confidence was gone and she was more naked to his touch than she had been in the garden posing for him. He touched each of her eyelids with an incredulous forefinger. He could feel the beat of pulse in the lids like twin hearts. He was like a man both blind and deaf feeling the skin of a thundering drum. As she hung on him to keep from falling, he felt the shudder of her rending begin, orgasmic but gentler and more profound than the convulsions of climax, like the incessant rebound of a bough full of blossoms beaten by rain.

"Please don't do anything to me," she said. "Please don't." It was the murmur of a woman terrified because she has no resistances left within her own power. And for a moment he stood glorified by the totality of her dependence on him. He held her erect while the shuddering rhythm intensified and she seemed to flow against him, molten as wax. "NO, no, no, no, no. Please! Nothing," she said. He knew it was not against him but against the rape her own body inflicted that she went on protesting. He felt her spasms crest and fade in her. And still, in her abandonment, she kept muttering those forlorn syllables of lamentation. "No, no, no, no, no, no!"

As tenderly as he could, he moved her back from him. "I love you very much, child," he said. "Now we have to go."

He meant to kiss her on the mouth. To give that much recognition to the fathomless surrender that had engulfed them both for a moment. She bent her head away, as if shamed, and the kiss fell on her cheekbone.

"I thought I could *tell* you," she said with a brutal harshness that was beyond remorse, lacerating herself for her failure. "I knew what I had to say."

"It's all right. It's all right."

Now she threw back her head to stare at his face. Even then she did not seem to be looking at him, but at his steel-rimmed glasses and maybe at her own reflection.

With a swift twist of her shoulders, she whipped her open fingers across his face, hooking off the glasses and letting them fly, catapulted by her rage, across the studio.

They both heard the glasses shatter as they struck the marble corner of his palette. But the suddenly blurred, altered form that he saw running from him, diminishing in scale, then silhouetted in bright purple against the opening door, did not pause or lose a step at the tinkle and light patter of fragments falling to the floor.

He would think in a few minutes, She was going for my eyes. Would think, If she had blinded me she would have stayed. Would think, She offered to blind me so I could see. . . .

He was not blinded. The purple afterimage of what had been golden sunlight in the door through which she fled was dimming briskly. The shapes of studio furniture and his two big canvases resumed appearances that were tentatively normal to his sight.

Yet all changed. The colors on his canvases were as bright and rich as they had been before the girl intruded. But now the shapes that defined their relationships were disrupted and vague so they were like scraps of bright wrapping paper kicked along by the feet of a holiday crowd. Suddenly vivid to him as to a child who might chase after them, guessing at a pattern that might be made if he could catch them, gather them, paste them down . . .

Prompted by bad dreams, he had begun something good today. It was not enough now.

He was a man prepared to know glory when he glimpsed it. As he went fumbling in a cupboard for a whole pair of glasses, stored for such emergency, a new pictorial combination already teased his inner eye.

He was not sure whether the furious girl had violated him or he had violated her. Neither assumption would quite hold. But he knew an elemental rape had been committed. As the girl fled, that truth took its full and irrefutable shape in his soul. His heart danced like a savage prancing and brandishing a spear in primitive ritual. He grimaced at the light, in triumph and without remorse.

Book III

Flight

Chapter 8

Sometime that night Tamisan came into his studio and tore up the watercolor he had painted in the garden. Then she ran away from North Atlantic in Jason's car.

She must have performed her vengeance late, because no one saw her come or go, though Jason was already hunting for her. She must have been in a state of hysterical fury. The watercolor paper was tough and she had torn it into thirty-two pieces, doubling the thick paper for some, if not all, of the rippings.

It was George Vendler who first discovered the destruction she left behind. He came into the studio at a comfortable hour the next morning, intending to begin an edition of prints from an intaglio plate Dean Goss had finished in 1953. Before he went downstairs to the print shop, he noted the two big new canvases started the day before.

He had gone to look them over—with some mystification and reservations about what he saw: wild stuff, like Nolde or Soutine reincarnated, but not like Goss—when he noticed he was standing on a patch of what might have been oversized confetti. Some of the pieces around his feet were creamy white. Others were tinted with dioxazine purple. Some with new gamboge. He did not have to fit pieces together to recognize the watercolor.

His first thought was that Goss might have ripped it apart himself. That happened often enough when the old man was disappointed with his work, but the litter usually went into a wastebasket or incinerator. Goss kept a clean shop if not always a neat one.

It was possible that some vandal hippie had got on the grounds last night. North Atlantic had no real security system. To be sure, it was off the beaten track of the summer hordes, but not very much. And it was one of Vendler's sad convictions that sooner or later the barbarians would spill in here, from sheer overflow if they lacked specific motives.

So he picked up the phone in his basement workshop and called Dean Goss at the mansion. He could tell the old man was just waking up. He didn't seem to get the message straight, for when he first heard it he crowed like a hoarse rooster. Then he offered, in a conspiratorial whisper, "I was expecting that!" And hung up. Evidently he had more important matters on his mind.

Susan would blame herself later for not having expected . . . well, if not this particular vandalism on Tamisan's part, something . . . well, something like an earthquake, a breaking dam, or the eruption of a volcano. After all, her intellect grasped what Dean Goss told her about the collisions between anarchic desires and fixed reality. She had heard his puzzling shout—"Collision!"—when she came on him watering the flowers and afterward had tried to puzzle out *all* that might have been implied beyond what she could expect him to tell her. She credited him with some sort of prophetic foresight, if not with clairvoyance.

Yet, before the news hit her, she had spent one of her nicest mornings at North Atlantic. No suspicions or anxieties either had bothered her while she was with Fiona. Fiona had at last been exposing some of her own paintings. The two women had been alone in Fiona's apartment on the top floor of the mansion.

They rode up in a charming, antique lift. "It's a bird cage!" Susan said in delight with its brass fittings and latticed walls. It was another of the amusing secrets of this grand old place, hidden from ordinary view by a perfectly plain door.

"I loved to ride in it as a child," Fiona said. "I hardly ever use it now. I can walk up faster than we're going." It was toylike, and its slow, creaking ascent made Fiona's rooms seem farther away from the busy-ness of North Atlantic than they really were.

And her rooms, too, were a jolt to Susan's expectations. She had expected an austerity that wasn't evident except in the studio itself. The other rooms—bedroom, parlor, bath and office—were luxuriously feminine. Silver and marble twinkled against the cool gray-green of wallpaper and drapes. The rugs were soft as coverlets. The bedroom was positively bridal—the nest of emotions that would never come to flower and therefore never fade.

"So you see I *do* pamper myself," Fiona said with a humble note. She was not apologizing for herself, merely signaling that here some enigma of her nature was being opened to Susan. The note of humility was a note of confidence. Susan felt honored by it and comfortably humbled herself.

Above the delicate, exquisite pieces of furniture Fiona's own paintings hung on the walls. And they were humble, too, in the midst of elegance. Humble—but by no means amateur or abject. Most of them were small. In color and design they were faithful rather than assertive. They had the direct, experienced honesty that makes the work of a good cook or a good carpenter seem so wonderful.

"They look like Mary Cassatts or—well, some of the early Matisse lithographs," Susan said, and then was sorry she had needed to make any comparisons at all. For Fiona wrinkled her nose and said, "They are what I wanted to do. I was never clever enough to be fashionable."

The paintings and drawings on her walls were almost exclusively of women—women dressed in the fashions of the twenties or thirties, a few candid nudes. Before Susan could ask or comment on this exclusive subject matter, Fiona said, "They're *his* women. Wives and . . . Jason teases me. He says I keep his father's harem up here."

"What a great idea!"

"Neither Vidal nor Godwin has ever seen most of these. Godwin would be condescending, so . . ."

"You don't need that."

"I wouldn't mind," Fiona said. "But you're right. I don't need it. They're all for myself, whether it's a harem or a private gallery or whatever you might call it."

"His . . . women?" Susan said huskily. She felt her pulse quicken with an oddly troublesome excitement as she turned from picture after picture to squint and marvel at more than the masterful draftsmanship.

"There haven't been so many in his life," Fiona said.

This assurance comforted Susan. It obliterated Bern Whitestar's suggestion that Dean Goss was Superstud, or had been. "I suppose there're not so many *considering* his age—how long he's lived—and his . . . his . . . his potency," she said.

"Potency?" If the word amused or startled Fiona, it certainly didn't bowl her over. Her curiosity remained humble and straightforward enough to make Susan feel devious in comparison.

"I don't mean sexual potency, of course," Susan said in a flustered rush and almost tripped on to ask, How would I know? "I meant the kind of . . . energy that everyone feels coming off him."

"That's very attractive to women," Fiona said gravely. "But really, in absolute numbers, there haven't been many. That's Maggie," she said of the elongated little canvas before which Susan had now paused. "Of course you recognize her, at least, from the many photos you've seen of her."

"This is so much more than a photograph could be," Susan said.

Again the older woman's marvelous honesty corrected her. "No," Fiona said. "No, it isn't. It's a literal representation. I don't know how to distort. Emotions never got into my work. They went the other way. Into my heart."

And it was exactly this homely, motherly refusal to distort that seemed to lift blinders from Susan's eyes and let her glimpse a vision in the unpretentious picture of the bride. Against the scrubbed umber and black background she saw Maggie naked as on her bridal night, a girl still in her teens, looking quizzically and almost plaintively to her left so that her exquisitely simple face would be in profile. The sheer elegance of her figure made her somehow pathetic, like a slave girl in an auction, like a wildflower that will die quickly enough whether it is picked or left alone. For an instant Susan knew that the body and its beauty were prophetic in themselves. Beauty and grief uttered in a single, undecipherable syllable that seemed the speech of eternity.

"That's true," Susan said.

Fiona's studio was neat and businesslike as a kitchen ought to be. If her living quarters were furnished to pamper her, this small, adjacent room was meant for nothing but work—"though I haven't picked up a brush for months," Fiona said. "I don't always need to. *He* experiments constantly. I never have. As long as I can come in here and smell turpentine my mind is peaceful."

It occurred to Susan that the racks and shelves in this modest-sized room might contain all the pictures Fiona had made in her life, while Dean Goss's had kept spilling out into galleries and museums around the world. But for the time she was with Fiona, the woman's world seemed as spacious as the man's.

"I suppose you'd be most interested in more souvenirs of Maggie," Fiona said. She had not missed Susan's galvanized response to the nude against the dark background. It was as if her broad nostrils had taken in a glandular response that Susan herself was not yet conscious of, some effluvium of desire that neither woman would wish to name. "There are a good many here. Too many for one morning. But you'll come back again and see the rest some other time. I'll mix you a martini if you'll give me a cigarette, my dear."

"Yes, a martini. Yes, Maggie," Susan said. Yet, when she settled with the drink in her hand and the plume of cigarette smoke swayed like the ghost of a charmed snake above her limp left hand, she was relieved that the first paintings Fiona drew from her shelves did not show Maggie in her nakedness.

There was Maggie in the door of a boathouse with the light of river and sky behind her. Maggie at a tea table. Pastel studies of Maggie with her hair twisted up and the delicate length of her neck *seeming* exaggerated until one realized the exaggeration had been nature's, not Fiona's.

Maggie standing in the grape arbor of their Pennsylvania farm with the color of ripened grapes reflected just detectably by her porcelain skin.

"It was taken for granted I had come to paint whenever I visited them. That got around the need for small talk," Fiona explained, talking around the cigarette held in her lips as her hands were busy pulling out the pictures. "I was never good at small talk. I preferred to be busy. Not to be noticed too much among the brilliant people he and Maggie attracted like flies."

"I envy you more than them," Susan said, aching with the possibility that too much of her summer here might already have been squandered in small talk. What realities had slipped away unnoticed because of her big mouth and big ears devoted to matters of secondary importance?

Then, as if in response to this itch of remorse, as if to challenge her willingness to admit the full shock of either truth or beauty, Fiona flipped from her shelves a canvas slightly larger than most of the others. "Oh," Fiona said, arching her brows. "Well, I'd almost forgotten this one. My, my! Goodness, goodness, goodness. My mind plays tricks on me now that I'm old. Well! Of course now that I see it again I remember quite well the time I painted it. Jason was just old enough to crawl and sit up." Her tone was that of a grandmother showing color snapshots from a dusty album.

Sly woman! Slyness in the midst of the humblest honesty; slyness of a sort impossible to achieve except on a bedrock of absolute candor.

Of course it was precisely *this* picture she had brought Susan up here to see. It was the instrument through which their serious communication was to be accomplished and small talk set aside.

Fiona sank heavily in a chair beside Susan and both of them stared through a silence in which meanings crackled like summer lightning. Now Susan felt herself unmistakably damp.

On Fiona's canvas she saw Maggie lying on her back, Maggie on the floor of some unidentifiable room, smooth as spilled cream on the lightly figured carpet. Her smile was at exactly the right angle, a smile of pity more than contempt for those who had not been loved as well as she. There was no mistaking the degree of fulfillment her body had known. In the painting her pubic hair was set discreetly and exactly in place like a bottle top replaced on a bottle, like a medal of honor.

Oh (said Susan to herself). Oh . . . that great, sexy smugness of early motherhood, that completeness defying the whole world in its clamor to intrude. . . . Oh, Susan knew the feeling well, as she would have known it ten years before she had given birth herself. Perhaps, she thought, we are born knowing we have to wait for that and hunger back for it when it goes.

And there beside Maggie was naked little Jason, crouched on all fours as if he meant to go for her as soon as he got the right instructions from his glands. The expression of his whole body was lust. Lust for the milky breast, the springy litheness of his mother's arms, the cloudy joys within where he had emerged from his father and shared ecstasy with both mother and father before the trinity was broken.

"Has Jason ever seen this? Since he's grown, I mean?" Susan asked at last.

Either Fiona did not hear her or chose not to answer an irrelevant question. Why would Jason *need* to see this painting on canvas when, of course, it was a fresco in the chapel of his soul? Whenever he withdrew to that chapel its lines and colors would be fresher to his eye than anything they were looking at this morning.

The painting before them was perfectly candid and simple. In no way was it a geometric hieroglyph. It was no surrealistic dip into the subconscious. Yes, a great and lucky photographer might have caught a picture of naked mother and naked son that would have leaked the same secret to the ready spectator. But in this moment that Fiona had prepared and staged it seemed no less than the key to Jason's sexual destiny, a Newtonian law governing the motion of all the stars in his universe.

This much Susan guessed and believed. Now I know him, she said to herself, quite simply, feeling she knew him as if he had been her lover, her son. Both.

Into this eerie certitude Fiona spoke. "They must marry," she said. Her voice was both humble and oracular. It was like a pronouncement coming out of the mouth of a cave where the speaker is invisible.

"Jason and Tamisan?" Who else could Fiona have meant?

Fiona went on, not to be argued with, though she was not so much giving orders as seeming to transmit them. "They must," she repeated. "It would be too much for Jason to lose her now."

Susan wanted to say, How nice. What a nice idea. How flattering! But she was afraid of the proposition so squarely put. "It might be too much for him if he was stuck with her!" It seemed a terrible flaw in herself that she had not simply agreed with the authority of the old woman's decree. Not Tamisan's fault, but her own. Sins of omission and commission came home to roost and soil with their droppings all her good hopes for her child. "Mustn't we let them make up their own minds about that? They're both so young." Her equivocations sounded shabby in her ears.

And the moment when she might have uttered a simple agreement with Fiona was gone—shattered and irretrievable. Now the painting in front of them began to look banal, ordinary, even old-fashioned in spite of its craftsmanship. It had provided an instant of vision. For an instant the ordinary barriers to communication had been cast down because of it. But the moment had not been seized. There was no hope that the painting, by itself, had magic powers to give back the chance that was lost.

With the dimming of the painting, Fiona's certainty faded at the same pace. "Wishful thinking," she admitted. "I suppose they would laugh at the idea of marriage. An old maid's idea! Certainly I'd be afraid to state it flatly to Jason, let alone your girl. I don't like to make myself ridiculous. I hope you won't think I was too silly in my daydreaming."

"No, no, no," Susan said. "No, no, no, no. *Please* don't imagine I thought that. I wish it could be so, too. So simple as that, I mean. Tamisan *is* good. That is, she would be if . . . That is . . . if she could get herself together. If she could . . . I don't know."

"You see," Fiona said in a tone that was close to grieving now, yet patient, "they *are* potent, he and his father, just as you said. An odd sort of potency! I think I know the extent of their dependency on women. Perhaps you've been amused by Dean Goss's habit of asking everyone for help. He calls out to people who are evidently much weaker than he. I think that both of them take on burdens of love and responsibility that are beyond their strength."

"That's what it means to be an artist," Susan said.

"We agree on that, at least," Fiona said, with the first note of bitter reproach Susan ever heard mingled with the patience of her voice. "Never mind."

"What does Jason's father think of . . . would he want Jason to marry her at this age, or . . . ?" Somehow Susan supposed that Fiona knew everything in Goss's mind. It even flashed through her mind that Fiona might have been asked to sound her out.

But Fiona said, "I have no idea. It's never been mentioned. Up here alone I get some eccentric notions. That's all it amounts to. Certainly I don't know much about men and women. I'm all confused by the relationships of young people these days. Please be tolerant if I've been absurd. Yet—I've seen how Jason depends on her. He follows her the way he followed Maggie. I don't know why. She's not the least like Maggie. Perhaps her voice sounds similar. Now and then it does. But they have nothing else in common. I hope you won't mention my follies to Tamisan. She'd take me for a meddling fool."

"No," Susan protested.

But, at any rate, that was where the matter was left. There had been a moment when they shared excited conjectures. Nothing at all had been changed by the intuitions they shared.

As things turned out on that day of jolts and reconsiderations, Susan did not even have time to ponder all that might have been implied by Fiona's cryptic command—"They must marry."

Surely it was a command—wasn't it?—though there was no force to back it up.

Susan was hardly back at her worktable in the guesthouse when Jason came knocking with the news that Tamisan had run away. "She's been gone since early last evening. I've been on the roads looking for her since about ten last night. I drove into New York to see if she'd showed up there. To your place and the studio. I phoned Janis Ward, who hasn't heard from her. I hunted the side roads and bars around here while they were open."

Then, as if to soften this disturbing account with something amusing, he said, "She tore up Dad's watercolor sometime during the night."

"Oh, my God," Susan said. She did not know which was worse—Jason's wish that she should not worry about her runaway daughter or his nonchalance about the destruction the girl had left behind her. He laughed giddily. But she saw he was very tired, too, from his night on the roads. His laughter was not far from the tears of an overwrought child. It fell into place with what Fiona had said about his vulnerability.

"Is the painting ruined beyond saving?" Susan had some thoughts of offering her talents with rubber cement and Scotch tape.

Jason nodded. "Shredded. You know how vehement she can be."

"The savage!"

"It began when Dad hurt her feelings. He's not altogether to blame either. She waltzed in on him last night when he'd worn himself out. He'd been working hard all day. He drains all his patience. I've seen it often. He had two big paintings started this time. And . . . as he reports their dialogue, she explained to him that he was 'not a serious artist.'"

"Great!" Susan said, surprised into a bitter cough of laughter. "I suppose he didn't think that was as hilarious as you and I do."

"It's not so gross as it sounds. You might say it came out of things that I planted in her mind. I've worried about him, you see. It's hard to put exactly. So, I guess she didn't express herself well. . . . It doesn't matter. It's my fault to begin with."

"Everything is," she said with sarcasm as broad as her despair. A fundamental embarrassment, originating exactly in the womb that had borne the damn-fool girl, was spreading through her nerves like sparks running a bunch of powder trains. "What does your father say?"

"That it's his fault. He's very repentant—or he was half an hour ago. So all we have to do is find her and he'll apologize."

"Sweet Jesus!" Susan said. She had a vision of berserk Dean Goss apologizing to her girl one minute, dropping her with a blow of his fist the next.

"He called her a 'fucking idiot,' " Jason said. "That much of their conversation I got verbatim."

"Continue. I see that it gets worse and worse." There was clearly blame enough to go around. A part of her anger swung to the arrogant old man. Were they going to deny her the minimal comfort of taking sides in their dogfight? "You know as well as I, Jason, that nothing gets to Tamisan faster than to be called stupid. Tell me the rest." She helped herself to scotch from a bottle in her drawer. She thought of her apartment in New York and covers of her own under which she could hide her head.

Jason explained that he had seen Tamisan running across the lawn from the studio toward the garage. She had been too wild then to give him a dependable version of her encounter with his father, but he had heard part of it.

"It seemed sensible to let her cool off and she didn't much want to tell me what had happened. She meant well. She was going to patch things up after my spat with him the other night. Even with what I know now I can't be sure what I ought to have done."

"You used common sense."

"Oh no." He seemed surprised that she would say common sense had anything to do with these richochets of personality. She admitted the egos involved were hardly to be kept in line by what *she* called common sense.

He said, "Don't you see it was absurd for me to drive in to New York? When she hadn't come back here near midnight I tried to fit into her thoughts so I'd get on the track. It was pure impulse."

"As good as anything else."

"I couldn't have helped the way things turned out," he conceded. "I'd looked earlier in the beach parking lots and the bars where she might have gone to cool down. Even country roads. I think now she must have come back here to tear up the painting while I was somewhere nearby, though that's only a guess."

"Do you know for sure she did it at all? If no one saw her . . ."

He looked at her almost reproachfully—as if it belittled Tamisan to think that anyone else might have dared leave such a clear sign of defiance. "I didn't know last night she'd done it," he said. She had to concede that what they were looking for was not legal evidence on that point.

"Your father is convinced she did and that's what counts."

"I told you he's more pleased than upset."

"That I have to see to believe."

"I'll go with you if you like," he offered.

"Please. Before he changes his mind again."

"He's with Vidal and Monica. They came in from Paris this morning."

"I knew they were coming. A grand time to meet them! Lead on."

It was Vidal she hated most to see again under such circumstances. He had seemed kind when they talked before. She had liked him and supposed he liked her. She had been looking forward to seeing Goss with his granddaughter. Monica was to stay here for an indefinite number of days while her father tended to business in New York and South America. A child, Susan had thought, with some fascinated anticipation, would be a light illuminating one more facet of the old man. But her idyllic preconceptions of this development were suddenly soured.

"Splendid!" she said to Jason. "Why shouldn't we face them too? And any other ticket holders. Only—do take my arm and hold me on my feet, please. Doesn't it make *you* mad that Tamisan would pull such a stunt?"

His breath quavered. "I've always been afraid . . . It's been so good between us, Susan, until we got here. I was afraid something would happen to blow it. Yes. I knew it would happen."

Dean Goss was neither repentant, angry nor depressed when they got to his studio. He was exultant. He was loud and possibly drunk. He was discoursing to his second son and his spindly, pretty granddaughter on the blessings of destruction and resurrection. He sounded like an old-time hell-and-brimstone preacher. The text of the sermon was the offending watercolor, its pieces still scattered like the debris of Sodom.

"In a word," Vidal said drolly, "whoever did it, it was divine intervention in your behalf."

"Pree-CISELY! And don't imagine you know the least little thing about that, my boy. She was spelling out the message she gave when she broke my glasses."

"She did that too?" Susan asked through clenched teeth.

"The girl was inspired!" he thundered at her.

Then he saw that he was scaring them all. Mostly he was scaring young Monica. The child had got off the plane only a couple of hours before. She looked as if airsickness was getting a second grip on her. As if she had arrived only to be told of a death in the family. Idolizing her grandfather, it was inconceivable to her that anyone might be depraved enough to lift a finger against his works.

Then he saw they weren't exactly scared by the messages from divinity that scared him. They were scared that he was putting them on with an irony that would lead on to anger.

No doubt poor Susan had good reason to expect his viciousness. Jason might see his act as distraction from proper concern about the feelings or whereabouts of his girl. Vidal would interpret it as loud clowning. And even Monica would soon enough give up trying to hear the truth in what he was saying.

He had cried wolf too often, experimented with too many masks. No one, any more, could believe in the simplicity of his heart. But, in fact, he was trying to be open and candid with everyone today. When he told George Vendler that he had expected the watercolor to be destroyed, that was the simple truth.

But, even then, he had guessed he could not make it stick without endless reiterations.

Vendler had not picked up the scraps before Goss arrived in the studio. They made a nice, though meaningless, design on the studio floor. "I wasn't sure you hadn't done it yourself," Vendler said.

"I've gone too soft to do what needs to be done. No wonder they laugh at me."

If Dean Goss hadn't done it, Vendler was very shocked indeed. "I knew we should have been more careful about locking up."

"It was someone who had a message for me. 'Get off your ass.' "

"It was a nice painting," Vendler said. Vendler was unlikely to be more extravagant in his praise if he had seen him paint the Mona Lisa with a brush held between his teeth.

"It was," Dean Goss agreed. "Otherwise what point would there be in her tearing it up?"

"Her? She?"

"Tamisan Vail." He was as sure of that as if he had been here and seen her scattering the pieces from her two furious hands. Only someone like her or me would have the nerve, he told himself. Would know it had to be done so I could get past it.

"George, what about these paintings I started yesterday?"

Before Vendler had a chance to ramble through his obvious uncertainty, Dean Goss said, "All right, all right. Can't you see what I've got going in them? Of course the value of that patch of orange is absurd. It should come down to bare canvas behind that one's head. Maya-Shakti, who creates and destroys, huh? The real woman. I was coming to terms with them yesterday. Green mother, red mother. With her great yoni among other fixtures and features. All the teeth among the roses. See Mary's milk flowing in the firmament? All the strut and sag their bellies can have, mmmmm? Mmmmmm? You don't see that?"

"Sure," George said, without assurance. Then he said sensibly, "It will take me a little while to know what I do see. It's always like that. But if you say it's there, it's there."

Nothing sensible was enough for Dean Goss this morning. He shook his head with a ghastly, humble smile. "That's not good enough. A lot of paintings grow on you. But what I have to do, what I thought I was doing, what I *will* do is something that gets a response as quick and unmistakable as a green traffic light. See?

"Not good enough. So, if you've got an hour to spare, will you help me scrape and wash them down with turp and Zip-Strip. I want to take both of them off. All the way back to the canvas. . . ."

So now when he was having difficulty getting his message through the preconceptions of his tolerant offspring and Susan, all he had to show them were the two big canvases Vendler had helped him erase and clean.

"Look!" he declaimed. Like a bear dragging a pack of tooth-less hounds, he took them with him around a partition of the studio. They came into a smell of solvents to see the ruins he had made, following the girl's example.

There was damn little left of yesterday's grand beginnings. Only thin, cloudy stains of color remained on the surfaces, a few smears of charcoal, a few stars of the older pigment on one of them, too stubborn to come out of the woven tissue of the canvas. "I knew when I saw what she'd done to the water-color, I had to wipe these out too."

Naturally it would be the two females, Susan and his grand-daughter, who would take this hard. Neither of them had seen the paintings in the state they were in last evening. Only in-tuition could have told them anything valuable was demolished by his whim. But Monica looked as shocked as if some elder busybody had just explained abortions to her. Susan asked, "Why?" as if she were accusing him of murder.

"Minimal art!" Vidal cheered. He was mocking fondly. "You do that, too, with your own distinctive swoop."

"Minimal art is nice for minimal people," his father said sternly. "This is only so I can start again. Clean." Now his face was genuinely woebegone. For the first time it dawned on him

163

that his response was not only irrational (which was fine) but rash (which was fine, also, but more questionable, harder to follow up on). It might have been downright stupid of him to obliterate his good beginnings. A fatal line separated quixotic rashness from stupidity; and he had bragged to Susan and others that luck had always saved him from pure stupidity.

Monica might be bewildered by what she saw and heard. Nevertheless she meant to help. "I like them just as they are," she lied stoutly. "Just tell people they're your avant-garde stuff. Everybody will think they're great."

His eyes locked with hers. "Now, Monica! Now, honey!"

"You could!" she said. Then she wavered. "That would be cheap, I guess."

They nodded at each other solemnly. Old man and little girl saluting each other from one mountaintop to another. They seemed to agree that, if what he was up to was rash, incomprehensible, or even stupid, at least it wasn't cheap.

He swooped her into his arms and swung her so fast her flying feet endangered the others.

Later, when Jason had gone with him to his room in the mansion, Dean Goss was still trying to wind his breakaway thoughts onto a spindle, counting on Jason to help straighten them as he wound them.

"Am I completely a fool? There are whole minutes on end when I deceive myself that I'm comprehensible, whether comprehended by anyone or not. I am not heartless. Selfish, yes. Why should I fret about manners or property when all this big stuff comes crowding in? You might give me the credit, Jason, to assume I know what I've run up against. Did you see Susan's face when I told her I'd washed out the paintings? They weren't as bad as you might think. I was ahead of them yesterday. They had come from great inner turbulence. How else would I know they were the real thing? But I'd got them under control. Then this morning it seemed to me I had to try something with no end in sight. Enormous. Is it fair to ask that of a man my age?"

"Did I ask?"

"You and your girl. You sent her in to tell me something and I know now what it was."

"She doesn't express herself well in words. That's why she's so hurt."

"She expresses herself!"

"She believes in signs."

"Signs and wonders. Paintings have to be signs. I have to respond, don't I?—sign for sign. That's what you wanted from me, she said. But she's hurt, you say, and we mustn't even think of the job cut out for me until we've found her. And I'm the one who ran her off! Shouldn't we call the police? How long has she been gone now?"

Jason threw up his hands with tired melancholy. "You don't call the police on Tamisan. She'd never forgive that. She'd think you were angry about the painting she tore up."

"I'm angry that you two didn't leave me in peace. But it's too late now. I believe what you sent her to tell me. The signs women give us! Who has any right to stop searching when he's seen something so beautiful?"

"She's not . . ."

"Miss America? Women aren't beautiful like flowers. Or rivers. Clouds. To whom do you think you're talking? But . . . there'll be time to work this out when we've got her back."

"I chased her all last night. There's nowhere else to look for her."

"That's a woman's power over us. The frightful mystery, pulling us hardest when they're beyond touch or sight. . . ."

"What if she's dead?" Jason asked abruptly. Their eyes locked in a kind of musing challenge, as if neither was entirely sure whether they were talking about runaway Tamisan or about Maggie Goss. The challenge was without hostility, as if between two young men questioning each other to see how openly they meant to name the dare of the shadows in their minds.

"She's all right," Dean Goss said tenderly. "We can't keep them from dying. Until they've done it, we have to do our best with them, even when it hurts. We do our best, Jason, and there's no pattern for it. Not for us. Everyone knows what to do about women and death except us. So we'll work until we find out."

"What if she's killed herself?"

"Who?"

Jason shook his head firmly to kill the cobwebs. "I shouldn't have said a thing like that. Bad sign."

"Why did you?"

"Because I'm weak. Everyone knows I'm weak. Why'd I let Tamisan come to talk to you if I had something I wanted said?"

"Honey, honey. No! Why did you say she might have harmed herself?"

"She's such a liar. But we've both talked about it. I'm more the liar. I suppose it excited us. Like all our lies."

The misery of destiny held them together like quicksand into which both had leaped. That the quicksand was partly imaginary made it no less treacherous for them because their shared destiny was to live or fail by the imagination.

"If she is—*were*—dead, why, I would have killed her," Dean Goss said.

"There's no use dividing up blame. I only don't want to lose her. I don't have anything more to lose," Jason said, almost penitently.

His father said, "We'll get her. And never mind if she lies. Women *are* liars. That's how you can tell the best ones. They lie to show us how shallow the truths are we try to live by. We've got to follow them beyond the lie. Yes, yes, yes, we've got to get her."

Somewhat later that day Susan had her turn. When she got to Dean Goss's room she found him sitting in an armchair in gray pajamas. The chair had been drawn near the window so he could watch the late afternoon showers and the exotic play of colors begin between the sea and clouds as the lowering sun struck through.

"The girl has harmed herself," he said in hushed apocalyptic tones as soon as Susan entered. For a bad brief moment she believed he had heard from police or hospital and was breaking the news to her.

No such thing. It was only another of the vivid possibilities playing as unpredictably as weather through the landscapes of his imagination. In today's moods it was as if he made even less than his usual distinction between possibility and reality.

Rather angrily she said, "You have no right to suggest such a thing." She, who had steeled herself to so many of Tamisan's irregularities, had at least paid for the privilege of entertaining such worries before anyone else.

"I have no right," he conceded. "No. She's probably as well off as usual. Damn girl is probably high on hallucinogens, shacked up with some hippie or tourist. Jason and I have to expect that! Offer a woman what we've *made* out of grief and art, offer them *ease* in their nudity, offer them the body purified of the shame of centuries and they have to run off for their one-night stands with glib, adulterous pseudo artists who'll throw them back in our faces after they've had their minute of pleasure and comfort. If we try to be artists . . . if we turn our backs for one minute to get the work done, the bitches knife us. . . ."

The target for his anger showed plainly enough, and it was not Tamisan. He was at last venting his anger and hurt with her for going off with Whitestar the other night. Cruel and unfair to both her and Tamisan to make this insulting confusion in his arrogance of judgment, but she welcomed her share of it as punishment deserved. She felt the burning sting of a switch on her legs. Wanted to kneel by him and whisper, "I'll be good," though it was too late for that. Many wandering years too late.

"Jason's frantic and the house is all disturbed," he said. "You have no idea where she is either. Have you no control over the little bitch?"

"Not much. I never locked her up. I'm not an idol to her as you are to Jason. I wanted her to have freedom, at least. . . ."

"Freedom!" he said with titanic bitterness. Then he repeated it like a love word, not offered to her. "Freedom!"

She turned to leave the room. "If that's all you have to say . . ."

167

"That's all. Let freedom ring."

"Perhaps I'll see you at dinner? You really must get some rest."

"Perhaps," he said.

He was staring out at the sea. Like a bereaved old king, she thought, who has brought his bereavement on himself by excesses of passion and less common sense than a smaller man would need. Why wouldn't the mean old fucker let her crawl to him and hug his knees?

As night came on he was not cooling off. She supposed he was drinking more. That more than drink was pumping energy into him. He was witty and boisterous with Fiona's friends, the Kaltmans, who had driven from Oyster Bay for dinner. He flirted like a pixy with his granddaughter. He spent an hour on the library phone with the poet Richard Luellen and reviewed this conversation with the dinner guests. He held Monica on his knee while they watched cuts of a film Vidal had brought from Paris.

It was only after the filming that he spoke to Susan again. Was there any word from the fugitive yet? None? "Then it seems only reasonable for you to go back to New York to wait for her there. Poor child needs someone to turn to if she has been treated discourteously here." Clearly this was a command. The anger stuck through his patriarchal manner like points of barbed wire snagging a silk shirt.

She took his recommendation as an order of banishment. When she went to pack a bag in the guest room, it occurred to her she might as well take everything of hers as she left—manuscript, typewriter and toothbrush. If she didn't, Dean Goss might come in and Zip-Strip them right out of existence as he had his paintings. He was certainly a man who, when his eye offended him, couldn't keep from plucking out any eye in reach.

Oh, what the hell! She had lived all her life by salvage—a real picker-up after typhoon and flood, she thought, bundling the swollen notebooks into her big briefcase. Of course she could salvage some sort of book for Hal Robinson out of material thus far accumulated. She'd had her glimpses, souvenirs, anecdotes—and above all she still had her wits about her, even after today. In a few weeks, by autumn, it might seem to her lucky that she had got away from Dean Goss while she still had them.

Then Jason came to help her load her patched and peeled Dodge in the opulent garage. He said, "Don't worry about what you've seen today. He's not going off his rocker. He doesn't have to go crazy, because all craziness is already part of his mind too."

She sighed and agreed. "I knew when he was so ecstatic about the ruined watercolor that the reaction would set in. Someone would have to pay."

"Hurt vanity is part of him," Jason agreed.

"If only he hadn't got carried away and destroyed the big paintings too," she lamented.

"That's no loss. You don't know how Dean Goss works. It's all part of his cycle."

Of course she understood that Jason meant to comfort her. He always meant to comfort. But that final cut . . . *You don't know how Dean Goss works.* It was true and, being true, it forbade her to even consider patching up a book out of her salvages. The balloon was sailing away and she was dropping back to earth.

At home in the hallway of her apartment building, her breath caught with an old familiar anxiety when she set the key in the lock of her own door. How many times when Tamisan was straying she had come home like this and opened the door hoping that at least the child would be physically safe, would let her provide shelter a little longer if there was nothing else the kid wanted or would accept.

But now, as she found the apartment empty, a queer, malevolent relief played in her thoughts. Wouldn't it be *nice* if, this time, Tamisan were gone for good?

She suppressed the pleasure of such hostility. She accepted the stuffiness of her rooms, closed up for so many weeks, as if she were pulling on old clothes the morning after an astonishing party. She tried to be grateful that the whiskey she was pouring for herself was her own. Never mind how raw and cheap.

It was only when she lay down in bed that she gave way to unmixed bitterness. She cried as she hadn't cried since she was a junior high school girl disappointed in her love for the basketball coach.

Remembering him in his godlike indifference made her laugh. She gave up her tears, realizing how comic grief can be without ceasing to be grief. It seemed to her this was what she would have to say if she made a book that was worthy of all she had learned from Dean Goss. She left her bed to write and get loftily drunk. She typed: I DO TOO KNOW HOW HE WORKS. WHATEVER IS HAPPENING NOW, TO US ALL, IS HOW HE WORKS.

That seemed to her, at the moment, overwhelmingly profound.

In the morning it seemed overwhelmingly profound and utterly indecipherable.

Chapter 9

Looking for her was one thing. Catching up with her was something else, Jason had told himself the first time he went into New York to try to intercept her. So he drove at great speed. The speedometer of Fiona's big convertible trembled above ninety.

A perfectly safe speed. The danger is never in the speed. Ninety would be perfectly safe if he knew how to drive. . . .

Two weeks after his mother's ashes had been scattered over the wintry fields of their farm in Pennsylvania, Jason had driven down there from New York to kill her red horse named Boss. He had driven down in a sleet storm that whinnied brutally on the windshield, loud as the summer wind shrieking on this first night of his search for Tamisan.

Driving to kill the horse was the first time he had ever driven a car. It seemed to him then—it seemed now—that not knowing how to drive did not matter as long as he sustained himself in exorbitant motion. If he slackened speed he might go over like a boy losing his balance on a stalled bicycle.

But how could he tell himself he knew how to drive now when he couldn't tell this night from the day he had sped to take care of the horse?

He had not gone then with any rational intent of killing it. What reason could there be? He was hurtled along by a desire beyond belief or disbelief either and certainly beyond any support that common sense might give him.

If he had been able to believe in any hereafter, any transcendence, even in a timeless eternity, the words of the funeral sermon for Maggie would have served him instead of the killing. "I am persuaded that neither life nor death, nor heights

171

nor depths, nor powers nor principalities can separate us from the love of God which is in Jesus Christ." That could be as true as anything else to those who were persuadable. He was not. Only he had to move to deny the separation that the blind impulse of desire would not accept.

Nunc manet in te—now she lives in thee. He did not perceive that she did. Memory was only memory. Example, influence, even his genes and the eyes that were said to resemble hers were not herself in him.

It's not even missing her, he thought. Not grief. Certainly it was not a delusion of rescuing her that sent the boy speeding down the winter-slick roads. It was only the artist's irrational need to put some design on the face of emptiness; to do something on a scale with his recognition of the void.

" 'The forehead and the little ears/ Have gone where Saturn keeps the years,' " his strong father had said. "We have to let her go." The mind would not even entertain the concept of departure until some pattern could be made for the concept to be based on.

Besides, he did not trust what his father said to him then as much as he trusted what his father seemed to be doing. Jason would believe later, when capacity for belief was restored, that his father was getting set to die himself. To *follow,* if he believed in a *going* as he said he did.

During the holiday season of that winter Dean Goss had got himself knocked down in the street by a parcel truck. And that would be his way, Jason thought—not that the old shaper and maker could be killed by a mere parcel truck, but that he would have invited, first, a brush with death so he could size it up, get it in view, then begin to work on it to give it the form and color he meant it to have.

He was only bruised by the truck. His face and forehead were cut and his left eye turned dark purple. While he still looked like a mauled pirate he developed pneumonia and encouraged it by lying at home in their New York duplex drinking gin. He was still in half-hallucinated stupor from the gin and toxins of his lung infection when he bought the revolver.

It was a monster, a .45-caliber hog leg that might have been deadly even as a club or a mace if it had lacked a firing pin. When Jason found it, only lightly hidden amid the rubble of unanswered mail on his father's desk, he did not conclude the old man meant actually to shoot himself with it either. It also was a sort of model he might handle and observe from the corner of his eye while he composed his artful way to death.

Even then it seemed to Jason his father would die painting—either before a canvas that was thick with unpatterned black pigment or whiter than swirling clouds. And then Jason had no way of caring whether his father died or not. So it was not even in a mood of shocking his father into a reconsideration of life that he stole the revolver and went to kill the horse.

It was a purely exploratory act to slip away with the gun and a car he did not know how to drive. It was incredible luck that he had sped safely through the storm to Philadelphia and the other fifty miles out to their farm. It was only after he had parked the car where the caretaker would not see it—at the end of the stone wall extending from the corner of the stable—that the myth or fable he needed began to take some satisfying shape.

He went into the chilly gloom of the stable by a side door. It was the horse, he would remember, who knew who he was, not himself. The horse recognized him. The recognition began to give back shape and meaning to his personal existence. Standing beside the animal in the stall, he felt the kinship of blood warmth with the brute as he called it by name and slipped past its side to untie the bridle rope from the feed rack. "Come on, Boss," he said.

He remembered the intense cold as he led the animal out of the stable into the winter pasture. The hoofs crunched in a rhythm to which the sounds of his own footsteps were counterpointed. The sleet storm had stopped but there were crystals of ice in the dead grass. The sky was like a seamless sheet of corroded lead.

He still did not know or ask himself why he had to do this but he was confident it had to be done. From the motion itself, the determination to see it through, he seemed to develop the conviction that his mother was waiting for him to lead Boss to her. Even that she would have to come part way back to take over the animal and mount. She would not thank him but there could be thankfulness again in the frozen universe.

He had seemed to know just how far he would have to go. He counted on the horse knowing too. But when the lead rope went slack in his hand, the animal shouldered into him from behind. Not stupidly or blindly but with a kind of inertia that was part of its trust in him. Halted, it lifted and turned its head to look back over the crystalline fields toward the stable and the black trees around the house.

Only then, turning the long bone beak of its head toward him again, did the animal show any sign of distrust. With its dark eye meeting his, it jerked once, twice, tautened the rope around his gloved hand and tried to tug free. It was then he recognized his own brute fear—felt coming back into him the capacity to be afraid again and the knowledge that he wanted to master that fear.

Again he calmed the horse by calling its name. He lifted the outrageously big revolver and set the muzzle against the sleek hair just at the joint of the skull and the neck. The eye of the horse rolled down as if trying to see what was touching it, as if in seeing the weapon it might understand the whole apparatus of necessity that had brought it here to die. He admitted its need for metaphysical comprehension and pitied it only because it must die without that.

Boss's ears were slanted forward as he strained to hear . . . the way they looked when Maggie whistled to it. His nostrils flared and the steam of his breath hung in the windless cold like another ghostly presence with them.

"Here's your horse if you want him," Jason called to her just before he fired. In the instant of the explosion the animal seemed to strain upward until it towered far beyond the hands that held the revolver and had let go the rope. Blood sprayed and cascaded from somewhere higher than the winter clouds.

Then the dying animal must have toppled on him as it fell, for he went down half under it in a heavy confusion of legs, warmth, bone chips and blood. He was still lying in this tangled

174

embrace when the caretaker came running from the house, alarmed by the revolver shot, and dragged him free.

Luckily it was Fiona who had driven down to get him that time. She had found his father in bad shape from pneumonia and put him in the hospital. She had taken the call the caretaker made to the New York apartment.

It was Fiona who had decided his father was not to be told of the episode. She had given no indication at all whether she thought she understood or whether she had any curiosity about why he had done it. She had let him believe it was the kind of fact that women could live with better than men. So, as far as the family went, it had remained their secret.

Of course on the morning he had come back from his first useless search for Tamisan he had understood with perfect clarity the difference between this night excursion and the one he had made to kill the horse. He had slipped in suggesting to his father that Tamisan might have killed herself.

All in all, he got through the first day of her absence pretty coolly. Susan had commended him for his common sense. She was right. He had plenty of common sense—along with a teeming and uncontrollable imagination that boiled out along all the lines of possibility as the day went by.

He could speak with calm rationality in his conversations with everyone except Fiona. When he spoke to her he asked, "Mightn't it be best for me to forget about it until Tamisan turns up again or we hear about her from Susan?"

That was just about all they said to each other. After a long and ponderous silence Fiona said, "Well . . ."

That was all they said to each other. It was from her silence, heavy with those secrets women could live with better than men, that he knew he was committed to the search, wherever it might lead him.

In his heart, in his secret fears, he was prepared for tragedy. It would have taken someone older and already more coarsened by life to be prepared for the degeneration of his pursuit into an all too human farce.

It was after Susan had already left in humiliation that one of the maids told him he was to call the model Jean Simons. Jean didn't answer her phone until after midnight.

"Jason? Look, I've got your car. You know Tamisan stayed with me last night." He had never seen the place Jean lived in through her summers out here. He knew it was a room over someone's garage in the scrub forest, the rural slum inland from the shore. It was less than five miles from North Atlantic.

"Is she gone now?"

"Took the bus into New York to stay with Janis. What happened, Jason?"

"A long story. Never mind the car. Drive it over sometime tomorrow and I'll give you a lift wherever you have to go."

With his heart pounding and breath coming fast, he called Janis and found her merely surprised. No, she had heard nothing. Had supposed Tamisan was over her tantrum by this time and back at North Atlantic. "Is it something more serious than you told me, Jason?"

"No, no, no. Nothing at all." Then he called Susan and felt he had increased her alarm to no purpose. She had nothing to report, was mostly concerned about his state of mind. She sounded a little drunk and promised to call him at any hour—at the very *instant*—the wandering child came rolling in. She repeated and repeated that this wasn't his worry and he must get a good night's sleep, as she meant to do.

He hung up accusing himself of losing his cool and alarming others. He had overshot badly in driving all the way to New York the night before when Tamisan was so near by. His intimations of disaster were some sort of contagion he was spreading. He had to zero in on the facts before he blew this all even further out of proportion.

So he called Jean Simons again. He got the impression she was in bed again—and probably not alone in bed. She was a little impatient with him this time, and not so careful to spare his feelings.

"Jason, all I *know* is what she told me. And she said she was going straight to Janis', you see. But she was pretty spooked. Maybe she doesn't want anyone to get on her trail so she lied to me too. Well, have you ever thought she might have, like, gone off with or to some other man?"

"I've tried to think of everything," he said hoarsely.

"I don't say she *did*. I actually wouldn't think so, considering all she's got to worry about if she tore up your father's painting. Did she actually do that?"

"That doesn't matter at all."

"It's what seemed to be worrying her most today. But last night . . . Well, the truth is we were both kind of high and she did call . . . well, some men. She called Bern Whitestar, but I don't think she could have gone to his place. His wife's back, I mean. But, Jason?"

"I'm listening."

"Does a name like Sanders mean anything to you?"

"Zach Sandler," he said.

"That's it. I'm sure that's it. She called him or tried to call him, too. It was pretty late and I'm not sure they talked. I wasn't listening, see?"

So he was driving again. Once more committing himself to the inextricable medley of dread and desire and sheer motion as he raced Fiona's car again toward New York. Once again he was speeding without knowing why.

He had not listened to Jean long enough for her to give him any reasonable clues that Tamisan might have gone to Sandler when she went into the city. As the sibilance of wind mixed with less material sounds in his mind, he was not even sure Jean had said Tamisan reached the man when she tried to call him.

And it was nothing Tamisan had ever told him that precisely determined him now to go look for her at Sandler's. It was as if he only remembered that Sandler's party was where he had seen her first, first been struck by her look of *waiting,* first guessed that, like himself, she was waiting for some miraculous opening in the walls of the world to show her where to go. As if he supposed that tonight it was possible to go back to the beginning of his love for her and find her waiting for him at the same spot on Sandler's carpet, wearing the same costume of jeans and pendant, looking like a woman his father might have painted in his youth.

Tamisan had never dwelt on Sandler's name, or told him what connection there was between her and Sandler. "Men," she had said. "Various men," she had called them, making it sound almost like the proper name of a fraternity. The Various Men of New York—like Robin Hood's Merry Men of Sherwood Forest. "I certainly didn't fuck everybody," she said. "I certainly fucked a lot of them before you."

It was not the least of her charms. It might have been the greatest.

Last night as the power of the car raged under him, emotions related to his killing of the horse had broken loose. Tonight, though his fatigue was greater, emotions just as strong broke through his common sense and reason.

"I'm going to make you a sensualist," Tamisan had said.

"I always was one. Long before I knew you. You said you masturbated when you thought of death. Don't you think I ever thought of death?"

"I'll teach you to beat him off whenever you think of me."

"All right."

"Whenever?"

"All right."

"Promise? You don't have to promise. You *will.*"

"All right."

"You *weren't* a sensualist. Not when I found you. Found *him* in the bulrushes. My little Moses that I found. You were just a soul with a prick on it."

It had never become literally true that he brought himself to orgasm whenever he thought of her. There was little need for that since she was so often and persistently present to assist and claim the creamy jet of ejaculation, receiving it in cunt or mouth or in the pink cup of her palm with adoration more frank than any she offered to him as a person—as if the curdling pearly drops she extracted might be the closest she would ever come to seeing his soul with her own eyes.

It was an adoration not unmixed with startling objectivity. "Your stuff tastes like peppermint," she said, not so much complimenting him as noting his singularity. "I never tasted any quite like it before."

Her eyes veiled in an effort of exact memory or evaluation before she gave that sharp peremptory nod which meant *Yes, I'm right.* His soul had a flavor all its own. That was the wisdom you arrived at by the path of sensualism.

"Don't be afraid of me," she pleaded. "Don't be afraid of your body." He was not afraid as long as her authority sheltered and guided and delighted him. It was the boldness as well as the sweetness of her erotic ingenuity that gave him confidence he would never have managed without her example. Boldness became sweetness, a honeycomb where every sip stirred perilous imaginings, sometimes lies, no doubt, sometimes the illicit recognition of trespasses beyond the limits truth is supposed to respect.

"It's thinking that makes you hot. It's thinking the right way and not being afraid of whatever thoughts you have that make you hot, if you want to be a *total* sensualist," she said.

"Yes."

"There are girls who have this terrific awareness of cunt," she instructed him. "It's like the Kingdom by the Sea. Like fairy lands forlorn where the real things are about to happen or just happened."

"Are there? You don't mean all girls."

"I mean me. I think about, for instance, what can it feel like to be inside my body?" She had spent more time than anyone could have guessed with astounding, absurd, profoundly real questions like that. She shared them with him as part of what they called their meditations, only partly spoken.

What does it feel like to have it in me? It must be like tracing the curling grain in a smooth piece of wood. Like a tiny plant uncurling its leaves toward a dark sun. The dissolving of ripples when water calms on the surface of a pond in September. A sound muffled by curtains of tissue and membranes. "Lightness in tightness."

179

"Yes," he said.

*Melted emeralds and honey. A mixture of napalm and cotton
candy. The falling walls of a Babylonian palace, silhouetted
against an invisibly burning city. The farthest edge of whispers.
The shape of silence after music melts a cave into it. The awed
discovery of a vast, dead animal carcass, like a bloated mammoth at the door of a cave man's cave.*

"It's like that," he confessed.

"You find me," she said in a voice awed by her thoughts.
"It *is* lightness in tightness, isn't it?"

"Light as a thistledown," he said.

"You're so alone in there," she cried out in pity and envy.

Not alone. They were two solitudes, mirroring each other.
Never alone. Never not thinking of her and always hot. His
soul—if that was what leaped urgently to seek her in the bowstring twang of orgasm—escaped its solitude and clung like a
sticky liquid to the shapes of a reality beyond the visible. Their
erotic frenzies woke hopes and intimations that never quite
flickered out when the tension of sex was past. When she
fucked him dry, it was not the end but a new beginning of
heated thought. The fables of the Kingdom by the Sea went on
to rouse a broader desire. Sensualism led straight on to mysticism and gave the colors of passion to metaphysical meditations
on death—never quite persuading him that all separation was
illusion, never quite bridging the silences with the voice he
listened for, but always tantalizing him with the possibility that
a little farther on his intimations would be as true as they were
desirable.

"You make me whole. Almost whole," he told her. "As long
as you're there."

"Where?"

"Anywhere, as long as I'm thinking of you."

"As long as I keep you hot," she said, delighted to find him
accepting her mystic formula. "I wouldn't want you to actually
idolize my cunt. She's not a goddess. She's a sacred prostitute.

She just works in the temple. Now you know even when I'm not with you she gives you signs you know what they mean because . . ."

"Because at least I'm an artist in reading the signs you leave me."

"Don't say at least. You're an artist more than any of them. More than your father."

"I don't have his strength."

"Ahead of him, so we can give him signs too."

She had never admitted she loved the soul attached to his prick more than the pleasure she took in training, fondling, cherishing it. "But you can't keep giving it to me all the time," she said.

"Soul?"

"I don't know how to talk about souls," she said with that tack-hammer nod of her head affirming she *did* know how to talk about pricks and cunts. That language would have to do.

Various Men had contributed to her sexual vocabulary, just as poets had told her about the Kingdom by the Sea or fairy lands forlorn, and other teachers had written that in some religions there had been sacred prostitutes. The Various Men seemed as anonymous, in her references to them, as the bards and troubadours who passed on the legends of old times before they dried up in written language. They were there—shadowy, remote, devout in lechery whether they were always virile or not —like voiceless actors in a pageant. They were the examples and the witnesses in the ceremonies that confirmed his manhood and Tamisan's womanliness. Not hostile or enviable either—he was incapable of jealousy as those are who have always known it is their superiority, not their inferiority, that makes them unsuited for the world—and not rivals, because whatever they had wanted from Tamisan it had not been a mirroring of souls. They were there like fictional characters invented to keep his thoughts and his devotion glowing.

There was the Man Who Really Knew How to Ball a Girl. "Always, always, always," Tamisan said, "there'd be this ritual. First—on from the front, missionary style. Then—my legs around his neck. When he saw I couldn't stand it any more, he'd turn me over. Put me on my hands and knees and *really* finish me."

There was the Man Who Liked Her to Describe. The Man Who Counted Orgasms. The Man Who Appreciated Costumes. The Man in the Snowdrift. The Man With the Vibrators. The Man Who Lathered Her. The Man Who Kept Talking. The Man Who Rode Like on Rocking Horses. Various Men.

It was as if she had never even bothered to learn their given names or anything of their personal qualities that was not translated into the language and gesture of eroticism, as if she had purposely been gleaning from them in preparing a vocabulary by which she and Jason could magnify the range of their communication. And they had not even seemed to be men who were walking and breathing in the same century with him, but like those she might have known in another existence. She brought their lore like honey gathered in the clover fields of an unnamed planet.

She had never needed to say to Jason, "You're different from any of them. All of them." She said, "I'm just the organ of whatever you're fucking." Her body was the table laid with bread for his hunger and mystic wine for a communion of spirits. She had wanted him to find in her boldness and sweetness those glimpses of an alternative existence that many of their generation claimed to have found in drugs. "You probably never needed drugs," she thought. "Various men gave them to me. They're supposed to make you hot. They never did me. It was always thinking that did it."

And on this second night of his search, hearing the berserk roar of the motor and feeling the hysterical tremble of the steering wheel against his palms, he felt his prick harden as if Tamisan were holding it in worshipful hands. As if the night itself had unfolded the clothing from his loins and lowered its dark mouth to engulf him.

Not yet, he thought. Gently! Gently! Gently! I'm at the edge, don't let it end yet, Tamisan. Let me linger. Don't let our night end until I know all about you.

The street in front of Sandler's house was silent. It was very late, but there was still a light showing in the ground-floor windows. If there had not been, Jason thought he might, once again, have wheeled the car back across the bridge and returned to North Atlantic, much as he had on the night before. He still had thought of no reason why Tamisan might have come here. No reason to suppose Sandler could tell him where he must look for her. This trip, too, was whim and hallucination.

He did not know how late it was, but he saw the morning star over the river at the end of the street when he stepped from Fiona's car. He had to wait several minutes after he rang the bell. Then there was a sound of blithe footsteps slithering near and the oak door was thrown wide with theatrical abruptness.

It seemed to be opening on a full-length mirror instead of on the hall that separated the downstairs rooms. The boy who opened it so recklessly looked astonishingly like himself.

"Yay-uss?" the boy asked.

"I'm looking for Mr. Sandler," Jason said. The boy looked like him, but he was wearing clothes like those Tamisan had worn to the party several months ago. Jeans and a knit top. There was a heavy pendant slung on a chain around his neck.

"I'm none other," the boy said. "I have the honor to be Zach Sandler."

"Then why are you barefoot?" Jason asked lightly. The bare feet, like the clothing, suggested Tamisan. The boy stood there like a phantom reflection of boy and girl melded in a single figure. He could be both of us, Jason thought.

"You have a point," the boy conceded. "Why would Zach Sandler take off his shoes? If I'm not Zach, who am I?" He blinked and said, "I'm not you, though the resemblance is shocking." He flicked the pendant on his chest. At least that distinguished him from Jason.

"I'm Jason Goss."

"Vidal's brother, to be sure. We know him well. Come in.

183

Entrez donc. If I'm not Zach Sandler—sorry!—I'm still a family friend. Any brother of Vidal's is a friend of mine. Please don't just stand there scrutinizing me. The street is full of muggers and the FBI."

"I came here looking for a girl," Jason said, still hesitating on the steps. Still ready to apologize and leave since he could not explain why he had chosen to look here.

The face so much like his own opened in a wise and arrogant grin. "Are you sure, dear boy? I thought you were looking for Herr Sandler, whom none may behold, for he is not with us, having descended to his father. Why seek ye the living among the dead? Come in, come in. Though this is no place for a nice boy to look for girls. There may be some in the house. I haven't searched the rooms today. . . . Come in. I am Vidal's friend. That much is true. I played with Vidal in one of his films. *The Long Spoon*—on which the poor dear lost so much money. Did you see it? Of course. I played a very minor part, or parts, since, if you saw it, you know that I impersonated several different lads and lassies there, as well, and must have caught the habit. *Do* come in. Not a bit of a joke about the FBI. I think that some of Zach's foundlings are in the basement making bombs. That's why I opened the door so gallantly—to make a proper show and allay suspicion. But their listening devices are surely picking up every syllable we utter!"

Jason followed the dancing bare feet into the room where Tamisan had first been pointed out to him.

There was no doubt that Jason was being subjected to seduction. The chattering boy insisted that the hour was right for them to drink Campari and sodas. He mixed them at the sideboard and turned with them in his hands, smiling with teeth as even and handsome as Tamisan's, swirling so that the medallion on his breast swung out flirtatiously.

"Why are the girls making bombs in the basement?" Jason asked.

"To hurl. To hurl. And does your girl make bombs? Is that why you came looking for her here? Actually I suppose they're here with their dynamite and gas pipe because Zach is not here to forbid it. He abhors violence. But people who interest him come and go in this house with a liberty hard to conceive. Never mind the basement bombers. I don't think they're political, though when I meet them on the stairs I call them Mizz out of discretion. Perhaps they're not actually making bombs but doing something else with those gas pipes. Come, sit here and tell me all about your girl."

He led Jason to the softest of brocaded sofas near the piano. He curled his legs under him as he sat down and wiggled his toes. He lifted his glass in a salute of fond welcome. "Is she a dear? Is she worth it? I've known right many utterly adequate girls. The truth is I switch, you see. Perhaps that's why I thought I was Zach Sandler, though his appetite is more legendary than real. A man who has abandoned effort. I think he is only waiting. But . . . perhaps I know the girl who led you to us?"

"Tamisan Vail."

"I'm sure she's not one of Zach's people, is she? I'm a vulture for gossip and I would have heard her name at least. Is she in films? Or perhaps wants to be? Vidal's spoken of you. You're the lamb, aren't you?"

"The youngest."

"Ah, you are a lamb! To go flying about this wicked city so late at night in search of a wandering girl. But I know the imperative of the drive. Do I not! 'Past reason hunted and in proof a very woe.' Is it not? The commandment of lust? May I fill your glass again?"

"Yes," Jason said. The room was faintly musty as air-cooled rooms in the city often are. There was an embalmed smell of flowers, of cigarette smoke and perfume. No smell of the sea.

And yet something else as subtle, foreboding and enticing as his thoughts of Tamisan was trying to speak to him, promising him he had not lost the track.

This time when the boy sat on the sofa, he threw his body languidly back over the arm. He knew he was being watched in every gesture and he supposed he knew what the yearning in Jason's eyes meant. "My true name is Schuyler Baron," he said. "You may call me *Red!* Woops. Sorry! I'm not all frivolity,

Jason. I'm not all lies. I detest people who think it funny to call me Red, so I attempt to forfend it, so to speak."

"She is here, isn't she?" Jason said somberly.

"She? Here? Who?"

"Tamisan."

The boy watched him from pale eyes, matching his gravity for the moment. "Ah. You think I'm merely trying to distract you. There are other little mice in the house, as I told you. There might be one down there in the basement called Tamisan. But she's certainly not here with Zach. He went to Nassau two days ago. Ah. You may call me Tamisan if you don't like Red or Schuyler. Schuyler is a bit off-putting for most of my friends. Are you as horny as I?"

"No," Jason said.

"I've seen you peering at my bangle," the boy said, fingering the medallion on his chest. "It has a history and an inscription I think might amuse you. Here." He slid closer on the couch so Jason could see. Jason took it in his hands and made out the delicately engraved letters. FOR THE CLEVEREST IMPERSONATOR.

Turning it between thumb and forefinger, Jason said, "All right. You are Sandler, impersonating Schuyler Baron. I see it now."

"Ha-ha. That's marvelous." The boy slapped him on the shoulders and left his arm resting lightly across their slope. "But I shouldn't joke about it. It was given to me by the person I care most about. It was not intended to be so derogatory as it might seem."

"You're Tamisan, impersonating Schuyler Baron." Jason let the medallion drop. It hit the boy's breast with a muffled thump.

"I might be." The boy had not removed his arm from Jason's shoulder. Now he writhed a little farther down the couch until the fly of his jeans was almost presented to Jason's hand. "I told you I was horny, Jason," he whispered, arching his back so the bulge of his crotch was fully demonstrated. "You may, if you like."

It seemed to Jason that it was not decision but bafflement that kept him from moving his hands. He felt very close to a discovery that he had to have. He was utterly unsure of how to make it.

"You *may*," Schuyler said more urgently. He tugged playfully at Jason's ear.

"May I . . . see?" Jason asked.

"See?"

"Only look, I mean."

Slowly the rarest of smiles formed on the boy's mouth. He sensed the strangely balanced delicacy of Jason's request and conformed to it delicately. "You may see," he said. With nimble fingers he opened his fly and tugged the jeans a little way down his thighs. He nearly closed his eyes and pursed his lips tautly. With motherly condescension he brushed his gleaming cock with one hand lightly and said, "The poor thing's blushing, see?"

There was a slamming rush of pity in Jason's mind as he saw the proud curve droop under his gaze, an indefinable sense that he had murdered some fragile possibility. A sense of overwhelming bereavement as if his own clumsiness, the slowness or fearfulness of his mind, had made him miss what would not come again.

"I'm sorry," he said. With a tearing effort he lurched to his feet. "I had no right. I had no right to let it go this far. I'm not good with people and sex. I don't know what I'm doing sometimes. I thought I had to see . . ."

". . . if I was Tommy son?"

"Not that. I don't know how to tell you." He waved his hands and blushed wildly.

"Don't say a word!"

"Well, I apologize. Only . . . it was eerie for me to come here and find you resembling the girl I really was looking for. You couldn't know how strong the resemblance seemed."

"Tut! Why should I know all your secrets? I'm not your master."

"I'm sorry if I disappointed you."

"I'm not sure you have. It was sweet, Jason."

"I have no right to disappoint people."

He began to shake uncontrollably. The boy said, "What is it? Let me guess. You still think she's here and with Zach. Is that it?"

"I don't know. I only came here on a hunch. I don't know why I came. No," he said when Baron held a glass to his mouth and urged him to drink. "No, I'll be all right. I'll get in control as soon as I'm out in the air."

Baron shook his head. "You're not going until I've proved to you Zach hasn't come home yet. His rooms are upstairs and locked. But . . . would you believe it? . . . I've stolen his keys. This is a most eccentric household. Come."

He led the way upstairs. Now his bare feet on the stair carpeting impersonated those of a mischievous farm boy leading his buddy on a Tom Sawyer adventure.

The last intense, disorienting surprise of the night for Jason was to face a painting of his mother in Sandler's ornately decorated bedroom. It was a medium-sized or even smallish canvas in a brown frame rubbed with white. It was not hung on a wall but positioned casually in an armchair. The feet of the armchair rested on a bearskin. A potted plant sat beside it.

"I didn't even realize your father had painted it," Baron said. "Sandler never mentioned it. Wow! I'm an utter fool about the visual art. How far would I get if I stole it? It must be worth . . . Sandler's *so* careless, leaving his keys about where I might find them." He began to laugh, a trilling, careless soprano outburst of mirth. "How marvelous—now that I know Dean Goss painted it. Look, it's alive!" His hand tilted the spotlight on a stem that he had turned to illuminate the painting, and the shadows moved around the edges of the frame.

They looked alive. The figure in the painting did not. It was Maggie, sitting or kneeling in the orchard of their Pennsylvania farm. She had an accordion open between her outstretched hands and her head was thrown back in a cartoon of song. Jason could not remember if he had seen the painting before or not. It must have been painted when he was very young.

Only, looking at it now, he thought, It was never intended to be like life. The greens in the picture were not the greens of living fruit trees. The arabesque black lines that swooped from Maggie's fingers to the keys of the instrument were heavy as the leading around the figures in a stained-glass window. The line of the uplifted throat was a line of praise for a form that could never bend with the suppleness of life.

"I'll help you steal it if you want," Schuyler offered with a low giggle. "What do I owe to Sandler? After all, it's your mother. Right? I suspect he's only acquired it as an investment. It can't mean as much to him as to you. No? Ah, you are a *pure* lamb." He put his hand on Jason's buttocks.

"I should have taken your word that Sandler was gone," Jason said. He moved away from the fondling touch. He felt with almost nauseous keenness his guilt in trespassing into these rooms. He picked his way out to the stairway as if any careless step might shatter crystal and leave a sign of his unlawful intrusion.

"Think nothing of it," Schuyler Baron said, yawning at the front door when he let Jason out. Suddenly he leaned to kiss Jason on the cheek. "I'll remember you. Remember me."

Jason did not know what he had found that night. As he drove, once again toward North Atlantic, he told himself it was nothing at all. Nothing. The sun was high before he got close enough to home to see the ocean. He was so tired that his grip on the steering wheel seemed necessary to hold him upright in the seat. But it wasn't fatigue that made him drive more slowly now. He was afraid to drive fast.

He was afraid to breathe for fear of catching again that smell of woman, of ocean, that had enticed him into this leg of his wild goose chase. Afraid to keep his eyes open or close them either. Afraid to remember what he had seen when Baron lowered his pants. Afraid to remember the painting he had seen in Sandler's bedroom.

Most of all, afraid to think of Tamisan in any way, shape or form until he was rested and could think straight enough about her to separate her from his passionate hallucinations.

Chapter 10

Vidal Goss had no intention of being involved in a family crisis. On principle, he refused to believe in crises, though he suspected that both his father and Jason had a penchant for taking the ordinary complications of life and jerking them into hard knots —the way impatient souls jerk at a badly tied shoelace until it is so tight no amount of patience will pick the knot loose and it has to be cut.

"Making up crises is your father's genius," his mother had told him. His mother had long ago been reconciled to the circumstances that led Dean Goss to desert her and the two sons she had given him. Almost as long ago, she had married the clever man who subsequently became the Danish ambassador to Rome. Her second marriage had suited her magnificently, partly because its even pace gave her time to measure and comprehend the rich bewilderment of the nine years she had been married to the painter. "When we are young no one tells us how vastly different human beings can be from each other. Using the same words doesn't mean we're talking the same language. When we kiss, it's often like two alien universes surprised to find that they can make any contact at all, my dear. He didn't go away with that ghastly Forbes woman because he was unhappy with us. He saw a chance to make a crisis and he couldn't resist it."

Life with Dean Goss had made Minna shrewd enough to define him with precision. She was still living the good life in Rome. His mother, Vidal thought, was not among the castoffs or failures left along the road of his father's pilgrimages. She had got her due—not without pain, not without fighting for it, not without claiming it by retiring far enough to watch the Goss spectacle from a comfortable box seat. She was a spicy, tart old lady, proud of her abilities to embalm the past in the amber of her wit. "Allowing for your father's overwhelming perceptions—and his cunning," she said to her middle-aged son, "it must be admitted that he is cunt-struck. Therefore, throughout life, blind to what most of us learn to manage without such an infernal hullabaloo."

And Jason was bound to be more like him than Godwin or I, thought Vidal, who loved his father and half brother without much trusting the ability of either to make treaties with life. He had never imagined that his stepfather, who was a very good ambassador for his little country, was in the same league with his father. But his own penchant for easing around confrontations was acquired and chosen rather than directly inherited. There was something awesome about the lines of destiny twining in the sequence of marriages, he thought, thinking sometimes that Fiona had come to play the same supporting role in his father's life that his mother might have in her old age, allowing for some superficial differences in the personalities of the two older women. And he himself—modeling his urbanity on the unflappable resilience of the ambassador—had he not, by just that choice, affirmed his genetic relationship to the still excitable old man who had got him from Minna's youthful loins?

Travel, personal contacts, telephones and hotels were the habitat in which he lived. He had an apartment on the Île St. Louis. His wife had gone to Auteuil to live with the woman she loved. His younger daughter, Monica, was still "at home" between the two Parisian households, but he felt, deeply and privately, that he was a roving ambassador. As an artist, too, Vidal had modified his heritage. His medium was film—more fluid than the media Dean Goss committed himself to. In film, Vidal was a colorist, and though the storytelling possibilities of film enchanted him, he knew as well as any of his critics that he dissolved comedy and tragedy both in landscape, in the play of light and shadow on faces, in street scenes prolonged for their own poetic or expressive sake.

A man who took his own sweet time about tying his shoelaces properly, frightened of tugging them into impossible knots. . . .

Before Vidal moved on from North Atlantic, his old friend Sandler called from New York.

"Vidal, sweetie, I came home to learn that your brother showed up on my doorstep night before last. Cross-gartered and distraught. Blasted with ecstasy. Is he all right?"

"I'm sure he is."

"Is he . . . there?"

"Do you want to talk to him? I think he's sailing with Monica. Or they've driven to Paumanok. I know he was up for breakfast."

"No, I'd rather *not* talk to him. There was a faint implication that he had come for my blood."

"That's unlike Jason."

"I'm sure of that. I'd be deeply grieved if he thought I'd in any way injured him."

"This . . . uh, has to do with Miss Vail, I suppose?"

"I suppose. I wish he could be assured that I have *not* seen her. *Not* heard from her."

"He can be assured of that if the subject comes up between us."

Sandler said, "I will see you when you're in the city, won't I? Friends in Hyannis have asked me Tuesday next, but until then . . ."

Vidal hung up thinking, How nasty. He refused to speculate on where the blame for the nastiness might be put. For all he wished to know, it might exist purely in excesses of the imagination. And yet there was melancholy in thinking that the miasmal nastiness of the world had touched Jason. If he had filmed the amorous life of his half brother, he would want to show him running in rapture through a field of tall grass toward a blue-green grove where an invisible nymph waited. Not chasing through the night slavering for scraps left over from Sandler's feasting. Or mine, he thought. He was unlikely to feel remorse for enjoying the youthful skins that went with travel, hotels and telephones. But still his eye, at least, hungered for the early summer colors of love, the single white cloud over the field of grass. . . .

"Jason is brokenhearted," Monica Goss said.

"Why . . . why . . . why . . . why no, he's not," her father said. He watched the blue smoke from his cigar rise up, trembling ever so faintly in the sunlight. He and Monica had taken a morning dip in the North Atlantic pool, and he could tell she wanted him to do something. Though they lived in Paris, Monica was not altogether insulated from the fads of young America. She often wanted him to "do something" to stop the pollution of the planet, the mistreatment of blacks, the endless war. "Your uncle Jason has a Hamlet streak. All boys that age have girl troubles. Heartbreak is something . . . different."

"What?"

"Not being able to do anything about wickedness," he said gently. "That's why your family got stuck with art instead of social action, honeybunch. There isn't always anything to be done."

"I harbor no regret for that," she said gravely. "Only . . ."

"Only," he said. "But Jason seems cheery enough to me. He's giving you a good time, as far as I can tell. Has he been pouring his woes in your virginal ear?"

She shook her head. "Grandpa says he's heartbroken."

"Your grandfather is a foul-mouthed old man, and if you start picking up his expressions I won't leave you here even to go into New York."

He set his teeth in the delicate brown leaves of his cigar. For an instant he remembered his mother saying, in her clear, always reasonable voice, "Your father has made a decision, boys. He loves you very much, but he thinks it would be better for his work if he didn't live with us any more."

He said, "Grandpa loves us all very much, honeybunch. But you've got to learn not to take literally what artists say. Jason's disappointed about his girl. That's all."

"I'm sure she'll turn up pretty soon," Monica said.
"They always turn up, honey."

Walking past the door of Jason's room, he heard the nimble, somber voice of a guitar. He knocked and Jason let him in, embarrassed and somehow shockingly surprised that he had been overheard. "It's . . . it's *her* guitar." The blue, curved body dangled from his hand like the body of a huge bird he had strangled without knowing his own strength. "I don't play the guitar," Jason said. He motioned for his brother to sit down. From the corner of his eye Vidal saw him armoring himself, drawing on his defenses like chain mail.

"Sounded like Segovia," Vidal said. "Is it blue because of Wallace Stevens' poem?"

Jason nodded.

Vidal chanted quietly:

"Things as they are, things as they are
Are changed upon the blue guitar."

Jason said, "The fantastic irony is that it's so *easy* for me to play the thing. She wanted *so much* to be able to have something she was good at. Better than anyone else. It's not that her fingers are clumsy. She can't get her music out."

"So you never played it, never showed how easy it is for you, while she was around," Vidal said.

"That wasn't condescending on my part," Jason said with frowning insistence.

"Of course not."

"But maybe it was," Jason said. "Maybe she felt I was belittling her by not ever playing any instrument. I'm taking a new look at everything."

"I gather her whereabouts are still unknown," Vidal said. "But I wouldn't think too much until she comes home. There's something to be said for gathering the facts before you leap to conclusions."

"Home?" Jason echoed with mocking blitheness. "Never more." His face looked rosy as if he had a moment ago roused up from refreshing sleep. "I think it's better if she doesn't ever come back here. It would humiliate her too much, now."

"It's an outrage," Dean Goss said. "Of course the little bitch is safe. No news from the coroner, is there? There is a little matter of dee-struck-shun of property involved. I want that girl dragged back here. To . . . To . . . All I ask is an explanation of what she thought the fuck she was up to, ruining my painting."

Vidal had brought a hand-held camera to his father's studio and was watching him through the view finder while he listened to his undulant ranting. Vidal was too good an ambassador to point up the contradictions he heard.

"To hell with her and Jason both," Dean Goss said. His beard stabbed at invisible offenders. "Now Jason won't even stir his ass to find her. He won't talk about where she could have gone. It's a generation of devils. But I still feel some responsibility. For having been rude to his girl, you know."

"I see," said Vidal. "I wouldn't worry about Jason's reticence. His heartbreak is temporary."

"Heartbreak?" his father sneered. "You know as well as I that Jason is a full-blown schizophrenic. I only hoped that if he was getting his ashes hauled regularly it would give him a re-mission of symptoms. Loony!" His beard swung in an illustrative circle, like the circling finger at the temple, the classic gesture describing madness.

In times past, when the terms were more thoughtfully chosen, Vidal had asked whether they should not push Jason to look for psychiatric help. The suggestion had not been met with a dia-tribe against the quackery of the profession—as it might have been if something less crucial than Jason's happiness was in-volved. "No," Goss had said. "If we were scientists we ought to seek for a scientific remedy. No question about it. But we're artists. The die is cast, isn't it? We have to seek and pray that art—his own growth as an artist—will heal him."

That had seemed wise to Vidal—wise enough as long as Jason's problems were not acute and immediate. Of course there were psychiatrists who specialized in treating artists; the good ones got swept into deep water themselves with no visible prospect of return to the shores of commonplace bread-and-beans reality; he had no evidence that such cures as the bad ones achieved were not more destructive than the suffering they aborted.

Now he said, "Jason ought to come back to Paris with Monica and me. Even more than you, I'm baffled by what's going on in him now." That suggestion had been made before, too. A year ago he had been convinced that Jason needed to get out of America. Jason was not the boy to find comradeship or community with the drop-outs of his generation here. He had, if anything, less in common with the formula life styles of his generation than with Vidal's. Vidal had hoped—and argued—that Jason's penchant for solitude could be cushioned and sweetened in Europe—kept from turning into the loneliness that he himself had always dreaded in America. But his "even more than you" had been the wrong thing to say to Dean Goss at this point.

The old man threw his brush down, wiped the paint from his hands and lit a cigarette as if he were touching a match to the fuse of a bomb. "Goddamn it, I know exactly what's going on with Jason, and don't kid yourself."

"Good," Vidal said. He put down his camera, ready for parley and hoping for the penetrating distillations of experience he knew his father was capable of pouring forth.

"The same fucking confusion that's killing me," Dean Goss bellowed. "That's what's going on with us. They've driven me bats too."

Burning his cigarette down to his beard in six powerful drags, he said pitifully, *"Nobody* helps me. They get me going and then run out on me. I've got to do it all alone. Why can't someone find that damned girl, kick her ass, and let me settle back down where I was?"

In New York the next afternoon, Vidal was chuckling with Susan Vail over his father's lamentable cries for help. He had arranged to meet Susan at the Behn Gallery, where she said she was going to look at two Goss paintings that had just come in.

They were the paintings Sandler had bought in South America. The gallery was to act as his agent in selling them.

The paintings were fine. Fine. But because they were finished and done, they interested Susan and Vidal less than the quandaries of the by no means finished artist who had painted them fifteen years before.

They spent only a few minutes together in the gallery before Vidal suggested they get a drink. In a hotel bar a few blocks down Madison Avenue Vidal put on his ambassadorial manner.

"We're not to understand that the Papa will sulk in his bedroom," Vidal said. "Oh no! He's in the studio from morning until night. You saw those two matched canvases he's set up . . ."

"The worst was that he scraped off those new beginnings." More and more Susan's curiosity had fixed on what had come and gone before she had even laid eyes on it.

Vidal waved away that concern with a despairing smile. The situation had evolved since Susan left North Atlantic.

"Isn't he sorry they're gone?" she demanded somberly.

"I expect he is. But that won't stop him. He's on the loose now and that's like being an Irishman on the drink. Lo and behold— instead of *two* canvases in his composition being worked up to complement each other, he's got *three*. There they stand, all in a row, like the Spanish Armada. And in his own words they're being attacked with a 'sheer outpouring of emotion, dream, inspiration, lettuce, tomatoes, catsup and dog puke.' Yes, he's got a new conception. Or it's got him by the ear and that's why he's hollering for help."

"But that's not all of it," Susan said, clicking her swizzle stick between her nails, wanting to laugh with a strange relief, afraid to laugh before she heard all Vidal might have to tell her.

"Certainly not. He's mad as a wet hen because, however excited he may be by the new paintings, he feels he was tricked, swindled and betrayed into ever starting them."

"Uh-huh!"

"He is too old for this. It may make his heart stop in mid-stroke."

"Do you think . . . ?" Susan said in sudden fear.

"No, no, no. That's only what he says. He has a heart like an enormous flea. If a flea was the size of a mouse it could whip Mohammed Ali. The trouble is not purely physical, though it seems to hurt him all over. He thinks that Jason—well, Jason and your girl—arrived on the premises recently to challenge him. He's convinced that Jason accused him of repeating his past successes."

"Better than repeating one's failures," Susan said, speaking as one who knows.

"No," Vidal said—speaking for all Gosses, as he had good right to do. "No. Copying yourself is more sterile than copying someone else."

"Even if you're Dean Goss?"

"Especially if you are. I think he may be truly scared that the young people have challenged him to risk failure again on a truly big scale."

"If he failed . . . who'd know?"

"Well, he would. He hasn't put it in just these terms. I've been learning to interpret him since childhood. You see, he and Jason try to live each other's lives. They're both terribly afraid of extinction. Haven't you seen that yet in my father?"

"No," she admitted.

"That's why they have to gamble with it whenever the bet's down on the table in front of them. They mean to cover every bet. And they talk to each other in ways even I haven't begun to get in on. If one of them died, the other wouldn't know for sure whose death it was."

"I don't know about that," she said, puzzling it out. "North Atlantic . . . your father's life . . . is so comfortable. So established. All this talk about life-and-death gambles . . ."

"It doesn't seem quite decent in bad times like these," he agreed. "My daughter keeps reminding me that it's wrong to talk about the importance of art in genocidal times."

"But it might be life and death for . . . someone?" she persisted. He saw how white she had got suddenly from the swift turning of her thought, how sharp the tip of her canine tooth looked as it dug the corner of her lip. "If someone *makes* it a life-or-death matter, then that's it, isn't it? Jason's taking the worst of the beating, isn't he?"

"He's not letting anything show. Now, now," Vidal said, "you were quite right to say they're comfortable at North Atlantic. There's a lot of cushioning around Jason and my father when they need it. There's Fiona. And more. Oh, I meant to ask . . . I hope you're going on with your plans for the book?"

"I'm *determined,*" she said, and her face went white again just as the color had started to come back.

And so he was glad he had not asked her a single thing about Zach Sandler. He might have. With the paintings Sandler had left at the gallery for his excuse, he might have gone on to mount a subtle inquisition about her daughter's past involvements with Sandler or others. In fact he had let their meeting go by without directly inquiring whether Susan yet knew her daughter's whereabouts. Susan was sweating out her stake in the gamble, he thought. He liked her. Since he was trying to mute the crisis, he must not heat it up by prying.

He did not pry when he had dinner with Sandler either. He sat for a long time at their table in Le Pavillon, wondering how one could imagine prying into the coagulated softness of Sandler's life and mind. That mind was a tropical swamp, afloat with gossip and theories, facts and rumors and the colorful dyes of fashion in all the arts. In such a mind there was nothing solid enough to set a pry against, no place to stand and fish in the fluid surge of his attention. For Vidal—and he was sure this was true of others—talking to him had the fascination and unpredictability of roulette. Sandler's life was his work; he claimed any given utterance to be part of his oral autobiography. The title of this self-destructing masterpiece, he admitted, was *Being Ahead.* He stayed ahead "so I'll only have to watch out for what is behind me."

He came from a wealthy Louisville family. In the late forties he had arrived in New York, fresh from Duke, with a swatch of family money in hand to try his luck at producing plays. His first production was famous; the very ease of his success had made him contemptuous of it. He had spent the decades since then staying ahead. "Not on the wave of the future," he once told an interviewer. "In New York we know what others don't. The future won't come with a wave but an ooze. I am what the patriots stormed the barricades for, what the Unknown Soldier died for. I'm a free man." The price of his chemically pure liberty was to stay ahead of everything and everyone. He was probably not rich, Vidal supposed, but he was easy with money. It oozed in and out of his hands. Ten years ago he had lost a quarter of a million dollars bankrolling a film for Vidal. He had made that—plus change—back in the years since, but it was the original loss that had somehow put a foundation under their friendship. Had made them comrades in arms. "But we are brothers," he said once. "You'd be astonished at how much I'm nagged by the idea of your father. He's the one man in America who has made it big without being part of a school or forming a group of followers. He fades back out of sight for a while. The smoke clears and there he is again as big and fresh as ever. That endurance is the rarest thing in America. I *hate* it. You understand? My generation—our generation, Vidal—has destroyed the ancestors. Got rid of the buffaloes. All gone. Then, we dissolve like a puff of smoke. We look at each other and we aren't there. A few tough old mastodons like your father—if there's anyone else quite like him—are still there, big and imperturbable as ever.

"I tell you I hate him. There's no use fighting with anyone in my own generation. It's no fun. My duel is with him. Yes. Did you know I came from a long line of duelists? The duel is my only remaining passion."

And why, Vidal wanted to know, did the metaphors of rivalry between generations have to be so bloody? Granted that the generations had to be adversaries, still he felt that he had made a workable truce with his father and that it had not crippled his own work to do so. Why should it be war to the knife?

"Ask your father," Sandler had scoffed. "He's a duelist too, I'm sure. But don't ever mention me if the subject comes up. He

201

doesn't know who I am. I prefer it that way. It gives me the advantage I need. The duelists I descend from were famous in Kentucky for firing from ambush. . . . No, thank you, I wouldn't want to meet your father face to face."

Tonight the self-styled duelist and bushwhacker was in one of the least aggressive moods Vidal had ever seen him in. What vitriol was left in his wit was directed at himself. His capacity for deriding the idiocies of the world sounded altogether like self-pity. The weaknesses of their acquaintances in the arts were not something to take advantage of, but a contagion that had settled in himself.

"Now it's our turn," he said. "The young have caught on to us. We tore down the walls for them. You've done your part, Vidal. Congratulations! So have I. Liberators. But now they've scampered away from us. Gone so far they can't hear the whistle any more."

"Are you referring to anyone in particular?"

"Anyone in particular?" Sandler's mocking, self-mocking tone took on an accent of surprise. "Do you know me as any respecter of persons? No, if you've seen one youth you've seen them all."

"And they've all fled beyond your whistle?"

"I'd be too disenchanted to blow it anyway. I don't want anything to come back. It's only that I never expected the party to be over so quickly. I thought it would last my time. The falling of walls is an exciting music."

"It's hard to settle for less once you've heard it."

"Anything less? Afterward I don't hear a thing. Only the endless silence."

"Maybe the new generation is whistling to us and we'd better try to listen to them."

Sandler grimaced in disgust. "You can't *mean* it. No, it isn't possible. Our generation, those of us who lived over from the times before, are fatally handicapped by fastidiousness. That's not a virtue, mind. I haven't descended to talking about virtue!

Goodness no. I'm talking about an indisposition that keeps us from taking nourishment in the slop they thrive on. Youth! The word itself can spoil my appetite."

"Last confessions of the immoralist," Vidal scoffed. "Let's eat. My appetite is fine and I'll avoid that offensive word if I see you turning green. I'm listening with fascination, getting a new idea for a film. There's always a new angle on the oldest stories. *Le grand séducteur de la jeunesse,* the Pied Piper himself, finds he can't stand the children he's led off into the mountain with him. The tables turned."

"Tables turned! Always a new angle! Haven't I thought of that? But the weariness of it! Don't you get tired? You want new angles? Why not do *Swan Lake* over again showing that the Evil Enchanter is really the victim of all those ravishing little swans and swanlets?"

"It's a deal," Vidal said, scanning the menu, seeing the rich offerings of barbecued swans and broiled enchanters, poached youth and middle age *à la crème.* "With a proper *mise en scène* we ought to be able to peddle that to the old lady from Dubuque. She's very cynical these days. *Très cynique,* like us."

"Ah, we've liberated her along with the other youth."

"Be careful of that poisoned word."

"It popped out of my mouth like a toad, all by itself. But, dear Vidal, do I understand you've promised to buy my idea? The fact is, I seem to need money. Money is above all a symptom of the vitality of the will, and the fact that I'm so wound up in bankruptcy litigations must be seen as a sign that someone has eroded mine close to zero."

"I've promised nothing," Vidal said. "Not even to pay the check here, though I might if you tell me more about how they managed to drown you in Swan Lake. Bleed for me. Make me feel it."

He did not mean that he wanted—or needed—to hear anything more specific about his brother or Tamisan Vail. He did not imagine he would get specifics if he asked. He might even lose his footing and be trapped in Sandler's endless deviousness if he was unwary enough to ask. The general and allusive term "youth" would serve them. Its use thus far had served to convince him that Sandler had indeed found the tables turned on him and was stricken by some hard-to-define loss of control.

And he would hear more about that when they had filled themselves with expensive food and the best of wines. The solace of a full belly did not sweep away Sandler's self-pity. It only humanized it, so what had been chilled with his characteristic derision before became more touching, almost a plea for sympathy.

"I must have had hope once. Surely I thought that the sheer energy in young people would create new forms that wouldn't bore me to death. Unleash them! I was a sentimentalist. Why are you laughing at that? Never mind. I've known you long enough so I don't have to define my terms. Don't tell me you've never *watched* while you were boffing them. Girls! Watched the girl, panting and hungering for freedom, pant and cry for subjection as the power in her turns around and pins her to the earth. Ah, their impulse to liberty is so wild and fierce—so beautiful, such an itch in the best of them!—that it becomes the one force in the cosmos that could betray her and turn her into a domestic beast.

"What an unbearable irony—the clutch at freedom is what puts her in chains. What are you thinking?"

"That you wanted them to be free. Why else destroy their past? Why else knock down the walls?"

"That was the sentimentalist in me. That's been kicked out of me long ago. I learned something worse than that irony. I learned that the monsters didn't need me to knock down any walls. They were going to be free anyway. That's the horror of it. When you begin to see you were only a tool, a dildo, that they can use and cast away, then you begin to realize the extent of their power. . . . The danger of it. They are pure chaos. Mother night. *Then* the ultimate seduction begins. You know they're capable of *anything*. We haven't seen it publicly yet, but I know. Boredom and bloodthirstiness at the same time. Any combination. You name it. And they make you envy them too. The envy of nothingness. I can't grasp it. But I want it. Ugh!"

"Wow," Vidal said with a flat restraint of emphasis. "You must have run into girls I haven't caught up to yet. I see I've been sheltering myself among the remnants of civilization."

His jest turned Sandler instantly away from whatever frankness he had bled into this conversation—as it may have been intended to do.

"You won't make me envy *you* and your Italian girls," he said. "For speed, bestiality and various other charms the new American girl is unmatched in the world. I love the new girls' names. Sheridan. Hilary. Elspeth. Megan. . . . It's the spice of irony for one who comes from the classical Kentucky tradition to bring off girls with such elegant names. They are so *good* to watch in their cute routines. . . ."

Vidal paid the check. As the men were waiting for taxis in the street he said, "I went this afternoon to see the Goss paintings you left at the Behn Gallery."

"You *will* get your father to settle this mess about their authenticity?"

"I will. No problem as far as I can see."

"I'm ashamed of selling them. My lawyer says I have to. Whatever I said about dueling with your father, I'd like to have something of his. I may be yearning for his blessing after my prodigal years. My own Papa was strong, too, but a sadist. So! I despise money but I despise even more being trapped for lack of it." He shrugged and left the rest unsaid in this distorted little apology.

Sandler took the first cab, and as he got into it he seemed to be deflating with a weariness beyond any he had let appear while they were at dinner. The Mephistophelean swagger he had managed through the years of their acquaintance seemed unconvincing at last, and when it was unconvincing it ceased to exist.

But Vidal refrained from pitying him for fear of pitying himself and all his own middle generation.

In his hotel room Vidal was thinking of the girls' names Sandler had reeled off. Sheridan, Hilary, Elspeth, Megan and . . . Tamisan, he thought. Of course Tamisan. Certainly Tamisan. Their names hung like ornaments on the emptiness of the night into which the taxi had taken Sandler. Little gold stars of bad conduct that Sandler had saved from his confident times.

Certainly Tamisan was among those that Sandler had *watched*. Tamisan, Tamisan. What bad dreams of the generation that Susan and he and Sandler belonged to had decked out its girls with such theatrical names and sent them out to live up to them? What venereal disease was passed on from one generation to its daughters by the images of womanhood it spawned with so much inventiveness? A generation of factory-finished devils, as his father said, babbling the truth like a drunk or a prophet.

He wanted to call Jason and tell him to break the guitar Tamisan had left behind in her flight. Break it three times and throw splinters and strings into the sterilizing fire.

Alone, Vidal was translating the evasive and allusive talk about "youth" passed over by his friend. They had, after all, communicated a great deal. The coded message had to be broken down and then, he supposed, made convincing to his unworldly brother.

It was Vidal's task to rephrase it in the workable jargons. Psychological: Don't fall in love with a neurotic. Social: Keep it in your pants until you've developed a congenial intrapersonal relationship that can stand without the support of sex.

It was much too late in the age to invoke the primitive warnings about dalliance with the strange woman. They all fucked now, or so it was agreed, and it was hopeless to quibble about how or with whom or with what they did it.

Vidal was not in a charitable or optimistic mood as he brushed his teeth in the bathroom, preparing for bed.

And yet, he said to his delicately spattered reflection in the bathroom mirror, through all the oblique and urbane contempt that had surfaced in Sandler's talk about the movie—which he just might find someone to make for him; not Vidal—there had been a note of yearning, too.

The most irrational yearning of all, which no profession except the arts was loony enough to offer to the sons of men. The lust for the will-o'-the-wisp, the unworthy object, the Siren, La

Belle Dame herself. The dream that had nothing to do with domesticity or health either. It was a wish to be fooled, misled, doomed even.

His phone rang and he answered. "Not tonight, chickabee. He told you I was here? Yes, until Saturday. There's *no* reason we can't have lunch, and we will! That's my lady. You did? You do? Ha-ha. That I must see. Well, I'm thinking of a film where the poor swan is seduced by Leda instead of raping her, and if you're not so ticklish that you mind a few feathers . . ."

It might have been Sheridan, Elspeth or Hilary calling him. The names did not matter after all. It was the voice of the telephone itself, reassuring as a cradle song, that soothed him to lie down and sleep in his hotel bed.

He woke uneasily in the late hours, remembering something else his father had said to him a day or so before. Dean Goss threw out sparks like a pinwheel when he was in a fit like the present one. The old man would convince himself of utterly contradictory positions and could not be persuaded that one of them canceled out another. He had gone foul-mouthed and savage about the girl from time to time. But now, waking, Vidal remembered another moment and a voice tuned to abysmal sorrow.

"She came to us with a gift of love we were too slow to grasp," Dean Goss had said.

Irritated by this memory as much as by the nasty spin-off of thoughts Sandler had inspired, Vidal got up and went to the bathroom to brush his teeth once more.

He took two Seconal capsules before he eased into bed again. The tranquillity they brought reminded him he was not in America for very long this time.

Some afternoon in September he would be sitting with his mother on her little balcony overlooking the Borghese Gardens. In the fine clear heat, looking out at the tops of pine trees, closer to black than green, they would sort the new chapters of the

207

Goss melodrama, making sense of it all in wry, barbed but unmalicious phrases. Mastering the ferment and beauty and grossness with the classic perspectives of skepticism.

In the meantime he saw no way he could usefully meddle in Jason's affairs or advise him either.

Chapter 11

Now I know the worst thing, Jason told himself. I didn't want to find her alive. And that terrified him as if he had glimpsed, in a mirror, blood dripping from his mouth, knowing it was not his own.

He could not very well forget the thrilling peaks of emotion that had dazzled him on both of his night drives into New York. He had been speeding in pursuit of some flying spirit of the night, teasing him with a trail of bright, phantasmal plumages. Tamisan transfigured by desires that afterward seemed perverse and morbid. It had all been a lie to tell himself he was anxious to catch up and console her for the humiliations she had suffered from his father—unless those humiliations were part of the inverted and deathly radiance his inner eye thirsted to see in its full glory.

I saw her blood streaming like the trail of a meteor. . . . Even now that thought or memory would not come clear to him. But it was there, lurking in the half-light of conscious recollection, at least as distinct as memories of things said and done in Sandler's house the night he had been there. He was sickened with an obscure guilt that had something to do with seeing the picture of his mother in Sandler's chair, something to do with the fevered erotic memories of Tamisan that had charged him up as he went to look for her at Sandler's house.

If he could put those disturbances clean out of his mind, still he could not erase the disappointment that flooded up when Susan called to say, "She's with some friend in the city. I'd guess Janis Ward, though Janis *told* me she was going away to Vermont. . . ."

"I'm glad," he told Susan. He was not glad. The bird of night was caught, its plumage drooping and dingy in the tedious light of day. . . .

At least Susan had not expected him to do anything with the information she relayed. He was in no shape to make a move. He was afraid to trust himself on the highway to New York again, though he had recovered the Toyota from Jean Simons by now. He was not going to make any phone calls that might oblige him to confront the ferocious traffic, the giddily converging lines of steel.

He had promised to help Monica with her tennis game, he remembered. He found clean white shorts, white shirt, white socks and put them on after bathing. The whiteness seemed ceremonial, and he had to force himself to remember he was only going to a game with an awkward twelve-year-old girl, not on a Kamikaze mission for the emperor.

When he left his room he did not go directly to pick up Monica in hers. He supposed his father had a right to be told that at last Susan had reported in with the news they had been waiting for. When that word was passed, he would be free to think of nothing but the white balls flying back and forth in the white, empty light of the morning. He did not feel the weight of his white sneakers on the grass as he headed across the lawn to Dean Goss's studio.

"You've done it again," Jason said in a voice all too much like that of a heartbroken five-year-old cheated of a promised holiday.

"Aren't they nice this way?" Dean Goss said. "Canvases are always most beautiful when they're empty."

Jason had come in to the blare of heroic music from the hi-fi in the studio. He had found his father arranging gladioluses in a tall brown vase on the floor. The three monstrous canvases on which he had been doling out paint with such a lordly hand just the afternoon before were empty again. Clean. Showing, expressing a sort of ferocious neatness all the more devastating because of the massive scale of the scrubbed surfaces. A lunar landscape, souvenir views of Hiroshima.

"You were going good," Jason said. "Why'd you have to strip them again?"

210

"I didn't have to," Dean Goss said, cupping a yellow gladiolus in his good hand. "There's nothing so annoying as to come close and *just* miss what you think you've seen." He was not wearing his glasses. He beat lightly at his eyes with his mutilated hand as if trying to pound them into greater effectiveness. "I wasn't doing too bad, was I, honey? Well . . . That was the trouble. The angel comes and sits for a while. . . . Ah, isn't she friendly? Doesn't she just smile and smile? You think you've got her . . . whoosh, she's gone. Up and away. There you are with egg on your face, and the mistake is clear. You've been watching her instead of what's been happening on the canvas while you painted. Just a *leetle* too charming she is, see? She fooled you after all. She didn't mean to have her picture took."

Apparently he got the gladioluses into a pose that suited him. He came over to stand with white-clad Jason in front of the bereaved canvases. He put his arm over his son's shoulders while they both looked up at the emptiness, but he did not bother to put on his glasses again.

"So," Goss said. "You've come close but you haven't done what you were supposed to do. The painting is mighty fine. Mighty fine. Why, the goddamned things are *successful!* Anyone can see that. So there's nothing in this world to do but wipe 'em out and go back next time just a mite farther behind the starting line so you can get a little more ump in your jump, right?"

The clarinets and drums spoke for them awhile. The long, preparatory rolling of a kettledrum, the fateful, blithe precision of clarinets like a file of soldiers, nimble in their white and red dress uniforms, wheeling into a skirmish line as the drumming beat once more at the headed grass of the field assigned for combat.

Goss showed his back teeth as the music flashed its pageantry through his mind. Horse teeth, Jason thought. He's showing me the molars he has to use if the incisors won't grind through.

His father began to hum and then went over to puddle with the paints piled up on his marble palette, fiddling with green and a yellow softer than that of the gladioluses, jerking a brush around the marble surface, sketching on it, obliterating his sketches by the same preoccupied motions that created them.

"I see my next step clearly," he said.

"You do?"

"Yep. Turn my back on the canvases. Let them think I'm not interested in them. That I gave them up. The pictures are women and must be given time, given a chance to think it's their own free will to appear. I'll clean up the studio while I let them think it over. There's too much junk in here. A painter always paints his studio interior—do you know that?—whatever he says the subject is. I'll get this place down to the varnish on the table tops. Stripped like a Mondrian. You know what I envied you last winter? The emptiness of the studio you were living in. That's the way to begin. You see, I do learn, Jason. I'll follow your example this time and I'll get her exactly right."

"If you follow my example," Jason said slowly, troubled, "what'll I follow?"

Again Dean Goss showed his molars in a ravenous, perturbed smile. "Ring around the rosy, isn't it? If that's the game, we'll play it."

"It sounds like Zen."

"I've got a little Zen in my blood," Goss admitted, "along with just a smidgin of Apache. Geronimo! Learning to hide himself in a desert where even the ants are visible from five miles away on an average day. That boy understood how to live! We've got to think Geronimo until we bring him in view."

His enthusiasm for the hiding warrior was not cheering Jason up. Neither was his father's intention of cleaning the studio. The photos, reproductions, flowers, tools, bits of driftwood, beach scavengings and historical tidbits Dean Goss accumulated around him seemed like part of his living tissue. They took on a charge of life from him. To get rid of them, even if they weren't literally destroyed, seemed like a mutilation. Jason blurted, "I know how Susan felt when she saw you'd scrubbed off the first two things."

"A woman of little faith!" his father said, sweeping that offending woman away with the other debris that was distracting his eye from its reckless search. "I had her tagged from the beginning as a string saver at heart. That kind of woman won't do. But look—she had a point. There should have been at least a photographic record of what I'd done. So I got Fiona to come help me before I slaughtered the poor things. We took some pictures. . . . What the hell will they prove? That I was there? Somewhere near the North Pole? But not *quite* there. Admiral Peary. There's another man we always have to think of when we're trying serious work. Geronimo and the admiral. . . ."

Jason left without mentioning Tamisan or his call from Susan. His father's professed confidence in what he was doing didn't cheer him. He mistrusted it as he had mistrusted the mammoth revolver Dean Goss acquired after Maggie's death. As he mistrusted his father's bad-mouthing loyal Susan. They were signs of gruesome disturbance.

But, as always, symptoms of his father's disturbance strengthened and stabilized him. They sat on some kind of emotional teeter-totter, rising and falling in a kind of intimate contrariness. Besides, he had wanted his father disturbed. For a long while, in his meditations, he had fretted about what he felt to be the artist's complacency. Bad signs were signs of life, weren't they? Soberly Jason went to teach Monica what he knew about tennis.

The beauty part was that he taught himself profound things that morning while he taught her to get a little more power in her forehand. "Back farther, Monica! Always swing your racket back farther than you think you ought to when the ball's coming. That's good! That's better. Reach *back*. . . ." As from a distance, he heard his own voice declaring the wisdom of the race—good for tennis, good for leaps of the spirit.

By the bucketful the spindly little girl whopped back the white balls he tossed to her. Presently she challenged him to a game. It was one-sided and unequal of course. Yet she was doing so well it seemed wrong to ease up and let her win. She was on her own and his heart welled with the joy of watching her fight for her points. Back, back, back—just as he had told her to do it—she reached with her borrowed racket. Whang!

213

She passed him with a forehand drive near the alley, though he spun like a released spring to retrieve it.

"I got it! I got it!" she called.

He paused to wipe the fine sweat from his forehead, thinking, I didn't really *wish* she was dead. It wasn't that at all. That sort of thing has to be stated precisely. I only wished she could have outrun the rat pack, have got where none of us could touch her. . . .

He was in his room at a little after nine that evening when his phone rang. He recognized the gay voice more quickly than he had a right to. It was Schuyler Baron.

"How *are* you, lamb? I was *cross* with myself for letting you go the other night . . . you were in no condition, none at all, to be abroad among gob-uh-luns. So glad you're all tickety-boo and comfy, and I've been thinking of you more than you'd *imag*ine. Have you felt the thought waves beating on your brow? Do you realize I sincerely doubted there *was* such a creature with a name like Tamisan? I *adore* that name. It keeps resounding in my *brain*. It chimes. There's a place in Mexico where I've never been called Tamazunchale. *Très exotique*. Tamisan Charlie . . . doesn't that meld the sexes enchantingly? Nevertheless . . .

"I want you to know I'm *your* friend. I'm your spy in this grotto of lost souls. I'm not above eavesdropping. There's hardly anything I am above, to confess the truth. Now listen, your naughty girl is at this number. . . ."

He paused in his breathless gush for a moment as if fumbling for something he had written down. It was a suspenseful pause, followed by disappointing anticlimax. The phone number he gave with succulent enunciation was Janis Ward's. Jason recognized it before Baron sang the last two digits.

"No," Jason said. "I've been in touch with the woman who lives there. Thanks anyway." He was sure Janis had been honest in reporting no contact with Tamisan. Besides, by now, Janis had gone to Vermont.

"She's there, alive and well," Baron insisted. "I must hang up now before I'm appre*hende*d."

I certainly want her to be alive, Jason thought, but I don't want to be fooled any more. He was very reluctant to pick up the phone again and ring Janis' number. The phone rested in its cradle like a booby trap—or maybe only like a prankster's gimmick planted to deride him.

But it was his duty to try, however much he doubted Baron's story. How had Baron got the information, supposing it to be valid? Had he eavesdropped? Had Sandler—or someone else in Sandler's house—deceptively arranged for the message to be passed along? The possibilities of deception buzzed around like fat, sated flies. He did not want to be deceived any more. He didn't want Tamisan deceived or tricked, either. Nor my father, he thought, admitting his father's stake in this entanglement. Further, he had a strong distaste for detective-story complications. The true mysteries of life, death, art and sex always seemed degraded and caricatured by attempts to pattern them on cold facts.

It was a relief, then, that Janis' phone rang on and on unanswered. He let it ring two full minutes, then three. It was, at least, a neutral omen that no one was home at Janis', and it seemed to him better now to trust omens than any suspect tips from Baron.

He spent the evening playing chess with Fiona in the library while his father read nearby. Monica made pen-and-ink sketches of all of them. It was a secure and pleasant evening. Early in the game he took Fiona's queen. By a little past eleven he had mated her with a knight-rook combination from which she could not break free.

Just to make sure, he told himself, to do the decent thing and leave no stone unturned, he dialed Janis' number again before he undressed for bed.

This time he got a busy signal. Odd.

Odd. But if it had any significance as an omen, he could not sense what it might be.

He sat down to wait before he tried again. While he waited, he idly turned the Tarot cards that Tamisan had left behind here among her things. He used the ancient Celtic method Tamisan had taught him.

The covering and crossing cards were the Devil and the World. After them came the Magician, the Ace of Wands and the Ace of Swords. The Four of Wands (which Tamisan called the "happiest" card in the deck). The Tower. The King of Pentacles. Knight of Swords. Knight of Cups. The High Priestess (unrevealed future, silence, mystery, duality; hidden influences at work). Finally the Hanged Man.

So many high-powered cards in a single layout would have kept Tamisan awake all night debating their portent. "Heavy!" she would have said. "Heh-VEE!"

Soothed and blessed by this intimate recollection of her, he fell asleep in his clothes, still propped up by a pillow, before he had a chance to dial again.

He woke with a thought that was neither omen nor dream, but a certainty that had matured in his long and heavy sleep. *Fiona gave me her queen! She purposely let me capture it. Because she knew I'd be beaten without it. She knows everything is worse than it looks.*

He was sweating. The sun was pouring into his room boisterously. He felt its moistened heat on his bare leg like the tongue of a huge yellow animal tasting him.

It was past nine o'clock. He had carelessly let himself fall asleep and slept past the time when he should have tried to phone again.

The phone was a dead thing in his sweating hands. The reiterant click of the dial as it returned after each number should have been a decipherable code, spelling forgiveness or condemnation. It meant nothing at all.

He got a busy signal again, a honking that was not even derisive, the mindless bray of nothingness, as if by mistake he was connected with an outpost beyond the fringe of the universe.

He dashed to the bathroom to throw water on his swollen face. Before he raced out, he grabbed nothing from the room but his car keys. Three hours later he was hammering at the beige door of Janis' apartment, shaken with premonitions he had felt only once in his life before.

He was in Paris with his young mother then. They had been there only two days on the trip that they had been talking about since he was very small. "When you're old enough to feel it in your bones, I'll show you my Paris," she had promised. She meant she would show him her adolescence, still unfinished when she married his father. They had been to Paris a number of times in his father's company. Many of the streets, restaurants, bridges, monuments and boulevards were familiar to Jason. What his mother promised was something else—a time beyond time, streets that the pavement hid, trees blowing in weather that only the heart could perceive.

On this second evening Maggie Goss had turned down an invitation to dine at the embassy with Senator Burke and Marian. "There's a restaurant in the arcade of the Place des Vosges," she said. "Tommy Peers took me there to eat before we went to the Opéra Comique and sat up very near the top for *Madame Butterfly,* poor thing. I think it may have been the only real date I ever had in Paris, though a few in London before Daddy carried me off." With Jason as escort she meant to retrace the path of that other evening, though it had been earlier in the spring and tonight *Madame Butterfly* was not playing.

Jason had come from his room in the hotel to hers and was reading the English papers while she got ready to go out. Through the sound of the shower and the closed door of the bathroom he heard her whistling fragments from the opera she would miss this time. Maggie was a great whistler and she sometimes shivered with fearful delight when she puckered her mouth to whistle that last hissing, transcending, soaring swish of cymbals that brought the tragic music to its close.

He was waiting to hear that when he heard her fall. A low, triple concussion of her light bones banging the tub's edge as she went down. He called her name before he tried the door.

He heard only the sibilance of the shower running. He remembered that his real panic had not begun until he put his hand on the doorknob and found it locked.

He had thrown himself repeatedly against the elegant door, feeling no pain in the shoulder that struck it, but seeming to have no more strength than a shadow. Afterward it seemed to him it had been more than wood and metal that made him so weak. He had been uncertain. Maybe robbed of certainty about what he might do if he had to take his mother's wet body in his hands. A dread that had made a coward and weakling of him and made him shudder with guilt when it came to his mind again. There was no greater accusation against his manhood than that he had wasted minutes when she might have needed him desperately to save her from drowning.

But then, just a little shakily, she had called, "Jason? I . . . I'm not hurt. Whew. I must have slipped. It's so ri*dic*ulous." He heard her clambering back into life. Heard her try to resume her whistling as she dried herself.

Since she had merely fainted and fallen, luckily, the oddness of her having locked the door to bathe made no practical difference in the outcome of that evening. They had gone out to the opera after all—only having to hurry more than Maggie intended with their dinner in the Place des Vosges because it was half an hour before she felt quite herself again. She went out with him into the streets that evening with no more bruises from her fall than he had got from trying to break through the door.

But after she was dead, in his nightmares he was often at that door feeling surprise explode into horrifying certainty when the ornamental knob failed to yield to his hand. Maggie had never hidden her nakedness from him. With his father they had always swum naked in the river at the farm. In all the houses and apartments he could remember she might whisk around without a stitch almost any time there were no servants or company with them.

It was death she meant to hide from him. The hand that had set the lock to keep him out had known she was going to die soon, even if her mind had not grasped it yet. Out of his nightmares he had confirmed this and admitted he had known it, too, from that evening on. Had known it and still betrayed her into going home to the hospitals in America instead of on to Rome and Greece and Persia, as she had so eagerly intended when they set out.

He heard the faintest rustle of bare feet before the knob was turned and Janis' door started to open. He saw it swing a few inches before the chain stopped it, and saw a long hank of Tamisan's pale hair swing in the gap between door and frame before he saw her bloodshot blue eye and a bright scarlet nipple. She tried to slam the door shut.

His shoulder was against it and his hand on the knob. His pulse was racing wildly and they were both silent as they fought for the door. She could not possibly have held it against his lunges without help from someone else. He took one short step back and hit it with shoulder and cheek. The chain tore loose from the doorframe.

There had been no one helping her keep him out. Only the chain and Tamisan's frenzied determination not to be caught as he found her now. He had broken both.

She was alone. She had not been able to keep him out, but she showed no intention of recognizing him.

"If you're another of Janis' sad, sick friends . . . she is not home. Definitely. She left for Vermont yesterday and I shall have to do. Well, do come in since you're in, and you can have your turn," she said with sullen defiance and the pathetic affectation of yet another make-believe. She slouched across the single room to the open, tangled day bed. "I thought you'd have too much sense to tear the door down." On her naked, retreating back he saw the red smear of an abrasion before she plopped gracelessly amid the covers and pulled a sheet over her insulted body and over her head.

He had been unable to speak at all until her face was covered. "Who were you expecting then? Who do you let in, naked?"

"You!" the voice from under the sheet sang. "Janis' druid friends. Druids all! Mama told me all men wanted the same thing. She didn't say not to give it to them. If you want your turn, just lift the sheet gently from the bottom, please. Never look at the face, Jason."

When she called him by name—*gave* him his name, he would think later—the crystalline paralysis of his senses seemed to open. He recognized the foulness of the room as a parallel part of his mind registered an awareness he had buried lower than dreams could reach and recover. Now, as the smells began to take separate identities in his nose, he *knew,* as if in legitimate memory, that his mother had not been alone when she locked that bathroom door in Paris. No boyish ghost of Tommy Peers clung to her wet limbs, no mustachioed Parisian seducer, but Death—Death standing in his naked bones under the luxurious spray from the shower, with bony fingers prying his mother's legs apart and tickling with cold fury. Himself and his father both cuckolded by her mouth puckering to take his kiss, opening so tooth rattled on tooth before she went down under the ravisher.

It was as if he had broken through two doors at once, as if he had known at the right moment how to outwit time itself. And he must be punished for his cleverness. He would remember later the vision flaring up onto the screen of his mind in a kind of binocular parallel or symmetry with what he saw and heard now.

He groped for a chair, reinforced his noodle legs by leaning on it as he pushed it close to the sheet-covered form on the day bed and sat down. "Well, I guess I had to find out sometime," he said. "I've been trying long enough."

In the silence which was either that time in Paris or this time, he sat among the impudent messages spread out for him to read. A cigar butt was stamped out in a white-edged ashtray on the floor beside the day bed. There was a sunflower shape of vomit on the floor near the dining table. The candelabrum that Janis usually kept on the table's top had been smashed to the floor, as if it had been swept down by some blind urgency that needed the table's surface for its enactment.

His nose went on sorting out the smells of whatever carnage had swept through here—reek of marijuana, tobacco, gin, a vomiting of Mexican spices, smell of shit, candle smoke, semen and the fish-counter variety of woman smells that embroidered all the others together. It was a den on the far side of life—either before or after—it smelled like birth or decomposition. The worst thing about it would seem to him later to be that Death had skipped away, leaving the two of them to inhabit it alone, without his wise company to explain how it had been or would be.

"Didn't you know I'd come looking for you?"

"I thought you *would*. How'd I know you'd come *here?*"

"Who'd you think was at the door?" He was not asking the same question he had asked before. He was asking for Death's common name, he thought.

"Hubert, Ivan, Gunther . . . One of them come back. Adrienne maybe. . . . In case anyone *omitted* anything." The chuckle from under the sheet was a mere whisper. "You better go, Jason. Hubert *might* come back."

"I'll kill him." He meant this as irony. A response to her unreal pretenses.

"He's bigger'n you. Cockwise particularly. Really, you didn't have to catch me now 'n' get hurt. Go. Please go."

He felt the flatness of the floor under his feet and realized he could hold himself upright in the chair without clutching its bottom in both his cold hands.

He said, "I suppose we—I—understand why you're doing this. No one blames you and we . . ."

She ripped the sheet away and sat up. The movement was like a released steel spring, whatever the scraped and skinned flesh might look like. "Gosses! Nobody understand me." It was not a complaint. It was a dare. *You'd better not.* "Have you been meditating on me, druidwise? I've been meditating too. What does Fiona say about me now?"

"She wants you to be all right."

"Go back and tell her and your father what you see."

"I won't."

"Tell them I'm just a girl who plays for keeps." As if this made its own mirthful rhythm in her mind, she sang it raggedly. "AHM jussaGIRRRRRRLLLLL who PLAAAAAAYS for-keeps. Will you go?"

"I guess they know that about you too," he said meekly. "They're not so callous as they may have seemed. I think my father would understand this, too. All this."

"I told you I'd gross you out sometime, Jason."

"I told you you couldn't."

"Words, words, words. Everyone is better at them than me."

"Some of them are poison, too. If you want to be through with us—me—let's not say them."

"Then PUH-lease go. Before Hubert might come back."

"I won't," he said again. He used up the last bit of his pride and confidence in himself by saying he wouldn't instead of admitting he couldn't. He might have got to his feet by now. They might have carried him to elevator or window or some other way down to the street. It was his blinded soul that was bound to stay here. He could not imagine where to go. The lewd ghastliness of this room at midday was overwhelmingly familiar to him. More familiar than the neatness Janis ordinarily preserved. Tamisan's scraped skin and chewed nipples were as familiar as his mother's rotting loveliness and the voice begging him—commanding him—to get out was familiarly inviting him to lie here. Rest here.

"You want to sock me. Sock me," Tamisan said.

"I want to kill you." Spoken like a lover, softly, softly.

"Go ahead. I invited you to take your turn and you won't fuck, so kill me."

"Please."

"Please *go,* I said."

Everything was familiar except quarreling between them. They had no practice or skill in that. It was overkill or nothing.

And he, desperately trying to cling to life and death with the same grip, realized she had known that before he did, too. In this also he was too late. And he wanted to hit her for letting him be too late to kill her at the prime, at some moment of ec-static guilt that neither of them could quite summon back now.

He watched her eyes change as she shifted stratagems and began to chatter—as if she were talking to a corrupt but disinterested girl friend who could be amused by understated sarcasm. She sniffed as her stuffy nose caught some of the stinks filling the ravaged apartment. "I guess we had a mini orgy here. Not so mini. There were five of us if you count Adrienne. Count her, but don't count on her. She passed out so quick. Leaving it all to me. I couldn't be this sore if it was mini. Can you fix me something? Anything. There's probably some of Hubert's gin. Hubert insists on Beefeater's. Nothing but the best. Beefeater's! I know them well. I'm about to crash if I don't . . . Once a girl I knew when I knew girls had a bad trip and I brought her out of it by talking in ape. Want to talk in ape or poetry? Ooon, ooonng, oooong. Never never never never never. Just *give* me the gin and I'll gross you out of the ball game. And then you've got to go because if they don't come back, I've got to *tahdy the house*. When I've slept. Oooooo."

He found gin for her in the kitchenette, finding below the icebox door a tangle of feminine underwear and pantyhose that were not Tamisan's, abandoned there not merely by carelessness, but placed like a clue to lead him back through the night just past. When he came back with ice tinkling in the glass in his hand, Tamisan was craning and twisting her neck to examine the long reddened abrasion that curved like an enormous, feeding flatworm toward the small of her back. "I think I've been abused," she said wonderingly. "I remember. That damned Hubert was pushing me across the rug. Bump, bump, bump! All he could think of, the bastard, was *push*. I dunno, boy. I dunno. . . ." She drained the gin in a gulp.

"I'd heard about Hubert from Janis or else when he called and was so sad she'd gone to Vermont I would never have said I was all alone 'n' hungry 'n' key-ute. . . . It's all Janis' fault— it's always someone else's fault in my life—for telling me about his dong. Hubert 'n' Janis never made it in college when she knew him in sorority days. So now when he's in Washington with HEW he visits her here and astonished her, since her sorority had never seen a cock that size. Which has to be seen to be believed. And his friend Ivan has a girl here which is Adrienne. He's a political science grad student from Princeton. With kinky hair. A real devil. Who incidentally happened to have the cocaine and knows where we can get an—ugh—Mexican dinner. And Mama says I should not be superior to people with nothing to show for it, so when I saw his kinky hair I decided I was inferior to everyone. Mexican dinner. Right. At which Adrienne could not stand Ivan's political views. Which I shared and we almost grossed her out before who was it—me?—said we might as well come back here since, though it wasn't my apartment, Hubert was such a dear friend to Janis in Vermont. And because she is a good liberal girl Adrienne might have thrown Ivan out early but we'd hardly got our clothes off when the cocaine hit her. She went to sleep over there and we kept stepping on her. She must have more bruises than me, wherever she is. Maybe in Vermont too. I dunno when they all went out. So, I've got them both on my hands, right?"

She is hearing me listen to her, Jason thought. As if she were creeping through nerves and tissue not only to see what was in his mind, to help sympathize and be patient, but to sense the unquiet of muscles, the pumping heart and the chemistries of fluid reserved in testicles, too. The gin she had taken seemed to have restored not only the narcotic level in her blood stream but some careless and truly superhuman detachment—bringing her to an apathy so staggering in its magnitude that she might have been the perverse Goddess of Love telling an immortal companion about the fruitless and always misguided worship performed in her honor. *Now she doesn't care if I go or hear the rest.*

" . . . pushing me across the floor. Bump with his huge cock. Bump, bump, bump. No doubt that skinned my poor back. But it turned out Ivan was the bear, because, see, I had to be indoctrinated with politics, since he took me for an intellectual, though immature. Wouldn't stop when Hubert went to sleep too, but has to go on all night. I think Hubert left with Adrienne. No! Gunther came and rang the bell because he is also in HEW and had to get Hubert on the early shuttle but came back after

Ivan and Adrienne left for Vermont. Also by shuttle. Gunther smokes cigars, which I told him must be against HEW policy and harmful to the system. He is not as big as Hubert, so if he should come back here instead of anyone else, I suppose you *could* fight with him. But that's all the story except for details that would make you hot and, as we always say, it is thinking that makes *you* hot, if not everybody. Not all men are like you, Jason."

He might have hit her for not telling him the details—he would think later. Because in the total carnage she had pulled down to serve as barrier between them it would have been some minimal kindness to let him imagine the splendor of destruction at its height. To hear, if even in echo, the ecstasy of abandonment as she fell away from him. To let him at least imagine that someday he might be humanly jealous of what she had given to strangers that she had never given him.

"Did you suck them all off?" he said.

"I'm not going to tell you everything. You said some words were poison. So is what I did. So I don't have to poison you any more. Jason? Will you go now? I'm all right. It's not the first time. You didn't believe me when I told you I was too dirty to love. Now you've seen it. What are you waiting for? It won't be the last time."

"All right," he said. He got up shakily. On legs full of glass splinters he started for the door. "It seems like a dirty thing to do to Janis. In her apartment."

"I'll clean it up."

He thought he would be all right as soon as he was in the hallway. What kept him going was that at least he hadn't hit her yet. He knew as his hand went out for the doorknob that his real motive for hitting her would have been that she made *him* be the one to catch her.

She had lured him here. Not by a deliberate plan. She had nevertheless lured him out of the solitude of his heated imagination to confront in sober daylight something that could not live except in the dark, something that changed its nature in the passage over from darkness to daylight. And it was not going to matter whether she could have foreseen or even guessed he might come to the door at this or that hour. She was not going to exist for him any more as a creature half made up of his romantic wishes.

Behold the woman on the morning after. Shake off the enchantments of erotic fables.

He could do that. Once past the door, he would start breathing again because it was so easy to breathe. Everyone else did it. He could too. He would believe he was alive because it was easy to do that, too.

"I didn't come here to take you back," he said without looking over his shoulder at her. "If I could only understand why you ran from my father and headed straight for Sandler . . ."

If she had answered this right away he would have kept on walking, descending, until his shoe leather touched the sidewalk. It was the rhythm of her hesitation and response that made him turn back.

"I did no such thing," she said. "I wouldn't do that." For the first time since he had come in, there was a look of contrition, doubt, on her face.

"You're a liar. You'd lie about anything. I told my father you were a liar and couldn't help it. He said . . . Never mind."

"I wouldn't have anything to do with Sandler."

"You were there the other night when I came looking for you." He stopped, shamed and shaken by what he had said. It was as if a voice he could not claim as his own had made the accusation. As if something alien, lurking, destructive in himself was ready to match lie for lie, until all clarity was renounced or muddled. How could he say that he had only been afraid, secretly, that she had intentionally plotted to lead him on his ridiculous chase to Sandler's door and up to the room where he had seen his mother's picture? He had no right to accuse her because his weakness muddled his faith in obvious reality. "You called him. And Bern Whitestar. And . . ."

"I don't *know* who all I called," she flared. "I was freaked out.

I guess I offered to fuck Whitestar, huh? Well, run tell Mama that."

"I don't want to hurt . . ."

". . . the innocent?" She began to laugh bitterly. "All names changed to protect the innocent. You're right. Mama is. That's her trouble, after all these years. But I called Sandler—only *called* him—to tell him if he ever said anything about me to any Gosses I'd kill him."

"Why'd you have to say that to him?"

"I dunno, Jason. I dunno."

"More lies."

"I'm a liar," she said absently, faithfully as a child repeating a catechism.

My father said . . .

"I'm not all lies, Jason."

I'm not all frivolity. I'm not all lies, Schuyler Baron said with ingratiating seductiveness.

My father said, "Believe their lies because they are trying to teach us the truths we live by are too shallow to appease the heart." He forgot to tell me what to believe when the lies lose their shape and cancel each other so there is nothing left except the heart wishing it had never beat, never been.

It was then that something convinced him everything would be all right if only he and Tamisan could flee away from here without a sound, leaving behind no trace that they had ever disturbed the ordinary neatness of Janis' apartment.

If we could go out by the window . . . Without the noise of the elevator cables giving us away as we went.

He thought that in a minute she was going to start to explain what reason she might have for killing Sandler. He did not want explanations. He might have hit her for abusing his ears with a history that changed nothing.

I'm not all lies, Jason.

It was not Tamisan who said it this time, or any memory of Baron's ingratiating earnestness. It was what music had said to him for so long and what his beloved silences said when he didn't choose to hear music any more.

"It doesn't matter," he told her gently. "Whatever you say is all right. I'm sorry my father was rude to you. He should have listened to you while he had a chance."

He did not go after that speech. He was never very sure what he did in the next moments until he heard Tamisan yelling, "Stop that! Stop it and get *out!* Oh, for God's sake, please!"

There he was on all fours below the edge of Janis' table, with what must have been someone's underwear in his hand, scrubbing at the impasto of vomit on the carpet.

"You are *not* going to clean up somebody's puke!" she commanded with all the frenzy of horror swelling her voice.

"All right," he said merrily. It seemed an enormous way up as he rose staggering to his full height, feeling the joints in his legs straighten like the mechanism of a terribly ingenious toy, sensing how miraculous it was that the weight of his head could be balanced so high and far above his shoes. "All right. I suppose someone else could do that better than I. That too." He let the wadded cloth fall obediently from his fingers.

He only meant to do one thing more before he left. Without even kneeling this time, he picked up the white ashtray with the cigar butt in it and headed for the wastebasket in the kitchenette.

"Jason!"

He knew, even as it was happening, that he could have controlled himself if she had not snatched the ashtray out of his hand and flung it, butt and all, into the sink. But hearing the smash of ceramic against enamel was too much for him.

He took a half step to get his balance and made the first fist that he could remember. "You should have let me do that for you," he said. He rolled on the balls of his feet and hit her square in the mouth.

It was bliss to see how truthful and astonished her eyes were as the blood welled over her teeth. She put her hand up to catch it, still watching him from over her fingertips with the wide gaze of one who has witnessed a murder but cannot remember how to scream.

"Hurry," he said. "Get some clothes on. I'll take you to your mother's place. You can tell her I skinned your back, too." His mind was all at once efficient and clear. "I'll come back and give the super some money to clean up in here. I want it to look as if we'd never been here, either of us. Hurry. Hurry now, hurry."

from Susan Vail's red notebook:

No, Jason said uncomfortably, he wouldn't come in, thanks.

Tamisan had run past me, into her bedroom. She had not been fast enough to keep me from seeing her burst lip. But wasn't it a relief to have her delivered home again with nothing worse? Not to get a package wrapped with maniacal perfection and addressed in Spencerian script containing her addled head?

"Jason, you're my friend as well as hers. She's out of sight if you're tired of looking at her. It's my apartment as much as hers. You look so worn."

"No. I'm tired. But I'd rather go on to my place and nap. Tamisan can provide the explanations. It was I who hit her, in case you're wondering."

"She undoubtedly deserved it."

He shook his head. There was a shape of pain repeated in all the lines of his face as he still stood outside my door in the hall. "Hitting's bad business," he said, and went away. I watched him square his shoulders. His shoulders looked like mine, and maybe the pity I felt was self-pity. I don't mind claiming my share.

No sooner had I shut the door than Tamisan came from her room to face me. Oh, not to ask for sympathy—supposing I had been ready to give it—but probably to prevent its expression.

She said sternly, "If you cry, I'll go again."

It was pure counterattack, defensive insult. Me cry over her woes? Her toughened Mama? Without some callus of the soul I would not have been able to answer a ringing phone since she achieved menarche. And her visible injuries now were no worse than a skinned knee when she came back from roller skating in the park.

229

She said, "Mama, I could have managed. I almost did. What tripped me up was knowing every minute what you were thinking. You were worried. I could handle everything but that."

"No."

"No what?"

"You're right, you could have managed, darling—whatever in hell it was you were managing, and once again you don't have to tell me. But no. It wasn't worry. It hasn't been for nineteen years. It was praying."

"Shit on pray," she said—most like a queen! "I am sorry I blew things for you and your book and all your work. Well! I'm going to sleep now."

We don't love strangers. What trick is played on us that we go on so evenly loving children when we encounter them as strangers? Sometimes it has seemed to me positively wrong to love Tamisan as I do when the love won't shape her or give her a viable pattern for her woman's life. It is like giving her a blank check or a gun.

Jason's dumping her back on my doorstep is only one more entry in the catalogue of nightmare encounters. Once (hilarious farce!) at Fiftieth Street and Madison I saw her being dragged into a taxi by a burly, red-faced man with curly sideburns and an executive air. Suddenly I recognized my child by her tie-dyed jeans and fringed leather vest. The sense of rape and ravishment was so strong in this scene, I would have called the police on the spot if I hadn't thought: She'd laugh it off if the police rescued her. Would claim she'd consented if they found her bound and gagged and locked in the bastard's closet.

I raced home with fever and chills—to find her sitting in the bathtub, doing her nails and reading *Soul on Ice*. She swore she had not left the apartment all day. All right, she could not have been the girl I saw dragged into the cab. Realizing this only made me madder. I suppose it was not an accident that I bumped the board she had laid across the tub, knocking her manicure set and her book into the water.

And she wasn't exactly fooled. "If you don't want me to read

Eldridge Cleaver, why don't you just burn the book?" she wanted to know.

"It's disgusting to pamper your body by sitting all day in the tub."

"Your racism shows in such petty ways it's really crude."

"What about your speech class at Hunter?"

"Fooling around with words when the system is fucking us over this way?"

At our worst we fall to such absurd bickering. If we could only get to the truth, however bad . . .

Was it my experience of bad luck the first time out that made me take her to Dr. Slade for BC pills before she went off to school in Massachusetts? I don't know. Reasons that seem clear at one time will fade, change or disappear altogether in the light of events. At any rate, it wasn't because I was afraid of the prep school boys, but that she would play more than guitar duets with the graying Spanish instructor. I was literally off the mark, though correct in essence. Her conquest there was poor Amos Hartshorne, who was paid to teach her creative writing. Poor Hartshorne with his poetic wife and three creative children. "I live in the cathedral shadow of your vagina," he wrote to Tamisan. (Eventually I saw the letter.) Who would be afraid, even at sixteen, of anyone who thought the damn thing casts a shadow?

The messengers and messages keep coming. Am I the Western Union or the addressee? And if there should be Someone Out There trying to tell me the ball game is over and I might as well give up, why can't He convey this in ten words or less?

Bern Whitestar was in town for the day and insisted with some urgency that I have lunch with him. I dolled up for the occasion, thinking it might be time to make good on what I'd skidded past that night at his place. When the milk is spilled, I have always mopped it up and wrung the mop out back in the pitcher. When I can't sell my soul, I am willing to barter.

Wishful thinking again. I'm still caught in the spider web.

There I had to sit, smiling with irony well worn as tattered under-wear, while Bern came across with the news that on her rampage Tamisan had phoned him twice. She had, in fact, tried to lure him to a rendezvous with her at Jean Simons' hideaway in the woods.

Bern's wife answered the first call very late at night and "had trouble getting back to sleep" after being thus awakened. Until Tamisan called again the next afternoon and insisted on the tryst, he only knew that "some female hippie" had tried to reach him in the indiscreet hours. When she got him on the wire, she made her invitation explicit enough. He did not repeat the conversation to me verbatim, but this prize line was delivered intact: "Would you like to try for two?" She took it for granted I had made it with him.

Bern said, "All my life I've wanted to score the famous mother-daughter combination, Susan. I'm still wondering why I didn't make a pass at you—and why I didn't dash right over to see Tamisan. It wasn't because she was Jason Goss's girl. I don't know how things stand between him and Tamisan."

"The evidence is in," I said. "You've made your case, counselor. She doesn't care about anyone. Why did you have to tell me this at all, Bern?"

The ancient Jewish wound appeared in his canny eyes. "Now, now, Susan. Pain haunts me. I can't inflict it. After I spoke to Tamisan I took a walk in the woods by my place and thought, I can't do this to Susan. Whether the kid cares about anyone or not, you do. You didn't sound like a mother the night you told me your story, but . . ."

"But what?"

"Like a woman in love. Now, now, Susan. I'm not the doctor, come to tell you about your latent lesbianism. . . . You're in love with the idea of someone who can win the woman game for you. Beat the odds. . . ."

Well . . . turn everything you've always believed exactly upside down and it looks pretty much the same. I always thought I had to kick my way through a man's world so Tamisan could waltz through barefooted. At least I began with that and no one told me when I was released from the responsibility.

He said, "It's damn near too much, isn't it, to think of her as both woman and child and worry about both?"

"Worry? Who? Me? Worry? She's home sleeping now. Literally. She's there getting her eighteen hours. Day after day. Eventually she'll wake up rosy-cheeked and think everything is all right. Whatever happens next is all right with them. Because they're young they can tear up the world and massacre the innocents. And that is all right with them. They can tear themselves up, too, and what does it matter? I *hate* the idea of youth. If I was ever in love with Tamisan, it was the child who was supposed to get through without being in this ghastly phase."

The best he could offer was to say sadly that this, too, would pass. Even Tamisan would be someday as reasonable as we two and as able to balance her impulses with the realities of the world as it is. As long as we sat there chewing the good food and drinking the good wine that did not seem the saddest thing. I thought it was dear and good of him to worry with me about Tamisan—he told me about the drug problems his kids are going through; I worried with him. I admired him for refusing to score the mother-daughter combination and mark F on the wall. The lunch was a limited success.

But walking away from it was the horror. The afternoon was hot. Fifty-third Street was a big heat gun aimed right at me. As soon as I came out onto it, I knew that all the people walking on it had been recruited to form a circle and start stoning me. The old riveting machine behind the Susan face was just as loud and hot as the construction we passed on Lexington Avenue. Bern thoughtfully caught a cab for me. I gave the driver the wrong address.

"Lady," he said, "you told me Riverside Drive."

There we were in front of the gray rock that Tamisan and I lived in eight years ago after I broke up with Bob F and we came home from Morocco. I did a brave thing in leaving Bob. (I.e., I did the necessary thing. By then we were infecting each other with each other's worst vices.) I was brave when I brought Tamisan to this apartment where she had a bedroom of her own from which she could see the river. ("See the river, Tamisan? Those are called the Palisades. Your bed will have a blue cover.") I was brave because I knew then that, though I was damn bad wife material (I was, I was), nevertheless I was a good woman.

"Okay, then, lady," the driver said, "no harm done. I get absent-minded myself sometimes, even. Just tell me the *right* address, I take you there."

No, damn it. I would get out here and walk home. I paid him off. But I snagged my hose getting out of the cab. It is ghastly to be forty-one fucking years old and snag your hose when you have absolutely nothing else left.

The information my dear Bern had given me at lunch was like one of those things they harpoon whales with. It doesn't hurt a bit more than the old-fashioned blade on the way in but there happens to be an explosive attached that goes off a little while later. ("See the parallel, Susan? See, see? The old meat felt good when they put it in you, but even though you read *The Scarlet Letter* you wouldn't admit it would do the same things to the insides of your life that it did to poor Hester in the novel.")

Before I had walked halfway home I knew the real reason Bern hadn't kept his date (date! Mama made it for her!) with Tamisan. They are wise, the Jews, and have been warned when the angel of death is approaching. She wasn't going to clasp him because she was hot. She was going to take his balls off or any man's who approached her in her tantrum. And would have known how to do it, too—probably by degradations of herself, since she knows so well that her best means of hurting others is damaging herself. However he knew that, he knew it. He put his mark on the door so my angel left him alone. And sure enough, our nice lunch had to be nice. It was his feast of the Passover.

I got the message. Found again no way to square it with the appearance of Tamisan still literally sleeping her undrugged sleep, rosy and innocent in her own bed with blue sheets when I came into the apartment. Obviously, with great truths brought down to me from Sinai, I was in no shape to work, or read or even think for the rest of the afternoon. All you can do with the tables of the law is stare at them, admit them, get drunk in front of them and smoke cigarettes relentlessly.

It was so rough that I put both *Madame Butterfly* and the *Kindertotenlieder* on the record player. They might as well have been *The Merry Widow* for all the good they did my mood. But when they had played through two or three times, Tamisan came running out of her bedroom and jerked the playing arm and needle across the Mahler record with a very expressive sound of scratching.

"You were playing them at me!" she said. "If you've got something to say, why can't you put it in honest words?"

"Why can't *I* talk to *you*? I've done nothing else for all these years. It's you who always leave the crucial things out when you're pretending to be frank. Always."

With an abominable sigh of patience she said, "If I have, in my negligence, omitted any *dee*tail of my recent scandalous behavior I am at your disposal now to fill it in. Though it bores me, frankly. What would you like to know? What? Give me a clue."

"Never mind."

"See? I offer to bare my sordid soul and there are no takers. I'll buy you a new record. Do you want to know who called while you were out? Fiona Trebbel called."

I declared I simply could not speak to Fiona in my low state.

"Oh," said Tamisan, "you don't have to. She wanted to talk to *me*. She wants me to meet her at the Behn Gallery tomorrow and have lunch with her and Mrs. Burke. Why is Fiona after me?"

"Like the rest of us, she's incredulous. She can't believe what appears to be the truth about you."

"I think she's trying to get me and Jason back together. Mama, that mustn't happen. I'm not good for him. I'm too much. I will *not* come between him and his father, who at least knew what I was. Jason and I have something immortal between us anyhow, because of the druid things we did and the way our stars are. We don't have to be in proximity just because we love each other."

But still the brat was humbled, softened by Fiona's call.

"You know," she said, "Fiona's the one I'd be like if I were rich. She's got the right relationship with men. But why don't they all leave me alone?"

I said what I still have to say. "Because you're precious."

"Mmmmm."

"That's what makes you able to do so much damage. If you'd simply concentrate on being bad you couldn't dent any of our skins."

"I've thought of that," she said—as if getting ready to stir the witch's brew again, deeply calculating how much goodness to stir in to make it truly lethal.

Chapter 12

"You've lived so many lives, Grandpa," said Monica.

"What brought that up?"

"I don't know," she said. She was his only breakfast companion this morning. His question did not bother her, but it stopped her. Pondering, she sat in a moment suspended from eternity. Her thin, tanned arms and the fingers that held her grapefruit spoon were immobile as those of a Dresden figurine as she tried to prepare a worthy answer to his irrelevant question.

He marveled that she truly did not know what secret currents of sleep had prepared her utterance. It was a morning thought, a gift vagrant and intangible as the touch of breeze on his cheek or some unprecedented color that the ocean shows when accidents of wind and sun stir it to quiet rapture. "I don't know why I thought of it now," she answered solemnly. "Fiona showed me a scrapbook of you in Europe when you were married to Grandmother Sorenson. Before Daddy was born. You've had so many good women . . ." She punched the spoon decisively into her grapefruit and took the juicy pulp into her mouth, narrowing her eyes at the taste.

"I have, huh? Well, where've they all gone?"

"Oh, we're still mostly *around*," the sprite said. "I think Grandmother Sorenson still cares about you though you never go see her. And I'm right here. And Fiona . . ."

"Waaal then . . . Waaaal then, I better live up to you all."

He had had more lives than two cats. There were lives lived in letters. Lives lived in photographs. In public reputation. In his sons' lives. Of course there were lives lived in wood, plaster and paint. In terminated marriages. In scrapbooks, too, not to mention other books more scholarly.

There were all these lives, see? But what about his *own* life? The life that refused to identify itself with any of these others to which there was objective and passionate testimony. It seemed to persist, furtive as a rat in the spacious complexity of a cathedral, scampering the lonely vastness of the interior when the worshipers had gone home, scavenging crumbs of communion bread, nibbling the votive candles and chewing the salt from vestments and rosaries when there was nothing more nourishing to be found.

After he had done his best to live up to the existing world around him, there was still that furtive life of his own, gone to hiding in some cranny or burrow under the filigreed vaulting and the well-trodden floor.

Mine . . .

These days as he went about purging his studio, fussily trying to eliminate all the excesses that had distracted him, it seemed to him sometimes he was literally expecting to find a rat in some cupboard or behind a stack of canvases, or even—cunningly—crouched in some jar or tin where he had mixed paint. And when he saw its beady eyes returning his gaze through whatever ultimate camouflage its instinct exploited, he must hope in that instant before it fled again to a further refuge that rat's eye or rat's grin would signal what the hell he was supposed to do now. The rat might know. He didn't.

Only a few days ago he had told Stan and Marian Burke he was headed for the showers after rounding third base. For once in his life—and high time—Dean Goss had been leaving well enough alone. Was rocking no more boats. Was keeping his genius in his pants. Was content to go on like a staunch craftsman, producing, in this assembly line, the artifacts of paint and plaster at which all the world marveled and for which they paid so much.

The hell he was.

He had turned third base, galloped for the showers and, when he opened the locker-room door, discovered that it opened on a wilderness opening on a wilderness. Those were not showers running comfortably. The sounds of primitive waterfalls only, gushing among dry stones and artificial foliage. The sound of water tormenting him where there was nothing to moisten his lips.

The hell he was content with any of these lives he was said to have lived. They were still mostly *around,* those lives, like the good women Monica reminded him of. They were too much around. The bustle of active human life kept the rat in hiding, and the rat was thirsting.

Only, for an instant, when that wild girl of Jason's snatched his glasses and disappeared in a burst of light and sundown color, he had supposed that his eyes and the rat's eyes had seen the same thing. Had been, for that second, the same greedy pair of eyes, dazzled with the same vision of woman that he was trying to coax onto his new canvases.

Lives lived in photographs . . .

The photographs he and Fiona had taken before this last purging and scraping of his big canvases turned out very well. Too well. Mercilessly well. They were prophetic in some disturbing way that he had no intention of interpreting.

"They ought to be part of Susan's book," Fiona thought.

"They'll do *instead* of a book," Goss said grimly. The photographs that showed him amid the monumental blank surfaces of the canvases made him look *nobler* than what Susan Vail knew of him.

In the glossy black and white, the barren canvases looked like the tables of the law before God had deigned to inscribe anything on them. In black and white Goss looked like a noble, vacuous Moses in an age that had outlived its interest in any laws he might bring to it.

The photos showed the artist purified of his quirks and hesitations. They made it seem as if his canvases were blank because of some decision on his part. They showed none of the terrors that had been unleashed to yip around his bearish flanks by Tamisan Vail's shenanigans and her apparently vengeful treatment of the innocent Jason. Ah, she had to know Jason very

239

well to know how vulnerably he was placed in the middle, catching it from both sides.

The photos also—coquettishly; as tauntingly as the vanished girl herself—made his false start look better than it had been. Goddamn them! Looking at the photos snapped before he started to scrape his canvases tormented him because they showed so powerfully what he had meant to do, what he might have done. The thing he had tried to capture was alive. No doubt of that. It was carrying on a malicious flirtation with him through these photos, like a woman keeping her distance but unwilling to let her suitor off the string.

"How elegant!" he said, fingering the photographs, despising the whole deceptive medium of photography. Servile, whorish, utterly shameless—photography was nevertheless an irrefutable testimony that somewhere and somehow reality could be rendered to the eye. It was another of the technological bribes that kept one running in pursuit of a constantly receding horizon.

He resented the photos, but he did not tear them up as part of his strict house cleaning. It did not seem worth the trouble. They would not bleed or weep as the images on canvas had done when he wiped them out.

He made his studio unbearably neat, then deserted it, hanging out in the library of the mansion like an adolescent hanging around a telephone waiting for a miraculous summons from a plump cheerleader. He pulled down dozens and hundreds of books of paintings, scanning modes from the decorations of Norwegian stave churches to Russian icons, Coptic burial portraits and Japanese pillow art, looking for clues to the vision that had fled.

Monica brought him a drawing she had made. She had stripped and posed in front of a full-length mirror in her room. The drawing was stiff and heavily labored. It showed her with a pencil in her left hand though she was right-handed. Her hair was stiff as that of a priestess in a Babylonian frieze. Yet there was something poignantly, yearningly alive in her rendition of the just budding breasts, limbs that were still cylindrical, and the very wide open eyes.

Most poignant of all when he realized it was brought as an offering, an offering of help in a distress that should have been altogether secret from her since it was so mysterious even to himself.

He waved the drawing in grandfatherly pride. "It's like some of those splendiferous paintings Munch made of young girls," he crowed flatteringly.

She nodded, totally unconcerned with flattery. "I'll . . . if you want, while I'm here, I'll pose for you." He had painted gay, impromptu souvenirs of her in years past. She meant something different now.

"In the . . . buff?"

She nodded again and licked her lips nervously.

Because he didn't know how to answer, she said quickly, "I'm pubescent and that's an age of a woman, too. You might not be so familiar with it as . . . you might have to be, I thought."

Then it dawned fully on him that she had nerved herself for this as for a martyrdom, a costly charity that she wouldn't even offer for his sake but only for the sake of those powers he was supposed to serve.

"I don't reckon I am familiar enough, sweetheart. I'd certainly like to take you up on it. But lifetimes aren't big enough to do everything we ought to do. Right now, you see, I'm trying to concentrate myself on an idea—one single idea, you see—that's trying to come clear in my head. I can't afford too many distractions."

He saw the gust of relief transfigure her. She sighed like a penitent absolved from sin. And went on nodding. "You can keep my drawing, anyway, if it's useful to you," she said.

"Useful?"

"Fiona says you're right on the brink and none of us can tell what ways we might contribute."

"You hang around with her gossiping about me," he teased.

"No. Naturally we discuss your well-being."

"Brink of what? You gossips want to contribute to my downfall."

"Of some great discovery."

"Like Edison discovered the light bulb? Like penicillin or the atomic bomb?"

"Of . . . *it*," she said reproachfully. If it wasn't discovered yet, how could she be expected to name it?

And then Jason came with the news that Tamisan Vail, at least, had been discovered. "I caught up with her," he said dispassionately. "There was never any reason to worry about her. She's okay and I'm okay. It's all over. I won't see her any more, I guess."

"That doesn't tell me very much."

"No, it doesn't."

"And it's not exactly my business."

"In some ways . . . everything is. I know you wanted it to come out . . . happily, I guess. Next best is just forget about it, right?"

If "next best" was good enough for any of them, Dean Goss would not have scraped the lovely paint from his canvases and prepared to start over. He could feel the rat's feet of anger roaming the nerves in his neck and the muscles around his elbows. How humiliating to admit he had expected Jason to bring the girl back—on almost any terms. Only that would have satisfied his superstitions, given him the confidence to begin on his canvases again. Begin to breathe the thin air past the brink.

Using only one third of the breath gathered in his big chest, he said, "Are *you* saying it is all over? Or is that what she says?"

"Both of us," Jason said, evidently holding most of his breath too. "We know it's over. Tamisan and I know the same things. It's true we're terribly alike."

"Then . . . ! Goddamn it! Then hold onto her!"

"I am," Jason said maddeningly. *"Nunc manet in te.* Now she lives in me. I keep her in my mind." Oh, goddamn his sweet smile, all the sweeter when he had transformed that succulent, spreadable, odiferous body into an abstract, ideal vulture to gnaw at his gut. Only the beak reminds me I'm alive, said his renouncing smile. Vulture, rat—what difference does it make what eats us? The vulture was sweet to Prometheus, wasn't it? His indispensable pet. . . . Dean Goss had known vulture keepers. Quite a few of them. And some of them were the best people and lived longest. Like Maggie, though, Jason had always spoiled the pets of his childhood by feeding them as much as they could gorge down. The vulture keepers who lived their lives out learned how to ration the horror and the pain.

"Whatever you thought, it wasn't just getting my rocks off with her," Jason said. "You didn't know her well enough to find what a kooky, fine head she's got. It wasn't the head, either. It's *spirit,* if you happen to believe in such things. For me she'll always be the symbol of . . ."

"Fuck symbols!" Goss snapped. Anyone who prattled about symbols was apt to begin talking about "principles" and then "taste." As an artist, purely as an artist, he had learned that neither principles nor taste worked when the chips were down. They produced symbols instead of the real thing.

"I know you can't eat them either," Jason said, giving his father a comforting slap on the shoulder, commiserating with him, showing that from his awful aloofness he could still understand the pain of those who couldn't let go. His father had no more use for commiseration than for inedible, unfuckable symbols.

It was unjust as a breach of natural law that now, when the boy's undoubted anguish was frozen, Jason should remind him more of Maggie than at any time since her death. Being with Jason now was like being with Maggie those last days in the hospital when she was perfectly anesthetized. You had to thank God she was not conscious of the signals of pain. You had to curse God, knowing the pain was there, perfect, undiminished by the blockage of drug in the nerves. Pain—royal and unperturbed, waiting for the roads to be cleared so its hideous chariots can ride out again.

Perhaps the worst of his frustration, the burning point that glowed at the back of his mind, was knowing that Jason knew the pain was shared between them and was trying to spare him.

"I went on like a fool making too many assumptions, not asking enough questions," Jason said. "Didn't know what I've always wanted to know about girls and been afraid to ask. It was a can of worms. Too many lies to count finally. You might as well know. I caught her with a man. . . ."

"I will beat the shit out of him," the original Goss said.

"The precise truth is I found her after she'd been with someone else. I beat her up."

"That's better. It is the women who always cause the trouble. They can't help it, though. But they must be reminded to guard and take care of that precious thing. They must only be beaten within an *inch* of their lives. Restraint is important. As important as storm. But nothing in this world is taken except by storm."

Bluster would not help, nor did Dean Goss suppose it could do more than give him delay until the real trouble was more fully exposed. It was like putting on a bad patch of color so his offended eye would be obliged to discover another painterly tactic of resolution.

"I don't care if you found her fucking a platoon of Marines," he thundered. "Are we jocks? Sinclair Lewis characters? Executives? Listen, there are more ways for women to be troublesome than by going down on their backs. I have loved more women than one. Consider Eileen Forbes. The madwoman. The poet. I must have loved her or I wouldn't have burned my hand for her. Exhibit A!" He waved his maimed hand before Jason's indolent eyes. "Evidence of love! Lately I've dreamed of her and thought of her. She's in what I am trying to paint now. I'm sorry I lost my hand, but what gives me satisfaction is that I tried to hold onto her. I went as far as she—and they go so far. Once I held her down in a bathtub and pissed on her. I am telling the truth. Even that was an effort to hold onto her."

Jason said, "If your point is that it was all right to hit Tamisan, you're wrong."

"Point? The point is that the memory of such anger is all that's left of the love I had for another woman who's gone from me. If that were gone, then nothing, nothing at all. It was in a chipped white tub. We were in some small town near Guadalajara, traveling. Not much light came in on us from the bedroom behind. A bulb on the end of a cord. And there were flies.

I twisted her arm to force her down. But then all at once she submitted and looked like an Umbrian saint praying for our salvation as she knelt. I pissed on her and that is good. It fixes the image and makes it last. Good, I say, because something has to last so I can tell you not to be driven off by some *little incident*. You say you know the same things and I believe you, so . . ."

"The Marines," Jason said out of his listening meditation. "Even if I didn't mind them, I might not get a turn. I'm not quick."

His flippancy was no more convincing than his sober reasoning. And both were as transparent to his father's eyes. If someone had brought his boy to him castrated and still bleeding from the knife, he would have raised both fists at once and pounded the earth out of its course and sent it reeling into the incinerating sun. There was no visible blood to give him excuse for such direct action. There was no discernible villain. He was only an artist, where a god of subtlety and power was needed.

Being that, he had best get on with art's impotent routines. One morning, working from memory, he painted another version of the watercolor Tamisan had shredded. He called Jason to come have a look at it.

"Better than the original," Jason said. "Something's been added! You know Strickland made some fascinating points, the night he was here, about how it fits into art history and the long tradition of nudes outdoors. Susan might find that very useful for her book if it could be reconstructed. When will you be in touch with her again? She's not to blame, you know, for any of all this."

Fuck art historians. Fuck fascinating points. Books. Susan. He had, he realized, done the watercolor over with the explicit intent of showing his youngest son that of course and to be sure it was no trick at all to put Humpty Dumpty together again. "I enjoyed having Susan here," he said. "It wouldn't be the same if she came back now. Let bygones be bygones. Where is it now, the visionary gleam . . . splendor in the grass . . .

treason is but trusted like the fox. . . . Best never to look back when love's first careless rapture's faded, my boy. . . ."

He knew by heart—however much he might mumble them —the famous quotes that said the golden bowls and the silver chords are irreparable, once shattered, once cut. What his heart knew by heart was another matter. It also quoted, saying, "What thou lovest well, remains."

He said, "Jason, it doesn't look like I'm doing anything these days. But I'm really winding up to lunge. Figures *will* appear on those canvases. The three I'm going to paint came from the three girls in the watercolor. No doubt about that. You said that was what you wanted, Jason, when I painted it. I'm trying to get the message you and—what's her name? Tamisan—wanted me to get. I'm slow to learn. I remember, though, every word she said to me the day I scared her."

"She told Jean Simons you tried to screw her."

If that was intended as a bombshell by Jason, it might as well not have been thrown. Goss came on past it, relentless as a tank. "She said you were religious. Never mind how eloquent she was. Or was not. I am on this earth to hear and see, not to criticize punctuation. If I am too slow to hear . . . then I am too slow to hear. But I am not so stiff-necked that I will not search to find what anyone at all has really meant. You're not the typical kids of your generation. Wait . . . ! Hush . . . ! No one at all is typical in things that count. I know that, love. We live and die one by one. Praise be. Bit by bit I'm trying to grasp what she meant. For my sake as much as yours. Hers. I believe the two of you were religious, which is better than having a religion. I haven't heard the high points of your meditations. I need them. I want to follow. I'm trying to turn myself around. You were right that my painting had turned into a hoax."

"I never said . . ."

But he saw he had caught Jason in a half lie at least and that gave him leverage. He went on, "At my weight and age it is not easy to turn around. I need you. Don't desert me now."

It was emotional blackmail of the crudest sort. Crude is

crude, but sometimes crude is best. It gained him . . . something.

He had found a thin spot, at least, in Jason's armor. "You already know everything we got to in our meditations," Jason said mournfully. "The difference is, you earned it. You learned it from a lifetime as an artist."

It was better for Jason to grieve about his own lack of accomplishment than to pretend it didn't matter. But yet it was a mistake to find any point where the armor was thin. It put Jason on guard and he wriggled like a caught eel. "Don't you see where I've got to, Dad? I'm drifting where there aren't any answers. All there is is facts. Who cares? I want *not* to understand. Not to understand. Not to understand."

His father saw it was not the girl's lies that had bled Jason or the world's lies, either. The boy had lied to himself from cowardice and the self cannot forgive that.

Knowing that, he knew the worst. That was some progress. "Anyone honestly religious believes in grace first of all, Jason."

"What do you believe in?"

"Work," Dean Goss said. Meaning art, which is not the same thing as grace, as Jason would know as well as or better than he. It is not even the same thing as prayer, which is confident that grace abounds. But in work, as he had once told Susan Vail and might tell others, there is a hope of discovering grace by surprise.

And if he could not be religious, he was overwhelmingly superstitious, as artists become with the advance of years. Superstition, he thought, was the causeway that primitives—like himself—started building into the ocean, hoping it would justify itself by reaching an island sometime. And now, taking Jason's predicament as his own, he laid on the line the mightiest and most awesome of his superstitions. He believed, with the force of nearly seventy unsatisfied years riding his back, that the challenge of his three canvases was the same challenge that Jason's life had come to be. To find the paintings was to find Jason, and a way for him to live. To lose . . .

He did not intend to lose.

He cheated and stole. He sneaked Monica's little drawing of her pubescent state into his pristine studio. He pinned it up on one of the big partitions—probably about where his well-loved Cézanne had hung before his house-cleaning frenzy started. He wasn't sure where things had been before. He had tried to erase the top layers of his mind as he went about cleaning up.

He tried to see something in the drawing that was not his charitable, learned granddaughter. Tried with incestuous lust to see the bestial and angelic aspects of womanhood she might have surmised behind her wide, earnest gaze in the mirror. He saw a shamed and shameful nakedness he would have been honor-bound not to notice if she had come in her skin to pose for him.

I oughtn't look, he thought.

With that realization, he knew he had made the right beginning.

Then he squeezed out some ivory black from a pound tube. With a two-inch bristle brush and a lightly thinned mix of the ivory black and raw sienna that seemed demanded—with exactly four sweeping contacts of the brush to the linen—he scrubbed a hieroglyphic shape onto the middle one of the three canvases. It glared at him like the desecration on a church door, scrawled by hard-breathing boys.

So he knew he had moved from the right beginning to the right second step. And he called Jason to see what he had painted.

"I guess you want me to laugh," Jason said when he saw what his father had done. The crude design scribbled on the middle canvas certainly warranted no response better than laughter. It was an ovoid shape with a single indented cleft to break its bulging contour, the shape of a toy balloon dented by the pressure of a clutching finger, maybe. All you could say of its startling simplicity was that it was unquestionably ribald. A bit of graffiti worthy of a toilet wall.

"Laughing wouldn't hurt," his father said, snorting lewdly at what he had contrived.

"I'm sorry if I've gone around looking depressed. Ha-ha then. It's undoubtedly female, whatever else it is. Ha-ha." It is very hard for the body not to mimic yawns or truly uncontrollable laughter, and it was his father's mirth, not what he saw, that made Jason chuckle. "It's got authority."

"Primitive authority . . . like the triad of notes Wagner used to start *The Ring of the Nibelungs,*" Goss declared amid wheezes. "It's that fundamental. Everything from here on is variation. I've got it whipped, Jason!"

"I knew you'd find a way."

"There *is* a way. That's all we need to know on earth." Even as he uttered this confident pronouncement Goss was back at his palette dumping a can of unbleached titanium on its surface. He stirred a soupy puddle of eggshell-colored paint and with this began to cover the talismanic design he had started with. "I have to get it out of sight before anyone else sees it. Even Fiona would say I'd gone too crazy this time. And I don't have time for psychoanalysis. No doubt psychiatry is helpful for those who want it. Like basket weaving. Collecting butterflies. Doing sandpaper wood carvings. Honey, it would take fifty years for a psychiatrist to catch up to us and cure what we can handle in forty-five. . . ."

Drunk with his confidence that he had made the necessary start on the paintings, he called Susan the next day. If he could master those vixen canvases, surely mortal women would fall like ripe wheat bending in the wind of truth on which he rode.

"Susan. We need you back here. You and Tamisan. To put it bluntly, I'm concerned about our young people. Jason is off in the clouds somewhere. A zombie. Is it true that he struck the girl? Bad business. Bad. Out of delicacy I shouldn't ask, but has she shown any disposition to put that unpleasantness behind her? You know they are very much alike. One's as stubborn as the other. Yet it seems to me, honey, that it's your responsibility as much as mine to hasten the inevitable. Don't you agree they should work out this misunderstanding instead of childishly not speaking to one another?"

"I don't know," Susan said.

"Here's a plan that occurred to me as I slept. Vidal should be coming back here soon. He's always sought a *theme* for the definitive documentary on me as I am and who I am. Here is the story: We'll put the girls to posing again in the rose garden. See the part for Tamisan? Again she'll be offended and destroy the watercolor. Your own creative imagination will help us shape up the story from that point. You can write the happy ending. Won't that appeal to your girl? The two of you must come at once. Today."

"No."

"My idea for the film is no good?" he asked incredulously.

"Oh, it's enchanting. You have so many good ideas." He heard her take a staunch, determined breath. "I'm doing my best with what's already started. My book. Yours. Whosever it is. My editor has faith in what I've done so far. But—that's enough. No, I'm not going to bring Tamisan back out there. I don't know who is to blame for all that happened. Someone was too rich for someone's blood in the combination we made. It mustn't ever happen again. I've wept my pints over Jason and Tamisan. It's clear she's not good for him."

He hung up the phone trembling with rage at yet another betrayal by the pettiness of Susan Vail. No *doubt* she was a reasonable woman. No doubt she cared about both the young people. Around, above, below, behind the reasonable façades of her liberal mentality—*and of all those New Yorkers,* he thought —swarmed the harpies, vultures and other winged abominations they didn't have a name for any more. If Jason went to pieces now, Susan, too, would probably advise psychiatric care. . . .

He swam for an hour from the beach to cool his head. Then he called Susan back.

"Give up the notion you're writing about me! I forbid you to publish anything. I direct you to return all notes of anything I said to you. Do you understand plain English? If you make a move to publish anywhere, I swear I'll have my lawyers on you and you will never publish any of your sentimental swill as long as you live. You know nothing about me. Do you admit that?"

He thought she was either choking with sobs or laughing out loud after he had delivered his ultimatum. The sounds were very eerie.

In a book of reproductions, among colored reproductions of pre-Colombian art, he found some photos of a stone wall the Incas had built high in the mountains at Sacsahuamán. It apparently sat disconnectedly in a high valley, walling off nothing from nothing, though the huge, faintly curved stones were exquisitely fitted. It seemed a discovery that would be of use to him in his paintings of woman, but he could not guess at what point he would be ready to fit it in.

"I can't work," he said to Fiona.

"You will again."

"Jason's life is spoiled."

"No, it isn't," she said. "I've watched him with Monica. He's so gentle, considerate. He's teaching her things and feeling rewarded by it."

"But Monica's a child. He's trying to become one too."

The wind of truth Goss had felt carrying him up was only briefly exhilarating. It was a wind that also swept aloft all sorts of garbage and waste paper. It soiled everything with spatterings and dust. All signs of tranquillity were whipped around like weathervanes, pointing back to where the storm had begun.

251

Jason, it seemed, had plans. "I should have gone to Paris last year," he told his father. He shrugged away the lost months. "Talking to Monica has convinced me I have to go there now. I'll be near her and Vidal. I'll get going. At what? I don't suppose I'd ever want a career as a performing artist. It's time I learned the piano. There are things . . . things have happened to me lately that only make sense musically. If I study music for a few years I might be some good as a composer. Does that sound all right?"

"You'd live with Vidal and Monica?"

"No! I'd want some place to be alone. Don't worry, it wouldn't be like last year. Just a place to sleep alone. I'd be near them."

"If it's what you want . . ."

"I know my weak spots. I don't want you to have to worry about me ever again."

"Well . . . well . . . Yes, you need to go somewhere to harden your heart. *'Dans ce monde il faut que le coeur se brise ou se bronze.'* It has to harden or break."

"I remember your saying that before."

"I've said everything. There's nothing new to say. Yet . . . I don't think I like the saying, even if I used it. Needed it. 'They love not poison that do poison need.' "

He saw Jason's face go far away without becoming smaller in his field of vision. The laws of perspective were no reliable indications of distance.

"It's harsh but it's useful," Jason said. "Like thinking about death. That helps. It's a stimulus, isn't that funny? I want to go because if I saw her again I'd have to face so many questions. Ask, I mean. I want not to understand except in music."

The heart has to harden and it will still break.

"I think you're wise, Jason. We have to use what's given us, and the worst is at least material for our work."

"I think I can learn that from you. I think that if I don't overestimate my strength again, then the things I really am strong in will have a chance to survive. My head is getting clearer every day."

And if it does not break by itself, if it is too hard for anything else to break it, what else can a man do but take a rock in his hand and break it? And when it is whole again, break it again, and when it is whole again, break it.

"I haven't taken it all as hard as you suppose," Jason said. "It's fascinating, really, how many neurotic elements were involved, and then, in chaotic times like these, there are bound to be all sorts of illusions imprinted on the psyche from dislocations that no one has time to trace out. Like, I can see there might be eighty-four, one hundred and twelve different and boring explanations of why she . . . wanted to spoil herself."

"Never ask," Dean Goss said.

"It's really not like a death in the family and I'm not taking it that way. Truly I'm not. It is not like Maggie dying. Mixed up as I may be I can still make distinctions of that sort. It's comically different from anyone's dying. In scale."

"I 'spect we've talked about it enough. If we say any more the music of it will disappear too."

And if it won't break finally, when you have hammered on it with stone and then steel, and blasted it and burned it and put it out for the water to erode and the sand blown by the wind to wear away, then you must stand and wait for grace, pure grace, to come along and break it for you. Because it must break.

"I think because I was naïve about the sexual part of it I made interpretations that were just rubbish. Like, you've said sometimes that dreams seem to mean more than they actually do."

"D' I say that?"

"You've said lots. A lot of it's been heard. You've given me a good life. You do that. You gave Maggie a good life, though she would have had one almost as good. So would we all. There's no way we can repay you. You see us through things. You can't carry us all. You're strong. That's the secret for an artist, isn't it? Doesn't it count more than talent or insight?"

And if there is no such thing as grace to break it at last, then you have to make that, too, because it must be broken.

"Well, I don't know," Dean Goss said. "I think sometimes that's it. Another time I wait to see. But now, I think I'll have a nightcap and go to bed. Will you have some whiskey with me?"

"I believe I will," Jason said.

Not his, mine, Goss thought.

It was his own heart he determined to see broken by Jason's pathos. Impudent old narcissist, he had never truly loved anyone at all except by considering them *his*—and when they were his he had loved them inordinately with the full fury of egotism and selfishness. It was *his son's* life that would be dimmed by the dimming of its early promises year by year until Jason was as dry as Godwin. Talents turning into dilettantism; juicy, eager boys turning into male spinsters because the very profusion of their gifts scared them away from life.

It was not in hope but in perverse despair that Goss agreed so smoothly that Jason ought to ease himself over to Paris and drop out of sight. *Heartbreaking,* Goss thought. *Fine . . .*

It would not be failure of lungs or gut that excused him from living. His arms and legs and eyes and even the barrel-sized cave of thorax that seemed to produce laughter of its own accord in the worst of circumstances would go on helplessly serving until somehow his treacherous heart was overcome and said, *Enough.*

Over the waste years, the spoiling of Jason would persuade it to yield.

It was Fiona, really, who would not let them settle for either tragedy or comedy, heartbreak or forgetfulness, madness or insensitivity. She would not intervene directly. She never had. She did not even concern herself with knowing where their fancies and their anguishes might be ranging at any particular time. She kept the house. That it was an extraordinary house, filled and surrounded by extravagances, made no difference as far as her primary intent was concerned.

She intended to have the best for herself and the men she loved.

Her determination in this respect was as simple as her father's had been. For gross old Henry Trebbel the best meant the most expensive, the fastest, the biggest. Horses, houses, women, guns, boats, political influence. His greed was on display. Flagrant. Hers was no less pure for being self-effaced, patient, never opinionated. It was true that most of her life had been vicarious. The marriages, children, fame, even most of the intellectual and creative passions of the Gosses had been enacted beyond the literal boundaries of her experience. If it was vicarious, that was because vicariousness was best for her, a purified version of the American Dream that Henry Trebbel drank straight, like raw whiskey.

Neither Jason nor his father expected her to advise them on matters of the heart. Sooner or later they knew what she wanted, and it counted with them like a law of nature—that is, it had to be obeyed whether or not one knew how.

"I phoned Tamisan," she told Jason. "We had a long chat. I never got the chance to have a long, quiet talk with her while she was here. I don't think that was fair."

"I'm glad you called her."

"Why?"

"Why am I glad? Doesn't that go without saying?"

"I suppose it does. Yes, yes. I suppose it goes without saying. There's no use talking about feelings, is there?"

"I can't trust my feelings. After I hit her, I knew I could have killed her. When I was looking for her I suppose I was glad to think she might be dead. That is true."

"Oh my."

"The thing about her . . ."

"Yes?"

"There's no way for me to protect what I think she is at her best. It doesn't fit into life. She isn't good. She's . . . great."

"Can you say that about a person so young?"

He could, but not as he wanted to say it. "She doesn't have any means to express herself."

"I think she has a very nice voice."

"She tries to get out what's in her. It makes trouble. It makes lies."

"That may be true. She hasn't lied to me. I suppose there was no occasion. I'm sure it will take her time to find . . . a means of expression. You know, dear, I was a very plain girl. Not like your mother. Or some other girls. I thought my homeliness was a terrible lie. I suppose many girls feel there is a goddess in themselves and the goddess ought to show. Everyone should recognize it. Well. I thought that whatever was best in myself would be expressed if I practiced an art. Then, wouldn't people throw up their hands and cover their eyes because they *saw!* Saw what I really was. It didn't happen. Then I think sometimes . . . that your father expresses me. That must be a lie too, one way or the other. I don't suppose there are so many different ways for a woman to express what it means to be a woman. Perhaps someday you'll express what it meant for Tamisan to feel there was—what did you call it? greatness?—inside her when there was nothing of the sort. Or at any rate, no way to express it. We have great faith in your future, Jason," she said, with placid, motherly cruelty. Goading him awake before he froze to death.

"There's nothing I can do now."

"I know," Fiona said. "It will be all right, dear. We must take things as they come along."

She only said to Dean Goss, "I know there's nothing to be done about it now, but I don't think it's fair that Jason's first love should end with a quarrel."

"His second. I agree that nothing should be done. He'll live through it."

"It isn't fair."

Chapter 13

Tamisan Vail had never feared or hated anyone as she hated Dean Goss the night she tore up his painting and ran. No one would ever grasp the magnitude of that rage, because no one had been witness to this scene:

A coltish, eleven-year-old girl and a plump ten-year-old boy come out of the pine woods on a sultry summer day, pushing a red bicycle between them. Tamisan Vail and Livingston (Livvy) Rice.

They ease the bicycle down a slope of sun-killed grass and cones and needles from the trees. It is midafternoon and they are returning to the playground where they got acquainted in the morning recreation program for children of the summer people. There is a softball diamond on the playground. Its chicken-wire backstop slumps in disrepair. Sunflowers are growing from a pile of topsoil that some parent with a truck dumped here in the spring so the ruts in the diamond could be filled in. There is a pole for a tether ball. There are swings and a backboard for basketball practice. There is a small shed used to store athletic equipment. But mostly there is the weedy, ominous air of abandonment and exposure. A threadbare patch of the universe where the shoddiness underneath can be seen with a child's eye.

The boy and the girl push the red bicycle down the dusty channel between home plate and first base. The tires make an irregular track, though their bare feet leave no distinguishable print in the soft dust. "Snake track," Livvy says. Tamisan says, "It *could* be that." There might be a snake or a dragon coming with them out of the silence of the dusty woods.

They sit in the swings suspended from an unpainted crossbar by chains that make a rusty sound while they wind up and then spin in partial rotations as the chains unwind. They have dumped the bicycle on which both of them leaned as they made their way in through the trees from the town road.

"Mama is writing her novel," Tamisan says. "That's why we're in the country this summer. So she can." She examines a new scratch on her leg where her sunburn is turning to bronze. She rubs her toe back and forth in the dust under her swing. She listens for whatever might come following them out of the woods.

"I thought so," Livvy says with the malevolence of one whose lewdest suspicions are confirmed. His family has snickered about Mrs. Vail in the white cottage by the bridge. He bunches his plump legs and with a great kick sets himself swinging. "I had a hamster last winter and took it to school. It died."

"I write mainly poetry. Mama has published one novel already. It was more an artistic than a commercial success. It was well received. The *Times* review compared it to Carson Mc-Cullers, but I suppose she is better. I've started something new this summer, also. Prudence Mayfair. It's about her true psychology. I don't write romantic shit."

Abruptly Livvy puts his feet down to stop his swinging and comes to a jolting halt. He lowers his chin against his plump chest. He seems to be hugging himself. Suddenly he begins to giggle uncontrollably.

"It is crucial to get away from New York," Tamisan says. "It's a rat race and various men distract Mama. This summer I can concentrate on my work. At home I play the piano but here mostly take walks. I like to walk at night and think about the stars. Man is really insignificant."

Girdled by its weeds, the playground seems to have no terrestrial connection with anything she knows to tell her possible friend.

"Mama and I are going to learn every one of the constellations this summer," Tamisan says. "Already I know Cassiopeia and the Swan and the Bear. The stars in them may appear close to each other, but they are not."

It is very, very quiet when she stops talking. The sound of the chains is like the sound of a very far-off place.

"Were most of the children in the program here last year as well?"

"I was," Livvy says.

With men it is important to make conversation on topics that are of interest to them. "I've had three or four hamsters, I suppose. Each one died each time we moved."

She does not hear the sound of chains from Livvy's swing any more. Only her own. He is not moving. Only watching her.

"Mama and I are more like sisters because I don't have a father. I'm a bastard." The word "bastard" is intended to provoke interest, as it has before. Here and now it has an uncanny, buzzing pungency in the midst of silence and the heat. It is like the black, insistent flies hovering by her leg. "We share the same interests in the arts. I suppose I might find a place in the theater, either an actress or something. I adapt to other people's personalities."

She flips her head in a way that makes her hair swing enchantingly around her shoulders. That gets no response from Livvy. He is still sitting exactly still. "I *like* some of the boys in the program. Buzz and the one they call Tom. They're exciting personalities. Everyone likes them, don't they? You're the only boy so far I can confide in."

Out of his profound immobility, Livvy says, "Let me tie you up."

Now she stops swinging and sits facing him with her hands up on the chains. He does not lift his chin, is still staring into the dust at her feet.

"You don't have a rope," she says tentatively.

"I got a rope."

"You didn't bring any."

He balks and will not answer.

"Silly," she says. "That's just make-believe. I don't make-believe any more. I haven't done it all year."

"I *got* a rope. Over behind the shed. Let me tie you up."

She closes her eyes and sees the color the sun turns her lids. "Are you going to tie me in the shed?"

He is already running for the rope. He finds it in the weeds behind the shed. Comes back at a dead run, with his teeth clenched.

Grunting and panting, he ties her to one of the weathered poles that supports the swings. He does a good job, fastening her wrists behind her, then looping the rope around her waist before he puts a final square knot behind the silver-gray wood, out of her reach.

They are both feverish and trembling while he works with the knots. Her mouth goes dry with nameless anticipation. "My feet. Tie them too," she whispers.

He pays no attention to her request. In any case there is no more rope.

Livvy gets on Tamisan's red bicycle.

He rides away down the lane connecting the playground with Krebosset Road. He is pumping very hard in his silent determination. He is riding as if something awful is chasing him. The playground is a bad dream and he is trying to wake. His knees flash like pistons.

He never came back to let her go. By ten that night when her mother and two state troopers with flashlights found her still tied to the swings, she was badly bitten by flies and mosquitoes.

She had known at the moment of release that Susan would not be satisfied without a full explanation. "That goddamn little creep should be whipped. . . ." Her mother's first reaction. Then: "You just stood there and *let* him tie you? Now, sweetie, maybe you thought it was just a game, but that kind of thing can be dangerous. So . . . if there had been an icebox, you'd just have crawled in and let him lock the door? We've talked about that, darling." Then: "You mean . . . you mean he didn't even promise to come back and let you go? That you didn't ask him to? That you never even thought of that until you got thirsty and the bugs . . . ?"

"No. It was a *game*. No, Mama. No. I'm *all right,* so leave me alone, please?"

She would admit any stupidity and then turn and fight to defend it, sobbing or raging, kicking or going to sleep to make her mother believe that stupidity was the end, that there was nothing more to find out.

She would never admit that she had asked Livvy to tie her feet too. Or that she had been glad to see him get away from her on the bicycle he had stolen from her. Why pick on one little fat boy she hardly knew? The hatred, clarifying and rising like a dark star in her mind, was for the entire world, where longings could be so unjustly crushed.

On that night at North Atlantic when she had those freak thoughts about becoming "visible" it had seemed to her she was on the verge of trusting men and letting them trust her.

And then . . . not only had Dean Goss humiliated her, misunderstood her generosity and best thoughts. He was going to go for the bod. She had no doubt of that. One minute more and he'd have been opening her clothes. Balling her right there on his studio floor to show her again what she was good for and all she was ever going to be good for. It had not been a pure lie for her to tell Jean Simons what the old man had done. It was a matter of unforgettable truth that she was fighting off an orgasm when she snatched his glasses and hurled them.

How much of the rest of what she had done until Jason caught up with her was, as they said, a matter for future historians to ponder. It was not *all* lies. On that feeble ground she had to stand as best she could until Gosses forgot her and quit harassing.

It was true, for instance, that she had only called Sandler's number intending to let him hear his share of her murderous feelings. Next to Dean Goss, she hated and feared Sandler most, because in another, sick way he'd made her visible too. Quite visible and for quite a sick, long time, if you cared to be specific. Which she would also leave to future historians. Among them Janis Ward, who had probably tipped off Jason where to catch her, and now would probably try to stay in good by spilling more heavy information about Sandler and his juvenile sex slave. Ah, the historians of the future would be lurider than anything seen so far.

It was true (she thought now it was true; she thought it could be true; she thought the truth couldn't always stand much penetrating corss-examination, and so be it) she had meant to get even with everybody by balling Bern Whitestar or who was available. At the peak of her fury she had been determined to make herself invisible again among people who didn't give a damn who she was. Who wouldn't use the bod as a damn microscope to peer through while they watched her soul like a crawling insect. An insect with glue on its feet that it kept rubbing together and waving in the air trying to clean the glue off.

She had better not try to explain such topsy-turvy motives to anyone. Or why, when it came right down to the nutty core of truth, there had been that what you might call spontaneous orgy that wrecked up Janis' apartment.

It might *not* have happened as easily as, in fact, it *had* happened. She thought it would not have happened if Janis had not had on her wall a reproduction of a Dean Goss painting.

Wh-wh-wh-wh-whaaaaaTTTTT?

Sure. Try making anyone believe that. But, finding it there—where she had seen it before without paying too much attention, except to know whose it was, of course—had made her mad all over again. As if she was being followed and spied on by the steel-rimmed glasses she thought she had escaped for good.

The picture was a little two-dollar reproduction from Marlboro bookstore, though nicely framed. Count on Janis for taking good care of her cheap treasures.

Weird, heavy colors. Heavy ochers and morbid violets and greens darker than just a song at twilight when the lights are low. There didn't seem to be any light coming into the painted room from outside, though there was a moon like in the Two of Swords of the Tarot deck visible through the window. The somber colors vibrated to produce their own kind of light, like the light that goes on in the head when you're high. A male figure, propped on one arm, leaned over the sleeping figure of a woman lying like stone in the bed beside him. A sharp-nosed dog slept at the woman's feet.

It's me, she had thought. He's got me in there between the dog and the man. And then she thought, He doesn't know which is dog and which is woman. Then she thought, And neither do I.

And that was why . . . ?

No, no, no, no. There really was no way to explain, beyond what she had already said to poor, beautiful Jason, whom she was not going to dump on with any more explanations, ever, or in any other ways.

The orgy had happened because lonesome Hubert had happened to pick up the Bell telephone at the precise instant one heavy star was crossing the port bows of another star just as heavy. A really trained astrologer would be more useful here than a future historian.

And what the stars wanted was okay. By definition. At least while the orgy had been happening, Tamisan Vail could not be accused of not living up to her full potential. She was a damn good woman as long as she was being simply female, like a sow. Pure body.

She would never see her fellow orgiers again now that the stars had neatly got by each other. For the sheer acrobatics of it she had no guilt at all. They had been sincere. Merry, but sincere. She too. There's nothing like a cock in your mouth to make you feel sincere. Hubert's enormous cock and his rhythm of attack had been undeniably a sincere tribute to what she had been brought to admit she was. Ivan, chewing on her nipples and standing barefoot on her ankles while he cheered her masturbation, had been a sincere performer. To say the least and not to speak of inspiration when you didn't need the term. To say all that had to be said. Ivan (last name unknown and never to rise from the subconscious because she didn't have one; whatever conscious she had was all one thing or the other; she never believed in the trinity) dragging her by the ears and pushing her face down to lick the cunt of the girl whose name she had also let slip. That was a warm thing to remember when she was falling asleep in her own bed at Mama's.

Ivan was clever. At one point she had led him by the hand to look at the Goss reproduction on Janis' wall. All she said to him was, "See?"

Something grave, awed and sincere to the eightieth power had passed over his prematurely wrinkled and freckled brow and she guessed that he saw what she had seen. Something heavy and fateful as the passing of stars. But he only said, merrily, "I see a dog in the manger. Permit me. I wish to put my dog in thy manger."

Later in that eclipse-lighted night he cheered his companions on by shouting: "Now we are living with the gods!"

She still believed he was right. Somehow pricks and cunts were always right in themselves, as much as gods were likely to be. Or pigs or dogs for that matter.

But let someone glimpse the visible pig, the visible dog, and the gods turned nastier than humans probably ever thought of being. And crueler. And not at all concerned about whom they butchered, flayed, burned, crushed, froze.

Which was why she would spare Jason forever and forever and forever. Oh, she was the Pharaoh's daughter and she had found him in the bulrushes, all pink and white, and it was only partly his prick she was talking about when she told him so.

And since she was human, she knew the only way to spare him the nastiness of the gods when they turned was to put him back in his floating cradle and let the parted bulrushes close again like a curtain, hiding his face from hers and hers from his, forever and forever.

Bullshit! There was no sister Miriam, for one thing, to wait and see if someone else would happen along to gather up cradle and all. She had not believed that bullshit since Livvy Rice tied her to the swings (like the Hanged Man in the Tarot; that was her card all right, thenk yew!).

But there was water for the cradle to rock and float in. There was forever, forever, forever.

There was sleep. Between the man and the dog, sleep was allowed her. That's what the picture said.

From sleep she could wake up forgetful and then—why not?—go on to become a credit to her sex and an asset to society. Why shouldn't she become a teacher like Janis? Grow a hump on her back and become an art historian. Maximal utilization of recent illuminating experiences among the masters.

Credit or not, as long as she stayed sleepy and loose, she would not mess up Mama's projects any more. It was for Susan's sake that she agreed to meet Fiona at the Behn Gallery. If there was one person in the world Tamisan did not want to know any more about her, it was Fiona.

"This is Jason's niece," Fiona said. Monica Goss put her small hand out to Tamisan with a frown like Jason's. "I think you met Marian Burke at North Atlantic the other evening."

"We didn't have a chance to be introduced," Mrs. Burke said. She shook hands with Tamisan too. "I saw a splendid painting of you and two other girls that evening. How nice to see you again in the flesh."

"I'm always in the flesh," Tamisan said. Mrs. Burke laughed as if this might be an intentional witticism. She stopped laughing as if it might have more than one intention. I can't open my mouth without sounding sly, Tamisan thought.

It comforted her, though, that Fiona had not come alone to meet her. The small talk of women and children at lunch might be contemptible and it might make her restless, but it was better than inquisition about what in heaven's name she thought she'd been up to.

Tamisan had got to the Behn Gallery ahead of them, almost demurely dressed for once. They had found her loitering in one of the upstairs rooms because one of the attendants had told her there were some Goss paintings displayed there for the summer. She had found three. The biggest of them, in the center of the wall, was the original of the one that hung in reproduction on Janis' wall. At least we didn't break that, Tamisan thought, spooked nevertheless to come here and confront what you might call a witness to her depravity.

The eyes of the man in the painting were lowered gravely to the body of the sleeping woman. But somehow there seemed to be more eyes in or about the painting than you'd guess from counting the heads in it.

As they all four stood in its ambience, Monica said, "Grandpa doesn't paint that way any more." The way she said it sounded protective of her grandpa and Tamisan liked her for that.

"This is good enough for me," she said.

265

"I like it very much," Monica said. "I like the dog in it, though I don't know why it's there. I like best that he's painted so many different ways."

Tamisan said, "What makes it for me is the man staying awake to keep watch. Someone has to. And . . ." She shut her mouth for fear of sounding sly again.

"Go on," Fiona urged.

"It's . . . like a holy family sheltered for the night on a journey they'll have to begin again next day. They're tired but they're stubborn. They're some kind of exiles. Maybe they deserve to be. The woman is sleeping for both. Or the baby." She stopped again, wondering why her mouth flapped out the word "baby" when there was no child to be seen there. "The dog's asleep because the others need his strength too. . . ."

"Keep going," Fiona said with a fixed smile on her heavily lipsticked mouth. So much lipstick looked eccentric on her. It had so little to do with her square face and muscular body, or her well-tanned skin on which big freckles floated like spots on a frog.

Tamisan shook her head as if she had already given too much away.

"The man who stays awake has got to be Grandpa," Monica said. "I keep seeing him in his paintings. I'm hard to fool. He'll never say whether I'm right or not. I think you're right, Tamisan. About the dog, too. He says in his new paintings the animal will be a rat."

"Oh-oh," said Marian Burke.

"Does he want me to pose for him again?" Tamisan asked.

It turned out that they had met here before going to lunch because there were some other Goss paintings, not on the walls but in Bruce Behn's office. There seemed to be some question whether they were forgeries, and Fiona had been asked for her opinion. It seemed that Dean Goss was not always to be relied on when asked about his past work. In a phone conversation he had told his dealer these paintings could not be his. *Could* not. Period.

"He has lapses of memory," Behn said to Mrs. Burke. "He takes whims."

"He's too busy to bother," Fiona said.

Bruce Behn was hardly taller than Monica. He was a beautiful old toy of a man. His white hair was delicate as the fibers from a milkweed pod. His eyes had the translucent shine of opals. His skin was rosy silk and he seemed to hold the precious collection of his body in the thin arms that were habitually folded across his chest.

"Vidal is convinced they are authentic," Behn said, in a voice that sounded like distant chamber music. "His friend, however, has a financial interest in them. The documentation Mr. Sandler was able to provide is not quite enough for certainty. There's a hiatus of time when no one is sure who owned them or where they were—assuming they are genuine, of course."

When she heard Sandler's name, there was a flickering instant when Tamisan thought it was her own authenticity that was being reviewed. No. But authenticity, not how good they were, was the prime question, because Mrs. Burke had a notion they ought to be purchased promptly by a museum she had something to do with.

Here they were, now, in Behn's office apartment at the back of the gallery, among the bronzes, icons, rare books, prints and paintings of Behn's personal collection. One of the framed paintings was sitting in a dark leather chair, like a queen of summer enthroned. The other was on an easel beside it.

"They are the real thing, aren't they, Fiona?" Monica asked. "They have to be, they're so good."

"We're very certain," Behn assured her. "I think, my dear, that your test is the only one that matters." A young man brought them aperitifs. From behind a desk that made him look even smaller, the precious old man said, "It's all part of a cloudy, endless romance for me. Personally, I'm enchanted, Mrs. Burke, by all the mystery that goes with attributions. In the ideal world we would not *care* whether it was the hand of Rubens or Botticelli that had laid the pigment on and traced the lineaments at which we marvel. It's the spirit of the artist that produces the masterpieces which we call by the names of men who will be forever mysterious to us, in any case. There's a certain Botticelli up in Boston for which no definitive attribution has ever been made. And yet—don't you agree, Fiona?—it's the purest, most certain revelation of that configuration of the spirit that we call Botticelli."

Marian Burke, rolling her shoulders in delight as she stood with glass in hand before the Goss paintings, laughed and said, "Are you trying to persuade me these *aren't* Dean's own work?"

"Not at all. Oh, not at all."

"I agree with Monica that they have to be the real thing because . . . I want them," Mrs. Burke said. "Of course you understand that it's a matter of the taxpayers' money. I'm only one vote on the museum board. But . . . it's all been discussed. Our curator is anxious, thank heaven. He'll be in to see you within the next several days."

"The taxpayers' money . . ." Bruce Behn's tone was a meditation in itself. The sound of lutes trembling in the Tuscan air. It was as if he marveled as much over the infinite mysteries of money as over the spirit of Botticelli, savoring both, certainly despising neither. And then he began to explain to Mrs. Burke some of the interweaving strands of commercial interest that had brought the paintings into his hands.

Tamisan, intermittently listening and wondering why they had really brought her here and got her in on this, was not at all precisely aware when she understood that Zach Sandler had bought the paintings from the South American dealer. That it was Sandler who stood to gain or lose most from the present transaction.

Nevertheless, she had that fact securely in mind among thoughts only faintly muddled by her aperitif by the time the women left the gallery to go to lunch. She still knew enough to keep her mouth shut and only gurgle admiration over the long-lost paintings when it seemed to be her turn to make any contribution at all.

Luxury and wine had muddled the thoughts considerably more by the time lunch was ending. So, there over the lunch table—without *exactly* being asked again what she thought of the paintings—she popped out the startling opinion, "They must be phony."

"You didn't like them!" Monica said with genuine hurt. She was trying very hard to be friends with Jason's "friend." Was going out of her way—as Fiona plainly was—to smooth over some quarrel whose outlines were very obscure to her.

"I liked them, but . . ."

But as always—all her damned life—she knew so much that she mustn't say. The old wish to blurt it all out and walk away was here again. Certainly it wasn't helping to clear her thoughts. "It doesn't matter what I think," she said shamefacedly to Monica.

Marian Burke, who probably had enough experience with boozy teen-agers not to worry about anything that slipped from their mouths, only said, "But, Fiona, you're satisfied they're really his, aren't you?"

"I believe they are," Fiona said. "You can tell your museum people not to worry about that, Marian."

Outside the restaurant, Fiona took her over. "Monica, I'll pick you up at six at Marian's hotel. Tamisan, I should have asked your plans for the afternoon. If you're not committed, I'd be grateful if you'd ride down to my apartment with me. It's not far."

Now it's coming, Tamisan thought as she got into the cab with the old woman. Now she'll start the questions and I'll tell her just enough to gross her out too. Then they will leave me alone. They will have to leave me alone. Will have to let it end where it had to end between Jason and me.

She stole a glance at the bulky figure riding now in silence beside her, the old unsmiling face that was not glowering or troubled either—a face that gave no sign of any curiosity or wish whatever.

She stared through the drowsiness of wine at Fiona's burly, freckled arms, thinking, I'll doubtless say something to enrage her and she will beat me up too. The Gosses will all have to go on and on beating at me until they've all had the turns they deserve.

To think of herself as their eternal punching bag reinforced her sense of justice considerably.

"Fiona and I couldn't be more perfect strangers," Tamisan told her mother later. "Not one word do we have in common that means the same to both. That's lucky. What I did say, I sounded like a fucking idiot again."

"What did Fiona say? If you can remember any words, I'll interpret."

"Words would only mix it up," Tamisan admitted wonderingly. "She sat there like Buddha and his grandmother. She leaned her personality on me."

And she had felt beaten, chastised with heavy, soft blows of concern, though Fiona had certainly not raised either her fist or her voice. Had not even meant to intimidate her by taking her to the apartment where they could be alone.

Probably it was the authority of Fiona's apartment, the authority of the good things her wealth commanded, that worked on Tamisan. The apartment was royally high in the air. The big living-room window that looked out toward Queens was wide enough to include views of the U.N. and two of the bridges. Against the outdoor brilliance, a boxy figure in dark wood loomed, a guardian figure standing at the threshold between the world of night and the world of day.

"Pluto," Fiona said, giving a name to the sculptured figure that needed none to do its work on Tamisan's submissive imagination. "Our friend Bern Whitestar carved it."

Our friend . . . It made Tamisan realize that at Fiona's height a woman could own everything without having to clutch at it. Things and people belonged to her because of who she was and what she was.

"If you're like Fiona, you don't have to *grab*," Tamisan told Susan later, not admitting how much it changed her to come to such an understanding.

There was a ruddy grand piano in the room guarded by the sculpture. It looked like a tank or battleship that would never have to fire its guns to conquer. Fiona admitted playing it— "When I have time. I don't go often to the theater or concerts. I play sometimes in the winter when I'm here."

"Will you play—just anything—for me?" Tamisan asked.

"Sometime," Fiona said. It was a promise that implied not so much a future of developing friendship as an already settled continuity of time that could be taken for granted.

Instead of playing, Fiona brought out wine. When Tamisan refused (thinking it would make her babble out all that was fighting in her mind) Fiona took none herself. They both settled to look at the limitless view beyond the figure in dark wood.

"I shouldn't have said the paintings weren't genuine," Tamisan volunteered after a while.

"I wondered about that."

"I say things that are *like* what I mean but aren't what I mean. It's awful to come close and not be right. I'm not always as stupid as I can make myself sound. I do things . . ."

"Yes," Fiona said mournfully.

". . . like tear up the painting because it means so much I can't stand it. Other people make things"—she reached out as if to touch the massive wood of the sculpture—"but I wreck 'em."

"Yes."

"That's why I ought to be in solitary confinement. Mama could never keep anything nice in the apartment because I'd somehow break it."

"Jason says you need an artist to express you."

"Mama says a zoo keeper. Every woman needs at least an artist if she isn't one herself. But I don't blame anyone else. I don't know why I said the paintings weren't genuine. It seemed true before I said it. I knew it was a lie when it popped out. Everybody catches onto how much I lie and that's why I have to keep moving on from one to another. Where it comes from is not inherited, because Mama is very straight. From being a woman is all I know."

"Your mother . . ."

"I know, there are other kinds of women. I guess it comes from fear. Whenever I'm afraid of dying I tell lies."

Fiona nodded—as if agreeing this might be a sensible thing to do. A thing beyond blame.

To hang onto her share of blame, Tamisan said, "That's only the beginning. One lie leads to another. As they do. It always happens the same. I keep putting one lie on another until it's utterly, utterly hopeless I'd ever be able to go back and straighten them out from the beginning. Then I have to run. There's no other way."

After a while Fiona said, *"Stop it."*

"Stop . . . what?"

"Lying."

Flustered out of her wits, Tamisan said, "I don't think I am lying right now. I didn't mean what I'm saying at this given moment isn't what I feel sincerely. . . ." She stopped, having said all this before it occurred to her that Fiona had meant to cast no aspersions on her present earnestness but was giving her a prescription for a new life. "I could," she said, "and hurt a lot of people. There are good motives for lying as well as bad ones, particularly in my case when things have got this tangled up."

"Just stop," Fiona said.

"I could stop lying but that isn't the only way I get entangled," Tamisan said. "My nature is, I go along with people until there's nothing left of myself. I'm practically a slave. Then what is there to do but rebel?"

Fiona said deliberately, "Some people don't know how to serve without becoming slaves."

This sounded like neither praise nor condemnation to Tamisan and she hastened on toward what she still supposed to be the central issue of their dialogue. "I'm sorry if you and Jason's father got the wrong impression of me. Mama says it was . . . the least it was was impudent of me to stay in his room out at North Atlantic. I get sick of being impudent after a while. But at least from your observations you can conclude that it's best for Jason and me not to—you know—plan anything permanent. I think I was good with Jason for a while, and then that got spoiled. Things caught up with me. He's so . . . clean, and I've lived a very freaked-out life. It seems like I've done everything already. Like I might be a thousand years old."

Fiona did not smile at the irony of Tamisan's claiming such age. She said, like a dowager empress, "We're not concerned with your morals."

More than anything else, that pronouncement left Tamisan floundering. Being good or being wicked were her stock in trade. Without those alternatives she was helpless among accomplished people. She wanted to cry out that they had to measure her morally or they wouldn't see her at all. Better to nauseate them than disappear altogether, it seemed now. But she saw this was useless with Fiona. "I'd expect Jason's father to be very cosmopolitan. You too, I mean. But still . . . !" She leaned dramatically into her interrupted confession, letting the implications ring like the Devil's anthem.

They didn't get through to Fiona. So Tamisan asked, "What does count then?"

From as far away as an imaginary throne, her voice sounding like an echo from the depths of a cave, Fiona said, "Power. The force in you."

"I don't know if I'm so strong." Again Tamisan was thinking in moral terms, thinking of all the temptations she had not resisted. But within the cluttered mishmash of her moral briar patch, she felt some stir of understanding. And it scared her worse than the notion of any punishment Fiona might have intended for her. As if the old woman might be probing close to the one secret she was absolutely forbidden to admit. As if morality and immorality both had been a set of distractions and stage tricks to keep anyone from seeing what Fiona had tried to name. "I'd be a good animal," she said with an ineffective laugh. "How d'ya turn that into being a person?"

No one has any instructions on that point, so Fiona was silent. But the silence reverberated now with a positively terrifying complicity between them. Something that had been running below the surface of their talk—a tide under the twinkle of waves—swept them both as they stared at each other. A furi-

ous warmth, like sexual excitement but more devastating, softened the girl so she felt she could not move from her chair.

It was against this that she summoned all her strength to
fight her way out of her chair and fling herself on her knees
beside Fiona, with her head coming to rest in the old woman's
lap. Convulsively she clung to Fiona's legs, feeling them motionless, passive, indomitable, whatever might come next.

She lifted her face to cry, "I'm not going to be to blame for
what Jason will do."

She saw the gallantly lipsticked old mouth tighten. There was
a resisted tic below Fiona's left eye . . . and then submission
to its cruel automatism.

"What?"

". . . will he do?" Tamisan asked. "I mean he'll do great
things. He's so talented and . . . He has such a great beginning
without me. He . . . he'll be better off without any woman to
hold him back, I suppose. He's . . . not like men. . . ."

"Nonsense," Fiona said, with an effort. "You'd both be all
right if . . . You're both so young. So young."

"I've hurt him but he'll get over it."

"Of course."

"You have to trust what I know. I know he'll make it fine
if he just goes on his way and I go mine."

"I trust you."

"Don't you think he will?"

Without a pause for reflection, Fiona said, "Yes." She moved
her knees restlessly as a signal that the girl was to release her.
Tamisan sat back. "We have to trust your judgment," Fiona
said.

"If it had been different, it could be different," Tamisan said.

"I suppose so," Fiona said absently.

"I learned a lot from the afternoon even if we didn't say anything to each other," Tamisan told her mother.

"You really picked her brains."

"Sometimes the best way to listen is to make a lot of noise!"

"For instance? What, for instance, did you learn? In your own words."

"That there's a lot of ways of being feminine I never thought of."

Agreeably, with a bitter sigh, Susan said, "That's a lot to learn."

"They'll always think, though, that I'm a witch who laid an enchantment on him. I saw that in her face, Mama. She's afraid for him. Someday they'll blame me more than they do now."

"Then you'd better wipe the enchantment off," Susan said.

"I tried that but I may not know how," said Tamisan, with a grief that left no room at all for vanity. "That part was torn out of the book I read."

from Susan Vail's red notebook:

D.G. came on Sunday morning.

If I have made that simple, declarative sentence sound like the Second Coming or like Zeus coming down from Olympus to ravish a heifer, it is more than half intentional. Let it stand. Considering all the other mysteries of how we are living now, maybe those myths of ravishment from on high are the most dependable and truthful accounts of reality.

It was one of those summer mornings that New York sometimes allows just to show how mean it can be on other occasions. There was a sort of premonitory majesty in the heat, a pause of silence over the streets. Our windows were open to the universe, in case it meant to come pouring in. The Sunday *Times* was spread over the orange juice glasses and toast scraps on the breakfast table. Across the street the wall of the Museum of Natural History was a curtain of blue-shadowed stone. Ah, that whole morning scene was a web of beauty, inciting the female to believe she is the spider at the center of it all.

The buzzer rang. Of course it was not part of his design to put us on guard by phoning first. Only the buzzer and the peremptory voice saying, "Dean Goss," on the intercom. Tamisan poked her head out of her bedroom to whisper, "Who?" when

I had already put my finger on the button to let him in the street door.

Then there he was, looming in our doorway, looking amazingly dapper. Not young. Ageless. His beard looked eight thousand years old—but most elegantly restored by the museum craftsmen who specialize in such things. Every red and white hair in it shone separately like those rays of power the comic strip artist puts around Superman's muscles. His steel-rimmed glasses shone at me like jewels in an idol's forehead. His figure was crisp as celery in his linen suit. In his gloved right hand he held a panama hat as big as the Ritz.

It is that hat I choose to celebrate as the badge of his authority. It came from other times—Caribbean mornings when the Old Planter visited his gibbering octoroon mistresses beneath the quiet murmur of ceiling fans. If the hat had flown in the window by itself, I would have knelt and said, "Thy servant."

"All set," he said. "Everything is fixed."

All's right with the world. By order of Dean Goss, Commanding General.

"Don't laugh at my hat!" he begged, misunderstanding my gaze of fascinated adoration. "Jason drove me in. He's waiting in the Toyota downstairs. Why doesn't he come up? Oh no, no! I told you everything is fixed. Everything must be ceremonious when we come to surrender."

If this was surrender, why did I feel so many big guns zeroed in on every open window of the apartment and so much cavalry surrounding the block in bright armor? Nevertheless I sustained some sort of welcome by nodding and grinning. He who laughs best laughs last, I do believe. And though we are still far from the end of the adventure, I mean to arrive there as I was that morning—with my teeth showing.

Tamisan came from her bedroom in the midst of this overbearing shower of good humor and enthusiasm. Came shyly. Her face was unbelievably pale, but she had quickly brushed her hair, even if she had been too confused by his unexpected arrival to put on underwear or anything else beneath her white robe with its embroidery of blue.

There was a real crack of silence when she came in. I mean the exact, metaphysical opposite of a crack of thunder. A grappling of wills. Defiances exchanged. A pregnant hush as if the quiet of the morning had been waiting just for this.

Without a sign of a smile she said, "I see you got new glasses."

He boomed with laughter. Jovian laughter. (I will clean up my vocabulary for another occasion. I am only doing the best with what is given me to account for the shudder I felt when he laughed like that. It was merriment on a scale I wouldn't have believed if I hadn't heard it.)

It signaled Tamisan that she had said exactly the right thing to him. She literally sprang into his arms, huddling and crying against his chest. I heard part of what came bubbling out of her mouth. "The painting . . . most wonderful thing that ever happened to me . . . and I had to tear it up. I want to die."

"You had to tear it up," he affirmed.

I did not mean to spy on them in this moment of sacred reunion. I was so dazzled by the emanation of light, I could not see perfectly. I must not swear that his arms embraced her *inside* the robe. Or that it made any difference. There was a terrific exchange of passionate energies. All I need say is I saw something happen that prepared me to believe what he told me later about the genesis of his new paintings.

I write prose. I am my lord's scribe, not his poet or his soothsayer or dream interpreter, either. Certainly not his musician, though I might try crashing cymbals to represent certain of his moments of greatest potency.

I write prose and when I come to those shatteringly brief moments of revelation which prose is too modest to represent, I leave blank spaces. But I have to live, too, with what other kinds of artists have branded on their souls by those chinks in the even flow of time. Revelations. I don't think it matters how much bare skin touched or rubbed his dazzling linen suit. It doesn't matter, even, if he was trying to fend her off to preserve the proprieties he had imagined for this ceremonial occasion.

I saw them touch. Saw him claim her for the Gosses. I

277

thought I knew what she had been running from since she ran out of his studio at North Atlantic.

But (the scribe reports) Tamisan was presently sitting on his knee in daughterly humility, listening to the boom of his commands.

" 'Stop thinking! Play the cards you've got,' I said to Jason. 'To hell with the past, except what you can use of it. Every new day is a living god. Move!' I said. He's waiting down there to take you to the farm in Pennsylvania, where life was good and can be good again. 'Why didn't you ever take her there before?' I said. It doesn't matter what he answered. You can go now and start from there. It doesn't matter where you go from there or when you go. You'll know what to do if neither of you is afraid of anything that's done and over. Let some air into the past. Let some air out of it. . . ."

She rode the tide of his confidence like a surfer gathering speed on a breaking swell. The sheer bullying drive of that confidence carried past the point that any argument or explanation could have reached with her. She didn't nod any agreements. She didn't question why he had come upstairs to fetch her instead of sending Jason. She hurried when he told her to throw things in a bag and rush out and zap the world. "Though you could go as you are. You're a girl who likes to go barefooted. Jason has your guitar. What more do you need than that?"

Only that seemed to embarrass her—of all that might have shamed her—provoked a minute of hesitation. "But I'm no good and I'll never be any good at playing anything, and I won't be laughed at."

"Then learn to play, you fucking idiot," he said. "You've got both hands. You've got time."

"That's true," she said—as if, of all he had to tell her, only that astonished her.

Then she hurried as she was bid to do. Only just before she left the apartment, he stopped her to plead, "Take care of Jason. Take care of each other. That's the great thing. Forget the rest I said. Take care."

"Yes," she said. "I can do that."

"Happy ending," I said when the door closed behind her. "Among your other creations you make happy endings, don't you?"

"I'm still strong in the clinch," he admitted. "They can still send me in to pick up inches for a first down." But almost as he uttered this justified brag, the air went out of him. He had come in looking big as a balloon in a Macy's parade. Now, in his swift deflation to human size, I first saw a way to love him. I mean that there and then it became *thinkable* for me to love him.

"What have I done?" he said.

"You've meddled in their lives in a way I wouldn't dare."

"Something had to be done. I meddled! Oh, I've done worse than that. Worse than that. You were right, to be sure. They are so strange. Wouldn't it be better to let them pick their own way? Nothing is clear to me. But something had to be done. I couldn't work. . . ."

"You mean you felt frustrated, stymied, and couldn't help meddling with them?" The enormity of experimenting with lives as if they were clay or metal or paint in his studio was beginning to dawn on me and I'm afraid that is just what he meant he was doing. "You mean you bullied Jason into taking her back the way you just faked her into going with him?"

"Oh yes. Yes, I did that." He was looking at me with terrible patience. There was not a pint left of that oceanic confidence with which he'd floated Tamisan away. "All that's clear to me is that, if they're going through a crisis, I am going through it with them. I can't paint what I can't live. And they came to me to challenge. Do you know that? Your girl said they wanted me to be as serious as they. That was the message from her and Jason. I didn't want to hear it. But I think I would have heard it anyway, sooner or later, if it had never been put in words at all. There's something as dreadful and bewildering about being old as about being young as they are. We get through to each other in ways you in the middle have forgot. We give signs to each other that have nothing to do with reason or common sense."

"Only with truth?"

"I have to believe that," he said in a voice more humble than I had ever heard from him. "We begin to believe in dreams again, impatient with anything else."

Earnestness by itself might not have persuaded me I was hearing the true voice. He has so many. But I had seen what I had seen flash between him and Tamisan, and a weird pity for him began to swell up uncontrollably. It was in pity I went to him and put my hand on his cheek. "Something had to be done for Tamisan or what's good in her would be totally lost," I told him. "You may feel the same about Jason. I only see the tip of that iceberg, so I mustn't say. But that excuses meddling and we'll hope for the best."

"Excuses won't help me," he said. I saw that his eyes behind his glasses were very clear this morning, clear enough to let me see the cindery depths way down in them, as if something was still smoldering from the time he burned his hand. He said, "I've never made anyone happy in my life. Happy endings? With any of them, what can you make but new beginnings? But, damn it, we *have* to bring it out right for these two. They need us. They have no shape to all that's swarming in their lives. It is terrible to be as young as they are and that wise. Only the old can stand wisdom."

I didn't want him to *stand* it either. I wanted him to sing it, paint it, dance it—live it *big*. I realized I wanted that more than I wanted to comfort him for any anxieties about whether he was doing the "right thing." I was grateful he had not stayed behind, to comfort or cheer me while our young ones dashed off into the open day he had given them. I was glad to be scared with the terrors of his wisdom. It put us where we belonged, facing each other as man and woman.

When he looked at me now it was like feeling a thumb of a blind man explore my face with a blind man's eager clumsiness.

"I've wasted your time and mine, Susan. I've been no use to you in making your book. I've said . . ."

"Great things."

"I haven't opened up for you."

"Well, now you're opening like a rose."

That seemed to startle him. He asked rather stiffly if, since he seemed to be here and dependent on my kindness, he might implore me for a fresh cup of coffee.

And now, so late, the great things began as simply as the coffee ran from the spout.

Choked with shyness. Stiff as a ramrod. Silent over coffee. . . . He was humming like a hive of bees in a rain-swept orchard on a day when they are wild to venture out. He was not a messenger with *something* to tell me. He had come to tell me everything. And naturally stuttered. For there is no beginning to everything.

He was literally choked about himself and what had turned the dynamos of his imagination since I saw him last. So he began to make noises about me. How could I keep plants growing in the apartment when I was so often and so long away? Did the super really do that for me? That antique flintlock pistol on the wall . . . had I ever played Hedda Gabler with it? Wasn't my father a captain? Ah, a *minister*. . . . That empty, gilded bird cage . . . it was from Morocco, was it? My midget Sony TV set on my writing desk . . . had he not been sure that's what I would have? The framed photographs . . . I should have expected that he would be intensely more interested in those than my paintings, since the paintings were not by Dean Goss.

It dawned on me while we were still on coffee that he is the most intense inhabiter I have ever known. All he had to be was *let in* and he began to fill the spaces of the apartment like a flood of water, seeking not only its own level but seeking all that had passed there.

What he made most of was the Museum of Natural History across the street. For the six years I have had this apartment (bad times and good) I have looked on those walls that keep natural history where it belongs and Susan over here in New York with her daughter and sundry.

The thing is, he paid no attention to the wall. Who else could visit a museum from the *outside?* God love him, he refuses the distinction between inside and outside.

Hippocampi began to run, over there, while he watched from my window with the sun streaming onto his face. Winged dinosaurs began to clatter and cackle (more like geese than you would imagine, though the sound of their reptilian wings in the air is far more eerie than the sound of feathers). The bones of *Tyrannosaurus rex* clothed themselves in meat and skin. The creature promptly began to eat everything in reach. Kodiak bears broke the glass of the vistoramas and began to gobble children. The elephants broke from their phony pose of charging *bwana sahib* and began to forage for food. I could smell Teddy Roosevelt's horse.

What has always saved my writing from excesses is the fact that I am a minister's daughter and never forget it. So it can be believed with confidence that the museum became a zoo of the ages, a zoo without walls but only the gap of the street to protect us from those big teeth and thundering herds—before we even got to the whiskey.

After that was broken out, neither we nor the creatures paid any attention to the street that had seemed to separate us. We were *among* them, he and I, lying down with the lambs, scaring the teeny horses into flight (like a pack of dogs running from us through the tall grass above a river that looked most awfully familiar), and trusting our friends the great apes to kill reptiles for us and swing us up to the safety of tall trees. We ran with the antelopes heading for the snow-covered slopes of Mount Kilimanjaro. (It seemed very far away to me, but whiter in the sun than I had realized. There really *is* a leopard up there in the snow.) Carl Akeley tried to round us up. Malvina Hoffman proposed doing a sculpture group that would include us among certain blacks.

All the human words I remember D.G. saying from his vantage point by the window were these: "Jason used to take me there when he was five or six. I said, 'Here we are, home at last,' and he smiled. I said, 'I don't know which side of the glass I belong on,' and he said, 'Isn't that funny'?"

Since I am, admittedly, a minister's daughter, what I have to say about the female orgasm can be trusted.

I am now able to confirm my lifelong suspicion that each of them has been there all the time, waiting to happen. Girls are born with a certain stock of them, which we sometimes dream about as a stock of fruits, vegetables, and meats put up in Mason jars shelved in a dark cellar. They are there on hand, waiting to be served to the wedding guests in case the bridegroom never cometh. Some are proffered, some are filched. Some recognized as offerings. Some we greedily enjoy by ourselves in private. More or less. Some turn out to have been hardly worth the preserving. Some are feasts. Others are *fit* for feasts, though we eat alone.

But in any event, each of them seems to have been there for longer than we have had custody of them, before we had memory, or at any rate before that memory knew how to say "I." They come from that dark cellar shelf that has no back except darkness and, fortunately, I believe, there seems to be no finite number or limit of those we may have. They all seem intended to mean something. But what they are supposed to mean is somehow directed to the wrong senses, as if we had to read with the sense of taste, listen with the sense of touch or interpret a texture with the sense of smell. Oh, they are tidings of great joy. Sometimes. But what *are* the tidings? the jilted, deserted mind asks after the spasm. What are you trying to tell me and why *can't* you just spell it out in so many words?

Orgasms are bigger and smaller, sweeter and more wrenching, shattering and composing, shapeless or as precise as the shape of a branding iron on the skin—thin, intense, scattered, unforgettable, casual, precious, loathsome—and often precious and loathsome at the same distressing time. They open and close doors in our lives like hospital attendants who may be Gestapo flunkies in disguise. They often seem to belong to no one. Sometimes they seem to be carried around by a particular man like an attaché case (his initials stamped on it in gold). They often seem inappropriate, like a football in a catcher's mitt (a tomboy thought). Some we would like to keep like flowers in a vase or wear like a ring. Some seem to erupt like volcanoes just beyond the horizon. Some are purses of stolen money; one wants to put them surreptitiously in the trash can after extracting the cash. Some are oppressions. Some are cheers that rock the whole stadium. Some are blessed relief, rain after drought. Some are utterly private, though technically shared. I have lain harassed, shamed and miserable under a man after the most glorious hosanna, because prosperity should only be shared with someone worthy. Those induced mechanically are not invariably the least moving. (Every art must provide room for the self-portrait, no?)

And then there are those that let you remember, possess, reclaim and lie open to all the rest. These are the queens of life. I bow my head—not at all repudiating the others, because each of them seems to have been prepared longer ago than dreams, fashioned out of more deeply disguised symbols, composed in the silence of the heart, in the voices of the children's choir.

All this is by way of saying I recognized ours—D.G.'s and mine—when, after the appropriate number of drinks, we clung to each other, delivered up our bodies to summon it out of the fabulous darkness.

More mysterious than all the rest, that orgasm. A passage of queens with veiled faces. Not at all like a "thing happening." It was there, waiting for its moment of mutual revelation. Everlasting unto everlasting.

We had been made vulnerable out of love for our headlong children. It was this vulnerability shared that helped us find each other. We communicate best when we use Tamisan and Jason as referents—almost as if we had been ghosts who borrowed their young bodies and lives to move us together.

It is a strange psychological fact that I am most aware—or best aware—of Tamisan when I am sexed up. I suppose that poor cheated Bern Whitestar had an inkling of that the night I told him my tale of Tamisan's conception by that other gambler who captivated my imagination so many years ago. And now, post-orgasmically, I felt I had given her to Dean Goss. I felt she had given him to me. It never could have happened *as* it happened if I had not seen what I saw as they embraced earlier in the day. "It's strange how identities get mixed up down there," I said, writing invisible things on the pillow, while he looked at something on the ceiling.

"What's in your mind?" he said from that distance men have to go to after the great ceremony has been accomplished.

"A million things. Woman thoughts about who I am and who's been there and who really got there." I felt it unnecessary to assure him he had got where no one really ever had before—or maybe I was not yet as sure as I am now that he had. Revelations take a while to sort out.

"Do you write those million things?"

"Part of them. Do you paint the million things that come up into your mind?"

"Part of them," he said brusquely. "One of my reasons for coming in today—to be frank—was that I need, I think I need, to read what you've been busily putting in your notebook about me."

"Oh no!"

"I wouldn't ask if it weren't important," he said in his patriarchal tone. "I've tried to explain to you that the artist needs people around him to help him imagine himself. I have to imagine myself—imagine my studio, too—before I can be sure of what I have to paint. And this time I can't start with anything ready made. You can help me put myself together."

"I know you use us all like mirrors." I was not so sure he had the *right* to do that, though. There's just a bit of a devilish suggestion that he reduces everyone near him to a *thing*. A doll or a puppet. That seemed, I suppose, more an injustice to himself than to the rest of us—as if he were cursed like Midas, who missed all the common goodies by turning them to gold.

"Then why can't I plunge into your notebooks?"

"Here and now?"

He brightened so at the possibility that I was hurt. "Brain picker," I called him. "Now your motives for softening me up begin to show."

"I don't have motives. Only wishes. I'm alone and all of you can see how *easy* my life is. Why should my wishes be granted?"

"It's not that. Of course you'll see what I've written when I have time to get the things in order."

"Now?"

"I don't know you well enough." Here we were again. Hilarious that once he'd asked to see my body and I wasn't ready. Now he had picked the secrets of the body if not the brain, and I couldn't have told myself for sure why I still wanted to hide anything at all. "For one thing, there's as much in the notebooks just now about Tamisan as about you. Lately I've tried to come to terms with her by writing."

Whatever he gleaned from this confession, it seemed to please him. I felt I'd been a good mirror by reflecting them side by side so to speak, bundling them within the cozy covers of one notebook. His foxy grin made me feel this way.

"Ah, you see she's like me, too?"

"She doesn't have such a beautiful beard."

"She's a real whore," he said with a satisfied chuckle. Giving me to understand it was his lifelong wish to be one—for the range of experience and the point of view it provides.

"I don't much care for the word, sir."

"It lacks precision," he admitted. "It has a hearty ring. Yes, yes, yes. The whore of the new American Babylon, the teen-age girl at liberty, the unfettered female, at last. That's a figure to hammer the brain! To paint her, as she is . . ." He kissed his fingertips and threw the kiss as his offering to the muse.

I wasn't going along with this enthusiasm. "If you think that's what she is, why the hell did you send her off with Jason? 'Take care of him,' you said. What did you have in mind? Sending him down to the famous farm, the great good happy place, to crawl into his mother's bed with a whore?"

"Ah," he sighed cheerily, "there's hardly any use talking until we get on dangerous ground and find out what words are worth. Don't you agree?"

I was too shocked and furious and frightened to agree or disagree at that moment. If that was what he'd thought of my battered child all this time she'd been with Jason, then the least *she* ought to do was tear up his comfortable life along with his paintings. I was leaping out of bed to take my stand for justice when he grabbed me and bore me down. So, he took me that second time speechless, furious, frightened, whorish, clinging to him because there seemed nothing else to cling to. He took me by surprise.

"We have a lot of things to get straightened out between us," I said when he let me sit up.

"It will take us a long time," he agreed. "A long, long time, I hope."

"They're our love story," he said of Jason and Tamisan.

He said, "I wouldn't have meddled except to honor what I believe is true. That they're neither of them at home in time. If they had met when they were five years older they might be ready for each other. The trouble is, they know this too. They've recognized each other. They salute. They pass in the night. They'll go on with the chase forever, chasing each other but finding . . . God knows what they'll find as they race along."

It sounded credible . . . as such things do at night. But if he saw them already in such a tragic inevitability, star-crossed, out of phase, and all the rest . . . "What's next in your plan for them?"

The beauty of it was that he had no plan at all and didn't pretend to. "Hell, Susan, what would you expect me to do but try what always has worked for me in painting—in the hard times? I put myself in an untenable position for which there is no solution. Then the hidden intelligence begins to work. Has a chance to work. It invents a solution. I don't."

If he was going to trust that, I wanted to. It sounded, in the night, one notch better than pure chance, anyway. Dangerous ground is better than none.

If he was not going to trust it when he got up to leave me, as men do, I wanted to trust his second thoughts. Seriatim. All the way. I wanted to offer my body like a grave where his furies could rest. What we had that night deserves a long blank space in my prose. It is not to be honored for its sensual aspects. It was something like pure knowledge. I knew his strength and its fragility. It was pure rebellion he offered to my womb. Like a blossom. Like a sword. I knew him then as I will know him at the hour of his death.

He said, "I sent them down there to fight for their lives."

Sweetly we fought for ours.

There was a strange man in my bed when I woke in the morning. I sat for an hour in my battered old easy chair in the front room staring across the street at the museum wall. It was a perfect blank. The face of nature. The perfect map for the future. A perfect mirror for a mind that had kept fewer traces than my body of whatever promises I had trusted or invented during the night.

Finally I heard him bumping around, sounding big, then calling in a small voice to ask if I could remember where his glasses had been laid for safety. As he put them on I panicked again at the thought he might be getting ready to read what I probably could not keep from him now. He had other calculations.

"Now," he said briskly as he sat down to the breakfast I fixed for him. "Now we must make some little arrangements. I want to get back to work. Get something settled. I've been indecisive too long with my painting. I want you to drive me back. And stay of course. Considering everything, I think it would be a shrewd move if we got married."

I didn't let go of the coffee pot or show otherwise that I was surprised again, but I wished he would meet my eyes, at least, when he delivered such utterances.

"Is this," I asked, "another of those ridiculous bad corners you want to paint yourself into so you can bring your genius into play to get out of it?"

"Not at all, Susan. Not at all. You know how well we were getting along before all this nonsense erupted. Fiona and Jason are very fond of you. I need things going smoothly. I need you. I've been thinking this over for a good long time now. I woke again in the night and couldn't sleep until I had my reasons totally marshaled and in good order. I think I have even got them phrased in language that will be convincing to you. First . . ."

"You old beauty," I said. "I'd marry you for any reason at all."

Chapter 14

Susan was back in Gossland and everything was changed by her return except herself. The mansion, the studio, the beach, the lawns at North Atlantic had been gilded as if Goss with a batch of elves to assist him had scurried around in the night with paintbrushes, touching up the flowers and grass, truing up the color of the sky and fiddling with perspective to make the buildings more expressive. Surely the tennis court was now a severe and geometric canvas from the painter's studio, spread flat for the delight of her eye as much as for the game she was playing again with Fiona.

It was all a work of art. But she was real. She had never been more real than she was now in the last game of the set. The score was real. She was leading Fiona 6–5 and had the ad in the game. Which could never have happened if even inanimate things had not undergone some miraculous change while she was away.

Take the tennis ball for example. . . .

The friendly, co-operative and clean white lamb of a ball flew up from her left hand to exactly the right height. It loitered in the bright, salt-smelling air, taking its time to give her time. It waited for further psychic commands. It moved ever so slightly to the left to put itself in perfect position to be slammed.

Sock me, Mrs. Vail! Oh, do it, *please!* the ball said to her just as the racket pulled her wrist exactly enough to cock it against her shoulder blade. She had everything and nothing to do with the flash of steel and gut that answered the ball's demand.

She was laughing so hard she had to squint. Yet every sense registered the perfection of her serve. She felt the intricate linkage of her female body released in an action as simple as the reflex of a fully drawn bow. The sound of the strings on the jolly ball was exactly as sweet as the sight of it flying straight to the corner of the service court. She saw Fiona turn like a heavy matador in immaculate whites, too slow to reach the sizzling bounce with her backhand stab.

"Yipes!" said Monica, running onto the court, dribbling a tennis ball with her palm. "Isn't she good, Fiona?"

"Improved," Fiona said, coming around the net wiping her forehead with the back of her wrist. She was smiling secretly, as if she understood precisely what had accounted for the improvement but was not going to mention it in front of a girl Monica's age.

Susan said, "Yep. I owe my victory to the thoughts of Chairman Goss. Unless you let me win out of charity."

That thought was shocking to Fiona. "I respect you too much for that. I always play to win."

"You let me win points," Monica said.

"Points," Fiona conceded massively and gravely. "Your time will come, Monica. In about—five years?—you can probably beat me legitimately. And that's the way it should be."

"Four," Monica said.

"It's a bet," said Fiona, setting her mouth hard and not smiling at all, though under her heavy, lowered lids her eyes might have been twinkling.

"Goss doesn't realize he's been coaching me at tennis," Susan said. "I take what he says about art and use it in other areas. I think I'll be a better cook than I used to be, too. He says there are times when the model and the painter both feel the geometry of the body simplified down to its essence. 'I have learned to wait for moments like that and then POUNCE!' My last serve was pure Goss pounce, Monica. The rest was luck. I'm not as good as Fiona and I'm not a born competitor."

"Why do you call him 'Goss' now that you're . . . ?" Monica wanted to know.

Now that I'm . . . what? Susan wondered merrily. Goss had said they would be married. Then, royally, had taken the intent for the deed. He had brought her back here as a wife. From the day of their return Fiona had treated her like a Dean Goss wife, not with any noticeable deference or startling changes in intimacy—Fiona was too solid and stately for that—but as if Susan had lost her right to be surprised by any depth or eccentricity of the protean old man; as if now, like Fiona herself, Susan must take him all in all as he was, however he showed himself. It was just this subtle sharing of ineffable risks that seemed more binding than the entry of a marriage contract on any official register. Susan took it as a sort of papal blessing on their union. There had been, before she got back here, a few minutes of bewildered worry about how Fiona would take this development. That had changed into a glad suspicion that Fiona must have known it was going to happen before she did.

"What *should* I call him?" she chafed Monica. "Call him 'Grandpa' just because that's his name?"

"I guess at your age and . . ."

". . . and fighting weight; I'm still a bantam."

". . . fighting weight," Monica concurred with a giggle, "it's kind of *nice* for you to call him 'Goss.' If you wrote a novel about him, Susan, what would you call him in the novel?"

"I've thought about that," Susan said honestly. "Maybe in a novel I'd just let him be a powerful influence who never really appeared on the scene and I'd give him a bunch of mysterious pseudonyms. Christopher for Columbus. Daniel for Daniel Boone. Modo. Mahu. What was Captain Ahab's first name?"

"Grandpa would have caught the whale barehanded," Monica said.

"I believe it," said his not-quite-wife.

"You will go on with your book?" Fiona asked. Or maybe she ordained it. Fiona kept things going on, with ever so gentle, elephantine pressures.

"On and on," Susan said. "It's going to take longer than I thought." And, sweated as she was from her game with Fiona, uncertain as she might sometimes be about where her little book was carrying her, she thought the idea of its going on and on was clearly the champion thing about it. "If I'm lucky, I'll never finish. And I am lucky, though I didn't always understand I was."

As the three of them ambled down from the court toward the mansion and studio where Goss was at work, she thought, Here come his women, old, middle-aged and young. It seemed to her there might be more than three in this happy procession of Goss women obedient to the pull of his gravity, though the others were invisible. Just for the moment, to feel that she was in his harem with Fiona and Monica was luck sufficient for the day.

The idea of a continuous procession of his women, filing through the decades of the artist's life, was emerging and taking more distinct shape in Susan's mind as a unifying image for the book that she was committed to writing. It was a persistent image—endlessly variable, sometimes comic to the point of farce, sometimes grave as the carvings on an ancient monument, where the original significance of tragedy has been bleached out by time, so that what remains has nothing pitiable about it, but only a sort of quiet majesty. We're like a frieze of women carved on the tomb of a loving old despot, she thought, effortlessly faithful to him in life and death.

According to Fiona, he had never been profligate after he married Minna, but he told Susan once, "I was a tireless fucker when I was Jason's age." Momentarily he shone with the memory of 1920s flappers and high school girls in rumble seats. But he gave no names or details. For the time being, as she roughed in the outlines of the feminine processional, her imagination would have to supply the individual facts. Her imagination was quite adequate—thank you!—for this sketch work.

She said to Fiona, "I'm going to get the best . . . no, the most essential thing about the man and the artist into my book if it takes twenty years." The chief luxury of her new status among the Goss women was freedom from her commitment to Finley, Schreiber, and McGrew to deliver a commercial property—*Inside Dean Goss* or *The Many Lives of Dean Goss*—to her publisher by any deadline. Her editor Hal was one of the very few of her acquaintances to whom she had confided that she was going to be the third Mrs. Dean Goss, and he had been excited out of his excitable skull at the possibilities this offered for publicizing her book. Couldn't she hurry? "Not in your lifetime, Hal," she teased him. Which depressed him on more than one count.

"The essential," Fiona mused. "I'm sure you will, Susan, because . . ."

"Because he wants me to? Wants to get at it himself?"

Fiona assented. "Though he knows himself so well, he needs others to help him sort it out. And . . . what do you think the essential thing is?"

"His women. What he makes of them. How he draws on them to feed his secret intelligence. I haven't got the right summary phrase for it yet, but . . . Do you think I'm on the right track?"

"Of course," Fiona said, showing no disappointment that Susan's current formulation sounded like no secret from anyone. She was a woman who cared very little for formulas or quick summaries. She had bought time to wait for the finished picture. "He won't *purposely* hide the track. From you or from anyone. I know some people have found him devious." She dismissed the weakness of their error with a sniff for those who had let themselves be outrun. "He's a remarkable teacher, a born teacher. He means to reveal things, not hide them."

And it seemed to Susan that the remarkable—fantastic—essential in Fiona's diligent life was that she had gone on for forty years seeing herself as a Goss student, never bothering to change that initial relationship though she had enriched, elaborated and solidified it almost beyond belief. After all, it seemed, the intimacy of the student and teacher relationship could be extended until it grew as tough, diverse and productive as any of the other intimacies between men and women—not exactly a substitute for the sexual intimacy, but maybe—why not admit it?—another manifestation of the way men and women got into and around each other. It was being altogether too literal to suppose that men had only one thing to push into women, or that between the legs was the only place women had to receive the thrust.

More than once these days as she eased into thinking of herself as wife, Susan found it amusing—and more—to think of Fiona as the other active wife on the premises. It amused her to think that Fiona had only scooted peaceably over to the other side of the bed to make room for her and her activities with the shared husband—though in her assessment of the literal history of the Goss women the evidence was persuasive that Goss and Fiona had never spoiled their intimacy by violating its eccentric rules.

"I'd like to meet Minna," she said once to Fiona, thinking of another wife displaced, yet still, for the imagination, keeping her place in the processional, whatever literal life she had had all these years in Rome.

"No reason you shouldn't," Fiona said. "I see her now and then when I'm nearby. She will like you. You'll find she's still bitter—at least she will speak bitterly—of his leaving her."

"She hasn't passed that on to her sons?"

"She'd have thought it unjust to belittle him to Godwin or Vidal. I think, in spite of what she says, something in her knows she wasn't the loser by her marriage to him."

"She still loves him."

"Do you write about love, Susan? I only know what happens. Things are as they are." By which she meant—once married to Goss, always married. Let time and distance and even bitterness fend for themselves as best they could. Yes, there was certainly a papal streak in Fiona's certainties.

So to speak, Fiona might have scooched over in bed to make room for Susan in the household. She gave no sign of yielding any of the prerogatives that years had established in her relationship with Goss. Let Susan sleep with him. Splendid! It was another of the exalted chores his women must do. And let her gain insights for her book by doing it. And feed them back into the life stream of the man working for them as they worked for him, on all the human ranges and some that seemed to happen past the border of the human. There were prerogatives and chores enough to go around, some of them intensely and physically pleasurable.

As for the managerial chores and prerogatives—things are as they are, whatever lines of authority may be drawn or wifely titles bestowed—these were inevitably Fiona's. She was eager to show Susan how the North Atlantic enterprise ran. Everything from keeping the staff of maids and cooks cheerfully efficient to assembling the help she needed intermittently with the archives and collection. The immense correspondence she carried on through the art world and with the people "who are part of his life" though he seemed to ignore their existence sturdily year after year. It seemed to Susan that Fiona's real artistry, her fulfillment and happiness as an artist, must come from the inventive orchestration of this world—which of course peaked in letting the man do and be whatever his whims dictated. It even seemed sometimes that the whimsical man and all his hearty physicality weren't necessary to the functions that Fiona kept in order.

It was unthinkable that Fiona could withdraw herself from this role if she had wanted to. There would be nothing left but the skin of the old lion. It was only now and then that Fiona hinted she would like to be set at liberty. "A time has to come when I do a bit more painting of my own. I have some ideas I haven't caught up with."

But since the day Fiona had shown her the enticing, enamored paintings of Maggie's nude body, there had lain in Susan's mind the germ of the idea that sometime Fiona might want to paint her in similar nakedness. If Fiona offered that, it would be the final seal of acceptance and approval that incorporated her in the imaginary harem as the creature of flesh. It would be the sign of recognition that she was not just a fellow student with Fiona in the Goss academy of art and occult sciences. It would be like an inspection of a younger wife by an older one in an honest-to-God harem—which Sultan Goss deserved as much as the metaphorical one that lived in Susan's mind. Posing for Fiona would be a kind of trial by embarrassment—thinking of it made Susan giddily uneasy. More than her natural modesty was involved. It would be a sacrifice and an initiation. If Fiona asked, Susan would make the sacrifice with suffering gladness, but it was a relief that, for the time being at least, Fiona never mentioned it.

But one day Fiona said, apropos of her neglected art, "The right model can make such a difference in one's style and enthusiasm for working. Over the years I've seen that again and again in his work. When you're thinking about essentials, Susan, don't forget that the relation between the painter and the model is the most promising of all questions. Sometime I'd like your Tamisan to pose for me. I suppose there'll never be an occasion. We can't be easy with each other as you and I are. Probably she doesn't like me at all." Fiona sighed and made a face of resignation. "Since I saw her in the garden with Jean and her friend, an idea has been gnawing at me. . . . As you've heard him say, each body is a hieroglyphic for us to decipher. Hers . . . speaks to me."

"I'm sure all you have to do is ask her," Susan said. For the moment she was a little hurt. A little jealous.

But she refused to be. After all, she could tell herself—she did—that the line of imaginative significance she attached to Fiona's paintings of the Goss women was only one of the possible lines that were woven in such profusion through this household of artists. There was some coincidence between her own reading of significant gestures and Fiona's. It would spoil too much to overread any one of them.

Daily and continuously there was so much going on here. It would have been sheer ingratitude to fate if she gave more importance to intangible nuances than to present blessings. Fiona was not interested in painting her body—but in the actual and sensuous nights Goss himself was in a near frenzy to know it and to teach it. She weighed his oversized balls in her hand—all the omens she could manage. His teeth and tongue deciphered the shape and taste of her nipples. He knelt upright in the bed like a colossus in the dimness and gave her his ponderous cock to suck erect so he could mount her again like a centaur, drunk and lunging.

She had an ample place among his women. She was cheated of nothing. And the pinnacle of her satisfactions was that he was working steadily, confidently now on his new canvases. After the days and weeks of nervous hesitation and all the evasions of cleaning up his studio, he had come back and gone at his paintings as confidently as a bricklayer following a stretched cord and a set of blueprints.

She might not understand just what her part was in this phase of his productivity. She hadn't the faintest doubt that her part was major. That in itself would have tipped the balance of her happiness.

She was happy to believe that the three gargantuan women now taking shape on Goss's three canvases were the truest manifestations of the parade she had thought of as the Goss women. Now the figures were declared by black outlines like the broad cuttings of a chisel in stone. Over most of the canvases there were great planes of color. Nothing was finished. Goss was not even willing to say flatly that this was the beginning he had waited for. But forms were surfacing from immeasurable depths. "They look like cow whales," he said contentedly, because it mattered so little what was said about them at this point. When they emerged fully they would not need names either.

"You're pulling them out from in back," George Vendler said, instead of saying he was awed by what he stopped to look at now and then as he came and went from the studio. "They scare me worse than what you had started before."

"They are weird sisters," Goss conceded. When the line was winding in to his reel, he did not mind flattering himself about the size of the creatures he had on his hooks. What he was angling for could still be lost, because the lords of the realm from which he was abducting his women were very jealous of him. "George, you'll have to admit what a cagey old man I am. It was good I didn't start prematurely. I have to be my own astrologer and pick the day to begin my great enterprises. I think I read this one right."

"All this time I've known you, I've never known you dabbled in the black arts too," George clucked. "Oh, Father William, what makes you so dreadfully clever?"

"Being in love," said young Dean Goss, with a little skip and a click of his heels. "That's where it all begins. You know that Susan and I are married in the eyes of God."

"That's the best way, isn't it?"

"It's like hotel fucking," said the crude old lecher, "than which there is nothing better except grand hotel fucking."

"Too rich for my blood, though I take your word for it . . . with all your experience to back it up. Seriously, I want to congratulate you for getting Susan. You couldn't have done better."

"Susan is a durable, tolerant, serviceable woman," Dean Goss said with deadpan loftiness.

As George Vendler or anyone else who learned his intentions toward Susan might readily have grasped, his *reasons* for marrying Susan now were impeccable. As they kept accumulating and he kept on faithfully enumerating them, the total got funnier and funnier to Susan, who said, "Did you have this many reasons for marrying your other wives?" And he answered with facile gallantry, "I'm sure I didn't." She said, "I'm glad. There's nothing like beginning with a winning score."

They were reasons befitting his age, his habits, his still vigorous appetites and—as far as he had been able to guess until lately—his weather-beaten soul. Having good reasons, he would abide by them.

What George Vendler and no one else in the living world was ever supposed to guess was that he did not refer to Susan Vail when he said he was in love.

He meant Tamisan.

He was purely, lustfully in love with the girl who was presumably, at this very moment, down on the farm in Pennsylvania giving her all to his best and best-loved son. The little whore-bitch, seer and poetess had *better* be giving her all to Jason or his headstrong gamble was sorely in jeopardy. If she was on her back in the grass, the hammock or any adequate horizontal surface, threshing that incredible ass with vigor while Jason rode, then she was exactly where Jason's monstrous father wanted her to be.

Still, the pure and bitter truth that had got him frenziedly to work was that he loved her as he had never expected to love a woman again. A lunatic love. An abomination. It was as if his belly had been slit open and he had to stand upright to face his paintings with the lewd and nauseating smell of his own intestines rank in his nostrils. Work, work, giant-killing work was his best distraction from that nauseating smell, though lovely times with Susan might be called his second-best relief.

It was humiliating and probably wicked to be in love at all. Adolescents could decently "fall" in love. Old men loved what earned their love, and he could not even securely tell himself that Tamisan was sweeter to his eye than her mother, though she had the advantage of youthful, tighter skin and a certain *weight* in the torso that Susan, admittedly, lacked.

No, it was not with anything that had met his eye that he had fallen in love. It was with an indefinable barbarity that she personified. It was, as far as he could tell, like falling in love with a bright-colored snake. . . .

He said to Susan, "Isn't there a story of Balzac's about a soldier in the Egyptian desert who falls in love with a she-leopard?"

"Yes. 'A Passion in the Desert.' I'm glad you haven't turned off all your Rodin-Balzac ideas."

"The hell I haven't. They were in another lifetime. If the new things go well . . . Christ, if I get started on something good, hundreds of things are apt to follow from it. No more Rodin. No more Balzac. Did you ever hear, as an example of American vernacular, anyone declare that he would fuck a snake if he could find someone to hold its head?"

"If I haven't heard it, I've read it in some novel or other. I've never seen it done, however. Sorry!"

Being a clever woman, she realized that he was chewing ideas that would feed back into his work—who knew in what form? in the cadmium and titanium banding of a coral snake?—and that these ideas had to do with romantic extravagances of erotic love.

Being less than clairvoyant, she would never know that their conversation had been about Tamisan.

He was crazily in love with a girl whose personality he neither knew nor cared to know. Jason loved her soul—and that was another matter. A matter into which Jason's father would never intrude, except kindly.

Dean Goss saw no problems arising from this complication of his old age, except the problems that he would fight to resolve on canvas, in his frenzied work. No need for him to vex himself with questions about how to treat the barbarous child who had meant to blind him and had given him a new set of eyes.

This obscene love was not even something he need ponder, once he had shrugged and admitted it. It was an eternal truth. He would paint it over—as he had painted over the crude, offensive symbol of the female he had showed to no one but Jason; that pudgy roundness with a cunt-slash, scribbled in crudest black until he had smeared it over with lightly tinted white.

"Titian," he said to Susan. "I'd like to take a knife sometime and scrape down into one of Titian's nudes. One of those Venuses with the lute player or the organ player. You see, painters like to bury something under the surface of their paintings. Sort of a talisman. I wonder what he put under those Venuses."

"Like sealing up a live animal in the cornerstone of a house," she said, shuddering a little at the thought.

He had buried love and symbol where no one was going to get at it with less than a knife. The black scrawl would remain forever secret from all but himself and Jason. Never intended to confuse the eyes of any onlooker at these paintings and never intended to confuse his reasonable love for Susan, or Jason, or Fiona . . . or . . . or . . . or for *mankind*.

But still his women—the real and the painted ones—were ruthless inquisitors. Even the adoring Monica came to challenge and unsettle him. She was particularly fascinated when he began to make huge paper cutouts to sketch new possibilities for the constantly changing women figures on his canvases. He had pinned these cutouts on various backgrounds, fastening some of them to the sliding partitions, hanging some of the others so they twisted free in space. They gave the interior of his studio the air of a circus pavilion where unearthly acrobats were rehearsing. It was obvious to Monica that these giant paper cutouts were paper dolls.

"But that's not all they are," she said to him. "Susan and I compare notes on you. We think you're telling the story of your life the way I used to tell mine by using paper dolls."

"That's it exactly, sweet. I can tell it but I can't read it. Did you always know what your life was when you were telling yourself stories?"

"I remembered part and I made up part," she said responsibly.

"Just like me."

"I haven't let on to Susan what I think you're really painting." Her voice sank to an awed crickety whisper. He waited with alarm to hear what the little witch might have guessed. She said, "They're three real goddesses and you're painting the 'Judgment of Paris' all over again."

"There's nothing new under the sun," he said—with some relief and some remaining apprehension.

"You haven't put all three goddesses in one painting, but that's modern art for you. It amounts to the same thing. And if I painted what I think, I'd put you and them all in the same picture."

"You'd throw me right in with those tigers?"

"Oh, you got yourself into it," she said with a slyness that seemed, for a moment, malicious enough for a female of any age. "I think you're like Paris."

"He was too young to know better."

Monica did not understand how age had anything to do with it. "I think you're trying to decide which goddess to choose, aren't you?"

"It would be my last judgment if that's what I did," old Foxy said to her with grandfatherly solemnity. "Poor old Paris certainly got the shaft for giving the golden apple to Aphrodite, didn't he?"

"He got what he deserved," Monica said, more in sorrow than in anger. "Women have other attributes than to be sexy."

"They certainly have."

"And brains aren't so important either."

"Gosh, no."

"But the other goddess was kind of a frump, I guess. What's her name?"

"I count on you for information like that, Monica. Or we could ask Susan when she comes around."

"Susan's the brainy one, isn't she?"

"Don't let her hear you say that!"

"Do you know what I'd have done if I was Paris and they all came at me and said I had to make my choice? I'd divide my apple three ways."

Grandpa Goss thought that Paris should have done just that if he hadn't been such a fool. "You mustn't judge me too harshly if I say I'd have kept the apple and eaten it by myself when the ladies had all gone back to Olympus where they belong."

Monica's outrage at such an answer was a small sampling of what the goddesses in question would have poured on him if they had been literally present to hear. "But the apple was gold, you couldn't have eaten it," she said with withering scorn.

"There's always something that keeps us from choosing right," he said, fixing her with hungry eyes and thinking he really wanted no more of Tamisan Vail—for himself—than to sit and have flirtatious grandfatherly conversations like this with her. Or with the daughter like herself she might bear sometime for Jason if all went as it should. As it had to.

Whatever the primer-simple myth said about the neat division of specialties among the competing goddesses who ruined the original Paris, in his specific, complex case he was bound to proclaim that the "brainy one" fucked like a champion. From the first time she clutched him, Susan had taught him things. Was there no end at all to what he had to learn? Was the body of the woman truly as populated with secrets and novelties as the galaxy-spotted universe? And he condemned forever to be the earth-bound astronomer with a short telescope?

"I like the way you fuck," he blurted. "You don't need all those trick acrobatic positions to . . ."

". . . do my tricks? I thought it was you doing tricks to me! The only trick she has is gratitude. But . . . I think you like the way I fuck," she said with that mixture of modesty and confidence she allowed herself these days. She nuzzled her head in his armpit, toyed contentedly with the shaggy patterns of hair on his chest and belly.

"You fuck like a long-lost daughter," he speculated.

"Your Cordelia, sir. How would you know? You never had a daughter."

"Some women are daughter women," he said, caught up in the compulsion to make categories for all the chaos into which his blind member had intruded. "It seems to me there are all these kinds: daughter women, mother women, wife women, widow women, sister women. Also, it is possible to divide them into types by their animal similarities: lion women, horse women, elk women, gazelle women, moose women, rabbit women, dog women, cat women, squirrel women, giraffe women, cheetah women, possum women, fox women, gopher women, camel women, sheep women."

Her face went crepey with sorrow, wrinkling like the skin of a swimmer immersed too long in the water. "I don't want you stuck with just me when I'm only one and you're universal."

"Precisely what a daughter woman would feel! However, I'll take care of the others in my painting. Susan, truly I'm much more aware of the differences in age with you than I ever was with Maggie. She was much younger than you are when I married her. I don't understand."

"She made you feel as young as she. That was her gift I can't match."

"I'm glad you don't. The worst horror that could come on me would be to find myself as young as Jason. Worse yet to imagine I was." He gave a heartfelt shudder that convinced both of them.

"Was Maggie . . . good cunt? Always?"

He wanted her to have the solemn truth on this point, so he said, "I can't remember."

"Then she was the best. Whatever we know that consumes itself in being and doesn't have to leave a memory must be . . ."

"Best," he agreed. "And it shouldn't be remembered. But if painting was all it was cracked up to be, it ought to put it all together again so it wouldn't have to be remembered. Just exist."

So they agreed. Susan, with her non-acrobatic tricks, gave him back expectations he had forgotten. And in mournful jest wished it could be more. "You *deserve* a giraffe woman," she insisted. "All those spots and spindly legs! And, oh, think how good and long Sunday afternoons would be with the elephant girl, brought to you by Sabu, your servant, riding on her big skull."

"Write it in your notebook, Susan. I can't visualize as you can. Sabu on the skull, huh? Yes, I can see him. Poor little fellow with his turban. Stop distracting me with what I can't use this year!"

He had gone into her body expecting distraction, requiring peace. Requiring it for the sake of his work, he told himself. For the new paintings intimidated him. The emerging figures were inquisitors who would not let him off as gently as Monica or Susan. The painted women demanded that he stand up to them for a final answer—abominable, or sweet, or fatal as it might be.

To them he had committed from the beginning his lunatic infatuation with Tamisan. They would not let him off until he had resolved it. Or so he thought now. And he answered to them what he could not fully divulge to Susan. They knew how good she was for him. He came to them still trembling from the excesses of his expanding lust.

Susan might mourn, "I'm not enough for you." And mean it or wish it to be denied.

But *they* knew.

They knew: the better it is, the more it's not enough. Knew that lust and desire feed on their own satisfaction, and expand abominably and immorally toward the infinite.

Chapter 15

No word at all came from Tamisan and Jason on the farm.

"They probably murdered each other or never went there," Goss grumbled. "Have you written to them, Susan?"

"They're about the only ones I *have* written to about you and me," she said. "Do you want me to phone?"

"Absolutely not! We mustn't meddle"—said the shameless meddler.

Instead of the word he was waiting for, the mail disgorged such picayune annoyances as Marian Burke's letter.

Dear Dean,

I have the Acquisitions Committee approval! We have the money for the two "lost" paintings. Larry Purdin, the museum curator, could not be happier, nor could I. "Maggie with Accordion" I must have near us, for obvious sentimental reasons, and "Children on the Roof" is just as haunting, though I don't know in what it originated. I wasn't there. The two paintings will go in a "Goss Room," Larry tells me. (Funds also available for that.) That will make nine Goss pieces along with the bronzes. Not bad for a provincial city like ours.

As you know from Fiona, they are the real thing. She, at least, has no doubt about it, and of course she is the authority. However, since there are state funds involved, the committee is reluctant to conclude the purchase without a letter from you or from Bruce Behn authenticating the two canvases.

By now I think Bruce is simply being evasive. Neither phone calls nor letters have produced any positive answer from him. Is he thinking of selling to someone else? Please don't let him

do that. And please, Dean, take the time to dictate the letter
we need and, when you're in town, sign the canvases.
Stan sends his best.

Love,
Marian

Earlier, Fiona might have taken it on herself to compose the
necessary letter, forging Goss's signature with complete confidence he would never bring the matter up again once he had
put it out of mind.

But he chose to make an issue out of Marian's "pushiness"
—revenging himself on her innocent enthusiasm because he got
her letter instead of what he was waiting to hear.

For the first time Susan felt she had to oppose him. "You're
being cranky, my dear. I'll write the letter for you and all you'll
have to do is sign it. We could even go into town overnight
for you to sign the canvases."

"No," he said brusquely. "I have too much on my mind right
now. You can write to Marian and tell her I'm too busy to
get involved with their horse trading."

As a matter of literal truth, when he spoke he had just been
spending two hours reconstructing a sand castle Monica had
built on the beach the day before.

"All that is the dealer's job," he said pettishly. "Why doesn't
Bruce do what he gets paid for?"

"He thinks you're tricky," Susan said firmly.

"*What?*" The hurt and outrage seemed genuine. He put his
head down in grief.

"You disclaimed those three things he sold to the Armitages,"
she said. She had heard the story from both Fiona and Vidal.

"That's true," Goss admitted. "I didn't like them. I might
not like these things if I saw them again."

"But you'd painted them! Bruce must have lost five years'
profit on you before the Armitages let him off the hook. It isn't
a matter of money, though. Marian's your friend. I think you
have to do the decent thing."

"I did that when I made the paintings. Let them carry on

from there. Oh, I know what they're talking about, and I don't doubt they're genuine. They're not fakes if Fiona says they're not. I suspect Bruce—or his client—is being devious. He's trying to work on my feelings. Maybe because he lost money to the Armitages. Do you expect me to submit to emotional blackmail?"

He seemed on the way to working himself into a convincing rage at all his exploiters and Susan went silent. But, after a while, when he had made Monica's sand castle more fit for the habitation of dreams, he said with soft yearning, "I wouldn't mind seeing the paintings again, to tell the truth. In the one of Maggie, I did some *very* thin overpainting on a thick impasto. It's against all the rules. I'm sure I used too much turp. All that nice overlay of color must be soaked in or blown away by now. Moth-wing stuff, played off against some *very* bold— massive—strokes. I could use that in what I'm doing now if I was sure it would hold up. . . . If I could only think of a way to get them without falling into Bruce's trap. . . ."

The small contentions and oppositions between them were not, Susan counseled herself, to be taken as more than guideposts by which she must find her way beside him as he moved. He was not being eaten by invisible teeth. He was only being nibbled. And, wisely, she supposed all the little riffles in his mood could be attributed to the turbulence naturally generated by his work. To look for explanations outside of that was to misunderstand him riskily. There was no man to be accounted for outside the artist. The core and the periphery of his life were linked, and had long been linked, by the devious fibers he had knitted in front of his easel.

She sorted the hints he gave her, guessing that those he let out inadvertently might be more important than those that came from intent. She did not mean to outsmart him in large things. So she followed Fiona's example—as well as she could—in outsmarting him amid those circumstances that he could not tend to himself.

It seemed to her a small but shrewd ploy to suggest that she drive in to the Behn Galleries and fetch back the two paintings still awaiting validation.

"I'd forgot about them again," he said when she mentioned her intent. "Why would I want to have them here?"

"The overpainting? The thin paint over the thick?"

He stared at her patiently, with nothing more than tolerance for her inexperience with the problems of his craft. "Go if you want," he said. "I must be getting on your nerves."

She was crestfallen. Decided not to go. Then he said, "You're quick, dear! You see what I need before I do. And if you drive into New York to fetch the pictures—wonderful idea—you might just as well swing on down to the farm and see what the *hell* those kids have done with it. That is, they wouldn't mind *your* intruding on them and I'd bungle it some way. Now, Susan, I know what I'm like when I'm this wrapped up in something I haven't solved. Inexcusable, but I can't help it. And if you spent a few days with them . . . You'll like the place. And . . . I've seen you're worried about them."

"I'm not worried about them," she said. She hesitated a couple of days to see if his mood or mind would shift again. Loving but leery, she suspected a trick. At least she would have liked to be assured of whether the proposed errands were of major or minor importance to him. Whether they were camouflage for something else he had in mind. She worried that she was, already, getting on his nerves. He gave no further sign that meant anything to her.

Before she left, she said, "Why haven't you had Jean Simons in to pose for you since I came back? One of the main theatrical diversions of your studio when I first came was watching Jean parade around naked while you paid no attention to her. You seemed to feel her body warmth and that was good for you."

"Oh, oh, oh," he said. "I haven't thought of *naked* women lately. Besides, I've got you."

"Not in the corner of your eye while you're working. Shall I call Jean back for you? Or some other girl?"

He thought this over for hours. "That girl who was out with your daughter," he said.

"Janis Ward?"

"My memory for names is failing. Pendulous breasts . . ."

"That's Janis," Susan confirmed. "You identify people with great precision. Janis is a pendular person." She was not at all pleased that he should even have thought of Janis as a model and not at all sure that Janis would accept the role. But it was his wish. Her command. She wrote a letter to Janis, taking thoughtful pains to include in this letter the information that she and the master were going to be married.

Susan drove all the way to Pennsylvania pondering the choice of Janis. Somewhere on the turnpike it seemed clear enough to her that Goss could hardly have been less interested in taking another look at that indifferent body. Of course, of course, what he had in mind was getting Janis in a position of vulnerability and seducing information from her. About Tamisan, of course. And Susan felt the same discomfort about this she had felt on the day she saw the girls posing in the garden, though so many, many crucial changes had been made all around.

Fretful about this, she was very glad to be able to phone back, as soon as she had reached the farm, that Jason and Tamisan had never seemed more tranquil.

"Like they'd grown up here and never been away," she confided into the phone, with a sincere lilt in her voice. "Your gamble with them paid off, old man. So far, it has paid off. Really, they're impossible. To have such anguishes and get over them with so little sign. Makes me want to thrash them."

To which Goss only said, "You will stay with them awhile, won't you? I want you to get the feel of the place too, love. Some of my happiest years lie around you there. Of course I miss you a hell of a lot. But as long as you're there . . ."

"Ha!"

"Now, Susan, they need you. I need you. We must try to spread you thin."

"Spread! I like that idea."

"Come back at once!" he commanded with a goatish chuckle. So she said she would do what he required, and stay at least a week.

She called him twice more during that week, once reporting, as an amusing afterthought, "They've become the same odd couple they were last winter. With an astounding difference. Tamisan affirms and swears they've been on a 'sex fast' ever since you sent them here."

"Jesus Christ!"

"I know it sounds very odd. And they roam the night naked as giraffes. They lie around the boathouse . . . *we* lie around the boathouse in a state of original innocence. It's all very easy here. We're all breathing your happy years."

"You mean . . . nothing at all?"

"I don't listen at their bedroom door. I think about you. But I pass on faithfully what I was told."

"My God. They don't even read books, either, do they?"

"They're never bored. Those things would distract them. They're trying to 'get through.' They're trying to 'achieve a state of being rather than doing.' They honestly want us to understand what nirvana or blessedness or extra-worldliness it is that they expect to achieve. They sit quietly in various rooms. They look at leaves. They try to memorize the shape of clouds. Looking for creation, Jason says. They count bees in the orchard. I'm making it sound goofy, and it's not for us, darling. But, you know, it's very, very sweet."

"The devils!"

"You want me to get them copulating, is that it? I'll pass it on as your wish and then I suppose . . ."

"Leave them to their fate. You won't forget to bring the paintings from Bruce's gallery, will you?"

"Forget? Who, me? That was my main mission when I left home. I know you didn't want me to come down here, and I will hurry back, but I'm so enjoying the sun and the slow, slow days, and I want you to miss me deliciously. Have you heard from Janis Ward?"

"Who?"

"Never mind," Susan said. "I'll come soon because I can't help it. And if they have any secrets, I couldn't dig them out anyway."

"You're a wise and splendid woman, Susan."

"Who doubts that?"

When she got back to North Atlantic, she found him anxiously waiting—for the paintings she brought in the back of the car. George Vendler helped uncrate them in the studio. Susan had never seen Goss's interweaving passions for his paintings and his human loves so nakedly on display. He was not in tears at this reappearance of his beloved things but softened to an excitement that tears would have expressed too violently.

"Well, well, well, well," he said, pulling his beard at the two paintings when they were propped against the feet of his easels. "That's our Maggie, fixing to entertain some of our bibulous friends at the farm. So many people used to come around, Susan, and it all seemed so easy then. How'd she manage? Of course the kids don't want crowds around them just now. It's all changed. . . ."

Of the other painting he said, "Well, of course that's Jason, and I could sit down and write out for you the names of those kids with him. They're on the roof of the boathouse you saw by the river. Probably what spoiled him was he always counted on Maggie to gather his friends for him. We knew how lonely he was. We did what we could. Hey, don't their summer shirts look like flags? Ho! It was late summer. Like now. Well, they look like a bunch of hydrocephalic minnows, and if I could only paint like Fiona, I should have. I should have caught them as they were—not butchered up into abstractions because I'm so stylish."

It was not just memories he was trying to accommodate. It was the paintings themselves, those labyrinths of style and distortion in which the once-upon-a-time faces had been intentionally lost. "Lord," he said, "all anyone who deserves these had to do was look at the signature to know they're mine."

When he spoke of the signature he did not literally mean the D.G. with which he signed most things. It wasn't visible on either canvas. He meant the black, gray and lavender outlines in which the colors of the accordion pleats and the uplifted arms of the girl bride were caught like treasures from Atlantis hauled up by surprise in a fisherman's net. The faun's ears in vermilion listening as much to the song of the grass as to the instrument. The accordion keys each in a different color and shape as if the music were in them, trembling with vibrations of light instead of vibrations on the air. The transparency of the fingers achieved by those casual, arabesque shapes of line over line.

He said to George, "I was not so bad in those days, was I?" He put his left hand flat on the impasto and let it roam while his palm was tickled by the hills and watercourses of old paint mounded on the limbs and curving throat. "Thank God, nobody got at it with varnish. Susan, most of the overpainting is there."

She had been sent to spy for him. On Tamisan and Jason. On Maggie. On the farm. The vanished and forbidden years. There was so much to tell him about her thoughts and experiences of the week away that, finally, she told him very little, and he asked few questions.

But he got what he needed. She was sure of that. Her true commission had been to go blind and to come back blind, bearing the rumor of a reality that the blind have a better chance of grasping than those distracted by spectacle.

Her body, the true body inside the illusions of the senses, was his net, lowered into the waters and retrieved by him full of lively, threshing fish. When he took her, she felt his hands freeing their strange, glittering flesh from the net with gratitude for the catch. She spilled onto him the alien, familiar truth of experiences that swim below the levels of memory. With her heels spread against his beautiful sheets, she clung to him and gave and gave.

She was an artist's wife. She was going to be a very good

one. Better and better. And what she gave him would be enough because it had to be. This total, blind release to him was her crowning accomplishment and she gloated in it, believing her trip had been a success though she could not have said how.

Later she suggested to him, "We could keep the paintings I brought back. We could buy them ourselves. Can't we? I'd like to feel in some way I've brought Maggie back to you and that would be a sign."

"We could," he said cautiously. "But we won't. I need them now. I'll only want them a little longer. Then we'll let them go out in the world again. No one must be cheated and they don't belong to me any more."

from Susan Vail's red notebook:

Maggie Goss's ashes are scattered over what is still called the Handy Farm. Her 1930 Ford station wagon is still parked in the garage. The furniture Maggie found to restore the farmhouse as it must have looked when the Handys built it in the 1850s is still placed in the rooms as it was when Maggie and Jason left it on their doomed trip to Paris five years ago this summer. In the boathouse (Maggie had it built on the little jog of river that indents a corner of the farm below the barn that Goss used as a studio in the summers they were all here) there is still the red canoe that is one of Jason's earliest memories. There is also the single scull that Goss used as a young man in California.

Layers of the past. Another maze into which the Gosses can retreat, or advance backward, or whatever they do—though neither Jason nor his father had been back there since her funeral.

"Yet another museum," Jason said when I stayed my few days with him and Tamisan. "Gosses make museums, don't they? Maggie's more alive for you, when you see her place this way, than she is for me." He was melancholy about this—a musing, peaceful melancholy that both Tamisan and I were tuned to share while we loafed about together and meditated as one can in any museum, breathing air that is both past and present,

313

listening to the tick of a clock that only specifies minutes and hours, never years. Looking at each other as museum pieces too, without grief or resentment.

No. I'll swear that the two of them, camping out on this borderland between past grief and happiness, were no more desperate than I was and no more menaced by ghosts of the place than I. Whatever was in Goss's mind when he badgered them into coming to the farm was working.

"It's easy enough to see his line of reasoning," Jason said with tolerant fondness and the pleasure he takes in being his father's pawn when he feels his father's imagination alive. "A matter of touching the right bases. We're talking of going to Paris after this, you know. He thought if I could shuck my fears of coming back here . . . oh, I'd be *open* and not afraid when I got to Paris, where the terrible stuff started with Maggie."

"Was he right?"

"Certainly. Except it was never just fear of coming back. His psychology was exactly right. But there's more to it than psychology."

"There always is. Maybe he's right about the rest, too."

"He's bound to be," Jason said. Convinced and convincing. "If we can only find the right signs to know what the rest is."

From that distance to which he'd sent us, we readjusted our views of Goss, back in his studio. And believed he had intended that too. At last I was taken in, I felt, to the meditations that had gone on last winter in that empty place in the middle of Manhattan. All three of us talked a lot about the man whose wife I had (essentially) become. We also knew him in layer on layer of silences. Wandering over the fields by night or day. Sitting in the boathouse dangling our feet in the water that comes into the horseshoe shape of decking under the rich brown gloom of the shingled roof. A thousand of the indoor and outdoor crannies that only we were inhabiting now.

At night I listened attentively to the house sounds. There were little creatures—maybe squirrels, the caretaker had told Jason—somewhere in the walls of the upper story or in the attic, and I used the sounds of their invisible creeping to make up ghosts of the place, as I did when I was a child at home. For I felt that I had been sent here by Goss to measure more than the mental health of our children. That I, just like them, was the sensing, spying apparatus that he was lowering into the underworld, the regions of the dead.

Was Maggie more alive for me there than for Jason? There were lovely, and I must say erotic, moments at the edge of sleep when I had very cozy hours with her, feeling without jealousy or alarm, either, that one wife was just as alive for him as another. Letting go in the spell of such meditations, I didn't need to envy Minna the spunk of his youth or Maggie the ceremonial yielding of her seventeen-year-old virginity. I knew (better than I know many less important things) Maggie's good years with Jason here. And have even come back from such states of trance knowing how much all her life was a triumphant make-believe.

Meditate, I say, on that 1930 Ford station wagon! (Because the *whole* of the Handy Farm is a subject for history and not meditation. Even the summers they spent here when Goss was at the height of his powers leads on to the distractions of a history I have not been directed to write.)

Pure make-believe in Maggie's hands. She bought that car in mint condition in 1960. An extravagance of the sort for which both husband and son adored her. "Maggie was a spendthrift." Goss never said a more revealing thing about her life and death than that. The true and honorable epitaph for a lovely woman dead of cancer at thirty-one.

The proletarian station wagon, so costly, and everything she did to make Handy Farm new by filling it with antiques—well, it strikes me as being more than a little bit like Marie Antoinette's having the simulated peasant cottages on the palace grounds at Versailles. I am not tempted to dismiss either one as vanity or showing off, but "make-believe" in another sense. Make-believe born out of a secret foreboding about things to come, an attempt to burrow back into the security of a time and a way of life further away from the dimly seen disaster.

Maggie, that rich English girl—in American farm country she

was a determined, self-styled populist. She was one of the neighbors. Though she and Jason and Goss lived most of the year in New York—sometimes Paris or Rome—many of her friends of the time were local farmers, teachers, merchants, and mechanics of nearby Story City. Maggie sometimes rode with the Philadelphia Hunt. But for years she managed the sharecropping of that part of the farm that is cultivated. According to Jason, she would have run for a place on the local school board if she could have met the residence requirements. (She settled her formal political passions by campaigning for Senator Burke in his state instead.) When she was not scampering around the community in her station wagon, she rode her Morgan stallion about the country byways, a make-believe country girl of the time she yearned back for.

At North Atlantic in the music room there is an equestrian portrait Goss painted of her—actually a sort of cartoon, one of those mammoth simplified statements that he sometimes used to complete in a single day's work. Against a green that might be evening light before a storm, a huge red horse is lunging away with its girl rider, fragile as a new moon. I asked once, because the painting is so ominous, if it had been his premonition of her death. "No, it was the way she looked," he told me then.

Here on the farm I spoke about the painting to Jason and we agreed that premonitions are only so called by people who believe that time goes in a regular, straightforward, measurable direction. At Handy Farm, while I was there, I resisted the pressure to believe anything that rational.

The boathouse is another of Maggie's Marie Antoinette creations. Jason has told me and Tamisan anecdotes of all the celebrated and splendid people who visited here over the years. (I have lists and may set all that down sometime.) The airport, twenty-five miles away, was an imaginary hub of a network spun over the globe to Vienna, Tokyo, Berlin and the other capitals. In the Maggie years Goss was riding the crest of some marvelous friendships and had more appetite for them than he has now. Maggie and Jason picked the visitors up in the station wagon. Maggie entertained them on the lawn or in the orchard with her accordion and hillbilly songs.

And one might think she built the boathouse, too, for the entertainment of those people who come more rarely now to North Atlantic.

Or—free choice—think her generous forethought added it to the older buildings of the farm as a place for the three of us to meditate together when we came back from swims out into the river. Its artful brown gloom is the enchanted hideaway for our daytime nudity. We undressed there and swam out the open end into the river and came back unobserved by neighbors— who in any case seem to have displayed a decent indifference to the return of Maggie Goss's son.

I sat on one side of the brown, twinkling, six feet of water between the two deck areas along the sides of the building, look- ing, not really looking, at the kids stretched on the deck across from me. "What we are doing, my children, is posing for Dean Goss. Showing him our bodies."

"Is he here too?" Tamisan asked drowsily and languidly. She rolled over, as if to hide her breasts and bush of hair.

"We're all, always, parts of his mind," I said. To say it aloud or not aloud could not have mattered less in that dreamy, mo- tionless heat inside the boathouse. "Tamisan, the paintings he is making now are his way of putting together the one you tore up. It was only three naked girls in a garden scene when you got at it. When he gets it back together again it will be all the women in his life. Everything that all of us can gather up and bring him. All we can bring of Maggie, too."

"True?" Tamisan asked Jason.

"Yes," he told her. "Susan always tells the truth."

I told Goss they were on a sex fast. That is what they told me and I see no good in disbelieving it. But there was this strange, good erotic tinge that the three of us laid over Handy Farm—not to bring Maggie back to life again, but to commune with her and, as I think, to serve her man. It sensitized us in the kind of innocent intimacy where words are only necessary to mark the points you have come to, not to scramble awkwardly toward them.

We were three transients camped in the buildings among the hilly thickets, orchard and meadows. We were in a "learning situation"—to use the phrase of those who helped miseducate my child. I need not say that Maggie's boathouse was our schoolhouse, or that as we idled nakedly on the quaint horseshoe decks inside it and paddled our feet in the water that we were like the School of Athens where all those famous fags ogled each other's penises while they developed their metaphysics.

Still, in that boathouse bodily awareness wove a mysterious, trustworthy connection among our thoughts. And what on earth were we doing if not exploring the good old standard question: What is art? The question which, in its ramifications, had paralyzed our Jason and made him, in some sense, impotent.

What is art and what does it mean to pose for an artist? To be his model? We had come some distance, at any rate, since that day in the garden when *posing* seemed only to mean dropping the towel to show the works to the sketchers and painters sitting cross-legged on Fiona's well-kept grass.

Out of the body, idea leads on to idea. My meditations from the boathouse (with its summery, country gloom) lead coherently on to thoughts that Maggie, the actor's daughter, was posing for her men all her life. What? Showing them with this plaything farm of hers what paradise on earth might be, if it were centered in the right woman? Teasing them beyond her life with intimations of how the paradise might be regained?

Goss says the best thing about her was her "gorgeous willingness." One must take it for granted that this includes the erotic and no doubt originated there, though it spread in all womanly ways beyond that and now into the crannies of memory. (I think of her as gorgeously willing when I pose my body for hers under his thumping tenderness in bed.)

Goss says he first met her at an exhibition of his paintings in London. She was there with an aunt, who introduced them. "Oh yes," he said, "you're the daughter of Sir Gregory Niles," and he expressed some adequately sincere respect for her father's movies. "Well," Maggie said, "yes, but he's only an actor." He says she gave him other signals on that first encounter. What sort of signals? "Body signals," he says. They were great on bodies, he and Maggie, and on the capacity of the body to convey a whole rich slew of metaphors and propositions which the arts, particularly the visual arts, can only approximate. All in all, she gave him to understand as quickly as he wanted to that she was quite ready to swap her actor father for the real thing, on whatever terms he might think appropriate.

"Sir Gregory was a very vain man," Goss says. "I could see it was a blow to him when he began to suspect I was calling around to see Maggie rather than to pay my tributes to his talents. But the speed of our consummation was the clinching factor in his hostility. Within a month, when Maggie announced she wanted to meet me in Paris, she told the old gent that she was pregnant and added as an afterthought that she had not been a virgin since the first evening I called at their flat to dine."

The resultant furor, he supposes now, resulted from "the clash of mighty egos," his and Sir Gregory's, over who should appear to be in the right. "It built up. The old fool got the police on us in Paris. The press came soon after them. Then in Rome, Copenhagen, Oslo and finally in Mexico City, on Sir Gregory's complaint that I was a notorious American who was probably keeping his child drugged and terrorized as I carted her about the world for my vicious pleasure." In Mexico City D.G. got off to the press some indiscreet remarks about what he had saved Maggie from at home. "Everyone knows what the senile English dandies are like."

Maggie was enjoying it all. And in retelling it to Jason, of course, made it part of the grandeur and romance of the times before his time, the clash of giants out of which he had been begotten. She intended for them all to live bigger than life. It was obligatory for Jason to be a prodigy. His musical ability cannot have been a surprise to her. Let's just say it was part of her merry intent, already gestating that day she contrived to be introduced to Dean Goss and signal her interest. She married a giant to have a giant son; she needed in her very personal world not only father and husband but a son who could have astonished the other world. Her father died a couple of years after Jason's birth. D.G. would die before she was old. Jason would go with her to the end. It was her imperial whim to consort with genius.

No—speaking as a woman in love, a writer in love, I can say it more bravely than this: after the first time he fucked her in her own bedroom before her father got home late from a board meeting of Unicorn Films and tidied up for dinner, she learned there is a potency of the spirit that only partly coincides with physical potency.

The same confidence, I suppose, is displayed by her neglecting to bear any brothers and sisters for Jason. "It was no one's conscious decision," I have been told. "We were at it all the time. All my wives have been so good in bed it obscures their other merits. She never used contraceptives." There was one sad stillbirth when Jason was two. After that, only nuptial joy. It was as if, in this matter, too, Maggie had said a heartfelt "Enough."

And yet, in her good and happy life, too, one has to reckon with an unappeasable hunger. I gather that finally when she knew she was going to die she began for the first time to show spite toward both husband and son. As if they had tricked her and denied her some common formula for survival that she deserved from them.

"From day to day it wasn't clear to me whether I ought to let Jason go to the hospital to see her," D.G. says. "She wanted to be remembered at her best—and she wanted all her resentments to be heard, like any jealous woman who is being deserted by unfaithful men. At the end it was not pretty."

D.G. remembers one chilly October afternoon when he and Jason had come to sit in a little concrete park across the street from the hospital, because they hadn't strength or heart to go any farther after their visit. He remembers that the park was surrounded by a palisaded steel fence—shapes of the lances he used in his painting of "The Surrender."

Jason said to him, "Is it true that we're killing her?"

"Did she say that?" He thought it just conceivable that in her pain and wasted courage Maggie might have said anything.

"Not in so many words."

"Then why do you think we are?"

"To get life for art or music . . . it has to come from some-where. Everything has to come from somewhere. Maybe we took hers. If she had only so much to start with . . ."

D.G. says that there and then he had no faith to argue that this superstitious judgment was not as good as any other. "But I just don't *want* it to be so. Because if art and life are hostile to each other . . . if every attempt to enhance life and make it fine uses up some unexpendable part of the vital basis . . . then to be human is a mistake and the artists are the greatest fools and criminals of all. I had to be very careful with Jason on that point, because if I had tried to answer him like a little boy I would have lost him. If I had told him there is no need to ask questions like that, it would have been the end. Because we *are* artists, he and I, and the need lies in that fact. I've given my answer. He is still thinking it over."

A whole cluster of superstitions seems to hover around that trip to Paris when Maggie first learned of her inoperable malig-nancy. It was her first major jaunt alone with her son. They visited family in England first, and it was her "reconciliation" with her father, though the old gent was dead. It was a "coming of age" for Jason, when he would be her companion at all sorts of grown-up delights in Europe. And it was a "dive into the past," for after she had collaborated with D.G. in writing his book *The Body's Eye,* she wanted to visit more scenes and friends of his young days in preparation for writing more about him, either on her own or with his or Jason's collaboration. And, like a diver going too deep, she seems to have encountered something fatal at a depth she could not stand.

I can be swayed and moved and caught up by the romantic melancholy of these notions—perhaps because I am far enough removed from the immediate emotional shock to see it all as art, as a story that I might have made up, a story whose theme or central meaning is still cloudy enough to nag at me and keep me searching for a way to end it. But perhaps because I am brought into it closer than I would have expected, I have been made to know Maggie better than I could have if I had seen her riding her big horse or driving her antique wagon.

And I hear her voice when she was dying and said to the man she loved more than anything, "Now you have made me old." It is a wound I share with her and with them too.

Death, too, is a pose that lovely women take.

More seductive than any other to the artist? Was that what Jason, Tamisan and I were meditating in the boathouse by the not quite restless backwater that fills its interior between the decks, while beyond the open end the full current of the river sweeps on without meditation?

Natural to the point of inevitability that I should breathe thoughts of Maggie—like breathing her fine ashes—those few days I spent at the farm. Meditate on her while I listened to the house sounds in the changing winds at night. Among her things . . . I need another word to name what I breathe when I am among her things or with her men. *Persuasions?*

Goss says—I think it is in my other notebook somewhere: "One must first persuade the body." Belief will not stick until the body is persuaded.

(Correction: I have looked it up since my return to North Atlantic. This time the quote is not from Goss but from Emerson. Ah well. He too derives from others. We all pose for each other. Wear each other's disguises when we are at our best.)

An oriental ceramic piece that Maggie found in Brussels once sits there on a Shaker pie chest she bought at a local auction. I touched it as I have never dared touch things in a museum.

Maggie's things persuade me.

Handy Farm would not have been enough if we had not had music. "Life without music would be a mistake." I suppose Goss did not say that either, and I must shake the habit of attributing every wise thing I recall to him.

Back here now I meditate on Tamisan sitting in the orchard playing her guitar and singing for us one morning while I counted the bees among the ripening pears. She had her blue guitar on her jean-clad knees, and I lounged there with a certain apprehension, because she had grumbled, "I'm still no damn good at it."

"Good enough," Jason said. As she began I only hoped she would not toss the guitar away into the grass as she has tossed away so much that thwarted her.

She sang:

> "Why should a foolish marriage vow
> That long ago was made
> Oblige us to each other now
> That passion has dee-cayyyyy-uddddd?"

She sang her song through to the end, blushed, and tried to disclaim the merit of her performance by saying, "Uh, Janis found me the lyrics. William Dryden? Joseph Dryden? John Dryden? Someone like that."

One night when the moon was in its second quarter, she led me out of the house into the dark orchard, saying, "We've got a surprise for you, Mama."

She held my elbow to keep me from being impatient. In a few minutes, then, we heard Jason's cello, the music coming from the house.

"It's the solo variation in D major from *Don Quixote*," Tamisan whispered.

The hell it was. It was the grass of the dark lawn and meadows finding its voice in the dark. It was the leaves talking to the moon. It was the damned earth itself complaining and rejoicing, dancing in its cold orbit.

"It's not the real thing," Jason said softly, from somewhere near us, though I did not even try to see him while I listened. It was a tape, but he was listening too.

"That," he said a while later, "that's an attack with the up-bow." He sounded like his father talking about the body of the painter working on a canvas.

When the tape was finished (not the music; it's still here, bothering me as I type), I said, "Could you still do it that well, Jason?"

"It's not just a matter of fingering. It's the right arm, too, Susan. It's . . . No. When I do something, I know it won't be the cello."

While I was there, I heard tapes, too, of Maggie playing her accordion. But not her voice. "Sure, we had some tapes," Jason said. "But maybe they got destroyed. I don't remember. Maybe Dad or I . . ."

They destroy so much, as Goss told me at the beginning.

It was a fine morning when I left them. There were still patches of mist in the river valley. The stones in the high wall that borders the lane were still damp from the night. There were dewy spider webs in the hedges. A smell of fruit on the breeze. The motor of the big car idling, murmuring just a bit unevenly with the involuntary motion of my foot on the pedal.

"You tell 'm I *am* taking care of Jason," Tamisan said.

I remember Jason's scoffing grin—like any common boy scoffing at the notion he needed taking care of.

He frowned and looked over the big morning and the hills. He had his arm around Tamisan's shoulders as they stood near the car window, saying a brief good-by as any children might. They had promised to come join the rest of us soon.

He looked at the morning world and said, "We *could* have all this."

Chapter 16

Tamisan woke late. Jason was up and outside before her. She was brushing her teeth when he climbed the stairs to bring her a letter that had come in the morning mail. With a mad-dog wreath of foam and a toothbrush handle jutting from her jaws, Tamisan put her head out the bathroom door and asked, "D'I ever tell you I won the tooth-brushing contest in fourth grade?"

Jason asked, "D'you brush more people's teeth than the rest of the kids?"

Tamisan clapped her thighs to stop herself from giggling. She reached to take the envelope he handed her, recognizing by its pale blue tint that it was from Janis Ward.

"I'll start our breakfast," Jason offered, and whisked away to leave her with her news from the world of calendars and clocks. "Two eggs?"

"At least," she said.

As she unfolded the blue pages of Janis' letter a clipping slithered out. From the *Times* obituary page.

Frankfurt, Aug. 10—Zachary Sandler, producer, critic, author and sponsor of many avant-garde movements in music and art, was found dead in his hotel room this morning, apparently from an overdose of barbiturates. He was 47 years old. . . .

Tamisan shook her head in violent denial. Her first wild thought was that Janis had written to accuse her of having killed Sandler. Her second thought was just as furtive and powerful and unreasonable: It's another trick he's pulled on me and now I can never get free of him. . . .

She started to read Janis' letter.

Your lucky and obviously happy mother has asked me to come back to North Atlantic for a while. Hope to see you there.

*She gave me the good news you and Jason are together again.
No surprise. I didn't take your overwrought emotional condition, when last I saw you, as the last word. . . .*

*. . . I enclose the clipping though I'm sure you don't want
to be reminded of Z since you broke so completely with him.
Actually—I never told you this; there was no need—I saw him
twice after our absurd "Black Mass" at his place. You can be
sure he was not interested in me. He wanted to hear how you
were getting on with Jason, since, he said resignedly, you would
not talk to him and had even run away once when he saw you
on the street. I would hardly say Z was remorseful for the part
he played in your life. Yet, as others do, he respected your
potential for becoming an extraordinary human being. . . .*

*. . . I send this news merely because I don't want you to be
confronted with it sometime when you're off guard. And want
to caution again that you* mustn't *make out of circumstances
and coincidences so much more than they require. An imagination like yours can run too far too fast with superstitious suggestions. Wasn't your running from Jason another example of
your overreacting to what you imagine? The Goss establishment may have overawed you, but they are worldly and generous people, not likely to be ruffled by the shadows you imagine.
Your imagination is what makes us all fascinated with you, but
it's a peril to yourself. While things are still delicate between
you and Jason, don't for heaven's sake fall to imagining Z's death
so far away means anything at all. Though it is cruel to put it
this way, I hope you are relieved. . . .*

*. . . what happened to my candelabrum? The apartment was
neat as a pin when I came back from Vermont (thanks) but
the candelabrum seems to have vanished. You see, my mind
is occupied with very trivial everyday mysteries. It had no real
value.*

Love,
J

Relieved? No, she was trapped. Janis' trivial, everyday opinions meant no more to her than the impersonal language of the

clipping. Some people managed to live by such bare selected facts, all right, and probably she could live with some people by counting only those few practical realities. But not with Jason. The truth he could survive by was not put together like a few rosary beads of fact to be fingered over and over again in public.

"Stop lying," Fiona had said. Just that simply. The grand simplicity of her prescription had been mighty impressive to Tamisan. It was elegant, it was queenly, to live by such commandments. Only the rich could afford to pay any attention to them.

Yet Tamisan had meant to imitate a good thing when she caught sight of it. If she had not meant to stop lying, she would not have come down here with Jason, whatever heavy pressure his father might have put on her. She had not lied to Jason—though it had to be said that he hadn't quizzed her, either. They had lived here in a quiet truce of silence, pretty much ignoring the immediate past while their pores took in whatever they could of more remote realities. Not much. They were happy together while the sun shone. At least they were not unhappy. They had sunk into the emptiness of being good together without any lies on her part. They were never going to get out of here without something more positive than that.

Jason had her breakfast ready for her in the sunny kitchen when she marched down to him with the obituary clipping in her hand. There were two white bowls set on opposite sides of the walnut table. In each bowl two boiled eggs gleamed and steamed. And even these common, good things seemed too terrifying to touch. Crack the shells with a knife . . . life or death might pop out and begin to crow.

She put the clipping announcing Sandler's death down beside Jason's napkin. "I lied to you about Sandler," she said. "It was true I only called him from Janis' to threaten him. I said I'd kill him. Now, maybe I have killed him. I lied to you, anyway, by not telling you any more. I never told you how he was involved with you."

Jason cut an egg in half. His clean, strong fingers held the halves of it as the golden yellow of the yolk flowed viscously into the white bowl. He seemed no more intent on listening to her than on puzzling at the mystery of egg colors, egg shapes, the delicate changes.

"You said a funny thing at Janis'," she reminded him. "You said I was at Sandler's when you went there looking for me."

"There was a boy I thought resembled you," Jason said lightly.

"Maybe I was there. I mean, maybe it was my presence you felt. How can you tell? What can you trust? There may have been a boy there. It wasn't an accident you thought he looked like me."

"You know him?"

She shook her head. "I know what Sandler's capable of. He fucks minds. How can you be sure it wasn't me?"

"I saw his prick," Jason said, his voice still light, almost careless, remote, and yet thrilling. There was no trace of joking in his tone and what he had just admitted terrified her. She nodded and said, "That sounds like Sandler's magic. Don't ask me how he manages to make things come together the way he does. You've got to believe he used me to take you in."

She was clearly not saying anything Jason was unready to consider seriously. She could feel a tremor like terror emanating from him, but it was as if the terror were something old and familiar, akin to the ecstatic sympathies they had shared in sex, the glimpses of inexplicable realities that their druid meditations had been founded on.

"I don't know if he's dead now," she said, meaning that she was not sure it was her own voice, mind and will speaking through her lips, or whether they gave life to Sandler's intent. Meaning that and being all too readily understood. Still, like someone trying to joke free of the encroachments of hypnotism, Jason said, "Even if you had a big affair with him . . . it ended, didn't it, when Janis delivered you to me?"

"Janis never knew what was going on. She thought she got you and me together. It had all been decided before she put her two cents in. I told him what she had in mind. I told him everything in those days. He just thought of using her to make it seem more innocent than it was. He loves to produce illusions. He's an artist. You know what Mama said about our all being a part of your father's mind? There isn't anything I can think of about your father I couldn't say about Sandler. 'Take care of Jason,' your father said. 'Take care of Jason,' Sandler said before I ever started living with you. When you first gave me a key to your place, I had to give Sandler a copy of it. He never went there. I'm sure he didn't. But it was to show I trusted him to leave us alone. To show I had faith in what he promised, that he wouldn't come actually watching you and me go at it. And even if I loved you, it was supposed to be because he wanted that to happen. He wanted me to remember he might have come in sometime when we were fucking. And he said thinking about that would keep me hot."

For Jason, listening, there was strangely more relief than surprise. It was as if he had known, heard it before. As if now a human voice might be repeating out loud what the wind had whistled to him the first night he had driven in to New York looking for her, not so much wishing her dead, probably, as knowing how she might appeal to him from the far side of death, luring him on with secrets no one else could share with him. "Did it?" he asked dreamily. He felt very hungry, but he made no move to eat the beautiful eggs in the beautiful bowl in front of him. Hunger seemed to have gone from his mouth to his eyes and then was displaced again so it was not in his body at all, but was like something around them in the room. "Was that what kept you hot?"

"I always *was* hot with you." She did not know how to divide one cause from another. He saw that she was not so much confessing to him something she was sure of as sharing a tormenting mystery, trying to hurt him so his pain would help disclose what she was determined now to know.

"Why did he care?"

"If I was hot with you? I was his gift to you. He wants to do favors for people. So they'll belong to him. He likes to own what nobody knows he owns."

"Did you catch me for him?"

"I don't know if I *did*, Jason. I have to tell you what he wanted because . . . really, you trust make-believe the way he does. And you know what's real and what isn't the same way. Sometimes I'm sure and sometimes I'm not. I wouldn't know if there really was a boy there the night you went to his house for me. You saw . . . did he fuck you?"

"No," Jason said, and saw her shiver with relief, as if she knew by that he had refused one of the baited hooks set to capture him. "But it made me hot thinking afterward that he might have. Those things melt in together."

"We're in just as deep one way or another," she agreed. "He wanted you seduced because he said you had an instinct for chastity. He says he heard it when you played the cello."

"It's what my second teacher used to say. Basil Grabehart. It wasn't supposed to be a fault in my playing. It amused Maggie and Dad when they heard what he said."

"Sandler had heard you play?"

"I don't remember if he did."

"Could he have told from that?"

"I played what I felt. In winter, wherever we were, I used to play to bring summer and bring us back here. I knew, even then, by the time we got here and started unpacking it was not going to be as good as the music promised."

Tamisan said, "He wanted you seduced because you had this chastity and he had to prove to himself there wasn't anything he couldn't get through to. He doesn't believe in anything. Except his 'concepts.' I was his concept and maybe I still am. Do you remember *exactly* that first night I came to your place with Janis?"

"We talked about death."

Tamisan's eyes got wider and more desperate at the promptness of his answer. "See what you remember? That's how he can control our minds. Why do you remember that instead of anything else said or done? Did it make you hot, talking to me about death?"

"Yes."

"Was I hot?"

"I knew you were when I thought back to it."

Tamisan gave a ghastly, breathless laugh, as if every new admission from either of them was another rivet of a cage they had ignored until now. "You got the sniff of death. He meant you to get it. We were still ahead of you then. I hadn't tried to break away from him yet. I didn't think there was a chance until I knew you. Didn't want to break. Well, you were hot because I was. He knew all the ways to make me think hot. I guess we invented most of them together when he saw what a good student I was. I wasn't so bad before I knew him, but . . . I'll tell you one way. . . ." She made a crescent horseshoe shape in the air with the thumb and forefinger of her right hand. "There was this little *device* from his collection that I used to think about so much. It was made of wood and he said he got it from Japan. The idea—*idea!*—was for me to wear it during the day before I was going to spend the night with him. One end of it in my ass and the other end in my cunt. I was supposed to walk around with it. On the subways. Go to class wearing it. Keep it hidden from Mama at home. You can see I had to think about it a lot, even if I didn't wear it much. So it would remind me all the time to be thinking of things I would do for him when I was with him. To be inventive. It makes you think! Actually wearing it turned into I would get hot *thinking* about wearing it for him even when it was hidden home in a book I hollowed out for it. Then there would be another circle of thinking hot around that until everything I thought or saw would be involved. And I began to make up rules about how I would be his slave. Thinking I was his slave made me hottest of all—though that's why I wanted to kill him finally."

She made the crescent shape again with thumb and finger, to show, if not the permanence of the sign, at least its persistence and its power to reappear as long as there was flesh and memory to repeat it. Now as she spoke about it there was slavish degradation in her voice. Rather thrilling. Their eyes were fixed hard on the shape her hand imitated.

She said, "I made up the rule to wear it, a while at least, before I went out with any new person he wanted to do a favor for. I wasn't wearing it the night I came to your place with Janis, but I had been. I wanted to be sure I caught you for him. That's why you paid any attention to me at all."

"No."

She agreed mournfully. "That wasn't all. It never was. There's you and me in this damn puzzle somewhere. If we didn't really love each other I wouldn't have got mixed up figuring ways we could break his hold. It's true I didn't go back to him after—you might as well hear the worst—the time he and one of his other girls shaved me."

How was he to tell that was the worst? Surely it was a confirmation of the snare she was describing that he believed her word automatically. "Who thought of the shaving?" he asked.

"It's all part of the concept. He was going to be way ahead of the conceptual artists, going faster than they to where there was nothing left. Pure idea. Nothing, nothing, nothing to hold onto, but just pure, pure, pure possession of things. He knew how smart I could be. As if he was my father. And maybe so. Maybe he is. My father who is in . . . whatever he's in. He wanted to fuck my mind and he knew how to get at it through my body. Who thought of shaving? *We* did. You and I know how it is to be so close you don't know whose mind is whose mind. Aren't we hot now? I lay there while they shaved me. He wouldn't let Marya laugh about it. Everything had to be solemn. I lay there while they shaved me thinking about you, but they were making me so hot you'd feel it and be caught. I couldn't separate minds then. I can't now. I only know about the powers that work in people and even calling it the stars that make you this or that isn't strong enough. I can't tell whether he's making me tell you this this morning. It's like you listening to music you can't hear. Where's my will power? Mama always said. It wasn't ever mine. That's all I know."

He listened with pain to her tales of Sandler, but it was far from the pain of simple male jealousy. It was a pain of yearning, of straining to grasp not merely what she had known as a female but something that had eluded her, too—a knowledge of powers and forces that human fables and religions and arts could only hint at, a knowledge that animals or grass or even the stones in the river might come to directly and without uncertainty. He felt it was his *privilege* to be shown even as much as she could show him of the underworld by her fanciful confessions. The turbulent pain that sometimes gripped his throat, his chest, his temples seemed to be a sign of that privilege, as if he had been brought to the verge of a new birth, as if he might be born again as a mole or the root of a tree, privileged to know the vast and simple kingdoms of darkness.

If he felt any jealousy of an individual named Sandler, it was only because now, by his death, Sandler had gone on from the adventures Tamisan was recalling, had sprinted past the threshold where they were still lingering.

He remembered the painting of his mother perched in the chair in Sandler's bedroom. That Sandler owned that painted image of Maggie and kept it in casual domesticity beside him as he slept—and dreamed—did not mean that Sandler was a prince of the house of death or keeper of those who inhabited its chambers. It might not even mean that Sandler was on the same wave length of premonitions and druidic insight as Tamisan and himself.

And yet the circumstances of seeing the painting there, the sense of having already peered illicitly out past the wall of the living world while the strange boy Baron hinted the eroticism of those unknown regions—well, the circumstances *fitted* with legends of the underworld, fitted together, while in the world of sense and proof they were merely part of a meaningless jumble of happenstance. As art they had meaning. . . . Once that was felt and admitted, truth was a matter of choice.

Most compelling of all was Tamisan's evident suffering as she tried to make truth out of her costly revelations. Like a girl without a tongue trying to imagine a tongue first so it can say what her mind wasn't meant to close in on and understand by itself. He saw her mutilated by the dark powers in herself she wanted to describe, to warn him against. He felt they would have to save each other or go down together, drowned in an ocean of lies and sick fantasies if they could not teach each other to swim in such depths.

Whatever reality had become, the morning weather at the farm was no more part of it than the invisible presences summoned by their passions. They wandered out of the house without particularly noticing the doorway or the steps that let them down to the lawn. They went to the boathouse and stood in the luminous shade of its interior, listening to the gurgle of river water around the pilings. To the voices of good and evil insects. The good insects said: Stop thinking! Stop it now! It will be a relief! The evil insects said: But you have to think of a way to stop thinking. How can you?

To his mild surprise Jason found they were presently walking hand in hand across the pasture from the stable, their feet following what was surely the exact path down which he had once led Maggie's horse before he killed it. He felt Tamisan's weight tug him back with that animal reluctance and brute distrust his arm remembered from the horse when its blood told it it was walking over the border line between life and death.

She said, "Mama used to smile sadly, shake her head and say, 'Oh, I hardly think you're old enough to claim to be a Great Sinner.' Some people know it's only children who *can* be. That's what Sandler and I knew."

When he led the horse out here, crystals of ice had crackled musically under their feet. His feet and Tamisan's moved almost soundlessly in the warm summer grass. Yet the warmth did not seem any more real than the cold. The two of them came to a certain point in the pasture. It might have been the place where the horse's blood had enriched the soil. It might not have been. In mute agreement, they gentled themselves down to lie on the grass, lying head to head. The feet of one were sprawled in one direction, the other's feet opposite, as bodies lie at random around the explosion point of a shellburst.

"All I know for sure is I want to die," Tamisan said.

"To follow him?"

"I don't know."

"Does thinking he's dead make you hot or cold?"

"Both," she said.

"If you wanted to kill him," Jason said, holding his hand over his closed eyes to cut the glow of the sun on his lids, "was that so nothing would get in the way of your loving him?"

"I never loved him. It was only my body and mind involved. I guess he'll always fuck my mind now."

Then they lay there for a long time without saying anything. Tamisan moved first. She rolled until she was near enough to kiss him.

"Your mouth tastes like the sun," he said. As if that, too, were as atonishing as what they had been thinking and talking about.

They went their separate ways in the afternoon. Jason took the canoe out on the river. Tamisan walked in the house and went from the stable to the barn and the other outbuildings to touch the wood. Each was enraptured with meditations of death, charmed to find that it was so near, so promising. They were playing a children's game, and they knew it. Recapturing and submitting to a fatal make-believe, and they loved it mournfully. Sandler was dead in Europe. Ashes and blood had been lost on the sturdy fields around the farmhouse. There was no odor of death to mix with the scents blowing to the house from the orchard. The clouds of late afternoon sported over the river valley, their colors richening as the evening came on.

Tamisan bathed herself leisurely before Jason came back. He told her he had swum in the river, down past the bend that had been his and Maggie's favorite place. It seemed they had both cleansed themselves for a ceremony.

The clouds were almost vanished when they went out to walk the dirt roads up the river after dark. They felt the soothing dust take the shape of their footprints as they idled along barefoot. In low voices they prompted each other on the names of the summer constellations overhead. Tamisan said, "I knew them all once. I've burned out so much of my brains, what with one thing and another. Do you think the stars have got stupider,

335

too, from having been up there too long? Look, there's the Swan. He's easy. He was my favorite in my poetry days. Flying down the Milky Way. Hercules is hard. Show me. I always faked knowing where he was. I never saw his body, if any."

"Move your eyes from Vega in the Lyre," he said. She stood against him to follow his pointing. His dim finger in the starshine traced the shape of the hero. Hercules was really there! Not there. Nothing was up there but what the hungering imagination wished to see. The stars were cold rocks, part of the cosmic make-believe hurled for no reason at all on the dark map of nothingness.

"They wouldn't help us if they could," she said.

"I suppose not."

She danced a little away from him, scuffing up barely visible puffs of dust from the road. "We have to help each other and it's no good being afraid. Look, Jason." She pointed at the stars again. "There's an easy constellation. The Virgin's Diamond. Ha! I can get that one for you if you like it. Come back to the house and I'll show you."

She laid a pattern of pills out on the dark wood of the kitchen table where the obituary clipping had lain in the morning. Four of them, small and white. With the tip of her fingers she poked them into positions that duplicated the imaginary shape of the diamond they had seen from the dark road. "Just like in the sky! The sky's crawling with Sandler tonight. Don't they look like what I showed you? Another of his *devices* to keep me true to him. They're poison. He gave them to me instead of an ordinary diamond. He knew death was my real sign though I said Virgo. I let him find out. It wasn't love, but we went a long, long way together. So I know him, too. He didn't kill himself with barbiturates, whatever the paper says. It was these. Four to match mine. See how I'm covered at all angles? I can't dodge."

"Were you? True to him? All the time with me?"

"I kept these," she said wearily. Proof enough within the

limits of the fairy tale, within the limits of the engagement she
had been explaining to him all day. "I brought them down here,
didn't I? Your father said take care of you. . . . I didn't know
what to expect after what we've been through. I brought what
I could trust most."

"All right," Jason said. "I believe you. I'm ready." He
reached out and carefully picked up two of the white pills,
shook them in his hand like dice. "We've made it this far together. We don't have to be separated again."

She had not watched him gather the pills from the table.
She didn't have to. It was as if all this had been rehearsed, decided, prepared by their whole time together. Yet she said, "I'll
take them all for you if you don't want to. I don't mean for you
to be cheated. I want to cheat him, if you can see any way. I
still thought, the night I ran away from your father, I could blot
out everything. Get lost where you and he and Fiona wouldn't
ever want to find me. Do you understand that?"

He nodded. He wanted death if that was what she wanted.
He wanted to share it. He wanted it to be an act of faith and
not of defeat. He wanted it as a testimony to the grandeur and
extravagance of all her desires that got so badly distorted when
she tried to satisfy them in life.

"He says they're painless," she told him. "He says he sat
with a girl in a Japanese geisha house once after she'd taken
them and watched her die. She held onto his hand. That was
all. We could hold each other's hands too. Jason, I tried to
warn you that first night. In different ways all along."

He shook his head. He had never wanted to be warned.
He had followed, trying to match the speed with which she fled.
She had taught him so much already. Never the whole thing.
Now it seemed that she was on the verge of revealing the beauty
that would blind all senses. He jiggled the pills in his hand.
Their barely audible clicking gave him the courage for a pure
honesty to match hers. She had promised she was not all lies.
Posed here like a silhouette against the shine of death, her true
self seemed close and naked enough to touch. "I was always
afraid, but it was what I always wanted," he said.

"You know what he was afraid of, Sandler?" she asked with sudden, imperial scorn. "To kiss! Make the body perform! Suck on anything! But not kissing. Did my mouth really taste like the sun, Jason?" She waited for his answer as if it made all the difference between salvation and despair.

"Like the sun," he said.

On this loyal affirmation, they kissed again now. It was not like tasting the dilute sweetness of the far-off sun, swelling the fruits of summer. It was like putting his mouth on the burning disk itself, sipping from the heart of fire.

They wanted mystic bodies to carry them for once—once and for all—to the end of those desires that begin in the senses but which the senses never fully gratify. In the burning totality of hunger they wanted to consume and be consumed. When she opened her legs for him, she wanted to offer a cunt through which he could pass in joy to nothingness. He wanted her to rise around the thrusting impact of his body like the evanescent splash of bubbles that a diver sees trailing behind him from the corner of his eye. They wanted to die. There was no doubt of that. Their kisses confirmed it. The glowing, gathering excitement of their belly nerves tightened like a bowstring drawn to send an arrow flying out of sight. She wanted him lost forever in the labyrinth of her pleasure. She wanted to consume him like food. He wanted to break her like an eggshell. They had waited and prepared a long time for this devastation that would free them simultaneously.

Perhaps it was tenderness that betrayed them. After all, they had only bodies where pain and delight were clumsily mixed in the same organs, muscles and nerves. The impulse to consume and destroy was clumsily mixed with impulses to cherish and be gentle. What were they, after all? Neither grass nor the fire that transforms it to ashes. A boy and a girl writhing together in human sweat and the pungency of smells that were both decay and health. Perhaps bodies always seek extinction in the appetites that renew them. Planets following a tug of gravity that swings them out toward the black extremities of space and gentles them back toward the comfortable center of life. They did their best. They were fulfilled. They were cheated.

They were lying in a strange, low-key light which she thought was like that in his father's painting in the Behn Gallery. She could feel the slow ooze of his semen, part of it flowing from her onto the carpet, sheet or bare floor, maybe grass. She was not sure where they were except they were in this light that wasn't exactly night or day either.

"Damn," she said. "If this could only be everything. I wanted . . . Was it the best I ever gave you?"

He couldn't answer. Both of them knew it had not been enough.

She said, "I care about you too much. It was always best when I knew I was doing something wrong, wicked. Sandler knew that. I used to scream and go wild. And that's the way I'm trapped. A woman can say ha-ha to all the mystical crap about the stars. But there's something . . . nature, I guess. The organs remember. The cunt remembers. That's where I can never get free. I wouldn't know if I was being true to you if you made me scream, or if it was still him. Do you see? Where are they?"

"The pills? I can find them."

"Are you truly not afraid of them?"

"No."

"Find them then. Find them."

He was gone for a while and she lay there, feeling the ooze like a bereavement. She wished desperately that she were the figure in the painting, from whom nothing could ever slip away. All motion, all change seemed to be part of a continuous waste that had gone on forever. All her wishes flowing away. Everything oozing.

"Here," Jason said, and dropped two pills into her palm.

"Would you be afraid if I had a baby?"

"Yes," he said.

"More afraid than of dying?"

His reproof was very gentle. "If we don't want life, can't make it, it would be awful to give it to someone else." He seemed to feel he shouldn't have had to say it, as if any kind of reasoning threatened the harmony of the longing that was what they had to count on most surely.

It was the sheer spontaneity of her rage now that woke them from the comfort of thinking they were already as good as dead. "You weren't afraid to kiss me!" she stormed. "Oh, goddamn, goddamn you all." She swept her hand to her mouth and felt something settle on her tongue. But then his hand was quick at her throat, squeezing, shutting off her wind, seeking her life. Wheezing, she spat out the pill. "Hit me! Fuck me! Choke me! You're all goddamn cowards. You don't know what a woman is, any of you."

"No," he said with a grandeur of humility that made her begin to cry—at last cry like a child whose stubbornness is broken.

"You don't know either," he scoffed lovingly.

"I know it," she said, leaning to nuzzle her teary face against his chest. "It's not easy to find out. But goddamn it, Sandler knew. He had this concept that worked. Click, click, click, like pushing buttons. He seemed always to know what my mind and body would do even if I didn't want it to."

"I don't suppose that's everything."

"How do I get him out of my mind? Now I'll have to think he's braver than we are."

"You don't have to think that."

"We won't get anywhere with lies. It's happened and what's happened is true. I won't have you shamed by what truly happened. I meant it when I told your father I'd take care of you."

"Poisoning me," he mused. "He might not like that."

"Jason, I want to learn how to serve you and your father. To learn whatever Fiona knows. I don't want to be a slave any more. Or to have to keep running away from being somebody's slave. Doesn't somebody know what I want? I don't. They didn't give me time to learn. That's why Sandler's got us coming or going. See—I've got this concept of him too. You've got to help me."

"I will."

"Don't just keep saying *yes*. Maybe if I had a baby . . . I could have. I could do that. If I'd been a sow, I'd've had litters and litters by this time, and I wouldn't have to care if they were all butchered, would I?"

They would not know that night—or ever—how to decide what was absolutely right and good and still possible. And at this age in their lives there was an agony that even a few years —even a few months—would begin to cool off. An agony of feeling they were free to choose the right thing—life or death— but unable to exercise their freedom. The agony of youth when it realizes that all the choices have been made for it and even death is no exemption.

Sometime in the night another decision seemed to have been made for them. They *would* have a child *because* they were more afraid of that than anything else. It didn't matter what they wanted. They lay together, still hot with their longing for death, for its ease, its heroism, its grandeur. But now that way seemed blocked, no longer open as an alternative always available. As with everything else, someone had beat them to it. Had claimed the territory because they had dallied too long. It would not be *theirs*. Past the dark of the night, death opened doors to kingdoms beyond the imagination. But they could enter only as slaves. It was unfair that they would have to take their chances with life. In sensuality and beyond it they had pursued some obscure miracle of conversion. Something to turn them around or let them out. Had found it, perhaps—and the miracle had turned out to be another injustice, a betrayal back into the patterns of living.

"Why aren't we like everybody else?" Tamisan used to ask when their meditations brought them far out and then stopped them with a riddle like a stone wall.

"Maybe we are," he had always answered. He had learned from his father—from the genes, from the voice—that artists are more like everybody than anybody. That they become artists by simply confessing the vast complexity of the common human fate.

In the morning the air seemed thinner. As if the ribs of rock far under the farm land might be expanding, raising the unchanged contours of the visible landscape a few thousand feet higher above sea level. It was both sobering and exalting to them to walk out and find the landscape so unfamiliar. It was a day when they felt obliged to give names to the strange animals grazing in the remote pastures visible from the hilltop lawn—names as strange and new as *horse, cow, pig.*

"Why do I feel like you're pregnant so soon?" Jason asked. He did not really want to be given a list of the symptoms he should look for.

In the next few days they kissed often in leafy places and on river sand bars. Under the rafters of the barn where pigeons murmured and went about their haunting business. In the boathouse and in the arbor where the grapes were just beginning to turn color. In the oak-beamed parlor of the farmhouse.

Anywhere.

As if no one had ever told them that kissing was not how babies were made.

They thought of going to Omaha or Dubuque—both blessed cities where Tamisan could get a job as waitress or chambermaid while he worked as a hod carrier or clerked in a supermarket. They would buy a color television, subscribe to *Life* and the *Reader's Digest.* They would decorate the walls of their apartment with pictures bought at the outlet stores. Sailing ships. Twilight landscapes.

The last dream of the imagination terrified by the dead end it has conceived . . . In fact, they agreed to go to Paris.

They were going back to Paris for Jason to resume a journey that had been halted when his mother sickened there. He said, "I was the one who tricked her into coming back, really. The doctors and our friends—the Burkes mainly—said we had to come back to New York to be sure she got the best care, the best chance to live, get well. As far as they knew then it wasn't a terminal illness. As far as they knew. But she knew. Her body knew. It was exactly like the horse before I killed him. It knew and had no way of expressing it even to its own mind. But afterward I knew what we both couldn't say that morning we were sitting with our *citrons pressés* at the Café de la Paix. We had to choose one make-believe or another because we couldn't say what her body knew. Only feel it. She said, 'Jason, we don't have to go back. Honey, I want to go on. Come on with me to Persia. Shall we? We can. All we have to do is go.' Persia was her make-believe. Theirs was that she had no choice but to come back here and try to stay alive. If I'd been man enough to say yes, we could have gone on to Persia. If I'd had faith in her body, I wouldn't have had to deny her that."

The sun had counted their days at the farm. The air had changed. They were on their wheels again. They were crossing the high bridge over the Narrows and there was Manhattan, off to the left, a mystifying sign that strangers had raised up and defied them to read. It was comforting to ride past New York and pretend you weren't noticing it.

He saw that Tamisan was clenching her hands tightly in her lap. Her knuckles whitened under the tanned skin of her hands. She had narrowed her eyes and thrown her head back a little so she could not see how precariously high above the water they were. She had always been afraid of high places. She knew the compulsive urge to rush for the railing of a bridge or a skyscraper and throw herself into space. He loved to catch her in moments when she was breathlessly fighting that urge. Their need for each other seemed clearest at such times.

"I know why my father made us go down to the farm together," he said with astonished happiness. "He guessed you'd kill me. You almost did."

It was still another harsh effort for her to free her attention from her phobia and answer him. But she managed without too much delay. "He didn't either. He couldn't know I had the pills. He loves you more than anything."

Jason nodded. "I know he does. But ever since Maggie died he's accepted my death too. He saw my living was a mistake. All right, maybe he didn't want you to murder me. . . ." He sought for the precise words to define what he knew. The car was moving delicately down the incline of the bridge now. Soon there would be solid earth and stone under the steel and concrete where the tires whined.

He said, "He wanted you to give me death. To let me in on it. You and he know as well as I that life isn't enough. Don't argue. That's true."

"It's all nonsense," she said, beginning to unclench her hands. "Don't ever say things like that any more."

"I don't mean he wants me dead on the spot. Not now. He thought you'd give me a running start, I guess."

"Then don't talk about it any more!" she said, letting all the tension go out of her, letting her voice break into a half sob. "I'm all in favor of life, now."

While they had been swooping so high over the arch of the bridge, she had kept herself blind to the terrors outside by concentrating on the image of a beautiful white young sow with a lovely, strong arch to her back and enchantingly pink folds and creases under her tail. The sort of pig that someone sometime must have told her about in fairy tales of China or Poland. A maiden pig with her four hoofs planted apart for steadiness as she waited for the champion white boar to mount and, with its big white balls chiming against her rump like porcelain eggs, fill her with squirming pink life.

"There was a time in my childhood when I used to identify with stuffed animals instead of dolls," she said matter-of-factly, hoping Jason would make more out of what she offered him than she could. Would incorporate it into the music that he was always composing about her.

Book IV

Trial

They came back to us, our Jason, our Tamisan, docile, sober, ready to talk to one and all about their plans for going soon to Europe. Pictures of health to gladden the old folks' eyes. Their similar skins are even more lusciously tanned than they were early in the summer. They are bright-eyed and responsive. At once Tamisan set about being friends with Monica and questioning her about Paris. They swim, sail, drive together and have plans for shopping together in New York before they all get airborne—the date for that departure no more certain than a wedding date for Goss and me. We have stopped living in the kind of time that requires fixing dates.

Jason told Janis Ward, who arrived almost a full week before they did, that of course, of course, of course he would play his cello for her, rusty though his technique might be by now. And she took this as sign enough that some psychological miracle had been wrought by the events of the summer. "Something's happened." Some subterranean shift of which we will catch only the reverberations. And I think she is essentially right, though I may not be as quick as she to believe that all is rosy now.

Goss says, "Ha, they look as if they'd witnessed a murder and are keeping their mouths shut about it. Or seen a crucifixion."

"Or faced the minotaur at the bottom of the labyrinth. Wasn't that what you sent them down to the farm to do?"

"I didn't send them there to dig up Maggie's grave. That's why we cremated her. To keep Jason from digging her up."

"You can be breath-taking in your cruelty sometimes."

"I don't know why I sent them anywhere. To get them out of my hair while I work something out. Look at them! They're

347

all right. I'm the one who's on trial. I've put myself on trial with these new paintings. I can't spend all my time worrying about two neurotic children."

Of course he cannot. Shouldn't. Doesn't. If their liberation or transfiguration is as promising as Janis—and probably Fiona, I'm not sure—take it to be, then none of us should worry ever again.

Goss rumbles, "They got me roped into this. Now they'll fly off, leaving me holding the bag."

"You mean me?"

"You're in this as deep as I am, Susan," he says, fixing me with glittering eye—sometimes glittering in a fearful, reckless gaiety and just as often shining with a cruelty I'd rather not fathom. Which has, anyway, nothing to do with how he treats me.

He sang such a different song about his new paintings before the young ones came back. Then the persistent theme I heard was: "They have to be convincing to Jason." Convincing . . . of what? "That if I can renew myself, make a start at my age on something that nobody's seen before, then it's possible for him. For anyone. They were right, damn it, they were right, they were right, they were right in saying I was only marking time before. Turning out Dean Goss copies for the trade. Making money. . . . I might as well have been using the etching press to turn out U.S. currency, putting my signature on money, money, money. That's not art, whatever else it may be."

The sheer conviction that he couldn't fool Jason made him scrape the last centimeter of his guts and turn his struggling with the canvases into a game which, I supposed, was as dangerous for him as anything could be. Oh, probably *more* dangerous for him, though my moments of real anxiety came when I saw how close he was to destroying the paintings at some peak of fury and frustration.

Those bitches on the three canvases would tempt him, tease him, promise to show themselves completely if only he would woo them a little more. And then, I suppose, they would start imperceptibly to fade, to go back into the incoherence from which he was trying to pull them. By now I could tell, partly, what it did to him when they began to elude his touch and sight. They might only make him deadly quiet while he sucked harder on a cigarette and stood over his palette, scraping and stirring the piles of color, waiting for everything to come together in the right moment—muscles, pigment, the taste of tobacco, the sound of music from his record player, that spot on the canvas toward which all the rest had to converge. Then his stubborn stalking as he went up to slap, caress, stab, slice, soothe the maddening temptresses. But then again he would scrape down huge areas in great and almost careless haste until there seemed nothing physically, visibly up there but a messy ruin that could not possibly be patched together again.

Sometimes I thought I was watching a boxer who kept coming on in spite of the punches he took in the face. Or a fencer. Maybe a battlefield surgeon with gore and guts draped over both elbows and sweat running into his eyes while he reached in, in, in to find the hidden wound from which the fatal loss of blood was coming. And even if he found that, could he get all the guts stuffed back in and the abdomen sewed up? Could he? Would he?

And even then—why should he? There were always people like me, not too far away, to remind him, "Rest. Do your thing some easier way. It's only art. It's only painting."

I didn't say that. Never quite.

The times I was not in the studio with him could be even worse—as when some premonition would tell me, *He's done it now.* It never occurred to me to suppose or wonder whether he might be boffing Janis Ward as she rambled too close to him in optimistic nakedness. (There was no embarrassment after all in persuading her to loiter as his model in case of need. She's filling her diary, too, with what she observed from that vantage point, I suppose.) The single horror was that I might go down there and find the canvases all neatly scrubbed back to their original emptiness. With *nothing* left to show Jason or the rest of us. Or would he slash the canvases this time, to show us there was no real blood in them after all?

I couldn't bear it. Things are worth what you pay for them, people tell us. For all the good it does, I tell people that. What I knew about those paintings was that Goss was paying into them everything he had left.

One way I knew that: the painting of Maggie I brought out from the Behn Gallery simply vanished. Bruce Behn called to find out why it had not come back as promptly as I promised. I suppose Marian Burke was still putting pressure on him. No crisis of course. But when I went looking for it and asked Goss why it wasn't any longer in the increasing clutter in the studio, he finally admitted he had started to paint on it again. "I screwed it up, my dear. I should have left well enough alone. Don't tell me. I wanted to see if my touch was the same. I wanted to see what a stripe of vermilion . . . Don't worry. We'll simply tell Bruce and Marian it was a forgery. Don't worry. . . ."

To be sure, I am in too deep with this family of high rollers to even think of measuring the stakes by any single loss or gain. It was unworthy timidity to feel that Goss would settle back just because Jason is "convinced"—as he appears to be.

"Don't you see, Susan?" Jason says in his euphoria. "These three canvases aren't the end of anything. They'll never be finished. Oh, he'll let up on them one of these days. We can take them away from him. Then he'll keep going on something else. For years and years, deeper and deeper and higher and higher. Besides, he got *you* out of the process."

It is hard to combat arguments so cunningly directed.

Chapter 17

"No rest for the struggling artist?" Tamisan asked. She had come looking for Goss to see if he wanted to spend the afternoon sailing with her and Jason and Monica. Jason and Monica were loading the sloop with picnic things. Either they would find some beach near the tip of the island where they could anchor and swim or they would have their goodies while they made a great circle in the open ocean. There was wine in the cooler for Dean Goss in case he could be persuaded to come along.

"Can you tell it's struggle?" He was probably being mocked now, though there was no use blaming her for it. He had been strong, lucky, wealthy all his life. There was little he could appeal to as the outward show of any battle against the odds. And just now he was not visibly at work on his three big canvases. He was whining and whistling at a much smaller new picture, so Tamisan or anyone else who came by had every right to believe he had finished with the big ones. It was kind of them to think he might be ready for a holiday after the effort.

He put aside his brushes for a while and said, "I'll go if you'll be kind enough to tell me whether my paintings of the ladies are done or not."

"Can't you tell?"

He shook his head and wiped his glasses. "Not at all. I don't dare leave them in case there's more work required."

She squinted whimsically. Opened her mouth two or three times without uttering a sound, then said warily, "Huh-uh. You won't catch me expressing any more opinions around here. You honestly haven't made up your mind?"

"Honestly."

"Then you'll have to ask *them*," she said of the painted women.

So the young people went without him or Susan on their excursion. And left him with the sour, sad conviction that if the presences in the paintings did not declare his trial to be over he would never hear it from anyone. But there they sat on their easels, mute as three playing-card queens. He might have laid out such cards and read as much or as little as he was yet able to understand from what he had painted.

Later it would seem to him and to Susan too that the painted women had begun to speak to him through a bad dream that now emerged from his obsession with them—a sort of parentheses for the creative process, repeating and matching his bad dream of the mummies on the night after his tiff with Jason. Whether the dreams prophesied the painting or the painting the dreams was not a question they needed to ask. But he would remember that this dream seemed to begin with the color combination from the left-hand canvas of his triptych.

But the colors were not so much those of figure or object as the dream began. They were the colors of atmosphere, the pervading tonality of a street scene in Manhattan that was still utterly familiar to him, though the automobiles passing were tall and ungainly and the people who glanced at him as he tried to hide himself beside the brownstone steps were dressed like farmers on a Saturday night. They did not seem like people who ought to be on East Seventieth Street.

He dreamed that a tall yellow and black taxi pulled up to the curb. From it, walking briskly toward the steps where Goss waited for him, came that handsome and gifted young painter Riley Donovan.

I thought you'd come this evening, Riley.

Thank God you're here. I hoped you'd be back by now. Eileen's been terribly worried.

Who could have worried her, Riley? With his big fucking mouth and his little-boy talk about how artists have to be free to live their big erotic lives. Who made her sick?

Dean, no one's known where you've been for three days. Not Glenda. Not Eileen. I've tried to explain. You're not your own best interpreter. You know I love you, Dean. It's because I love you that I ever talk about you with her. No secrets, Dean, I swear.

He dreamed that the crowd of urban hicks began to close in around them, every mouth leering, every ear tipped like a bucket to catch these slops.

Reasons! Reasons! Sure you have reasons, Riley.

Come inside, Dean.

And we'll discuss it all with Eileen, shall we? Take your hand off my sleeve, you chickenshit Judas. I have my reasons. Here!

With that exultant *Here!* he dreamed he hit big Riley Donovan with a right-hand smash to the jaw and caught him again with a left to the body as he started to go down.

Then, as the battered traitor sprawled at his feet, he saw it was not Riley he had hit. It was Jason who lay there on the sidewalk.

The hand that had struck the boy began to burn.

Beside Susan's evenly breathing form, Goss sat up in his bed and in the early morning light looked at his right hand to see if the dream was true. It must have been. There were the stumps of the burned fingers on a hand that had not looked like the hand of either human or animal for more than thirty years, except for the usable thumb.

The dream was true and false. The most repulsive thing about it was that it was cowardly in its distortions. As if his unconscious mind was ashamed for him, glossing over what he had to bring to consciousness if the old story of his fight with Riley was ever to be brought straight.

It was cowardly to represent Riley as bigger than himself. In those days he outweighed Riley by thirty pounds. He had fought as a heavyweight in intercollegiate boxing matches. He was in better physical condition, though he was almost ten years older than his friend. Beyond question he *could* have dropped Riley with the one-two punch he dreamed he had delivered.

In reality he had held a club of knotted elm while he waited beside the steps for Riley to make his appearance. It had not been necessary—only symbolic, only appropriate, *artful,* as his rage had judged it then—to beat Riley with a stick, beat him like a dog, to demonstrate the enormity of Riley's offense.

No great harm in beating Riley. The bastard deserved it. He could still say that. But it was the artfulness, the elaborate and complicated imagination of the form of punishment, that shamed his basic nature. That was the worst of it. It was just the perverse ingredient of the imagination that remained unforgiven, unforgivable.

"Is it time?" Susan murmured sleepily from her pillow.

"No," he said. "Rest awhile. The sun's not up. It's not time yet."

He knew then that he had brought the dream on himself. Induced labor, he thought. Induced by the labor of his painting —which had no intention, after all, of leading him on to a contemplation of the rich, fulfilled years that memory might like to dwell on. It meant to lead him right back to the most shameful of his catastrophes. His painted bastard women, litter of his imagination, knew what perversions they sprang from, after all. They were going to sentence him to hard labor again, to crawling in the stink of his greatest humiliations before he was finished with them. It was not true, after all, that an artist got rid of the bad things in his life by painting or writing about them either. It was the other way around. He used his work to dig his way down to them, at the same time eager and afraid to find them because he knew, was brought time and again to the confession, that they were the sources of his power.

He knew now he had induced the dream of Riley Donovan and now he did not have to sleep again for it to proceed as relentlessly as it had gone in reality. The dream led on to sequences of memory in which the blackish-lavender light prevailed. In that light he stepped over Riley and climbed the steps into the brownstone where he was then living with Eileen Forbes. As he came into the apartment the light changed, heightened and began to flicker. She was burning the paintings and drawings he had given her.

I caught Riley downstairs.

I saw, I saw. You have to prove your manhood every day, don't you? Because you doubt it, don't you? And now you've murdered that poor boy. It wasn't he who wanted me to know about your Glenda. I went to him because I guessed.

Then—he would have been ashamed to dream this; it was part of his pride to remember the absolute and hideous grotesquery of it in plain consciousness—he had stood there like an ox while the crazed woman opened his fly, pulled out his cock and jerked on it as if she were pulling a bell rope.

See? See? See? It won't stand up for me any more. You can't prove you're a man that way. How will you prove it to me? How? By your pay-uhn-teengs? Let me watch you stick it in that whore? Hit me the way you beat little Riley with your stick?

Surely the most shameful thing to remember was the quiet of his own voice. Submission to what anyone else would have known was already insanity.

Riley lied to you. There was nothing between Glenda and me.

You lie.

Now she was dragging him this way and that way with her nails dug into his agonized cock. A pure white cord of spittle hung from her fragile mouth. It was terrible to remember what an ecstasy of pity for her had welled from the sheer physical pain she was causing him. Terrible to remember he had been too young to trust pity.

But he tore himself free. He remembered reaching into the fireplace thinking he could still convince her that he had been true to her. Thinking at least there must be something that would hush her, overshadow her torment.

He remembered racing her to the fireplace, she thinking he only wanted to save his precious paintings and drawings, no doubt, he reaching in and pulling out a burning cross that must have been, in actuality, the bracing for a canvas stretcher.

The slow wonder of acceptance in her eyes.

I . . .

The terrible stink of live meat burning. But no pain.

. . . believe . . .

He remembered no pain.

. . . you.

He remembered tossing the burning wood and some pieces
of his fingers into the fireplace then. Ah, for the moment he
had been dramatically convincing! He had never been more the
artist. But the shame now, in remembering, was that it had accomplished nothing at all. Thinking, If I were whole now, if
I had my right hand as it was before that—I'd be able to finish
these paintings as they should be done. There was such a mixture of past and present yearnings, griefs and anxieties, it
seemed he could bear them no longer without sharing. And
along with this—as if it were a gift of grace long denied him—
a sudden confidence that it would be all right to share his most
secret responsibilities with the patient woman who lay beside
him.

She seemed to him, in that gray hour, a sister to the women
he had conceived and created, worthy as they to share the grotesque secrets of his creative mania. I wouldn't have had the
courage for so bad a dream if she weren't here with me, he
thought.

"Susan?"

"Yes?"

"Didn't you go to sleep again?"

"No."

"Will you listen gently?" She put her hand on his chest. It
lay there quietly alert as if it, too, might be listening to the even,
sturdy beat of his heart. "I've had an absurd dream and it's
put me onto a line of thinking. It has to do with something
that happened when I was living with Eileen Forbes and burned
my hand. There's a long story there, too. Why'd I walk out
of a happy marriage to go live with someone as difficult as
Eileen, anyhow? Never mind. Too many long stories and I
haven't time for them all. Eileen and I—well, it wasn't a big
sex jag as some of my friends liked to believe. It was . . . an
intensity. Just believe there was something that made us fascinating to each other. Oh yes, an intensity. Living with that
woman was like living on a window ledge with a suicide who's

trying to make up her mind to jump. You have to believe there's something enthralling in it. Do you understand at all?" He felt the faintest of tremors in Susan's hand, neither a full affirmation nor a negative. Only a readiness to accept what was given while she waited for more.

"I loved Eileen. She might have been a great poet. She had the sensibilities for it. I suppose that's what I wanted in her, to attach a poet's sensibility to my own. No matter about that either. The point is that I had made a headlong, total commitment to her. I wasn't holding anything back. I wanted to cherish her and support her as well as possess.

"Yes, yes. We have loved people in other times, other places, Susan. Places and times change and the love is either gone or it is not gone but still groping for other people with other faces, other names.

"The point I'm coming to is that Eileen and I got involved with a younger pair—Riley Donovan and Glenda Burnett—in somewhat the same way you and I are involved with our amorous children."

Now there was a definite twitch in Susan's quiet hand. He took it as objection and said, "There are always differences in any parallel situations. Thank God. I only meant we've said that Jason and Tamisan are our love story. I suppose that means they act out things that go beyond us. We watch them like any film or play—or painting for that matter—to see personifications of what's invisible, unsayable in ourselves or between us. Wrong?"

"Go on."

"I don't minimize the differences between our present situation and the one I'm telling you about. All is changed. But, in my dream, it was Jason I struck down, not Riley Donovan."

from Susan Vail's red notebook:

Parallels in the situation indeed! Were they found by the observing artist, or were they slyly, unintentionally, compulsively *made?* Where does the shaping impulse begin?

It's a *story* he has to tell about Eileen, Riley, Glenda. Yet I'm as much inside of it as outside it. Names are changed to protect the innocent, if any. It's a story, and an unveiling, and a prophecy, perhaps. A Goss happening. A laboratory demonstration of the metabolism by which the Goss imagination works. The breaking of the seals on—at least—two portfolios of drawings he made of Glenda and Riley in poses satanically pornographic and, at the same time, pathetically, heroically human.

A story drained of much of its shock by the perspective of time—that perspective stood right on its head by the parallels his dream nudged out into the light.

"They were featherweight people," he says of Riley and Glenda. "Neither had Eileen's capacity for tragic dignity, suffering, endurance in the constant torment of her suspicions. They were the kind of people meant for the eye. Summer insects, summer flowers. Delightful."

They might never have got to him at all if he had not been, then, vulnerable to trivial kindness and proffers of friendship from superficial people. In divorcing and taking up with Eileen, he had made a clean sweep of most of his friendships that had mattered up to that time. Outside the intense spiritual blaze of his relationship with Eileen he was almost as lonely as Jason made himself last year, he supposes. He was working then in the same studio that Jason took for his hermitage; so he would have seen Glenda Burnett thirty years ago just where he first laid eyes on Tamisan.

Riley was not only his mischievous younger friend. He had a facile talent as a painter and learned quickly. He was assisting Goss on some murals that had been commissioned for a university library in Baltimore. The subjects were of the greatest dignity: Christ at Emmaus, Socrates with his friends, Galileo before the Inquisition, Voltaire at Ferney, scholars of the Enlightenment. The cartoons for these murals were in a nearly finished state when Riley first brought his redheaded girl there to inspect them. Big charcoal drawings on oversize sheets of brown wrapping paper. (These, too, still preserved somewhere rolled up in the storerooms of North Atlantic waiting for Judgment Day or other appropriate occasion for display.)

He says: "Of course I was envious of Riley from the minute I saw Glenda's plump little face and red hair, cut in a kind of Dutch bob, you know. She was the real, the true country girl. From Iowa, though she'd come to New York to be an artist like the rest of us. I knew, because I'd heard him brag about it, that Riley was getting into some good country quiff. Light-hearted Riley was kind. Compassionate. Made of the right stuff and fit for life. Both of them were. I don't think for a minute they plotted to seduce me. In the beginning, with his college boy stories, Riley surely only wanted to brighten my life."

Bound to Eileen Forbes by his own volition, Goss nevertheless felt the friction of bondage. "I was not exactly the picture of gaiety. Compared to me, Voltaire and Socrates must have looked like satyrs at a bacchanal to anyone who came into the studio at that time."

Out of sheer respect for his older friend and teacher, Riley wanted to pass along the good news of his discovery that sex was fun. Furthermore, he and Eileen disliked each other with the natural hostility of those meant for the world and those who find that the world has soiled them. He seemed to be disparaging Eileen when he praised Glenda as the ideal liberated woman of the thirties. "Dean, I cry, literally, when I think of her. Why? Somehow in spite of her Midwestern upbringing she's honest as a man. How often do you find that? She doesn't want to marry me just because she likes to go at it with me. She has appetites. She admits them. She's healthy through and through. She's not such a bad painter, either. She's come a long way since she got away from Grant Wood." In his spill of generosity Riley hoped that the influence of Goss would make his girl a better artist.

He was not *exactly* pimping for her.

Goss remembers that on her first visit to his workplace her face beneath the bonnet of short red hair flamed with innocent envy as she looked and listened and hungrily touched the furniture in front of his austere murals. "Oh," she said, "oh"—promising everything for the chance to do such work herself.

Afterward, he remembers, they had drinks together at Goody's Bar. With prayerfully folded hands Glenda ventured to talk about her own painting. She worked in her apartment on Jones Street. She had two rooms on the top floor. The climb was long. But there was so much light up there . . . She blushed and tried to describe her difficulties in trying to loosen up her figure work when she couldn't afford models. It was clear she was in love with the smell of turpentine. The emotions of the budding artist intensified the lovely frankness of her broad face and smiling eyes. "I paint myself sometimes in the mirror, but . . ."

Suddenly they were talking about the possibility of her posing for Riley and his good friend Dean Goss on her Thursday afternoons off from her job. "She has a strong figure, Dean, not just a *nifty* figure," Riley said.

Ever so slyly the girl preened her thick mop of hair in the mirror of the booth. "Why do artists always talk that way? 'Strong figures!' It's prudish. Like doctors calling things by Latin names. I like *nifty* figures. I like to paint myself—if I'd only hold still."

"You'll hold still for us," Riley said.

To Goss she said, "I think a painter can really learn about his craft from being a model." He thought she must be right; he was impressed with her mind as she went on to explain, "You can learn how the weight of the body hangs from the bony structure. You can feel it when you're posing and the feeling is the beginning of seeing."

To a man whose temperament inclined him to respect men, women, children, dogs, old ladies—not to mention Socrates, Jesus, dragonflies and wild flowers—this display of insight was as seductive as the prospect of seeing the light gleam on her nifty breasts.

But—"They didn't seduce me any more than I seduced them. That was demonstrated later, when we'd seduced Eileen, who suffered from it most."

Now dead and gone, like Maggie Goss and Cleopatra, like all the lovely girls we can hardly bear to remember or forget,

Glenda Burnett was ripe that year. Summer-apple ripe. She had
—the painter does not forget—a skin that did magic things with
whatever light fell on it. Probably because she was a painter
herself and a born mime, Goss found her wondrously imaginative in her poses.

A strange thing: he thought this was the body Eileen wrote
about in verses that set his imagination tingling like a sniff of
strong, invisible spices.

Her body told him stories of a woman's life, so that watching
her move from pose to pose while he and Riley sketched was
like the intimacy of having lived with her as closely as an ob-
servant sister since puberty. The smug idleness of her curled
reclining poses, the vanity and expectancy of her leaning on a
chair back, the tensions with which she responded to her territory near a wall or a doorway—no technique of his could be
precise or swift enough to put down those human vistas she
opened to his imagination. So: "I knew I had to go beyond
anything I had learned yet. I began to invent again. That was
the joy that extended the seduction."

The dignity of a single female's life in America "whistled"
to him. It seemed to him, in those times, that he knew at last
what Walt Whitman was about when he celebrated the body
electric and the pioneer women in their prairie houses. The restless young women who would contrive their escape from Sinclair Lewis' Main Street. The rebel girls from Fitzgerald, who
would never quite know what lured them to the big city, but
put themselves in position to let it happen. He loved them all
so much, while he was intently working, that it never occurred
to him to feel anything special about one Glenda Burnett from
Storm Lake, Iowa.

His lighthearted young friends had more than that in store
for him.

One November day when Glenda was leaning on a chair
back like a Fitzgerald heroine counting the number of boys
she had kissed, Riley threw down his sketchbook and walked,
fully clothed, into the imaginary room where she stood naked.
At first he did not embrace her. He simply cupped her breasts

in both hands and stood with his eyes fixed on her face in an expression of mastery.

She glanced once—and only once—at Dean Goss. To see if I would take it, he thought. To see if I would accept the offense they were doing to me.

He started to joke. "It's become the Temptation of St. Anthony, hasn't it?" The joke could not have stopped what was going to happen. It might, merely, have taken the curse off it.

He said nothing, made no joke. He accepted the curse that they, probably, had never intended. Lightweights do not bother about curses. Paranoiacs on the other hand—or artists—come into their own when they notice a web around the spider and admit he is not floating weightless in the middle of the air.

Instead of uttering a joke, Dean Goss entertained a vision. In it his lusts began to come down from their perches around the studio, a smelly swarm of featherless, winged creatures. They shuddered their obscene wings in front of the mural images of Christ and Voltaire and the multiracial workers. If he had Bosch to help him, Dean Goss might have spent the rest of his life painting variations on that scene in the thinning light of November.

"Now, now, Riley," Glenda said in mild protest. "This isn't moving pictures." The sound of her voice was already testimony to the swollen tumescence of her throat. For a moment her hands fluttered as if she meant to push him away.

He whispered something to her. Then waited for what they must have rehearsed. Her lower spine began to sag toward him, her toes splaying with the unbalance of her body as she let her arched belly search toward the wool of his buttoned trousers. She was frowning with embarrassment. The flick of her eyelids showed nothing beneath but white.

Dean Goss wiped his oil brushes clean. Cautiously and with the human detachment of a bird watcher permitted by chance to stumble on the mating of condors in a mountain nest, he went to get a sketchbook, ink and a bamboo pen.

With her arms absolutely limp from her shoulders, Glenda reached with her belly and spread thighs. It was the obstinate, intent grapple of a creature humbled by the lack of hands, sent back to a primeval beginning and commanded to improvise the clutch for what it must have or perish. "I'm going to get it, Riley," she whispered in a breath that cut the silence like a siren.

She could fumble the smiling Riley with the hairy bluntness of her mound. The eagerness of her nude legs grappling after him only emphasized the brutal severity of the barrier made by his clothing—let him stand on one side of an iron fence like a bad boy tormenting a hungry animal in the zoo.

She played herself against his clothed erection and clucked encouragement. He still held her breasts as if supporting her that way, guiding her thought, giving her grudging permissions by the authority of his stimulation.

At last she shook her head groggily and took permission to use her hands. She unbuttoned his shirt and belt. She knelt to unlace his shoes.

The first drawing Dean Goss put in the sketchbook that would be filled before the winter was over showed the purest Platonic abstraction of a female—merely an ovoid shape with a single indented cleft to break its Euclidean perfection. A child's balloon dimpled by the pressure of a finger. A pure hunger. An icon for emptiness. An image that in the subhuman world would be a schematic representation of an unfertilized egg. The artist set it down that way first because he saw exactly that. Saw her in that transformation to a formal origin.

But now, to catch her kneeling over the shoelaces, he set down a swift Lautrec line of sepia ink to stand for the slanted curve of her spine and the compression of her buttocks against her naked heels.

Riley swung her to a position astraddle the wooden bench set out for her posing. The sepia line flowing from Goss's hand caught the awkwardness of Riley's waddle as he dropped shorts and trousers to his knees and moved onto the girl.

Now her legs and torso, which had seemed so unwieldy in groping for their desire, became sure and swift and nimble. The miracle of the sepia line was to catch the synchronization of muscles that danced with such ancient cunning between the plane of the bench and the compressing thrust of the man. As if the muscles of the artist's hand had understood that thrilling co-ordination without any prompting from the eye . . . yet rendering it so the eye that saw the drawing would recognize the interior and the invisible.

"That's true!" Glenda said later, when the spent pair came to stand beside Dean Goss's chair and admire what he had made of them. Her fingernail traced the power of the line from waist through stretched buttock and up the straightened leg to the toe pointed in rigid spasm.

How extravagantly the two of them had admired his draw-ings that day! Had they not, by their recklessness if nothing else, broken him through to a new creation? He could smell the semen on Glenda's leg as she stood brushing lightly against his sleeve and turning the pages of his sketchbook. Lion smell.

He could hear the hollowness of Riley's praise jangling like an empty can kicked down the pavement. He knew already, he supposed, that what he had watched was a trespass that would have a price no one but he could pay. That he could pay only with the coin of art. Not legal tender for everyone!

It was their offering of youth and recklessness, carelessness. If they had baited him with the display, they intended that their caper should crest and froth away in merely playful conse-quences. Again that afternoon, while Glenda was dressing be-hind the screen at the far end of the loft, Riley had spoken of her "healthy attitude" and hinted openly that she would stay after he had left to satisfy whatever healthy cravings had been stirred up in Goss. "We've thought about you. I'm sure she would."

It was their invitation to be human and take life as it came. No harm or offense intended. But it was exactly the *offense,* the defiance, the exposure of images never intended to be seen that had appealed to Goss's imagination.

"I must have known from that first day that I had to shed skin and change myself. Shed off the old techniques of the murals, yes. But much more than that. Change my body. Change my way of being. An artist works on himself, or lets himself be worked on, before he reports on canvas what has happened inside. I wasn't going to paint fuckers all the rest of my life. That's not it. I was going to paint the whole visible world *ob-scenely*. I was going to strip off the clothes of conventional appearances and show how one form spawned new ones, generation after generation. I wasn't ever again going to be content to be the detached observer I had been. I wanted sorcery, magic. And I wasn't about to let my apprentices haul me down to their level of health.

"It was health that I rejected. . . . That was the nature of the bargain struck. A choice for which I'm still on trial."

Children flaunting not only their lovely skin but their recklessness under father's gaze . . . It is easy enough to grasp the parallel between that couple and Jason and Tamisan. If the parallel is not visible to the eye, it is inescapable for the imagination fed by the eye.

Youth flaunting its liberation . . . Glenda and Riley were not demons sent to tempt St. Anthony in his solitude, or sent to tempt Goss to break his precarious alliance with the fine, tormented woman he loved. They weren't sent at all.

It was he who chose to emphasize, then isolate, then cherish what was demonic in the display they staged for him. Who chose to ignore Riley's offer of "fun," in the name of art. Goss who chose mania—in its old, plain sense—instead. He remembers his conviction that he was "too strong" to take advantage of Glenda's "very healthy attitude." It was not a matter of moral choice or of intellectual principle that kept him off Glenda's willing body. It was a maniac faith that he could and must see something beyond the limits of natural vision. So he could begin to "paint the impossible."

It was he who chose that the sexual carnival should go on as it had begun, week after week, through that winter. He was, of course, continuing the murals—competently, in the manner consistent with their conception. They were the shell, the dry husk, the camouflage for the change he was inducing in himself by insisting that every Thursday Riley and Glenda repeat their erotic satyr play. Excuse, also, for the decrease in his attentions to Eileen. She was supposed to believe that Socrates, Voltaire and the glories of the Enlightenment had sublimated his bodily passions. For a while this fiction satisfied her.

"The truth is I'd never been so hot before, though I never laid hands on Glenda. Everything was happening in my work—that great co-ordination between body and eye—knowing, without having to think, how to blur away whatever was obvious or banal and exaggerate the essential. Well, that winter I was crazier than Eileen ever became. Lewder than the boy who was humping away at Glenda before my eyes. I thought I was God Almighty making the universe over again from the beginning. Starting with the principles of male and female. . . .

"They were healthy. They wouldn't have tempted me into it if they weren't. I made them sick. Sick of each other. Bewildered them by keeping them at it."

He made himself, for most of that winter, quite impotent with Eileen Forbes.

I've seen the drawings. Learned from them how to clarify a little better the distinction between what an artist draws *on* and what he draws *from*. Between the potency and the visible form. Between the source and the resources of his craft and experience.

And also the distinction between the obscene and the pornographic.

The drawings have been here all the while. Two fat and bulging portfolios that have been sealed on all their edges with wide black tape. No one else has ever seen them except himself, Riley and Glenda. Not Fiona. Not Maggie. "I never *had* to show them before," he says. And he had not looked at them himself since early in the 1940s when he glued the black tape on.

We brought them up from the vault beside Vendler's print room in the basement of the studio. As I watched him slit the tapes and fold back the cardboard sides of the portfolios I knew it was like watching an Indian shaman open his medicine pouch and expose the magic contents to the withering effect of ordinary light. "I always kept these somewhere near when I was working. They were always at the back of my eye," he said.

I watched his disappointment as sheet after sheet of charcoal paper and board came out and we tacked them on the partitions or set them against the feet of the easels from where his great women watched us.

They were, somehow, like those tropical fish that lose their iridescence when they're hooked and lifted out of the water, turning to something as dull as shoe soles as they dry in the bottom of the boat. I could see them turning into pornography for him as one by one he brought them out of thirty years of invisibility, and I felt an awful pity for him—as if the destruction I was witnessing was more costly even than the destruction of the painting of Maggie. All part of what he paid to fight for the life of what he is creating now.

Yes . . . but as they turned into common pornography (common memory) for him they turned into obscenity for me. They were flickers of life from beyond the fringes of what even memory will hold of the exaltation in the sexual contact.

There, on a sketchbook page, the paper looking antique in spite of its long protection from the decomposition of light, drawn with the precise black of a carbon pencil, a girl's face with a little gleaming pearl of semen below the fishhook corner of her lips . . . a pearl like a tear falling through the dark and light reaches of the firmament. Infinitely huger than any star. Infinitely tiny and impermanent, to be rubbed away by the back of a girl's hand as she rose to her feet and shook her young red head defiantly and went about her pert business with the other lively women of her country and time.

The transfer of power from the male standing behind the marelike spread of the girl's legs as she leans on an ordinary kitchen chair—the lines of the outward body not less expressive of the way it all happens than the lines of the hand of God drooping toward Adam's erect forefinger on the Sistine ceiling, the gesture unmistakable when it appears again in Caravaggio's profane painting of the Calling of Matthew.

The fearful and evasive turn of Glenda's body on the studio bench as the college boy cock went in—not less than the submission to awe and terror every one of us Leda types feels when the swan mounts and batters at our faces with his wings.

Truly obscene matter. I began to cry.

"Here, here," he said. "They're not as bad as all that. They're not as wild as I thought they were, but they're not bad in spots. I like that dark mass against those converging leg lines."

"I want to show them to Tamisan and Jason," I said.

"Ah!" he said. "I've thought about that." On his face I saw a pure, unguarded yearning. "I thought about that all the year he was in the studio where these things were done. I thought these things—this part of my life—was what he wanted to find. I hoped he never would. Susan, love, these drawings must seem pretty banal. Now you can buy stuff on every newsstand . . ."

"They scare the hell out of me."

He began to shake his head ponderously. "Jason would see what they really meant to me. In doing these—I wish I could joke about this—I was learning the awful price of survival. That's one thing I never want him to know."

Surely he couldn't quite mean that as he stated it. Surely he could and did. "No man wants his son to know what he's paid to go where he's gone. We want a little discount or we wouldn't dare have sons. We want our children to be good *and* survive. It can't be. One rules out the other. I delivered myself in doing these things. Against nature. I made the bad bargain for the sake of art. I traded off some human claims. They scare the hell out of me too. Or they did until just now when I looked at them and saw . . ."

I suppose he saw how even evil loses its value in the inflationary spiral. I believe he thought he had violated his own nature to make these drawings—and had done a terrible wrong to the people who counted on him to be true to his nature. But . . . that formula sounds banal as the pictures must have looked to him when he saw them with his eyes in the plain light. What do we think of the serpent's tempting Eve and of the fall of man? Ho-hum. Hitler was more recent, not to mention the massacres from the sky in Vietnam.

And that *Ho-hum* was what threatened to demoralize him completely.

"Oh, show them to Jason," he said with a mean grunt. "Why not publish them as a book? They might cause a little sensation. Put them in a cookbook with other recipes. . . ."

On reflection, I don't suppose I want the drawings published or put on display in any gallery. Or shown to anyone else who would make the wrong comparisons. I know their force for me depended on the theatrical way they were offered to my sight, as part of something else, a larger whole of sacrifice and dedication that others would not comprehend even as well as I. I wish they could go back into the intactness of the sealed portfolios. Knowing it is too late for that, too.

"I only wanted to show you I was telling you about real people," Goss said, standing surrounded by his pornography. "So you'd know what it means to feel you're a vampire meant to live always on other people's blood."

He told me how he had "planted"—buried and painted over in his present work—that ovoid, indented shape he had put in his sketchbook the first time he watched Riley working over Glenda. The invisible signature. The invisible parallel to the name he will sign on the surface any day he wants to declare himself finished with this summer's task. Otherwise there is no visible similarity between the present manner and that of the drawings from the portfolios. But nevertheless says, "Oh, they're the same. The same thing. Over and over again we do the same things."

The only way out of the cycle is to go *beyond*.

He remembers that his impotence with Eileen came on in perfect parallel with the growing addiction to those Thursday afternoon sessions in the studio with Glenda and Riley. "I was mad for what I was doing. No detachment at all. And watch-

369

ing them gave me no noticeable erection. Waal, I sat or stood there drawing with every cell in my body tumescent. My hand was swollen with blood. I thought it was. The paper I drew on felt like bellies, tits! Better! And I knew nothing I was meant to do thereafter could be done without some erotic prompting like that they gave me. That stimulus behind all other stimuli of the senses. . . ."

Along with that infatuation, it was his overt detachment that baffled and misled the other three involved. One night near Christmas of that year he ran into Glenda alone in the shopping crowd on Eighth Street. It was literally the first time they had seen each other without Riley present. Goss remembers that when the girl saw him her face lit up with interior lights appropriate to the Christmas season. Her arms were full of gifts. He remembers the smell of snow on her face and cheap fur collar when she kissed him right there among the passing shoppers. She insisted he come home with her then and there to her apartment on Jones Street to see her paintings and have a Christmas drink.

They climbed four flights of tenement stairs to a tiny apartment as clean and forthright as the girl herself. A romantic setting, where opportunity and invitation amounted to the same thing. He could have taken her as simply as he would have picked a melon from the vine. It was the perfect chance to deny the demonic aspect of their involvement. Reclaim the equilibrium of health. Watching the girl move gracefully as she knelt to scatter packages under her little tree, he felt a perfectly normal erection begin. His last until long after he had burned his hand.

"Again I declined the natural thing. I was going to be true. Not to Eileen, but to the passion I got from those two in the studio. You can't believe how meticulously formal I was with Glenda that night. Big brother! Father! I played the role of detached artist there, all right. The perfect gentleman."

In February of that year Riley went with Dean Goss and Eileen to Philadelphia for the installation of the murals and their dedication in the college library.

There, while he and Riley were smearing a wall with white lead to paste up the last of the big canvases, Riley broke the silence of their labor to turn and remark with a grin, "It's done now. Now you can play, Dean."

The remark may have been offhand. Easy. Merely well-intentioned. It is certainly not, for most men, a telling bit of evidence to be kept intact for half a lifetime. But Goss, in his state of inflated tension—"pure creative paranoia," he says— took it as a sly reminder that he would be asked to pay for his indulgences as voyeur, as spectator, as artist. The offhand remark set off a rage at the younger man—all the worse because he had no terms to make it intelligible.

Riley would never guess how intensely he was hated, but he noticed something. "What's the matter? Are you feeling dizzy? Hell, you don't have to do this journeyman kind of work. I'll get someone else to help finish."

Goss smiled and said he felt all right.

Now you can play. . . . Now the Devil was demanding payment for having allowed the artist privileges denied to ordinary men.

In the dedication ceremonies of that occasion, a little spot had been made for Riley Donovan to add his tribute to the artist who had created the murals.

More double-edged and hellishly coded commonplaces from that smiling mouth.

Here, sitting under the painted images of the great teachers of human history, was the teacher who had shown him, Riley Donovan, how to make new images, for our time, of what might have been only a tired repetition of Renaissance formulas in painting. "He took me on as an assistant, not because I was so great as a technician. I wasn't," Riley said charmingly. "I was dumb and therefore teachable. That is Dean Goss's way, with men, women and dogs. He is a great teacher because he loves ignorance the way a doctor loves disease. He is not afraid to turn the artist's eye on what most of us would keep behind the curtain. He demands of himself the abstention from ordinary delusions. And even pleasures. As you look at the great work he has now brought to its conclusion, you ought to tell yourself there's more to Socrates—and to other teachers of youth—than meets the eye. Believe me. There's more to Dean Goss than meets the eye. . . ." On and on, charming the good academic audience with his easy humility. Telling the artist to come back now and take his place among good ordinary folks.

Now you can play, Dean.

As if, at best, the work of an artist was something to be polished off and sold. As if now the last excuse Dean Goss had for not wallowing with him and Glenda had been used up.

Now you can play, Dean. Now everything is permitted. All that is asked in return is that you see no more than the rest of us. Admit the obscene prompting leads only to getting your ashes hauled. Dropping your load. Feeling the old log chain pulled out of your asshole. . . . Be a man among men, for we have got your number. . . .

It was what Eileen might have said to him as well, in more poignant language. The paintings were done. He had no more excuses to withhold himself from her. Nor did he really want to, now that it was too late. If she was the spiritual antithesis of Glenda's healthy sensuality she was still a woman and wanted at least the "evidence" of the senses to confirm their higher commitment.

Goss sees that she had no choice now but to believe he was giving her due to another woman. It must have been an inordinate humiliation for her to have to ask the truth from Riley Donovan, for whom she had so little respect. It must have frightened Riley to be called on as an informer. And in his panic, he obliged her with lies. The simple sort. The kind that would seem forgivable to him. Yes, yes. There was another woman. Of course Dean Goss was a man who lived above and beyond bourgeois conventions. Riley named Glenda. And having been frightened and having lied, he took this turn of events as excuse for breaking off with the girl. "Of course I'd made them hate the touch and sight of each other," Goss says. "I thought that showed in my drawings too, as I pushed them farther and farther toward a pure eroticism with no sentiment left. I saw it happening and didn't want to understand."

And yet the cruelty of his obsession with his work had not even dimmed the pity, the decent compassion he felt for both women he had dragged along into this monstrous entanglement. What happened had merely separated one set of powerful emotions from another as—I agree—they can't be separated without some kind of disaster.

After the posing stopped abruptly, he took it as a matter of duty to go on being fatherly, being responsible to Glenda.

"So, when the showdown came, Eileen was right in charging that I had gone on seeing the girl. She never knew what I thought I had really seen—the task and the power in myself to accomplish it that every artist prays for. . . ."

A Wednesday afternoon in April, then.

A day of reckoning toward which the last months, with the sun in its different orbit, had been slithering and twisting through a screen of lush weeds, dragging something new and appallingly strange toward its moment of revelation. . . .

Eileen was visiting the painter's studio, a woman haggard and taut. A winter woman, sniffing for the invisible sun. Looking at the walls where the murals had hung, shockingly empty now, except for a few photographs and insignificant sketches.

Have you done nothing at all since the murals were finished? Do you come down here merely to daydream then? To stay away from me?

I've been working very hard.

Show me. If it's only sketches, show me. Don't you think I will comprehend them?

Not yet. Not yet. I'll bring out the drawings when I've got a little farther on.

Am I a threat to something that fragile, that precious?

You'll see everything if you can wait. But not yet, please.

Are they all paintings of that girl? I gather from Riley that you're still seeing her.

She's having a rough season. Our friend Riley has ditched her. I talk to her now and then. To keep her cheered up.

I'm told she's a painter herself. Any good?

She has talent. Lots of young people have.

I hadn't observed you being very cheerful lately. I'm astonished you have cheer to spread around.

She's demoralized at the moment. She's talking about giving up New York and going home.

Because Riley has dropped her? I don't understand why Dean Goss still finds her so interesting if even Riley Donovan doesn't.

I'm very angry at him for leaving her the way he did.

He seems to have found her not very fastidious.

Fastidious!

I'm sorry if my awkward expression troubles you . . . who are so fastidious yourself!

I hang on to some sense of decent fairness.

Fairness!

She's done nothing that Riley can decently fault her for.

Decently!

She's basically a glad little human being. Did Riley explain to you why he's afraid of her?

Riley doesn't tell tales.

He plants suspicions and blows on them to keep them hot.

The suspicions are mine. May I see the drawings you made of her?

It wouldn't be fair to show you while we're quarreling.

You trust no one but yourself to be fair.

I trust myself.

That's it! Don't you see that's why no one can stand you? Why you're losing the friends you had when I first knew you? Why am I laughing? I thought of something funny. You're going to forbid me to see Riley. Talk to him any more. He's one of the few who still cares about you.

I don't forbid anything.

As if this were a cue in the drama they were condemned to act out, she began to remove her clothes. There was a smile of utter sorrow on her mouth as she mimicked the enticements of the strip teaser. A lunatic smile.

I'm going to be your model again. Your woman-flower. Your inspiration.

He remembers he meant to act out this charade. To soothe her suspicions and her anguish once again by at least using the one skill that would not fail him. But even before he started to work, he knew that what he saw would be the last and unbearable humiliation for her. Her body was sufficient. If he could have drawn her nakedness glibly—in what he already thought of as "the old way"—some shred of vanity might be preserved to disguise the ghastly nudity of bereavement that he saw.

When she was undressed he saw the poverty within, the scrawniness of her womanhood, the doomed and pathetic artifice of her sexuality—and the bravery with which her soul endured the body's defilement.

She posed coquettishly on the bench from which light-hearted Riley had sanded the spots to keep them from her eyes. She twisted provocatively to another pose.

Do you like this better, Dean? Show me how the Burnett girl poses for you, Dean.

She saw that he was not working. The sketch pad was open on his knees. His right hand was motionless.

Or do I have to get Riley to do this for me too?

"I had at least some sense of justice left, if nothing else to rely on. I could have borne the fact that she'd taken Riley for a lover if I could have made myself believe there was the least joy in it for her. If they'd had 'good times,' as Riley liked to say it. I've always respected symmetry. . . .

"That wouldn't wash. On the face of it, in the depths of it, it was the ultimate humiliation for her. Pure crucifixion with nothing to redeem it.

"It wasn't enough for me then to suppose she had chosen it all by herself in revenge for what I'd done to her. I had to have someone else to blame. I had confidence in my strength to bear and endure what was coming to me. That at least. What I blamed Riley for was not having the imagination to see it would humiliate her, as I'd blame someone for not keeping strychnine away from her in her worst depressions. I wanted to make the punishment fit the crime. That's why I thought of beating him with a stick. Thought nothing less would do."

The perspectives of time are very strict. They reduce everything in scale, blur out the interludes, deny the complications of personality. From so many years after the event, the burning of his hand seems part of the single uninterrupted gesture of swinging his club at Riley's back, as if it were that piece of wood itself that burst into flames and made his wild scheme of justice merely the climax of a cycle of self-punishment.

But seeing things in a time perspective rouses only an intellectual pity. Besides, there is always a scattering of attention in trying to focus reasonably on remote events and names that are only for a moment caught in the vortex of passion that moves on. In his season of prophetic fury and mania he may have been convinced beyond reason that he was a vampire, a soul-stealer. Look, though . . . in the perspective of historic time it surely does appear that Glenda and Riley went on with their lives unaware of what he snatched.

Riley is still painting. He teaches in the art department of a large Western university. In Haupt-Eisinger's book—where all the chronology of Goss's life is meticulously accounted for—Riley is quoted. He not only confirms that Goss once laid on him with a stick "at the climax of a deep spiritual crisis"—he seems to cherish the memory. As if he had been knighted by a tap of the sword instead of cudgeled. "Beyond question Dean Goss was undergoing a grave personality change, possibly the presaging of those later styles that we all admire so much. But though his suspicions of me were groundless, I bear him no grudge. Let me make it clear that in the period I knew him he was for the most part an irresistibly generous man. Everyone responded to his magnetic dynamism—men, women, dogs and cats, pigeons in the park. . . ."

And so on and on. Time and minor artists heal all wounds.

Glenda went home to the Midwest. Within a year she was married to a doctor in Red Oak, Iowa. She mothered five chil-

dren and continued her painting. She won many prizes in the
Iowa State Fair art show and exhibited with distinction at the
Chicago Art Institute and the "Artists along the Mississippi"
shows of the 1940s and 1950s. In her lifetime she advanced
from Regionalism to Abstract Expressionism and might well
have gone on into Pop and Op if she had not died just as they
were becoming fashionable. She died among small honors and
the affections of her family and many friends. She had no way
of knowing whether or not Goss even kept the drawings that
celebrated her in her prime.

Eileen, of course, is a different story. Larger, cloudier, more
ineffable among the shadows he has left behind, even, than
Maggie. The gruesome testimony of burning his hand for her
seemed to be of a magnitude that stabilized her mind for a while
—like any shock therapy. It seemed to be no less than the renunciation of his whole career for her. He had given the hand
that his art depended on—or so it seemed then. Yes, yes, they
knew Renoir had painted gloriously with both hands as badly
crippled as his right hand would be. But thoughts of martyrdom
were more in Eileen's style of imagination than any remote
practical comforts.

He saved her only for a season. The next year when they
went wandering in Mexico she was worse. What had been pri-
marily a sexual jealousy grew back, tougher than ever, among
the political agitations of those times. He had made friends with
the Mexican painters, who were extremely political. Eileen
felt herself the target of all their Communist intriguing.

"But it wasn't the outward tensions that broke her. She only
took them as pretext for the constantly more metaphysical
quarrel she had with me and with life. I don't know when to
say she 'went' insane. It never appears as a sudden thing with
someone you've lived close to and loved. She had the smell of
other worlds in her nose. She couldn't resist them or bear them
either. We had other fights and reconciliations. She had hold
of me. She was trying to take me over the edge with her. Off the
ledge."

Eventually Eileen went back to New York alone. Two weeks
after they agreed this was a "reasonable" temporary measure, he

got a wire from her psychiatrist. It would be advisable for him to come at once.

He saw her face to face in the asylum only a few times. It was hopeless. What communication of a rational sort was still possible came through the intermediary interpretations of her doctors.

"She's full of accusations against you," Dr. Bowen told him at the beginning. "Nothing she has done or bought for herself or written or felt since she met you is 'hers.' She says you drank her blood and ate her flesh."

For his part, Goss admired the precision of such metaphors. "Hadn't she come to the truth when she was no longer able to handle it?"

But the sturdy physician of the mind dismissed such messages from beyond in favor of others that he seemed to have made up from his talks with the demented woman. He said, "Do you realize that several times in your life together she has planned or tried to kill you? Once she and a man named Riley Donovan had a plan to execute you. You foiled the scheme on the very evening it was to have been carried out."

Goss says, "I left the doctor happy in his low-grade detective story fiction. He got paid for thinking he had ferreted out some crucial secret that should have reconciled me to parting with Eileen. Hell, I knew her and Riley both too well to believe for a moment they wanted me out of the way. After all, I'd loved her and shared with her all the big destructive fantasies that threatened my going on. At bottom she wanted . . . oh, to take me out of a world that's boring and painful at the same time. She wanted me safe, so we could be pure artists together.

"That kind of love has to be accounted for, better than the psychiatrists can do. In the picture I'd like to make of women it would be there. I'd like to put everything I've learned from women together in one field of vision."

Chapter 18

Whatever you love is never finished. Paintings to which passion has attached itself can't be finished. They can only be abandoned or destroyed. The painting of Maggie that had come back to him so unpredictably through Bruce Behn and the trackless currents of the art market had showed up like a living hound, like a pet dog of his early days sniffing its way back to its proper master along dark roads that he himself could not begin to retrace. There it was one day, licking and nuzzling his hand, demanding . . .

Demanding what? Well, old paintings, old loves—like dreams —never made it clear what they demanded, except that they *be continued*. Be caught up in the life stream again. And that demand, for a man like him, was precisely the one that had to be honored, whatever anyone else might make of his monstrous ways of honoring it.

He had felt the guilt of desecration that day he started to repaint the picture of Maggie. Had felt the sacrilege of refusing to leave well enough alone. A damn fine painting . . . until he tried to refashion it into what it still demanded to be. Then it turned into a mess, as muddled and again pointless as one of his messy palettes. And as challenging. Then it began to whisper, whine and nag again, and, out of the mess, out of his troubled obligation to its urge to live, he had transferred its vitality to these new paintings.

Now they were hounding him fondly and imperatively, mockingly. Saying, You'll never be finished with us, though you've done what you supposed you set out to do. You thought you'd learn from us when you could quit. But we'll never tell. So you'll never know. Sell us too. Forget us if you can. We'll find our way back.

What did they look like? Some days he was so blind to them

he couldn't make out any resemblances to living forms at all on the canvases. But he knew they were women, like other women, and the endless trial was to account for them and all the women in his life. The passers-by, the wives, mothers, daughters of his friends. Strangers. Women of the private imagination and of the imagination of the race. The nearness and farness of the female. Their everlasting hold on the reins and bridles of the imagination. Their fidelities and deceptions, fragility and persistence.

All about women . . . for without women as reality, dream and idea there would never have been such a thing as art. He admitted that. Admitted the impossibility of a full accounting. Only wished someone would lock him out of his studio and say, "Enough."

Yet there was the obligation to defend himself still for having ever begun to paint. Therefore he was not going to clean his own brushes and say, "Done." All he would ever be allowed to say was "I've made a map of buried treasure. Dig here." Then . . . start a new map with the significant X placed somewhere else.

"I bring you tidings of great joy," Jason said impishly to his father.

"I've heard some noises," Goss said. From the window of Jason's room in the last few days, the sound of his cello had spread over the lawns and gardens of North Atlantic. Now and then Goss had heard it on the stairways inside the mansion. He knew from Susan and Fiona that Monica and Tamisan had been attending Jason in his room while he practiced.

"Oh sure," Jason scoffed. "You would be the first to know. I'm here to confirm whatever you've heard me playing."

"Am I supposed to guess?"

"Tamisan's pregnant."

Goss had not guessed any such fact as this. He felt a swift deflation of confidence in his insight, his gifts of prophecy, the authority of his imagination to range where it pleased.

"Does Susan know?" he asked humbly—humbled right back down to being the most ordinary of potential grandfathers.

"She's being told this instant. In fact Monica was the first one we told."

"Little girls shouldn't be confronted with more than they can comprehend."

"We knew Monica would be pleased whether anyone else was or not. She adores Tamisan. They're my little women. You have yours. Everything has got magically incestuous here. We might as well face that too. Well. Are you pleased?"

"I don't know if I am."

"It's as awful as anything you ever did," Jason said agreeably.

"Worse."

"Worse then. You know we wouldn't have done it if we hadn't had you for an example."

"No one should have me for an example."

"I've been warned of that," Jason said. "I know you think I'm not fit for life. Wait. That life's not fit for me." Both of them remembered a time soon after Maggie's death when the reckless old man had actually said, "I wish you had died instead of her." Now they were resuming precisely that conversation as if nothing had ever interrupted it. "I've thought a lot about death. Lately more than ever. You knew last winter how easy it would be for me to go. We never said it then."

"I suppose I knew, but . . ."

"You think only you can walk the tightrope without falling. Be a Goss and stay alive. That's what it's all about, isn't it? 'Steer always for deep water.' We either mean that or we don't. By now there isn't any choice for me. You and Maggie did that to me. There was never any way back from all the good things you let me know. It wasn't her death that stopped me cold. I don't think it was. Everybody accepts death. That there should be so much promise and then it not go on . . ."

"All right. You're there. That's what we can't accept, isn't it?"

"There's nothing you can think of that I haven't thought by now."

"All right, honey, but . . ."

"But there's another life involved now," Jason said. "That's what Susan is saying to Tamisan, right this instant, isn't it?"

"It's the thing that has to be said, honey."

Suddenly Jason's face went very white. "I take the responsibility for that life, even if he turns out like me."

It was not an oath—any more than the hypothetical embryo in the girl's womb was a human being. The whiteness of the boy's face meant only the clenching of his heart. It was nothing yet, except a fleeting instant when blessings were exchanged. Something more fugitive than forgiveness or apprehension about the future.

Goss said, "Good, good. Let's go find her and Susan. I've got to let on to them I'm pleased unless Susan has already talked her into an abortion. Susan has more sense than the rest of us."

Jason stood in his way. "You've got to say it to me."

"Words aren't that important. You know."

"You've got to tell me you believe."

"I'm a very heavy creature, honey. It takes me awhile."

"What does it cost to tell me you believe we're right?"

"Just about everything."

"Say it."

"I'll try."

Later, when he and Susan discussed the matter as reasonably as they could, Goss laughed. "I might have known our vixen would have to show me she could do one more thing I couldn't even think of before she did. She's a center-stage person. That has to be acknowledged. I yield."

"Do you think it was her idea, not Jason's?"

"It was theirs. I'm convinced of that. Dear God, woman, how could we let it go on if we thought Jason was dragging his feet?"

"Will it . . . ?"

"Work out happily? Don't ask, Susan. It's what they have to do. It's the absolute triumph of the imagination to conceive what it is we have to do."

"Then let us be as lucky as they."

"And all men," he said in the serenity of his good mood, a

mood of reconciliation related to the ebb of emotion and idea that compelled him to his painting. Related as well to the release of his responsibility for Jason. The two things were not the same; they had merely been interlaced, he saw now, like the fingers of folded hands. Strange, he remarked to himself again, how the creative impulse lost its force as he began to understand it better.

"We're fucking less and talking better," Susan remarked. It was neither uttered nor heard as a complaint. One of the dearest things about the woman was that she observed even while participating in either or both. "Do put that in your notebook," he instructed her. Because it sounded so much like what was happening between him and his painted women.

He saw that the actual women of his household, in their great subtlety, were weaning him away from his absorption in the painting. Fiona planned one of her formal-informal galas. Jason would play his cello for the family and a few others. Bruce Behn and Godwin would have a chance to appraise the summer's work in the studio. No doubt of it, Fiona was summoning those formidable critics to voice the conclusion she had already come to. That is: it was time to stop work on these canvases and take a breath before tending to the innumerable possibilities for still more pictures and sculpture that he had now opened. He was glad someone else was going to blow the whistle.

Before Jason's concert, Goss permitted Tamisan to lure him out for a drive. He had, after all, said nothing definitive to her about her pregnancy. Nothing that could even be stretched beyond the courtly kiss on the cheek the day he learned the news.

"I've got to have a heart-to-heart with you before we go off to Paris," she said. They drove out in broad daylight so there could be no misunderstanding on anyone's part.

He sat prissily on the far side of the seat of the big convertible. She tenderized him with fright by swooping amid the traffic like a cyclist. Finally she pulled into a public parking lot behind a beach. Between an aluminum-sided camper and a Chevrolet from Ohio, in a storm of tears, she burst almost instantly into a declaration that he was the true father of her unborn child. *"You* did something to me the day I broke your glasses. *You* came up to get me the day we went to the farm. I've *felt* pregnant ever since."

"Now, now." He offered her his handkerchief to mop her tears. She had something to say and he heard her out.

"It all began back in that other studio. The first time I was there with Janis to meet Jason, I thought I'd been there before. At the farm the same thing. I'd seen it."

"Déjà vu," he said. "It's a common phenomenon."

"Oh, go ahead and explain it! And maybe while I was there I got to know you so well because Jason talked about you and made you a god. And when we were making love we must have meditated you, so it was always like it was you coming into me. And after you'd painted me, I knew you knew it too. I'll stop in a minute. I've caused you all the trouble I'm ever going to, and I know that girls are always hysterical when they know they're pregnant so you won't have to pay any attention. But it's true I've always known things I'm not supposed to know. That's why I'm good *and* bad for Jason both. I made him a sensualist. But that only made us both more mystical. How do I know we won't keep going farther out? Things that keep happening fit better with what I know mystically than with anything I learned in school."

"Yes," he said, "but we must be careful about the people we tell."

Far down among the crowd of cars they saw the flash of sun on the water, dazzling, blinding. A signal of dimensions that overlapped the common geography of the island and the long-domesticated ocean. The other worlds were never as far away or as hard to see as people fearfully pretended. Tamisan's trouble was for him what it must often be for Jason—sheer temptation to let go the life line of reason altogether and go swirling away in the alternative worlds. "Yes, I'm the father of your child. Why not? It makes as much sense as telling the story another way. I'm glad you said it. That opens the way back. I suppose it's only the courage to go on and on that makes me trust you and Jason most. Jason's destiny is to be an artist. An artist goes on to the limits of fantasy. I trust you both to find them."

"There were never any limits for you!"

"I imagined them too, Tamisan."

"Curling up with Susan so you'd have to keep your mitts off me!"

"I'm proud of that," Goss said. "I'm proud of you for seeing through me so easily. Now we can go on from there. Stop grinning! I'd much rather you cried some more. There's enough to cry over and enough to laugh about. I have some respect for my age though you may not. I'm talking to you now as I talk to your mother and that has to be enough for you. If you laugh at me I'll hike up your skirts and spank you."

"You wouldn't spank me!"

"I can't imagine what I might do. Therefore I won't do it."

She thought awhile, bending her face down toward the steering wheel to hide any shadow of thought that might show on the surface.

"Can you believe I got pregnant so you'd keep your mitts off me?"

"I imagine you did it because you love Jason and trust him."

She struck the steering wheel a light blow with her fist—not exactly frustration, not exactly to show satisfaction with his answer. "This is just the way Jason and I get along. I mean how easy we can catch what the other's thinking and wants to hear. So don't you dare spoil it now if I say you and Jason and I and Mama are caught up in something very strange and I'm trying to save him. Do you believe that without my—uh—giving a lot of embarrassing evidence?"

"You're trying to save him."

"You have your own mumbo jumbo about art and I can't go along very far when you talk about it. But it's not just art we're talking about. More like enchantments or religion. Are you with me?"

"There's more to art than what we make and sell. Yes."

"Whatever happens, will you watch out for Mama and I'll take care of Jason and the other Jason—we're going to call him Jason because that's his druid name. Will you?"

"I'll take care of Susan."

"You and I are stronger than they are."

"Tougher."

"No one can help them if we can't."

"We can," he promised.

The sun moved. The light stopped blinking in their faces from off the sea. Tamisan gave a great gulping sigh like that of a child trying to halt the convulsion of tears. "I'm glad there wasn't ever anything physical between you and me. It's weird enough anyway, Pop. Will it be too lèse-majesté if I call you Pop when you get around to doing the right thing with Susan? No? Then let's settle for that. But something freaky did happen between you and me?"

"Very strange," he said tenderly. "I don't think you're an idiot. I think you'll save Jason when the time comes. I think he needs you and will need you."

"Don't expect too much of him, huh? He's very weak and very strong. If you and Mama hadn't expected so much of us, we might not have got so funny."

"I see that," Dean Goss said.

She turned the key in the starter and wiped her face. The starter whined with a high sibilance but the engine didn't start at once. She waited then, with her hand on the key. Managed a grin. "Will you tell me sometime who I am?" she asked.

"Sometime."

She waited a little longer. Then said, "Mama I've always loved, and she might have got along better if she'd met you sooner and had more courage. The best things she writes, sometimes she throws away. Once I found something in her wastebasket about swans. Did you know that when swans meet and want to have at it they get all messed up? They come at each other breast to breast instead of one on the other's back like sensible ducks. They practically climb out of the water trying to be at each other. Mama wrote that they make a ghastly noise. I found that in her wastebasket and I kept it in my scrapbook for a long time until I was afraid she'd find I'd stolen it. So I burned it of course. Or tore it up. Who remembers? What do you think, Pop?"

"I think they come at each other breast to breast."

"And that's idiot, isn't it?"

"No," he said. "That's part of it too."

He had put himself on trial before the demons in himself. By
nudging his son and the girl into their present responsibilities—
and by the recklessness of his new paintings—he had offered
his neck to jealous gods whose very existence was doubted by
an age too tame to seek them. Now it looked as if he had escaped condemnation. At least the verdict was postponed. But
now he was being hounded to pay the costs of his defense.

Marian Burke called again. Her impatient earnestness was
turning to outrage or even to doubt of his sanity. Couldn't
he say yes or no to the plain question of the authenticity of the
paintings she wanted to acquire? He lied again to put her off. In
doing so, again he felt like a rat—a rat cut off from his hole.

Then Vidal learned that one of the paintings had been destroyed. "You can't stop mutilating yourself, can you?" he said
to his father in exasperation. But that wasn't all that troubled
him. "The man who owned the painting killed himself while he
was waiting for you to make up your mind."

Goss blinked in anguish. "A friend of yours, was it?"

"A friend of mine," Vidal affirmed, a little uncertainly. "Now,
don't grab hold of this and make a big issue of it. I know he had
some money troubles, but I'm not saying that had any connection . . . No one knows what motivates a suicide."

"Well, it troubles you, doesn't it? So there must be a connection. Otherwise you wouldn't have brought it up to me."

"I brought it up because Jason knew this man too. Jason's
been after me for my opinions about him. He seems, I might say,
a lot more curious about Sandler dead than he was about Sandler
alive."

"So Jason thinks I may have done the poor fellow in by my
. . . irresponsibility?"

"I said no such thing. Jason didn't either. You know, though,
that Jason has his own peculiar ways of sizing things up. I only
mention this because I think you ought to talk to Jason and per-

suade him there's no connection. Now's no time for Jason to go sniffing after his morbid fantasies."

"No connection?" Goss said plaintively. "Oh, but there is a connection. Oh my, yes. Yes, indeed."

"Stop it," Vidal said. "Just stop it, please. I'm sorry I brought the matter up at all. Well . . . how do you know there's a connection? Did Susan or Tamisan ever . . ."

". . . ever mention to me that the girl had been mixed up with your friend? Why, no. No one ever *mentioned* that to me until this very instant, Vidal, when you told me."

He saw Vidal's mouth open to protest or deny he had said, implied or let slip any such thing. Then he saw a kind of horror begin in Vidal's eyes, as if—for just once in his life—he had seen his father truly and wholly. Had seen the rat's teeth. The rat's cunning and the infinite cruelty of that cunning when the creature had to fight for survival. While that intolerable knowledge linked them Vidal *knew* his father had killed Sandler.

"Now, now," Goss said tenderly. "I don't want you to feel I tricked you into giving information that should have been kept from the old man. It certainly *ought* to be kept from me, for if either Susan or the girl knew I knew it, why, that might cause them pain. And I'll tell you this. When I'm painting, a lot of things get through into my mind that come by ways I don't yet understand. I think I knew I'd killed the feller before you ever gave me a clue. What are you thinking, son?"

Vidal clenched his fists, unclenched them, shrugged and smiled sorrowfully. Slowly he said, "I was thinking that once Sandler told me he was in a duel with you."

"Duel? He said that? Why, he was a very shrewd feller, your friend was. Sorry I never had the chance to meet him"—said Dean Goss, who knew as well as Vidal that there had been a meeting, a trial at arms somewhere in those ambushes of the dream world which only artists know to be real.

"Not a word to Jason," Dean Goss cautioned. "Whatever happened to her, the girl's as healthy as a heifer. Any fool can see that. Whatever happens to them flows away like water. Now she's pure as the mountain dew."

"Is *that* what you see?" Vidal said, recovering himself enough to joke.

"I told you any fool can see it," his father insisted staunchly.

The matter of Sandler's interest in the paintings was handled professionally, in the end, by professionals. Marian Burke got the painting of Jason and his childhood friends for the museum collection. A fair market value for the destroyed canvas was established by negotiation among Fiona, Bruce Behn and various lawyers. Money for Sandler's heirs—if any—was put in escrow.

The whole deal handled fairly.

from Susan Vail's blue notebook:

DEAN GOSS: What I would like to do . . . is go into the dream. And into reality. Both at the same time.

SUSAN: Isn't that hard?

DEAN GOSS (who will not admit anything is impossible): It is like putting one pool ball into two pockets. With the same shot. It takes luck.

Chapter 19

"You'll have to take Jason over today," Tamisan told Monica. "I'm going to Southampton with Fiona and Mama. Take him sailing." It might have sounded comic to anyone but the girls to suggest that Jason had to be watched, or tended, on a minute-to-minute basis. But they were in agreement that if they didn't hold him to it he might not play his cello for the guests Fiona was expecting in the evening.

On his own initiative he had prepared a concert program, had practiced it, perfected it to his satisfaction—then told Tamisan that the concert was already over, though no one but himself had heard it being performed.

"He's got stage fright," Monica said. "I know about that."

"He's not afraid of anything. *I* think he's right, but no one else would understand. So he's got to perform."

"If he's going to be a father he's got to do *some* ordinary things," Monica agreed, with rocklike conviction.

So she took Jason sailing on the afternoon before he was to play. As it turned out, she had other things to lecture him on besides his obligation to Fiona's guests.

"Whatever your father says, you have to marry her. I mean an honest-to-goodness marriage," she told Jason. "Whatever you two think, the baby has some rights as well."

"My father hasn't said boo about a ceremony," Jason countered. "You don't see him rushing to church with Susan, do you?"

"He's a dirty old man and everyone accepts that. They're not going to have a baby, are they?"

"We've already had our ceremony," Jason mused. His arguments weren't at all combative. They weren't intended to tease his niece, either. They were his honest musings and that was what made them so exasperating to deal with.

"That's like saying you don't really have to play your cello tonight because you've already played."

"Exactly the same. We had a druid marriage. There *was* a ceremony before we came back here. When we were down on the farm."

"I'll *bet*," Monica sniffed. "I'll bet you did. Every night and three times a day, but . . ."

"I don't mean making love. I mean something else. A holy ceremony . . ."

"Are you a believer?"

Very seriously, looking her straight in the eye, he said, "Yes."

"You probably believe in Providence and natural beauty and things like that," Monica said. "Or you believe in art because of the family. But you're not a Christian."

"I don't think I am. Maybe."

"I'm not either, yet. But I'm going to be a Catholic. Daddy says all girls go through this at puberty. I think he also worries it's a reaction to his dissolute life. But it's truly *me,* and I will be one, though I hope not strait-laced. It isn't because the Church says so that I think you have to marry her."

"You don't believe we had a druid ceremony?"

"I do," she said, and her brown-green eyes got as round as flowers. "That's what scares me. I have bad dreams and I dreamed the Devil married you."

"Maybe," Jason said, with his sweetest and most thoughtful smile. "That might be so, Monica. I haven't had a dream like that but I know what your dream must have been like."

He did not *have* dreams these days. Dreams weren't delivered to his mind like parcels set on his doorstep or like babies delivered from the bodies of women. The dreaming part of his mind was fused with his waking perceptions. He was either unable to wake from the dream begun the night he and Tamisan had played with death, or else reality was different from what he had grasped before. The change might not show, even to Tamisan, even to his father. He might not be constantly sure of it himself, but he believed it must have happened.

Now, as their sloop ran down the wind a few miles offshore he listened to the chiding of his niece with genuine alertness. At the same time he was alert to the wind, gusting from the west—a little tricky, a little stronger than they had expected when they set out. He was alert to the other boats scattering widely around them as they made for the ocean. Two with bright spinnakers, one with a scarlet mainsail. All of them on independent courses, all diverging on the same wind.

And while he was alert to all that his intelligence and senses brought him from this sunny world, he was just as alert to some kind of dark life going on between him and Tamisan, though they were separated today, and between them and the unborn child and all the invisible sea life below the boat and all the living and dead people beyond the range of his sight.

"You say the Devil married us and that's very funny, Monica, because . . ."

"I don't want to talk about it. I just want you two to get decently married in any church you want to."

. . . because it was Sandler who married us. He married us both. And was in her when I went into her, so the child will have two fathers and one will be the Devil and the other will be me.

And were you true to him?

I kept these, Tamisan had said while she tossed the poison pills in her hand before she took them into her mouth.

"I've thought a lot about the Devil," he said sweetly to Monica. "Are you sure he's as bad as they say? Or that he couldn't perform a marriage that would turn out to be holy if . . ."

She was not going to be shaken on that point. "I know there's poetry about the Devil being creative," she said, "but that's only poetry."

"If it's good poetry it must be true."

"No," she said. "Huh-*uh!*"

Spray showered up from the prow of the running boat. The cables sounded an uneasy sibilance in the sea wind, strings of an instrument constantly being tuned from one key to another.

The organs remember, Tamisan said. *I used to scream and go wild for them. I might forget but my cunt would remember.*

It was Sandler, Devil or not, who had married him to that silence within her in which the screams of her ecstasy still sounded, though his sensuous ear would never hear them.

If she was only for me alone, he thought, *there couldn't have been a true marriage. And it's from those screams, whatever he did, she did to make those screams, that the child was conceived even if it's my seed. So we both are its father. It took both life and death to give it life, let it start away from the silence on the path to being born.*

"There really was a ceremony of marriage," he said to Monica. "You have to take my word for it because I couldn't really explain it to you."

"You don't have to explain, if you're sure," she conceded. "But at least you are going to play your cello tonight, aren't you? Everyone would be disappointed."

"I'll play. I don't think I'll disappoint people any more. Not as much as I used to. I'm sure I'm stronger than I used to be. I can't explain in what way I'm strong, either. Do you feel I am?"

"Maybe," Monica said. "If you're so strong, you better haul in the sail before it rips."

"I'll turn us around. It's probably time to turn back and get ready for tonight."

Those who heard him play that night agreed Jason had lost nothing of importance in the years he had put his cello aside. "I'm no fit judge of technique," Fiona said cautiously to Susan later. But she was a fit judge of other things that matter as much as technique, and Susan saw the older woman's reservations were partly a deliberate balancing for a pride and relief she did not choose to proclaim too openly. "What I felt," Fiona said, "was that we heard a man playing instead of a child. Perhaps . . . sometimes I used to think Jason was too gifted. That when we listened to him we were listening to something he hadn't earned for himself. It came through him instead of out of him. Does that make sense? I suppose not. I've been so inundated

with Goss superstitions. One of them was that Jason learned to
play—made such a swift start—by listening to his mother's voice.
I listened tonight for the echo of Maggie. It isn't there, Susan.
Not any more. Now he's his own man. I can't say yet whether
I'm glad of that or not, but it changes things. Oh my. It changes.
Whatever it means, I'm proud of him."

The others who listened were those who should have heard, in
Fiona's tempered judgment, and they were the ones she had
selected to go afterward, to Goss's studio to see his paintings
of the women.

Some of the people she had brought to the North Atlantic
music room after dinner were family. Godwin Goss sat next to
Vidal on a red settee near the ormolu of the mantel though
Fiona had kept them at different tables at dinner. Tamisan and
Monica, who had chosen to wear almost identical white taffeta
dresses and come barefoot, took places on the floor under a tall
white window drape that swayed above them like smoke as the
warm breeze caught its lower hem. Diana Rothman and Vincent
Berg sat with Fiona and Susan, and before Jason came in lugging
his cello from his room upstairs, Diana reminded Susan that she
had once written a very favorable review of Susan's second
novel. Richard Luellen had flown over from Connecticut the day
before because he was fed up with the trivial reasons that had
kept him from drinking with Dean Goss for too long. The
Bargers, the Considines, Herman Rosenfeld, Alvarez Valloton,
the Springers, Janis Ward, Gloria and Bern Whitestar, Hunter
Ashley, George Vendler, four maids, the gardener and Fiona's
new secretary, Lillian Krause, Connor Bryce, Eudora Macklin
were all there because their splendid lives had been interwoven
with the Gosses' and Fiona's and could, for this little while, be
woven back in again.

There was a tall lithe girl named Steinbeck who had spent
the afternoon playing tennis with Connor Bryce and the earlier
part of the evening explaining to various new acquaintances
that she was not John Steinbeck's daughter, though somehow
that rumor had got fixed in several minds. It was thought she was
there because she was a dear friend of Vidal's.

Bruce Behn came into the music room nimbly enough for a man of his years, but in the huge and ornate chair he selected for himself, he sat with his toes hardly reaching to the floor. He sat there in the fragile beauty of his age, his fingertips set delicately together as if he might have been a figure carved of jade that had been brought in by porters and placed merely for display.

It was neither a random company nor a cross section of any definable world that Susan could find a name for. She might guess that Fiona had been guided by some mysterious principle when she assembled them. They were not there together like ships that pass in the night. There were indefinable linkages that one sensed and lost track of in bafflement. You could only say for certain they were in the gravitational field that emanated from Goss. Might as well try to interpret Richard Luellen's asthmatic wheezing and try to correlate that with his verses as to go further in explaining what gave coherence to this gathering of bodies.

And yet when Jason began to play, without accompaniment, one had to feel the coherence of the group. And think the music itself was the true reason they were here. While it lasted, it made them a single body. Two ears instead of many. No eyes at all, since eyes were for the time being irrelevant. No use wondering about the minds that interpreted what was heard. There it all went scattering again. Only in the authority of the cello—yet unmistakably there—was their communion.

Jason began with the cello part of the *Meistersinger* overture. There was no applause when he finished and looked around, flushed and smiling. There might have been, Susan thought, if the music hadn't told us that no applause was needed, told us to be at ease with one another.

He played, with a few errors, Tersarin's *Vivace*. His face was getting redder and redder. His bowing arm, bare beyond the sleeve of his soft white shirt, seemed also tinted darker. His shirt was sticking to his back and now his smile was unmistakably apologetic, as if he might be shamed a little by the interference of bodily clumsiness between the music itself and those good enough to sit and listen.

"I want to go down to the studio with you and see my father's paintings in a little while," he said. "There's only one other thing I'd like to try. It's an improvisation. Not quite an improvisation, since I think it's already composed completely in my mind. I haven't practiced it, though. I was sailing in the ocean with Monica this afternoon. She asked me questions I couldn't give her true answers for. I don't want to answer any questions. I want to play—as well as I can—what the boat ride was like."

So that was what he gave his listeners, as well as he could. The music both hid and revealed the truth of that boat ride with his niece. Anyone who wanted to understand the voice of the cello would not be mistaken. No one had any certainty to carry away and translate into another medium. No one was as disturbed as all of them might have been if he had tried to account for the mental and physical and total reality of that little ride in words. Anyone could concede its beauty without having to pay a thing for the concession.

The improvisation ended with a single questioning, quavering, dwindling note. A high G as pure as it was faint.

No, it didn't quite end there. He lifted the bow, turned to make an impish face at his father, who was standing nearby with Susan. Then he dropped the bow beyond the bridge and sawed back and forth three times in a shrill, cacophonous shriek.

"Thank you all," he said. "That's as far as I can go with it. So let it go."

"Jason's is a hard act to follow," Janis Ward said to Goss later when the guests had moved to the studio and nearly everyone was drinking champagne instead of communing with the paintings they were presumably there to admire. Or else, he thought, his women had veiled themselves from all eyes. He didn't see much in them himself right now.

"Don't be absurd. I preceded him. I invented the act." That was his boast. His happiness for the evening was to settle down in the faith that it was no longer a matter of either following the other. For the instant they were abreast. Something had convinced Jason to get on the outside of his experience and rule it instead of huddling toward the center of it. His father wanted no credit for making that happen. He took credit for the intelligence to see that it had. He couldn't, any more than anyone else, spell out all the cello might have said. He had heard its authority. Had heard it say, "I am." Whatever the boy might do from here on out—and he talked one day of writing, another of making films; what did it matter if he triumphed visibly or not?—his life would show that "I am" like a brand. If he had to take his fist to Tamisan again—the chances seemed very great he would—the blow would not land on his own glass chin.

A heartening conviction. To celebrate it Goss swallowed the champagne he was holding and demanded that Susan get him more.

It was his svelte son Godwin who clicked glasses with him this time. Saying: "Father, I have been receiving rumors through the summer that you might have abandoned the Rodin-Balzac series. It was even suggested that you had disavowed it as a hoax, which I was hardly inclined to believe. Mergenthaler at the Met assumed that your lack of response to his feelers about a retrospective must confirm what Harold Strickland hinted about a change of mind. I'm glad to see there's nothing to it."

"What the hell are you talking about?" Goss turned to the big paintings on their easels at the center of the studio. "Are you altogether blind? These are like nothing I ever did before." But even as he said it, he saw that the canvases were only painted backdrops in front of which his Gadarene friends and family guzzled and posed. But still . . . different backdrops? At least novelties, please? "Use your eyes, my boy."

"No," Godwin said. "No. You must concede that I'm perfectly capable of seeing what you've done. Bless your heart. Mergenthaler and I know you're one of an endangered species and value you accordingly. You are the last of the painters for the eye. The eye is obsolete now, as I was saying to . . ."

"You mean my kind of thing isn't being done any more?"

"You're still doing it," Godwin said. "How could we fail to pay attention? Certainly I see *superficial* differences in these paintings from what you were doing last spring. Nevertheless, it's evident to me this evening that what you've done is a variation on the series, not a renunciation."

"You mean *anything* I might heave or smear onto the canvas would still be part of that series?" Goss could feel the beginning of an immense laughter convulsing his gut—himself the butt of the joke to be sure. Yet the laughter made him immune. If Godwin was right and he could outwit neither destiny nor time, yet laughter made him the ruler of both. "Ah, now you're the one who's fallen into the trap of mere evidence for the eye." He took Godwin's elbow and steered him close to the canvases, close enough so he could reach up and tap the center of one with his knuckles. "You know what's under there?"

Godwin was smiling as he had smiled long ago in every game of wits with his father. "We know your tricks. No doubt you've buried some symbol known to you alone."

"A *cunt!*" It was neither bellow nor whisper nor simple exposition. The utterance was, simply, continuation of the impulse that had laid the lines and plated them with colors in the making of the paintings.

"Knowing you," Godwin said, "there could have been little doubt as to the tendency of your symbolic preparation. Certainly I guessed that."

"But I said it! Sounded it out loud. And you were afraid to."

"A matter of manners. . . ."

"The difference between art and nothing!"

Part of the difference, then. A bluntness that spread the laughter out from the convulsions within, forcing the few who were near enough to hear to join, uniting them however briefly and ephemerally with his willingness to accept the sentence of his grimmest trials. No, neither he nor they were going to escape from what they must be. And that was why they *had* to laugh as he had always laughed, finally, at the whole web of his destiny, burying and then slyly revealing his joke as God himself had hidden it and revealed it. Laughing to affirm that eternally comic passage by which the man escapes himself and is transformed in the life of his sons.

The laughter was as transient as Jason's music had been. It only seemed to make the guests a little more at home with the paintings. At ease—but more wary of standing too near the painted creatures for fear of various temptations and embarrassments.

On the next round of champagne Goss listened while Bruce Behn praised him in lilting voice to Lillian Krause and the Bargers. "*Terribilità,*" Bruce was saying. "As you know, his contemporaries attributed and prized this quality above all others in Michelangelo's work. His figures were human and yet supernatural, consorts of angels and demons brought into the habitations of men. He did not think he was representing such beings. Not he! He supposed he was *releasing* them from the marble or evoking them from the pristine canvas. You must ask Dean Goss if he does not sometimes entertain the same assurances and—hope he will answer you! For my part, I anticipated what I would see tonight. I came like one of the shepherds of old following a star to the Nativity. You will forgive an old man his eccentricities of expression? Perhaps I may say that a work of art has a bouquet, like wine. The fragrance precedes the taste. Fame spreads and entices the imagination, then lingers beyond the moment of revelation through times to come. From the moment Fiona described these new canvases, I understood they ought to be installed in a chapel, though I would be hard put to say what religion would accommodate them."

"Are you always sure in advance?" It was Tamisan, circulating back into sight.

The frail man clasped his hands and beamed. "I am not always right. Is there a right and wrong in matters of the spirit, the realm of art? Magnitudes call. Magnitudes call. Yes, child, I'm always sure of what it is most necessary to know."

Already I'm being sold, Goss thought, and the laughter went on in his belly—not a bit more cynical than Bruce's praise. Not cynical at all, or resigned, but submissive as he felt himself being harnessed into the sincere community of men, women and children he would never know. Bruce was selling. It was not at all a matter of asking for a bid from the Bargers or Lillian Krause or expecting them to pass the word of a hot property to their moneyed or influential friends. No, the selling was far more ethereal than that, though the sharp rocks of commercial necessity had to be negotiated somewhere along the line. Bruce was tuning his voice to praise, tuning so finely that salesmanship became, to start with, a process indistinguishable from the rest of the creative deed. Another stream, flowing out in another direction, down from the dangerous peaks onto the flat lands it would water. The ceremony of yielding his painted women over to Bruce was as subtle as yielding the role of father to Jason. And just as fateful, profound. Both were too solemn for mockery. Both worthy of his best laughter.

He sat up late with Dick Luellen as the others drove away or went to their beds in the mansion or guesthouse. He would feel later that the poet and he had said their best things to each other that night, but he would not even try to remember what they were. What they said was like music, like laughter.

Susan woke to see him standing in pensive, bulky silhouette by one of the windows that looked seaward. He said, "Oh hell, there's still so many things that went into the paintings that you don't know about. There was the night I saw Jason and Tamisan run out bare ass to go swimming . . ." He gave a little snort that sounded like astonishment. "Susan, are we too old? Mmmmm . . . follow in their footsteps? Could we run out now, you and me?"

"If you want to."

He snorted again. "I really don't. I'm tired. I'm content. Let them go. I'm glad they're going. We agree it is better to be glad than happy."

He was too sleepy to indicate whether he was talking about letting his paintings or his children go—whether the agreement was with his women, or might have been something repeated in his talk with Dick Luellen.

from Susan Vail's green notebook:

D.G.'s wedding days: Minna Karbin Goss   May 14, 1925
                             Margaret Niles Goss March 30, 1951
                             Susan Goss   October 5, 1970

Book V

Mortality

Chapter 20

It had been almost fifty years since the first time Dean Goss went up the steps of a Paris apartment house two at a time, breathing smells of varnish and wax and wallpaper. Now the pattern in the wallpaper and its air of heroic, genteel decay took the place of memory—as if in the narrow shadow of the stair well the figured paper and the highlights on the varnished banister would remember for him what his life had been and leave his mind free to romp in pure expectation.

He was breathing hard and his heart was knocking amorously against his ribs when he went down a corridor of the *deuxième* and rapped with his knuckles on a varnished door.

And when Tamisan opened it, grinning her fine, expensive teeth at him, she only said, "Ha! You thought you'd surprise me again like the day you came to Mama's! The same trick never works twice."

Then she was in his arms. . . . Not quite. It was March and she was very pregnant. They both had to lean over the bulge of her pregnancy, like diplomats bowing to each other over a table, while they hugged.

"Oh yes. You're clairvoyant," he said.

"Not so much. Mama sent a telegram from Rome." She welcomed him into the apartment with a swooping gesture that also served to point out the table where the telegram lay among glasses and apples lit by the March sun outside.

"She didn't even know that I'd come in from the airport in Paris," he grumbled.

"Ha-*ha*," said Tamisan. She kicked at the cat that was flirting and hiding around her ankles under the hem of her ivory robe. "Go to your box, Puvis," she commanded. Then she swept the cat up into her arms and with her long, fine fingers teased his ears and the sensitive arch of his spine until he closed his eyes to the luxury of her caress. Then she lifted a foot to hook a newspaper from a doilied armchair so Goss could sit down if he wished. "We call the cat Pewvis dee Shuh-vawn-ees because he's not exactly my favorite painter in the world," she said. "Let's have some wine, now that you're here, sweet thaaaaang."

Taking off his coat and accepting the chair she had cleared for him—and the cat fur that would undoubtedly cling to his trousers—he said, "The concierge wanted to know if I was the grandfather. *'Vous êtes le grandpère?'* "

"She's an awful flirt. Well, you're *his* grandfather, anyway," she said, comfortably patting the person in her belly, "if not mine and Jason's, which the concierge surely didn't mean, but was only teasing you, too. I've got some champagne on the window ledge, if that's what you'd like more than anything in the world," she said with a teasing air. She tossed the cat down as she headed for the kitchen.

"The best thing in the world is to see you so nicely swelled up," he said lazily, easing his big shoulders down into the back of the chair. He meant it totally. The round completeness of her belly just simply looked like the platonic ideal of fulfillment. To his imaginative eye it looked like the rounding out, the intended culmination, of his passionate sojourn on the earth. And for a moment, with no chill at all, he felt himself absolutely ready to die.

"Really?" she asked, more flattered by his eyes on her than his casual words. "The French seem to like the looks of pregnant women. So we came to the right place. My doctor smacks his lips."

Dean Goss smacked his. "Really. You came to the right place."

As if the approval of his eye were a command, she paused at the kitchen door. Very deliberately she turned and opened her ivory robe wide so he could see even better what her pregnancy had done to her. She lowered her eyes—not at all out of modesty, but so there would be no distraction from the simple, fecund bulge protruding from the pedestal of her legs and the downy nest of pubic hair. Or perhaps she was looking down so their gazes could meet on the skin drawn so tight and shiny that it almost mirrored the room. "Jason says it looks like a roc's egg in a wren's nest," she said in an awed tone. "I think it looks like the Taj Mahal from above."

"Like a snow hill in the air," Goss said. "It swims among enticements." Desires chirped in his veins like the songbirds of an imagined Eden. Desires that wakened and gratified the impulses of his senses simultaneously, as art is supposed to do. There was absolutely no unappeased desire that could have moved him then even to wish for the possession of touch. All was consummated in his eye and behind his eye.

She did not let the robe fall closed until he nodded like an approving sultan. She was smiling with satisfaction when she lifted her gaze at last to meet his, then swirled out of sight into the kitchen.

Presently he heard her normal voice through the kitchen door. "Jason should be back any time. He's either walking or gone to Montmartre. He likes to get up high where he can see Paris from bird's eye. But not from the Eiffel Tower. It's too modern arty, don't you think? We think it is."

Goss was looking at the redness of the apples on the table. They remembered Cézanne and the south: the grays and highlights of the glassware remembered Renoir and his cheerful canoers resting for lunch; the whole interior remembered Goss's good days in Paris fifty years ago.

And now the fifty years were all there in one instantaneous package, like a gift wheedled from the god of time by this always surprising girl. Years that had been tamed so they could never flee again like frightened creatures disturbed from their grazing by his passage. The great clock of the world had stopped precisely at noon. Its stopping seemed to blur out the distinctions between youth and age, life and death.

Then he heard the tick of time again and called to the sounds in the kitchen, "Your mother stayed in Rome to visit with Minna. My old wives seem to have so much in common. They'll be fast friends and God knows what gossip Susan will retrieve for her book. There's been so much."

The great pearl of Tamisan's belly, in its eighth-month ripeness, remembered all the best painting of women he had done in fifty years. And how much exaltation as well as grief there had been in that work, now put behind him.

With the champagne they were toasting success, though neither of them had to say so, and they might not have known whose to call it. It was theirs in that they could meet with such fond familiarity, an ease that encompassed all sorts of domestic intimacy between male and female. Like father and daughter, grandfather and granddaughter, brother and sister, husband and wife. Like lovers who remembered the coziness of Paris when it was younger, fifty years ago, and need not bother very much with gossip about the intervening time.

They were toasting their success with Jason, perhaps. Or his success with life. He had had a good year, and there was just a bit of melancholy smugness in their realization that they had conspired to give it to him. They sipped like two spies at the successful end of a mission that can never be fully revealed to history. They did not forget Susan, whose year had also been a success.

"You know, Jason did some painting through the winter, too," Tamisan said, "though I'm sure he wouldn't want you to see what he painted."

Goss nodded happily to that. As a child, Jason had resolutely held back from painting, as if he had known from the first that that area was used up by his father. To hear now that Jason had enrolled for a few months at the Grande Chaumière and equipped himself with paints and canvas was to hear that the boy had reclaimed another part of his own identity.

"You're not surprised?" Tamisan asked.

Goss shook his head. He had seen neither Jason nor the girl since fall when they drove from Munich to spend a few days with him and Susan in Madrid, but he was not here to be surprised by any of the good news Tamisan had to offer with her champagne. In Madrid he had seen Jason eager as a convalescent, delighting in the responses of his senses and his mind to the Europe he and Tamisan were claiming as they had tried to claim America by driving its highways.

Then his father had seen the young artist unleashed, ready to test his powers. Jason had soberly discussed what he was beginning to write—"a journal, a novel, travel diary; we'll have to see where it goes." He was turning over the possibilities of making films with Vidal. Without haste or anxiety he was preparing for a career that would involve him more with the world than music could. "I want my boy to have a complete set of ancestors," Jason had said. "It would be too silly if there was a blank spot in the line of descent right before him."

When the weather began to get too chilly, Jason and Tamisan had found this comfortable apartment on the Rue de la Boétie and settled in with their cat Puvis. With Monica they had gone to concerts and the opera and a great many movies. Now and then they played mice-in-the-corner at parties Vidal threw in his apartment on the Île St. Louis or in one or another of the luxury hotels. It appeared they had involved themselves no more with new friendships than they had the winter before in New York. But the tone of their lives was different. Now, because of the expected child, they were trying to be as bourgeois as they could. They were going to be sufficient unto themselves because Jason must work. Tamisan had concentrated on learning how to market and becoming a good cook. Occasionally Jason played his cello. The taboo on that was forgotten. "I'm plodding along with my guitar," Tamisan said, "but you're not going to hear that any more than see his paintings. Some things are too private"—said the girl who had opened her robe to show the secret shapes of her body. "How long can you stay?"

He started to glance at his watch. Then, letting her refill his glass with champagne, he made up his mind. "Why not two or three days? The rest of the week."

"Oh," she said, shaking her head as if startled.

"I won't camp on you. I suppose I'll get a room at the George V for old times' sake. I thought you and Jason might drive me to Fontainebleau tomorrow if you feel like it. I'm fond of that place in early spring before any leaves have started. I like to wallow in the melancholy of it."

"Oh. Mama said you had to go on to London this evening."

"I *was* scheduled to go over to meet Vidal. But there's no

409

need. I like it here. No need in the world to go to London. Dreary place."

"Oh," she sighed. Her grin was tormented. He guessed at once that she had been acting out some important lie. She frowned and said, "Well . . . see . . . Jason isn't just out walking. Though he *does* like to be up high on Montmartre and I don't always know when he'll come back. It looks like I wasn't telling you the truth. . . . He's in Persia."

"Persia?" The sound of the name came straight from a fairy tale.

"Iran. Whatever they call it now. Or maybe he's in Egypt today. I haven't had a letter from him this week. But he's all right. I always know *that*. Honestly, I can feel it. He's all right except he has this bad cold he can't seem to get rid of. But that's nothing to worry about."

"What shall we worry about then?" He questioned her as gently as he could, wanting to offer her support without asking any reassurance for himself.

"It would spoil it all if you worried about *anything*," she said, just as firm as he in refusing to admit any personal need. All that was clear was that she had meant to shuffle him cheerfully along to London without any suspicions of Jason's absence. He saw that every move and probably every word she had uttered since his arrival had been calculated in advance. The recklessness of opening her robe for him had been finely calculated . . . he had been meant to understand that of course she would not have risked that if Jason were not expected momentarily to return.

And now his whimsical decision to stay over had ruined her scenario. She was left like a tightrope walker whose rope is suddenly cut away. He was sure she did not mean to explain all she knew or felt about Jason's absence. He was afraid that in the disappointment she felt at the collapse of her strategy she might fall on him in sheer bewilderment and dismay. Might come to him and sit on his knees. Hide her troubled eyes against his shoulder. Offer to his hands the unendurable warmth of her body. For a moment he imagined both of them falling from the broken tightrope in an embrace bitter as the shrieks of the damned falling into a pit of fire. And he saw his thought mirrored in the desperation of her eyes.

From this fatal—and all too possible—plunge, she saved them by going again into the kitchen and returning this time with a thin sheaf of manuscript on yellow paper in her hands. She said, "You know he's been writing. And in fact it's in connection with his work he had to go to Persia and Egypt. In fact . . . it isn't exactly research. But what he's writing is about . . ."

"His mother."

She nodded and offered the manuscript to him—surely not to read here and now, but as some concrete evidence that there was a good and honorable explanation for what she could not discuss openly with him.

His eyes caught the first line as he took the manuscript from her hand and laid it on his knee.

In Paris the dead mother called to him incessantly.

Tamisan sat on the carpet beside his chair, caressing the cat, which had come back to snuggle against her warmth. "You know he *is* finding himself. That's why you mustn't misjudge or ask for things too soon, and I'm sorry I'm such a lousy liar. I better quit it altogether unless I can improve. Good intentions don't help."

"Maybe they do."

She went on as if she did not need his encouragement. "He started something new—really—after we were down on the farm last summer. He knew he had to come to terms with his mother's death—with death itself, you might say—and still not refuse to live like all of us. And maybe that's what the baby was all about. See, the baby was part of an idea. . . ." She shook her head at the impossibility of straight explanation. "Coming to Paris where all the bad things started was part of it. Writing about it was part of it for him. We'd quit all that occult stuff we used to try. The druid stuff. But you know, when you've been through certain experiences, why, that's what you'd naturally use and write about. What he's done, starting to write

411

about Maggie and her 'calling' to him here, isn't so grim as you'd think. You'll see, these pages are all full of anecdotes and child-hood memories of Paris that she told him. It's like a scenario that goes back with skips through a lot of lives, back to his grandfather Niles who was a boy here when Santos-Dumont flew his dirigible around the Eiffel Tower.

"Things like that. But what I like, of course, was that he was getting so healthy, writing about it. Getting it out of his system. You know all about this, you. You've done it yourself, I'll bet.

"Well . . ." she said with a huge sigh. "He was coming to terms with it all and how life goes on. Then, about a month ago, he came home sick one day. From the Louvre. I don't know exactly what had happened, but what he thought was that, for once, out of the blue, his mother really *had* spoken to him."

She seemed uncertain about going on, as if she had already stretched the thread of credulity to the breaking point and might snap it altogether if she tried to hang any more weight on it. After a while Goss said, "So he went off to Persia to see if she would speak again, is that it?"

Tamisan nodded. "He'll go and he'll come back. He'll cer-tainly be back before the baby is due. You've got to believe how much he takes care of me and wants to be a father."

"I believe," Goss said.

"Do you believe Maggie really called him?"

"You told me you were through with the occult stuff."

"Yeah." Her eyes got very wide, looking inward. "What if it's not through with us?"

As he had before with her, he felt the power of her belief tugging at him like a physical weight. He thought, No one be-lieves in ghosts or magic by himself, but there are other people, some others, who can persuade us they have seen them and drag us after them. Beyond her now, he felt the gravitational tug of Jason's quest for belief tugging at the fringes of his mind like the beloved hand of a child who does not want to be led into the cold or the light of day.

The girl—and through her, Jason—seemed to be begging him not to utterly deny the reality of those fairyland, imaginary realms where separation and loss melted away. As an artist, could he deny what the girl called "the occult," those imperatives that only the unfettered imagination will justify?

He said slowly, "You're a temptress, daughter. You pose such indecent questions. Do I think Maggie's called him off to Persia now? They both told me, before she died, that they almost decided to go to Persia when she got sick. Do you mean that, though she said it then, he's only—really—hearing her say it now? That it was, all this time, a sort of delayed-reaction time bomb planted in his mind?"

That was not what she had meant. It was not a good enough conjecture and Tamisan sat stroking the cat waiting for something better. He said, "Well now, we don't know as much about time as we pretend to. Nor all about communication—or 'calling.' No, we don't. Dogs can hear whistles we can't. Sometimes I'm not very sensitive to signals that come through loud and clear for others. I guess if I'd been with Joan of Arc at Domremy when the angel came to speak to her . . . I wouldn't have heard a syllable. *I* wouldn't have heard, but I believe Joan heard. I believe she did. And, yes, I think Jason heard Maggie if he says he did. But I believe this, sweet: If Maggie called him, she wasn't summoning him to any harm. She wouldn't do that."

Tamisan's eyes were shining now. This was what she wanted to hear, and the mere eagerness with which she absorbed it seemed to guarantee that he was moving toward the truth, even if he hadn't hit it squarely yet. Breathless, she asked, "Even if he never came back?"

"Well . . ."

"That wouldn't be bad, would it, if it was her he was following? Listening to her all the way?"

"Well . . . wouldn't it be very bad for *you?*"

She blinked like someone coming awake. Shook her head vehemently. "I have the baby now. What does anybody need except someone to pour out their feelings on so they don't go sour inside?" Her claim was so ruthless and so sincere that it pierced the last of his doubts about the stuff she was made of. Now it was as if she had shed the last rags of her personality, too, and sat there on the floor with her cat as the pure embodiment of the nameless female, the source of a love that only needed "someone" for its expenditure, that might flash down unpredictably, destructive or life-giving by the same capricious accident or chance. For that moment, when her ruthless cry was still in his ears, he thought he had never known any woman as well as he knew her.

"Well," he said stubbornly, "babies are fine. I'm all for them. But you need a man."

"Oh, I didn't mean Jason wasn't coming back. He is! He is! It was only a 'what if' kind of question. He'll be back well before the baby is due. You'll see! And as far as needing a man, Jason takes care of aw-uh-ull my needs, thank you. He's a chip off the old block, I guess, and you don't need to worry in that department."

"No, no," Goss said, chuckling with a certain amount of relief at this swift passage from the occult to the bawdy. "Look, I won't ask questions I don't need to. I have time for just one more glass of champagne. Then I'll have to dash if I'm going to catch my plane for London."

Tamisan was neither smiling nor frowning when she filled his glass the last time. She was going to let him go in peace, but yet her lips were pursed as if she might be on the verge of some further revelation that would keep him with her. As if, in spite of her show of bravery, she needed to be held in his arms for a little until the terror of being herself ebbed away. As she bent toward him with the bottle in her hand, that tricksy robe of hers opened just enough to show the iridescent glow of her swollen breasts in their envelope of shadow. Breasts the color of death, he thought, yearning for their honeyed taste, contenting himself with the sweet vigor of champagne.

"Do you want Susan to come and be with you until the baby is born?"

She seemed angered by the suggestion. "Jason will be back any day now. We want you both to come *after* we've got this here detail taken care of. Glory be! It is kind of astonishing it's going to happen to me, isn't it? What if it's a little pink pig instead of a baby?"

414

"We'll exhibit it," he said. "Mmmmm. I always have been curious what really happened when you and Jason went to the farm. But don't tell me any secrets about that, either."

"Ooooh," she said, wincing. "The baby just kicked. Want to feel him kick before you leave, Pop?"

"I think I'll wait for that too," he said, just a little bit crossly.

"You're sure you've got to go?" Her smile was harlotish, teasing.

"I told you I didn't *have* to. I think London is going to depress me a great deal. I'll miss your mother."

"Miss me a little too," she said as she kissed him good-by.

"I'm damned if I will," he said.

His plane had crossed the channel and was descending toward Heathrow Airport by London before he even tried to sort out the contradictory impressions of his visit with the girl. If he had begun to think about anything revealed to him he might have begun to worry, and he preferred, rather, to savor the varied tones of excitement and calm that had colored the encounter.

But as he heard the groan of the landing gear lowered he thought: Now it's clear she's always known completely what she does to me. And could do. Known every kink of my impossible feelings about her.

And considering the strangeness of that, the strangeness of her position between him and Jason, she was handling everything like a champion.

The groan of the landing gear continued until it was fully extended.

Home in America two weeks later he got a note from Jason explaining that he had returned from a rather dull junket to Bagdad and Cairo.

"Tamisan is afraid she made me sound like a character in *Dracula Meets Wolf Man*. The truth is—I'm disciplining myself day by day, in ways I've learned from you, and I've learned

415

more from you than I can very easily put to use. I'm trying to be a good writer this season. My prose description of the magic carpet I flew on ought to be good enough for *Scientific American.* I didn't find any ghosts, if that's what I was looking for. . . .

"Tamisan is grumpy that you saw her in such swollen condition and promises her old, sylphlike figure before she will let you lay eyes on her again. . . ."

So . . . the girl who knew how she had dazzled him had told a little bitty lie about that to her Jason, his Jason, had she? And somehow tricked Jason into passing the teasing little lie along.

Harmless enough, no doubt. Wasn't it . . . ?

But as Goss's eye swept the banalities of the note, his hand began to tremble. A sudden icy sweat flowed under his shirt.

If I'd gone for her, he thought, if I'd touched her when I might have, Jason would never have come back alive.

The two of them don't necessarily want me damned. They are just going to give me every chance to be, from here on out to the end of my life.

from Susan Vail's red notebook:

There was a moment when everything was put together. For Goss and me. For those wild birds of passage we have tried to claim as our children. I know there was such a golden, perfect crystallized moment—or a year—because I remember feeling it begin to pass.

Now I remember that I was given so much. All the loot of his lifetime was packed into one big sack of treasure and tied up tight and laid in my lap. Mine! And the irony is that I couldn't really claim it until the string on the sack was loosened and the treasure began to spill and scatter.

Now, with each bewildering loss, I see more clearly that I was not meant to claim what was given me in any stable or permanent form. I'll claim it as mine by chasing after it as it scatters and rolls away out of reach. . . .

Goss says, sure, you can get art into a museum—but you can't keep it there. It seeps out under the doors, and the artist had better follow it back into the street and down all the streets that branch out and away endlessly and forever.

Chapter 21

In Paris the dead mother called to him incessantly. . . .

Jason had written the line one day with no more premeditation than is ever required to let a genie out of a bottle. He was finding himself—just as Tamisan swore to his father. The things he wrote and painted that year were legitimate self-discovery, whatever they might amount to in the long run. He never worried about whether he was writing for publication or how long he might go on writing.

He had written that line and as soon as it was down on paper it began to obsess and charm him like some mystic inscription he might have come on amid ancient stone carvings while he was exploring a cave or a tomb.

It was true, he thought. The truest words he could have possibly written.

It was false. It was pure fiction. Though he could summon a host of memories of Maggie on Parisian streets and in the changes of weather that modulated the sky above the rooftops that had enchanted him and his mother in years gone by—still, it was absolutely clear to him that it was he who was summoning those memories. He who was alive while she, who was dead, was utterly silent.

It was true-false, as he tried to explain to Tamisan—confusing her in exact proportion to his own confusion. "Stop the nonsense," she said. "Just do it, don't explain. Just write, or whatever you want."

As far as his intentions were concerned, he was quite willing to stop his efforts at explanation. It was in his blood and his mind from his father to know that the artist must say: Let it *be*. It was either a comic or a tragic waste to scratch for explanations of the artist's enigma. "I'm producing. You produce," Tamisan said with her hand on her growing belly. As long as they were visibly productive, they were doing what they were supposed to.

Yet his enigmatic line itched and itched, deep in his enfolded nature where it was maddeningly difficult to reach.

In Paris the dead mother called to him incessantly.

That itched when he thought of it as true. It itched a little worse when he thought it was false. Worst of all when he knew it to be true-false.

In the course of those late winter months while they waited for the showers and the chestnut buds to signal the resurrection of spring, Jason carried his dilemma to others besides Tamisan.

"I want to go to Paris," he complained once to Monica. Of course he was laughing as he said it.

"But you're here!" Monica exploded in vexation. "You've been here all winter and you've got Tamisan and everything is *great*. I know. You're just anxious to see the baby."

"I'm anxious to see . . . something. I know I've got to wait until he's born before I can see him. I *know* I'm in Paris, Monica, but I don't feel I'm there."

The gray walls in the winter rains, the bright, musty, scented interiors of apartments, restaurants, churches, subways and theaters seemed to him to be an opaque curtain behind which was hidden the Paris he wanted to go to. Yes, he knew that Paris of past times was dead, just as everyone else knew it was. Yet he felt it stirring behind the curtain of the visible Paris as if *it* didn't know it was dead.

Once, looking down on the whole sweep of the city from his favorite spot high on the slopes of Montmartre, he had seen some stir of movement far off, near the Pantheon maybe, clear across the city, and for a little while it seemed to him that what he had seen was what he was straining so hard for. Another time inside the towering vaults of Notre Dame he had heard people murmuring in a language that, for a moment, seemed to him not merely foreign but from another time, as if it were being spoken in the Paris he longed to enter. And once on a gray, frosty morning while he was walking alone along the banks of the canal heading for the Père Lachaise cemetery, it had seemed to him that the brown, chill water was flowing through that other Paris, not the one he lived in with Tamisan that winter.

These were very fragile, vanishing intimations. They only increased the itch in his mind. But they led on to the strange thought: If I could get through to that other Paris, the dead Paris, then, in that city, the dead mother would call to Jason incessantly. Then it would be true.

Once that winter Tamisan wrote in a letter to her mother: "There are a lot of people I could name who *fall short* of being sane. Jason tends to go out on the *far side* of it. Naturally I go with him because his people are my people and his god my god as someone taught me and don't imagine I wasn't listening to anything. Do you find the same true of Pop?"

Her mother wrote back, "I'm not sure they go out *past* sanity. They go past other people's borders, maybe, but I like to think they stretch sanity and drag it along with them and give it a bigger scope."

To which Tamisan wrote back, "Bullshit!"

Which her mother understood to be an expression of delight and agreement, the equivalent of declaring, "Enough said."

In that winter Tamisan and Susan seemed to understand each other better than they ever had before.

"I want art to be true instead of being a pretense," Jason said to Vidal. "That's my trouble. That's why I don't know if I'll ever be like you and Dad. I've been meditating the Egyptian art in the Louvre. Those dumb, wonderful Egyptians never made the distinction between stone figures or the little clay figures they put on their ships of death and actual, breathing animals and people. They knew something we don't."

"We ought to be Egyptians," Vidal agreed. But even in this sympathetic reply language itself forced the distinction between *ought* and *be*. Only total hallucination could dissolve that frustrating distinction. And the better his work, the better his life with Tamisan, the less capacity Jason had for hallucination.

421

"What do you want your son to be?" Tamisan asked as they lay in the dark with his hand cupped to the curve of her bulge, feeling now and then the kick of life signaling mysteriously from beyond.

"An Egyptian," he said.

"All right."

"Promise?"

"Whatever you most want."

She was trying—and trying very well—to give him anything he wanted. They were rich, they were young, they could have anything they wanted.

But the itch was always there. While she slept he lay awake alone knowing he would want something else language could not name without ceasing to be language. Something he could not think of because the processes of thought could not conceive it.

When he had come to Paris on his aborted adventure with Maggie, they had missed almost everything they had planned to do. But, like ordinary tourists, they had made the obligatory visit to the Louvre before they flew hastily home. And when his mother was dying in the New York hospital she had comforted them both by saying, "That may have made up for what we missed. The rest might have disappointed us, Jason. I lie here and think about what we liked best that day. I liked the Egyptian things best. Don't you remember that huge cat goddess we said looked like Fiona?"

Now as the present winter passed without event, Jason went back several times to retrace the actual path he and Maggie had walked through the museum. Trying to fake up the emotions, the memories—he told himself—in the stubborn hope that out of the fake he might catch at least a clue of the true path he had lost. The forms were there to his eyes. Painting, sculpture, ornaments, hieroglyphics. The whole warehouse of priceless, worthless shapes. If he wanted, the visual memory of Maggie among these things was not hard for him to summon. Just there she had stood on the chill marble stairway. Thus, she had swung her long dark hair as she began to grin, balancing on her high heels coltishly, flinging out her beautiful hand to point at the cat-headed lump of basalt. "Look, it's Fiona. Isn't it, Jason? Isn't it? Isn't it?" He could hear, perfectly, the enchanted merriment of her voice as she made the recognition and ignored the fact that she must go back to America on the morning plane because the doctor said she must. Her voice was the very best thing about her. *I admit I have a nice voice,* she said to her smiling husband and grave son. *Where does it come from, Maggie?*

It comes from . . . your wanting it.

But that doesn't make sense. I couldn't want it until after it was.

I don't know about that.

Whatever made sense or did not, it was from that voice he had learned to play the cello. It was the secret no one else could quite fathom, however much they marveled at how quickly he had learned the technique. To this day his ear could reconstruct that voice as easily as his fingers had ever got music from the box of varnished wood between his knees. He could stand looking at the cat-headed basalt goddess and make believe he heard Maggie's living delight as she spotted Fiona right there in front of them, pretending not to notice. And there the pretenses that went with art ended in the inflexible frustration.

Until one February day he was standing there in a reverie when he heard that voice, unmistakably real, call his name, "Jason, Jason. Here you are."

When he looked around, he saw the crudeness of his mistake. The only other person in sight was a young man his own age whom he didn't recognize. An American-looking boy about his own height. Perhaps not quite so plump. A gringy, grinning loose-jointed fellow who now came tripping down the wide marble steps with just a trace of uncertainty as to whether it would be shaken.

He was a stranger and when he spoke again the voice had no trace of resemblance to Maggie's. "I'm Schuyler Baron. You've got to remember! We met under such *strange* circumstances. Or were you more zonked out than you seemed?"

Jason shook his head. The name was instantly recognized, but if there was one thing he was sure of, it was that he had never seen this person in his life.

"No, you don't recognize me," Baron said. "No doubt I was wearing a wig when you waltzed in out of the night. Oh yes. I was. A sweet wig! It's back in the dear U. S. of A. with so much of my worldly possessions. Don't you remember? You were looking for a girl with an enchanting name."

"It's not the wig. . . . It was your voice that startled me."

"I just can't help it. I am an impersonator. At any given moment, well . . ."

But how did he know the voice he impersonated any more than he had known the other night how to resemble Tamisan, wig or not? There was nothing, now, in the shapes of his face or smile or yellow and uneven teeth that was at all like Tamisan. I wanted them to be him. It's not his impersonations. It's what I wanted, want, to believe, he thought. The sweat and dizziness began with that rational admission.

"Sandler thought I'd run into you here sometime."

"Sandler's dead."

"So I heard," Baron said. "He's a very devious person and I wouldn't believe anything about him I didn't see with my own eyes. I told him about our meeting and he laughed and laughed. I was only pleased that you weren't dreadfully angry. You're not, are you?"

Then he put his arm around Jason's shoulder and brought his face close—not at all aggressively, but like a beggar wheedling, testing the tolerance of someone who might have something to give. Jason smelled his clothes, a dull sourness like the fog that came to his nostrils when he walked alone in the Père Lachaise cemetery.

"Sandler said I'd be here?"

"In Paris sometime. Not today. How could he know either of us would be here on a rainy day if he's dead and gone?"

"You said he might not be."

The arm was withdrawn from his shoulder but the eyes watching his were more confident now. As if Baron had caught sight of a thread that might unravel something good for him. "What's this thing between you and Sandler? Honestly, I think he's dead. Slip of the tongue. Come out for a coffee and I'll tell you all I know. I'm living right across the river. Not far. I'll give you coffee. Come."

Jason shook his head. He was feeling very shaky and unwell now. He wanted only to hold himself intact until Baron left him alone.

The simple refusal was accepted lightly, but now he was to be harried on another tack. "I know you're deep in thought, so come another time. When you like. I'm living with a troupe of mimes on the Rue de Ciseaux." From somewhere inside jacket and raincoat he produced a little tablet and pencil, tore off a page and thrust it into Jason's pocket. "Our address," he said. Then he rolled back on his heel and squinted at the sculpture. "I like Egyptian things best."

Again Jason believed it was Maggie's voice being impersonated. Again he thought it a flaw in himself that he accepted the impersonation, but felt the other knew where the flaw was and had begun to probe. And he wanted not to be afraid of submission to that, either, as if submission might open the way to the reality that eluded him.

Nevertheless, he began giddily to climb the stairs to the main floor. Baron caught his sleeve, not so much to hold him there as to keep his attention.

"Ooops, I'm a fool and a flop, Jason Goss. Did it again. Bad jokes I make and should seal my mouth—at which time I'm better. You know I'm only a clown. But yet I'm a jolly good mime. So are the rest of my gang. We've got acts! Many. And where does it get us? I've been to producers. I've licked some very sandy pisspots. Sandier here than in New York. At any straw I clutch, holding my group together, I hope, until we can sell ourselves. I have laid in wait for your brother. If you could put in a word with him, Jason . . . that's the only reason I've been trailing you. If Vidal Goss says we're no good, we quit. Finish. We break up or learn to be acrobats. But we're best as mimes. If Vidal could use us . . . I know I told you once I was a friend of his. A lie, too, but I'm not all lies. . . ."

"I know you're not." Jason tried to keep on climbing. The

stone steps heaved under his feet like a moving boat. "I'm late. I'm expected at home."

"I'll find you a taxi. Shit, man, I don't know if even Vidal could help us. Forget it. We're already dead and might as well admit it. Good though. If my troupe was only Frogs, we'd be staying at the George V. You and your girl come see us sometime, and if you don't like the act, forget us. No? Well, you're missing something. We do a Leda and the Swan you wouldn't believe. Jackie and Onassis. George and Dwight. Norman and Cassie. Maggie and Jiggs. There's a huge black woman from Detroit who's filed her teeth and wears an orange wig to do the Goddess of Liberty. . . ."

As Jason passed the Winged Victory and came into the scatter of museum visitors in the lobby, he began to trot. His friend kept pace. They went out that way and across the courtyard of the Louvre to the Rue de Rivoli. There Baron whistled and a cab stopped almost immediately. Jason was afraid Baron meant to climb in with him, but the still unrecognized face grinned and disappeared as the cab drove away.

The driver had to help him climb the one flight of stairs to the apartment. To Tamisan he would explain, at first, only that he had had a waking nightmare in which for a couple of minutes he had been convinced that his mother had called to him. He had heard her voice.

No wonder, Tamisan thought when she felt his forehead. He was burning with fever and when she called a doctor it was determined that his temperature had reached 103. The diagnosis was pneumonitis. Not serious enough to require hospitalization, the doctor thought, since Monsieur could expect good care at home.

For five days while Tamisan pampered and steamed his lungs, he kept sorting over his memories of this encounter and the earlier one with Baron—and once again came out with an even balance between the explicable and what could be discounted as excess of imagination or waking dream.

Being sick was no more and no less than taking a drug, in

terms of its effect on the mind. But yet, this was left over—
he had been feeling fine until he heard the voice call to him.
Why had the illness come on at just that time?

Very painstakingly he made up for Tamisan an altered account of what he remembered. He was afraid now to identify
Baron or mention Sandler at all. They were getting along too
well to risk poisoning her thoughts with any further meditations
of that sort.

She found in his raincoat pocket the address Baron had given,
but he identified Baron only as a down-and-out actor who had
asked him to drop by. "I promised to ask Vidal to have a look
at the act sometime. It's a bunch of mimes. I don't want to
see them myself."

A few days later he announced to Tamisan he wanted to fly
to the Mideast and "look around." Her one and only protest
was that he hadn't regained his health. The fever was gone, but
his head cold persisted week after week. "It will do me good
to be in a warmer climate," he said. "It will be better for you
if I'm out of the house for a while. We don't want you catching
anything awful from me just now."

With such frivolous, unnecessary explanations he went away.
A few days after his father had passed through Paris, he came
back with the same light cough and congested nose. His absence
made her more acutely aware of how the cold changed his voice.
"You left your voice in Persia," she said. And it was strange
that he sounded always as if he were speaking from a distance
greater than the eye measured or from behind something.

"There's not much to tell you about my trip anyway," he
said. "I was just another bug-eyed tourist making the rounds."

"You're always something besides that."

"A couple of times in Bagdad, alone in my bed, I got so
restless I sat up—wanting to go to Bagdad! It's no better than
Paris."

Finally, carefully avoiding any emphasis, he said, "It wasn't
just pyramids and desert I saw. I went to Frankfurt, too. I
looked up the hotel where Sandler killed himself."

"What did you find there?" she asked with a strange, thin anger that might have passed for jealousy.

"Nothing, nothing," he said, in haste to placate her. "It was the same as in Egypt and Iran. Nothing. There isn't anything *there*. What I'm looking for is inside me. I didn't even go into the hotel. I only walked back and forth in front of it. What could I have learned by going in and asking questions?"

"Spying!" she burst out. "What'd you want to know about Sandler I haven't told you?"

The explosiveness of her vehemence shocked Jason into silence. He sat there with his hands fumbling blindly in the air and with no voice at all. He had made himself defenseless by admitting his odd secret, by exposing the utter frailty of the whims that guided his search.

She saw this but went on. "Sandler's on your mind. You haven't fucked me since the day you came home sick. And that's when you began to think and blame me. I might have known how it would go."

"I thought with the baby so near . . ." He found enough breath to say that, enough voice to yield to her rage, to give in to whatever she required of him. But not enough confidence to try to share with her the perilous siftings of imagination that had become his beacon. This might have been the occasion for him to give her the full account of his meeting with Baron in the Louvre and—more important—how his own compelling fantasies had swarmed out from the suggestions given him in his sickness. He might not have managed a fully coherent story. Too much was still obscure to him, and he had gone on his Mideast wanderings like a sleepwalker following commands that would be forgotten on waking. Yet the sympathy between them had served before to communicate things forever incomprehensible to others. They both knew they failed each other in this decisive moment.

"I wouldn't be jealous of him for you," Jason breathed.

"I know. I know," she said miserably. "It's just . . . Come lie down with me now and we'll take care of you. I still have so many ways."

His face brightened with the suggestion, but both understood the fraction of falsity in his smile. There was still joy in their caresses, a furnace of warmth in the inventive joining of their bodies. "Aiiiiii–eee-OH!"–a cry to welcome spring when she took the pure white jet of his semen between her humming breasts.

A cry of welcome and mourning, as if she had seen a bright, immortal figure blow them a kiss across the roofs of Paris and then turn away.

Charging him with jealousy of Sandler was her one real infidelity to the bargain they had lived by in their good months together. Later it was the one thing that shamed her, that made her feel sometimes like Lot's wife, who has turned back for one look at the corrupt cities—maybe only to assure herself they have been left far behind.

Once in a quiet moment he had said to her, "My father took the big risks all his life. That's how he found himself." And she would be shamed everlastingly to remember that in such a moment of exquisite risk as only artists can define for themselves she had turned away from Jason and denied him.

And yet she had known the alternative. By provoking their small, profound rupture she had tried to divert him from it. "I wouldn't be jealous of him for you," Jason had said, truly.

Hadn't she known that? And had she not, with the same costly, female cunning, hidden her knowledge from his father's wise guesses?

Jason would be jealous of Sandler's death. Jealous that this enigmatic figure should be once again ahead of him among those ultimate erotic majesties forbidden to the living, veiled by life and its comfortable sensuality.

from Susan Vail's red notebook:

How can you tell a mirror is there until you see an actual face in it, or hear an echo without being sure you have heard a voice? Reality gets terribly real—TERRIBLY, I said—when it is repeated and echoed, and now I know nothing is more puzzling to us than reality seen with the twists and repetitions he makes me see.

How queer it was that for so long we never asked: Was I to have a child for him? Did I want? Did he want? Could we?

Not a word was said about it for months. As far as I can honestly recall, there were no cues given by either of us. I went on with my pills until the supply ran out. I bought some more and still have them all. It made no difference.

The realization that we *hadn't* talked about a matter so important made me mention it. And all the devil answered me was: "Oh. Yes. To be sure. But we *are* having one."

As if I had better admit that Jason and Tamisan are *we*.

Chapter 22

Tamisan's labor pains began one evening in Vidal Goss's apartment on the Île St. Louis. A fine April rain was falling on Paris that night, glazing the chestnut buds, making the dark hedges shine around the nearby cathedral, and giving a pastel softness to the lines of traffic headlights moving on either side of the Seine.

Monica Goss was at work on a clay portrait of Jason. To oblige her, he was sitting stiffly upright, looking as spiritual as she wanted him to be. Tamisan was writing to her mother when she paused to look at herself mirrored among branches by one of the windows that faced toward the Left Bank and said, "Ouch."

"Has it begun?" Jason wanted to know. He had been all the while more attentive than she to the obstetrician's instructions and forecasts of what they were to expect.

Monica wiped her hands clean and said she would get a taxi right away. This was a family pregnancy and she meant to see that it went off right. In her view, Jason and Tamisan had done their part by yielding their bodies to love. That was their specialty—something like that of acrobats somersaulting on a high wire. When they had finished their star turn, someone ought to be on hand with capes to cover their glitter. The mundane consequences ought to be handled by professionals and artisans like herself. In the past winter she had taken them very much in hand, being in their apartment almost as much as here or in her mother's place in Auteuil.

"Not yet, Monica. It was a tiny pain from far away," Tamisan said. She rolled amorously under the globe of her belly, the only part of her that had been significantly reshaped by the months of gestation. "I only said 'ouch' to let you know we were here.

It might be days or hours yet. The waters haven't even broken
. . . maybe you'd better get me a towel to sit on, Monica."

She concentrated again on her letter. She wanted it to be
worthy of the occasion. She wanted to affirm that bearing this
child was the best thing she had ever done.

She had written:

*I'm glad you're not coming until it is all over. Then we can
all be as sentimental about the little one as whoever would like
to be, including Pop. He will not be so scared of me as mother-
with-child and should admit at least I am good for his work.*

*I guess it is part of our make-believe, which goes on and
on, to keep it to ourselves pretty much until then. I even like
to think it will be a genuine bastard, since I liked to think I
was a bastard, which gave certain advantages.*

*We hope you will not think this has been like last year be-
cause we haven't much to show except just another of the bil-
lions of people already cluttering up the place. We know it is
all different.*

*We only belong to ourselves. We only care if people are beau-
tiful or not and that keeps us from getting involved. More and
more of them get to be beautiful and that is the difference. The
main thing is we are not contemptuous or superior of anyone
and can take them or leave them alone.*

*It is not like last year. Jason is not worried about his father
since he has you to keep him really company and instead of
loneliness it can be solitude, which is what we have and surely
deserve. For two people it is the best thing and as a prenatal
influence also surely best. It is strange how many children we
have who are already friends. On the nice days I go to sit in
the parks as far as Montsouris to be with children. I like to
watch them to see which have loneliness and which have solitude. They all have one or the other.*

*Monica's friends her age are some of our friends and best
to go places with, as to Fontainebleau where we had a picnic
by the moat and all threw bread to the carps. If you have to
be with someone besides yourself, children are the best bet.*

*We say we will take the new Jason back to Handy Farm
so he can grow up where he was conceived, but that is all very*

vague and does not have to be so. We are here now and are
all right. Tell Pop it all worked out just as he wanted and he
will see.

Your loving
T

"Finished!" Monica said, sometime after ten. She stood back
from her little clay sculpture and squinted at it very hopefully.
"Tamisan, tell me if I haven't got him finished."

Tamisan stretched and got up to share in this act of adoration. "I can't tell him from the real one."

"You've made me a doll," he said. He was teasing without
wanting to spoil Monica's pride in her work. "No, you've made
me what I always wanted to look like."

"It isn't very modern," Monica said doubtfully. "I could have
done something more like Brancusi but it isn't so much fun.
Why is it more fun to make things real?"

Jason pulled her head against his shoulder and laughed. "My
mother had no patience with what she called 'modern art.' She
made a total exception of Dad's work. Paid no attention at all
to what it looked like or anyone's labels for it. She concentrated
on him. It was no trick at all to fit him to her prejudices.
I think it pleased her when he used to say she was blind."

Tamisan didn't want them to talk about his mother on this
night, so she said "Ouch" again, though she felt nothing at all
unusual.

They were lightly arguing again about whether they would
go home by taxi when Vidal came in. His hat and umbrella
were glittering handsomely with rain. He had come from watching "Jason's friends" run through some of their acts in a borrowed studio in Montparnasse. Tamisan and Jason lingered to
hear his report on Schuyler Baron's troupe of mimes. Monica
made coffee for all of them as they lounged around her father's
chair.

"Oh, they are *wicked,*" Vidal said with a glitter of appreciation in his soft eyes. "There's no doubt about their talent.
There's no doubt that they are funny. They were being quite

hilarious this evening, miming prisoners, paraplegics, the blind . . ." What he had seen had excited him, no doubt of that, and his thoughtful voice communicated the quality of that excitement—at the same time as it expressed his satisfaction at being able to come home from it to the stability of comfort and position and the quiet attention of the younger members of his family. "They replace all sorts of pity with comedy. I think you could say that's their guiding principle. They make the graves fly open."

"Disgusting," Monica said.

Her father smiled tolerantly at her. "At any rate, I came away from them feeling older than when I went. No, it isn't all disgusting, Monica. If a moral judgment has to be made, I think it could be said in their favor that they've found something alive in those human areas that society has wanted to discard as dead rubbish."

"Sounds like maggots," his daughter insisted.

"You mustn't judge until you've seen, Monica. They'd make you laugh too."

"They couldn't if I stayed away from them!"

"Stay far away from evil!" he agreed, to please her. "Surely that's a good idea, but I'm too old or steeped in sin to be affected by it. The only part of the evening that left me feeling a bit nasty—and puzzled—is a part in which our friend Baron did an impersonation of Zach Sandler involving this huge woman black as coal—glittering black! Knowing that I knew Sandler. Trying to get at me, give me some message? I don't know. I feel crawly still. I can't make it out."

"A message from Sandler?" Jason mused.

"Of course not," Vidal said. "I'm making it sound melodramatic. Baron and one or two of the others supply voices and commentary. They are diabolically clever. I admit that. I merely resent their directing anything personally at me." He waved his hand to dismiss the phantoms from his mind and lowered his mouth to the steaming coffee.

Since Tamisan felt no more labor pangs, she and Jason were going to walk home. Monica walked part way with them. The three of them cut through the park behind Notre Dame. The cathedral buttresses and walls rose beside them like the immensity of a great ship tied at anchor, its towers misted with the sweetness of the night, its gargoyles lost to view in the dark. On the Left Bank, in front of the Librairie Mistral, they said good night to Monica and sent her back.

"Good night, angel," Jason said, kissing her on the forehead.

"Good night, good night, good night," they all echoed as she skipped back the way she had come. The rain had lightened since earlier in the evening and they waited to watch her out of sight, her head and shoulders moving above the rail of the bridge as she crossed to the safe shore, her blue rain hat winking like a tiny blue beacon as she moved from the glow of one street light to the next.

Then they walked in silence as far as St. Michel and turned toward Odéon before Tamisan said, "You're thinking about Sandler."

"How did he put himself in our minds tonight of all nights? I should have gone with Vidal to see them."

"To see Sandler with the black woman?"

"To see if Sandler was there. Hear his voice." Then he laughed shakily and said, "Make me stop this. I'll stop. You've got to rest and take care of yourself."

"I have to take care of all of us," she said with a catch of anxiety in her voice. "We've been good all this while. We've outrun the bad dreams."

"Yes, yes. It's nothing. I know that. I think I'm sure." But as he put his arm around her thick waist she felt it was to comfort himself and not her.

She did not think she had slept long when she woke to find herself alone in bed. There was a light on in the kitchen of their apartment where he sometimes wrote or read at night. But he was not there either.

He had been, she noted. On the dark table top he had left pencils and paper. The sheet on top might have been a note for her, of the sort he sometimes left when he went out by himself, but when she bent to it she read:

The child does not belong to life. Could not be. The conception was from death.

"No," she said, but there was no one to hear her. She began to dress. She could feel no movement, no quickening inside her, but it had been explained to her clearly that this was normal just before delivery. As so many things had been explained to her. . . . Always everything was clear except what absolutely had to be known, and Jason had gone roaming the night to find that out.

Before she went out herself, she read part of another sheet he had left on the table:

The black woman was Egyptian. The cat head in the Louvre. I am inside her, not separate, so I can see her relation to other things. She is the dark in which I wake when I know. The horse has come to take me to Paris. This is no dream but the beginning of knowledge. If it were a dream Tamisan would not have been sleeping beside me when I heard the hoofs in the street. The cat could not have been already prowling awake beside the bed. The cat heard too. I have already been downstairs once and the horse seemed angry that I am already late. Horse without tail or mane. Blue eyes like Tamisan's. Hard to hold onto when he gallops and the little boy would have grabbed the mane if there had been one. Shaved away. Only skin, smooth as oil, and blood between his legs. Must ride all the way to Paris to bargain with Sandler for the child. If I am willing to die he will surely live.

For a wild moment what she read made her glad. Then, as if someone had drenched her with ice water, she caught her breath and said, "No!" again. She could not let him go. This was the night when she had to keep her promise to take care of him. She had broken faith with him when they last spoke of Sandler. Not again. If he was sniffing through the dark streets of Paris on the trail of death, she had to catch up and go with him.

She was terrified, but if she trusted her terror it seemed to speak to her, telling her step by step and street by street where she had to go. Terror itself could have led her to the door she must find. Besides that she had the address that weeks before she had found in Jason's raincoat pocket.

There was no concierge and she came in from the crooked little street across a dim courtyard paved with stone. She knocked at a door that showed no chink of light at the sill. After her third or fourth knocking there was a faint rustling of response within—something that might have been voices or maybe only the movement of someone approaching the door from the other side. Then the door was opened confidently, as if she had been expected. Someone in a robe with a candle in hand confronted her.

"I came looking for Jason Goss," she said. "I'm his wife and I need to find him right away."

"Why should you look for him here?"

"He came here to meet someone."

"At this time of night? Fancy that! Whom did he expect to meet in such a place?"

She thought she said, "Death," and she thought when she said it the candle seemed almost to go out as if it had been cupped under a glass that shut off the air. Then its light grew again and she said, "Sandler. Zach Sandler. That's what he would have told you if he came here, I mean."

The dim face that could have been either male or female said, "Are you supposed to meet Sandler too? Because if you are . . ."

"No," Tamisan said, and the candle seemed now much brighter than any real candle ought to be. So she said, "Yes," and the light dimmed to a level her anxiety could stand.

The candle bearer stepped back with a theatrical swish and beckoned her in. "I'm Schuyler Baron, Mrs. Goss. And in case you don't know, I must inform you that the man you are seeking in my dingy abode is dead. Departed. Fled from the mortal scene, to wit."

"He's not!" Tamisan said fiercely, thinking he meant Jason. "Oh no, you don't!"

"I tell the tale that I heard told," her guide said, not turning his head as he led her down a chilly corridor. "Dead by his own hand and choice, I believe. But I never get these things straight. To the right, please."

They passed into a room where another candle was burning on a heavy table. "Why seek ye the dead among the living? Most pregnant question, I observe," Baron said jovially. "For the last two hours I've been at my philosophical end trying to make it out. Am I in the yellow pages that everyone must bring their quandaries to my door tonight?"

"You mean he's here?" Tamisan asked. "Is he here?"

"Who?"

"Jason."

"But you told me you were here to meet Sandler. No wonder I'm confused. Confusing to you. For which my humblest apologies. No, Jason isn't dead, if that's who or whom it seemed in my natural confusion I meant or you meant or we both meant. No, no! The lad is livelier, I might say, than I would have anticipated. Lively! Oh, you have a *lively* husband, Mrs. Goss."

In the face of this indecent mockery Tamisan managed to say evenly, "Where've you got him? And I'll kill you, too, if . . ."

"We haven't *got* him, poor lad. He's quite safe here. Certainly came of his own free will among consenting adults, as it were, and all that. Do we look like people who would harm anyone?" Through a masonry arch opening off one side of the cold room there was an even dimmer room where nearly a dozen figures nodded on benches or sat on the floor in corners, not exactly deathlike but somnolent, entranced, caught as if in some spell or dream that she might enter as peacefully as they. Baron swept his arm at them to indicate the peaceable kingdom over which he presided. "Poor angels, every one. We all smoked when we got back here tonight. Yes, I smoked with them and

though I give no sign—do I? don't I?—I'm also higher than a
kite. And am your servant, dear lady. Will you smoke? Can
I offer you wine? Opium of noble Persian origin? Wine then."
The bottle that he offered was open on the table, but there were
no glasses in sight.

Baron held the bottle out to Tamisan and, when she did not
lift a hand to accept it, he thrust it up to her mouth. She drank,
feeling it ice cold in her mouth, searing as it went into her
stomach. She gulped again from the bottle in his hand in a gesture of supplication and submission.

Then he said benignly, "Your Jason is here. Be not or naught
afraid, my child, as wonders never cease. We haven't drugged
him. He only partook the communion, like you. I was concerned
about his cough when he burst in and gave him something for
his throat. He is tranquil now. Upstairs, as you will see." Now,
for the first time, Baron seemed to turn his attention fully on
her as the warmth of the wine spread out through her veins.
"You shouldn't be out in the weather, either, love. Looking for
Sandler? You must be Tamisan. If so . . . You of all people
should know that Sandler is dead. Dead when you knew him
. . . best."

"That's not true. I want to see Jason," she said.

Baron drank from the bottle and wiped his mouth with the
back of his hand in a motion that seemed deliberately coarse,
as though he were rubbing from his lips something foul and
viscous.

"When Sandler used to fuck me, *I* knew," Baron said. "Quite
a special thrill to lie in the embrace of death. *Ah, oui! Oo-
la! N'est-ce pas?*"

"Let me go up to Jason!"

She saw another doorway to the room and, thinking it led
to stairs, started for it. Baron skipped to block her way. He
was not going to keep her away from the stairs by force, probably, but merely to force her will to follow his direction. "In
a moment," he promised gleefully. "You'll find your lively lad.
You certainly will. In all his glory. But we've just met, darling.
And we have so much in common, from our days with Sandler.
Now more than ever. We certainly have something in common,

though we're most uncommon persons, aren't we, Ta-mee-san?"

"Yes," she said humbly. "We do. Now, please . . ."

"Do you *know* all we have in common?" She could see the points of the candle flames reflected in his eyes as his face came close to hers, bright sulphurous points sharp as spearheads.

"Sandler *was* dead. I knew that every time," she said, as if reciting some litany learned long ago. "I knew it as well as you. Sure."

"What else?" Their breath seemed to sizzle together, like the sound of grease in a wet skillet.

"You've had Jason," she said in a voice of total despair.

Baron shook his head. He started to speak, but the uncanny excitement he had generated seemed to choke him. "Not yet. Not yet." His eyes, his position that blocked her way to the stairs, commanded, *Guess again.*

"You said you'd . . . given him something for his throat," she said.

The fine, deadly shape of the candle flames in his eyes exploded into showers of sparks as his head jerked with gurgling laughter. "You learned from Sandler. I can see! I can see that. You learned! The sewer runs right through your brain." He put his long finger on the middle of her forehead. The touch was delicate, priestly, cold. "I only meant I had given him wine. Ha! He drank from the bottle you drank from. But you thought . . . I'd like to hear more of what you thought. But come up! Come up the stairs. We'll see if your lively lad is ready to receive us both!"

They climbed stone stairs to a room identical with that one below, but even emptier of furniture. On a smaller table another candle burned. There were no chairs. Near one scaling, empty wall was the sort of screen used as a prop by mimes who use nothing else. A screen to disappear behind during the interludes of their acts, disappearances and reappearances signaling a shift of impersonated identities.

If Jason was in this room to which they came, he was no-

where except behind that screen. But his clothing, with underwear dropped on top of the pile, lay haphazard on the floor.
When Tamisan saw the discarded clothing, a hiss of anger and
compassion passed her gritted teeth.

"He was sick and you did this." She lunged toward the screen
but Baron caught her arm. It astonished her to find him stronger
than she, to find herself helpless in the clutch of his hand.

"We'll spoil it all if we're hasty," he said, holding her by force
until she stood still in submission. "Sandler taught us we must
be veh-uh-urry, veh-uh-urry slow and deliberate to get the full
flavor and the ecstasy. Didn't he?"

"Yes," she said. "Damn you, yes."

He held her in silence that dripped with the cold moisture of
the walls of the ancient house. Then he said, "He may be gone.
If he'd heard your voice he would have come out to you.
Wouldn't he?"

She saw there was no door to the room except the one by
which they had entered. "He's there," she said, bowing her head
toward the blankness of the screen.

Baron nodded agreement. "He's back there communing with
Sandler. Communing! Isn't he?"

"Yes," she whispered obediently. "Let me go to him. Please."

Baron nodded but still held her for a moment until she understood his intent fully. "Go," he said. "But go fitly." He held
his right hand before her face, rotating it slowly from the wrist,
contorting it, tightening the tendons until knuckles rose sharply
and it looked like a claw or the hand of a skeleton. "Go fitly,"
he repeated and began to loosen and remove her clothes.

When, after his elegant and deliberate hand had dropped the
last warm wisp of nylon to the littered floor, she heard the
rustling of steps on the stairway she knew that the sleepers below had been roused to witness the humiliations to come.

The witnesses were mimes, actors, and they were far gone
in the intoxication of whatever drug they had smoked tonight

441

and for a long series of nights that no one would ever suppose it worth while to count. They were not, after all, a pack of slavering animals gathered for the kill, or robots, or zombies, or vampires or any of the other bogeys of the popular imagination.

They were half a dozen young men Baron's age or a little older or a little younger, and five girls and a giant black woman who came in next to last wearing an orange robe and showing the points of her filed teeth in a smile that was neither bored nor fanatic, but merely loosened to the whim of the drug in her blood. They were not a pack of perversion-hungry tourists, either, lured from the corners of the bourgeois world to see last gimmick of corruption enacted live. As for sex and its varieties, they had had as much of that, seen and felt, as they had had of other intoxicants.

They were—however sodden or hallucinated—some species of artist, committed to mirroring whatever came into their souls from nature. And when Tamisan had lifted Jason from his curled repose on the floor and led him out from behind the screen, she knew she could win with them as jury.

She knew from their attitude of waiting that the bedrock of humiliation or illness or abandonment to which she had come with Jason might sit beneath their naked feet like a stepping-stone.

I went to him fitly, she thought. Not afraid.

It seemed a miracle to her that even Baron's mockery could be transformed to have another meaning. The choice was still and always hers. Holding Jason's hand as they stepped into view, she felt no impulse to cover his nakedness or her own, and she took the first free, full breath she had had since she came in from the street.

She heard a turbulence she believed was her own expanding breath until she understood it came from those who had crowded into the room to witness the spectacle.

"Now!" Baron said. He was standing among the others crowded into the room. His voice was a command for action or movement, but not a prescription. A whisper of shuffling feet followed his single syllable.

Then he called Jason's name. It was like the signal of a hypnotist, the crack of a whip, the blast of a whistle, commanding the obedience of the subject's obliterated or smothered will. Tamisan felt Jason's hand pulse and twist in hers, but there was no other motion of his body. They were merely standing there, submitting to the waiting eyes.

"He has a prick like the morning star," Baron sang. "She has a belly like the great globe itself."

"Yeh!" The ejaculation seemed to come from the grotesque mouth of the black woman. It did not matter where it came from. It was the voice of desire that might be either lust or worship.

"I've got to fuck them both," Baron wailed.

He was shedding his grotesque robe when the others of his gang mustered in the room began, one by one, to sink to their knees and shuffle forward.

What happened then was pure ceremony. Folly. Art. Recognition. Even a glimpse of truth that could not have been purchased more cheaply.

If Tamisan and Jason had come from behind the screen shamed of the spectacle they made in their nakedness, at having been duped into this shabby and sick mummery or at having duped themselves, the response would have been in keeping.

They had come instead in shy and bewildered humility. The boy unaccustomed to his nakedness, the girl disfigured by her pregnancy. He defiant for her sake. She for his. They offered themselves as criminal and outcast, denying nothing. Pretending nothing. Without pride except that of standing erect and side by side. A momentary offer of themselves to the derision of gods who might be watching from outside this shabby room.

And as the others shuffled on their knees toward them, the muttering still had no distinctive tone. There was a luscious, slavering flicker of tongues. A deliberate and hungry advance while Baron, also fully naked now, deliberately held back to watch.

Heads rose out of the shuffling, singular mass of the group.

443

Faces became defined around the eyes that held on the figure of the pregnant girl. The movement that had been reptilian, or animal at least, changed to hesitation in full awe of her power.

"Praise the unborn one. Praise the neverborn!"

The voice was over them, echoing like silver from the shabby walls of the room. It made no difference who had uttered it or how briefly it sounded. It was their common voice. A decision. Command and reprieve.

"They mine, you devils!" This was clearly the voice of the huge black woman. She reared up brutally to her full height and lunged to embrace Jason and Tamisan against a bosom bigger than both of them.

What they heard while her giantess breath enveloped their faces was a wondering chuckle and her voice saying, "Now, y'all get outa this wicked place. Fun's all over and glory be!"

The air in the dark streets was sharp as ammonia in their nostrils as Jason and Tamisan walked toward home. They had no idea of the time. The true morning star was over them and its shining seemed to emanate from the spaceless darkness where they had been lost. It was a tiny, mellow planet to the eye as it would be to remembrance later, yet intensely distinct.

They were coming back chastened and silent, and yet in their sobriety there was some kernel of intoxication to console them for the weirdness through which they had passed. They were coming back from another ceremony that could never be made intelligible and had best not even be remembered though it had changed them and they would never pass out of its spell. It had been grotesque. It had also been solemn. It was like a ceremony of marriage to all that was most rare, eccentric and impossible in their life with each other. Worship and sacrilege blended into a single spectacle. Exaltation and shame fused in a single rite.

They had stumbled—or been lured—into trespassing on something forbidden to be seen. It was beyond belief that they had been spared at all, but at least the penalty was that they could never tell even each other what they had known at the summit of revelation.

They were very tired and walked slowly, as if the fatigue of their steps expressed how hard it was to come back from the terrors of revelation into the ordinary world. They had made their way to within two blocks of their apartment when Jason turned his face to say, "I'm sorry, I . . ."

"No!" Tamisan said fiercely. "I don't want to ever talk about it. It happened. It was true."

"All right," he said. "Just hear this, though." When she looked at him, she thought his face looked like a blind man's. She thought it had the color of starlight. "Now I'm certain that I can know all I have to know."

His declaration of faith meant everything and nothing to her. Then and later it struck her as the key to the riddles he would leave her with—and as the riddle itself.

She was not going to question him further on it tonight. Both fell gratefully asleep as soon as they got into their bed. Through the night neither riddles nor phantoms disturbed them. They slept through the morning. In the afternoon she was wakened by the resumption of her labor pains. By four o'clock she was admitted to the hospital. In that excitement the night before was as good as forgotten and all seemed to be well.

from Susan Vail's red notebook:

The infant they meant to call Jason Vail was not born alive. By the time Goss and I had heard this dreadful news and flown to Paris, Jason was gone too. We expected him to meet us at the airport, but Vidal and Monica were there instead to tell us that Jason had vanished. Vanished into thin air, as it seemed in that startling moment when we heard of it—and as it still seems, though we now tell each other he is alive somewhere and, in his own way, well. He must have got out of Paris very shortly after his phone call to us. A call that I remember as strangely calm, almost joyful, as if glad tidings were all he *could* report.

I have never seen Vidal more shaken than when he described Jason's disappearance to his father. Clearly it seemed a tragedy

to him, all of a piece with the stillbirth of the baby. And I think
he may have expected it to finish off his father there and then,
dropping him right on the terminal floor.

But Goss only took off his glasses, holding them gingerly
at arm's length and studying them to see if they had been
smudged or misted by our journey. "Well," he said. "Well, yes.
Well. Jason's lit out, has he? We'll have to wait and see where
he turns up." From the steady rumble of his tone I knew he
did not mean to join the rest of us in frantic speculation about
Jason's mental condition or health, and he did not mean to
grieve with the rest of us about the dead child.

We found that Jason had not called us for two days after the
delivery. Vidal had to force it then, saying that if Jason was not
up to calling he would. It was too cruel to Goss and me to leave
us uninformed.

I took that call at 2 A.M. Goss was asleep. I didn't wake him
until I supposed I had digested the facts and felt ready to share
them. I remember thinking how gallant it was of Jason to keep
insisting that Tamisan was "perfectly fine, perfectly all right"
though the baby's heart had probably stopped before she went
to the hospital. The doctors insisted, he said, that there was not
the slightest worry in the world as far as the mother was concerned. So I wanted to know why she had not called or was not
on the phone with him.

"I believe she thought Dad would blame her for not keeping
her promise to take care of us. But she did! You've got to make
him see that. She's cried a lot. I've cried too, but that's over."
I believed him. I had to. There was no trace of sorrow in his voice
as he spoke—or rather, no *more* sorrow than all of us had heard
sometimes from him in the midst of casual or jolly circumstances.

"Susan, the baby was fine too. A perfectly developed boy,
according to Dr. Vidaux. Perfect. We've got to be thankful."
I couldn't answer that. The word "perfect" shut me up. In the
circumstances the irony of it was too heavy. Jason had to resume
the dialogue by asking, almost with a consoling chuckle, "Do I
sound too much like Monica, Susan? Monica says the boy has

entered eternity without being dirtied by life. Monica has been wonderful. It's a comfort just seeing her try to comfort us. She's with Tamisan now, so Tamisan will be fine. We're taking it better than you might expect. So you and Dad don't need to come at all unless you'd feel better. There's nothing to come for, is there?"

"Nothing to go for," his father said when I had wakened him and tearily repeated what I'd learned. "We've trusted them to go all the way themselves. We better not quit now when trust is what they need most from us." I'm convinced he would not have made the flight to Paris if I had not insisted.

Vidal still blames himself for not being warned by Jason's outward calm. In hindsight he wishes even that he had had Jason confined in the mental ward of the hospital to prevent his going away. "He should have been kept until Father could have talked to him at least. I don't say that psychiatry could have reached him. We've been through that argument before. Yes, Jason's a law unto himself. The thing is—Father knows that law. It was Father who kept him going on borrowed time after Maggie died. Who always gave enough gravitational pull to keep him from flying off to the moon. Jason was into strange things. Stranger than we'll ever know. I told him—more than once and in different ways—that he was playing with fire. Asking too much of himself. Once he answered in perfect seriousness, 'Yes, I'm supposed to. My father held fire in his hand.' Only Father could stay even with him when he began to take such ideas literally."

Vidal simply believes that Jason is dead. He has no evidence of that. His first-rate mind merely brought him to that idea and he takes it literally.

God knows how or when we'll ever be sure, one way or the other. Still, as the hurts fade, I find myself less and less anxious to be sure. It seems Jason has taken pains—wherever he's gone—to keep us from being sure. This matter of his disappearance seems more and more a matter of deliberate artifice on his part. An exact balance between threat and promise, between dismay and relief. A riddle deliberately posed for the rest of us.

I sometimes even come to the ironic fancy that Jason took a

hint from his stillborn son. I remember his insistence that the little one was "perfect."

In this illusion he's given us of being alive and dead at the same time, that's what Jason has made himself—perfect.

Of course, nothing could be harder than that to live up to.

Certainly Jason left behind him no signs of desperation. He told Dr. Vidaux quite matter-of-factly that the child had not been intended for life. If the second Jason was only alive he could only die. The doctor took this to be a paraphrase of "some verse or sermon the lad had saved for a time of extreme trial." As, of course, it is. When the doctor learned that Tamisan had been "deserted"—she didn't take it quite that way, but the term was bound to come up—he wished, like Vidal, that he had not dismissed the words as "merely poetic" but had taken them as a symptom of another calamity to come.

Yet Vidaux also mentioned the "inner glow" that emanated from Jason after the ordeal of waiting had confirmed what the doctors feared soon after Tamisan went into the hospital. "One sees it in the very devout," Vidaux said. I extracted from him the opinion that the child might have been dead in the womb for as much as three days before delivery.

Then—in our first days in Paris—I was very busy in my search for any certainties that could be gathered up from the smash. Goss says it's nonsense to suppose people can't live with uncertainty. "The planet would be uninhabited if that was so." Yeah. But someone had to paste together at least an illusion of certainty for Tamisan. I knew that when I told her Vidaux's opinion about the time of the baby's death.

I saw her let go some awful tension. She closed her eyes awhile, pretty soon tried to grin cockily, didn't quite make it. The tears started to come pretty fast and she said, "At least we didn't kill him with that stupid scene the night before."

"He wasn't killed," I said. "Nobody knows why he died."

"Jason knew. Maybe I did too and wouldn't admit it. Mama, you better make the sign of the cross and get out of this room."

"Hush, I wouldn't do that."

"Never take a warning . . . Then you're asking for it. But we tried, when it was too late. That's why we went out at all. To try to make a bargain to get him back."

"That's in your imagination," I said.

She looked like a witch when she grinned at me then. The canine tooth on the left side of her mouth somehow looked twice as long as it really is. "Yup. It's in my imagination. That's where it is, all right. That's where it always was. There never was a real live kid in me. So what's all the fuss about?"

Only, the tears on her face were real enough, and that's what you make a fuss about.

"And they're what you make everything else out of," Goss said when I reported the scene to him. "Yah-uss. Start with a few tears and stir them together right and you can make it all come true over and over again. Yah-uss. That can be done."

"But not your tears," I said.

"I don't have any," he said. "I don't seem to need any of my own. Not now. Not any more."

There are enough without his. Never enough imagination to see what can be made of them.

Goss will not admit anything has been done wrong at all. He approaches Tamisan as he would a painting, where the "mistakes" are at least as interesting as an intentional success could be. And it has been he and Monica who helped Tamisan most. The veins of trust and distrust that always ran side by side in her nature have been utterly exposed by what she has been through. "She didn't hold anything back from Jason," Goss says. "She didn't save anything out for herself." It is his fullest tribute.

But it is also the description of a condition that makes her as dependent as a newborn child. Someone with no orientation to life. At first she seemed to be "looking back" at us, as we might imagine Jason looking back from wherever he's gone. There were days when one had to feel she was with him and not with her own body. To come back, she had to rest her trust with the aging man and the child until some trust in herself as a woman could be built again.

In their different ways both Goss and Monica support her faith in unknown levels and modes of reality where she and Jason and the child are not separated—off in that "Persia" that Jason went looking for unsuccessfully before the child died. The old man and the little girl have kept perfect pace with such fancies. As for me, it doesn't matter much whether I am persuaded or not. At least I listen. "Mama," she said. "It's just not true that all our meditations ended up in zero. It's certainly not true that Jason meant to die. He wants to know death. What the Egyptians knew and maybe some others who are still around. He'll be with them. That's what he meant when he told you we were fine. Oh, we were. It *was* a perfect baby. I knew him even if I never saw him."

She clings stubbornly to what Jason left in place of a farewell note. Two sheets he must have written before he locked the apartment and walked out with one suitcase and a plane ticket for Athens. (That much I know about the circumstances of his departure; that much learned before I admitted that playing detective would be downright impudent in this matter.)

She produced them one warm May afternoon when we met Goss at a café on the square at St. Sulpice, a place that he had cared very much for since the twenties.

"Here's the bible," she said, smoothing the pages out on the table in front of Goss. She watched his face with absolutely hypnotic concentration while he read it. As far as I could tell, his face showed nothing. Then I read it.

In his elegant, well-shaped handwriting Jason had put down this much:

The Perfect Life—a letter to be buried with my son.

You lived mine and I lived yours. Between us we had it all.

We were immortal until you died. Immortal is not forever and death is a door that leads two ways. Passing one way through it is to intersect the life in time. Going the other way completes life outside of time. I always doubted that before. Between us you and I got rid of doubt.

You were immortal while you lived in the womb. A little golden bee in the best hive. You only came out for the death in

*time. Being immortal, you turned back to the delight of the
other death, which creatures know best in the womb. The delight
of never emerging, never leaving the honey of the beginning.*

*It was my mistake to look in time for my mother or to go into
the streets to look for Sandler. Now that mistake is behind me.
But . . . suppose a person who might, all his life, make such
mistakes. He mistakes people for gods and tells himself they are
the lords of life and death. He mistakes what his senses and his
hungers tell him for what he already perfectly knows and always
knew. Then suppose that everything in his life turns out as if the
people he loved and feared were the masks of various gods.*

*That has happened in my life and I will not be fooled any
longer. The masks will teach me and not deceive.*

*But when I am fully persuaded I can persuade no one. The
bad cold took my voice away, little by little, and what I know
now couldn't be heard by anyone.*

When I had finished reading, I looked up to see Goss smiling
at me and Tamisan was smiling because he was. The shadows of
leaves were trembling on the marble top of the table and on the
daisy-colored wine in the glass he was lifting steadily to his
mouth.

Their smiles made me feel like an idiot who has been caught
pretending to understand a language completely foreign to her.

"Well, it's very obscure," I said defensively. "It's beautiful.
It's like Jason. It's his voice. But you have to admit it's obscure."

Goss nodded patiently. "I think we can understand it if we
want to."

"Yes," Tamisan said—not quite as confident as he sounded.

"I like the way he ended it," I said. "I like that."

"Why?" he asked—like my first-grade teacher, more or less
prompting me.

"It means he might come back sometime," I blurted. "When
he's done what he has to do."

"But not to me," Tamisan said. She was very near tears again,
though she kept smiling.

"Your mother's right," Goss said. "On that point, at least, it's very obscure, Tamisan. There's some things we'll never know until they happen." He drained his wineglass and set it down on the marble with a little silvery clink.

In the midst of the uncertainties we have to interpret as best we can, it was Fiona—naturally Fiona—who was chosen to take some of the eeriness out of a situation that will never be reducible to the terms of normal curiosity. Near the end of June she heard from Jason. From Tokyo. He needed her to transfer some money for him to his account there. He wondered if, through Senator Burke or some other connection, she might help him get into China "before cold weather came."

That was all. No mention of the past, no detail of his plans for the future, though his mention of the cold weather suggested blithely that he meant to go walking "in China."

Goss was outraged at my relief in knowing Jason was, at least, alive. "You women think if a man needs money he has no other serious problems."

I didn't reply to such nonsense. It's merely that I'd rather know Jason was wandering around the bends of the Great Wall, barefoot and wearing saffron robes, than ending as a bloody spot on the pavement.

It was Fiona who suggested—then arranged—that we bring Tamisan here to the farm in Pennsylvania when we three came back from Paris. We'll spend the last weeks of summer here before we go back to North Atlantic.

Fiona was here four days with us. In her clear, careful manner she painted a small portrait of Tamisan in the orchard. "To put with the other Goss women," she said. I suppose, also, that she intended it as some sort of replacement for the painting of Maggie in the orchard that Goss destroyed a year ago. Of course Tamisan does not resemble Maggie in her youth, but somehow Fiona's little picture conveyed a sisterly kinship, all the more impressive, I thought, because Fiona does not intentionally distort anything she paints. She finds and shows the elemental secrets in common daylight.

The painting was her way of communicating an elemental

confidence to Tamisan. They still find it very difficult to talk to each other, but if Tamisan has confided her wishes for the future to anyone, it must be to Fiona. I can't guess which way she'll go, though by this time I'm worrying again.

The dangerous pride in her has not been destroyed by the tragedy. Perhaps it will have been strengthened by the months she carried the child. She's felt what it means to be a complete woman. But what else, now, has she got to count on? There is so much time, so much empty freedom ahead of her. Deserts of it. She seems strong, confident. Like a hard statue that could shatter if it took one step.

I think there's no question of her ever living with Jason again. But, as for the rest of us, it seems to be a question of living *up* to him.

Chapter 23

Time would never come back and the seasons would always return. His painting perhaps had nothing to do with either seasons or time. The paintings came out of time and seasons. No one except Jason—his son, his equal—could quite comprehend how much he depended on nature and events to make him paint. He had to have the tit of Mother Nature right in his mouth oozing milk or the work went flat. But the paintings that came *from* time and seasons and the excitement of circumstance *went* somewhere else. He couldn't say just where.

The big canvas he was working on now was an architecture of yellows. If he had time to waste he might have made a catalogue of where each patch of cadmium, lemon or tinted ocher came from. For instance, there was a long, wide pebbly stroke of pigment the exact hue of the wine he had been drinking that day in the square by St. Sulpice when he read the pages Jason had written. It bordered the riper yellow of the fields ready for harvest within view of the barn where he was working. If there was time for it, he could have gone from corner to corner of the painting, verbalizing the origins of the colors and shapes. But he had time only to do things. Make what had to be made and send it along to wherever art went.

"I think it means something that as soon as we came back you started a bigger picture than anything yet," Susan said.

"It means I'll never get it out of this barn without knocking the walls down," he said, and went on laying up his yellows like a workman putting stucco on the wall of an imaginary palace. There was nothing that Susan couldn't see that she needed explained. So he bantered absently, "This one I'll sell to the government to camouflage Rhode Island in event of enemy attack."

The damn thing was big. And, sure enough, that must mean

something. So did the pile of yellow pigment he was thinning with white and tinting with umber.

It meant that painting was the continuity he required to live and the force to pass on his vitality through the women who had attended his life. That among other things. It didn't have to be said again to one of them as quick as Susan.

Each of these mornings while he was at Handy Farm with Susan and Tamisan he came to the loft of the barn where he had begun to work the first summer he and Maggie brought Jason here. From season to season in the time of their best happiness alterations had been made—a skylight added, shelving, table space and cupboards built in. Much of that original furniture remained for his convenience now, just as the other buildings of the farm and the enduring contours of the land remained.

It was a place that made him work. The emptiness of its years of abandonment made him, as if automatically, set about to fill it. The loft was big so he tried to fill it with his big painting. There were other paintings started besides this dominant one—more canvases from his series of women who descended from the giantesses of the summer before. They sat around him as he labored—half idols, half caricatures. They satisfied him, they tormented him with their imperfections. But, at least, only damn fool critics would say of them that they were good or bad. They were tokens and fragments of reality, which a sensible man does not call good or bad as long as he is working on it or in it.

The incompleted images of women, like the component colors from which they were made by his hand, had come to him from things around him. You could say—if you wanted to—they had all taken shape out of his various frenzies. It was just as true to say they came from the shapes of clouds over the river valley. The acts of creation had not begun with him. Still, he was necessary to their completion. Knowing that was all the happiness he would ever have and all he needed.

His labors of the morning justified the idleness of the afternoons he shared with Susan and the girl. On one afternoon, like others of those weeks, he was on the river with the two of them.

They had taken the canoe from the boathouse. Susan and Tamisan paddled while he sat between them on the varnished boards of the craft, admiring the sparkle of the varnish, the evanescent ripples and the great sun that made them sparkle.

Overhead and on both shores a multiplying variety of lights and colors enticed him on. An hour downstream, thunderheads loomed from the west, battlements of cloud endlessly changing as they rose and finally covered the sun. Then single rays, distinct as the beams of searchlights, played from behind the gilded edges of cloud through the moist air of the valley.

The women rowed him under a highway bridge, edged toward a cutbank shore where an alfalfa field sloped imperceptibly down and a farmer's tractor pulled a baler that seemed strange as a vehicle designed for moon landings. The river ran shallow and they were between islands where driftwood and brush made miniature jungles.

"Rain!" Tamisan called from the bow.

They all felt a few scattered drops, though the sky could not have been more brilliantly adorned with irregular lights and colors.

"Shall we head back?" Susan wanted to be told.

"For these sprinkles?" Goss scoffed.

"There'll be more," she said, tranquilly content to go on as long and as far as he wished. "What could it matter if we get soaked?"

"I want it! I want it!" Tamisan chortled in an ecstasy of childish expectation. "Rain, rain, don't go away!"

The rain paid no attention to her. If she wanted the adventure of a drenching, she would not get it by twisting schoolgirl incantations. The clouds swelled and maneuvered like an emperor's cavalry on parade with banners and bright uniforms, turned out for show and not for action.

It was to be an adventure only for their eyes, the senses responsive to the balm and color of unthreatening nature. What might have turned into a storm with really dangerous lightning only softened, at last, into a uniform gray overhead, soft as the lining of a purse. If there was to be tension and danger it would not come from nature.

457

No contest. What they saw as they rowed down and back reminded them as much of art as of other demanding realities. Goss found himself talking to mother and daughter about the painters of American rivers. The Hudson Valley school. Bingham and the Mississippi. And then about Thomas Eakins, who had been a friend of his father's. About the haunting realism of the paintings Eakins had made of men sculling on another river not far from this one. A river that flowed where this one went.

"I know those. I know the pictures you're talking about," Tamisan called over her shoulder, her young voice chanting the excitement that comes from being on an actual river that *might be* a painted one. "There's an orange steel bridge in the background. The men have wrinkled skin on their elbows. . . ."

None of them would remember anything more historic or flamboyant about this day's excursion than this low-keyed sharing of recognitions.

The melting, softening, lowering face of the cloud was just overhead when they eventually got back to the boathouse. Its freshness perfumed the smell of the river and mixed it with the smell of trees and dry fields as the wind came up ahead of the advancing rain.

They dragged the canoe onto one of the interior docks and then sat down to watch the rain approach from the other shore. It came on with mild and tentative overtures, first dimpling the brown river with delicate craters that vanished instantly in the current. Then with a swish of authority it swirled gray veils over the trees on the bank across from them. Out of its whispering on foliage and water emerged the kettledrum sound of big drops thumping on the shingled roof and the arrhythmic splatter of runoff as the gutters filled beyond their capacity.

"I want it!" Tamisan called out in a changed voice, laughing in melancholy now at the fate that made her a woman instead of a flowered field prostrate under the weight of the rain. "That's all I ever wanted. May I have it, Mama?" she asked, wrinkling her nose.

"I'll give you jelly beans instead," Susan said. But she saw her daughter was in an ecstasy that deserved anything but mockery. She felt in herself the hunger to be made of simpler elements, to welcome the rain on its own terms. To receive it without thought, to take its caress without consciousness.

"Perfect," Goss said—not of what his eyes saw, peering contentedly into the depths without perspective in the heart of the rain, but of the moment, of which the rain was a part like himself.

"Too beautiful to lose," Susan said. "I want it too."

"It always comes again," her husband said drowsily. He accepted Susan's arm, sliding behind his head, her palm lying against his cheek, her fingertips brushing his beard with a delicacy that seemed imitated from the rain itself.

The heaviness of his body, the heaviness of his long, great life, reclined against the small bones of her shoulder. She felt the familiarity of his breathing as his ribs flexed and slowly closed over the cavern where his heart beat. And she wanted him with the same mindless passion as she and Tamisan had wanted the rain. She wanted him within her, totally within, to match the whisper of ecstasy with the shouting ecstasy of nerves that came with full possession. She felt something like the urgency of the rain in her breasts and loins and turned her face to hide its flush in the cover of his beard.

Tamisan, sitting a little apart from them, uttered a faint, involuntary cry as she half turned to see them nestling together. The sound came from far down in her throat, as of something wakening, not yet certain of its whereabouts or welcome.

To Susan, her breasts seemed loud. As if both the others must hear them over the steady music of the rain, hear their need and their supplication. She felt Goss's weight shift a little as he knew what was happening and responded. He put his big left hand on her leg and left it there. Motionless, undemanding, unbearable without motion to complete what was begun. Her throat was too swollen to speak for a moment, and she thought, Now it's got to happen and it must not.

It was the mindless, obscure voice in the rain that asked, *Why not?*

Susan had nothing to tell herself except that it was the rain which prompted her then. In a minute she said, "I'm going to the house."

"Yes," her husband said. "Yes."

She stirred to get up, freeing her leg from the tickling weight of his hand as she moved. His fingers closed around her ankle as she got to her feet. She could feel his pulse surge faster in his fingers as they clutched her. "Yes," he said. "Yes. I'll come with you."

She could not bring herself to look at Tamisan. But it was not shame that kept her eyes averted, though the girl could have no doubt of the passion she was submitting to. It was sheer acceptance of the necessity of the moment, to the overwhelming glory that might be squandered unless she submitted perfectly.

"No," she said. "Stay with her."

Still his grip held her ankle. She thought he was waiting for her to take back her offer, to change her mind. And she wanted to cry to him that she didn't want a mind. She wanted the truth.

She felt him let go her ankle. She knew he had heard her.

"You heard her say what she wants," she murmured without opening her eyes. "You heard as well as I. Give it to her."

As she left them there together, she said again, "I'll go to the house. I'll be there."

The rain was still falling in modest cadences as Tamisan sat alone that night amid the paraphernalia of Goss's painting in the barn loft studio. She had brought her guitar with her when she slipped out of the house, and the poor thing was likely to warp from its moistening. She had not tried it to see if it was already going out of tune. From time to time she had run her fingers along the tight strings to test their readiness.

She waited patiently, knowing that either her mother or her mother's husband would have to come looking for her presently.

She thought she was ready with what she had to say to either of them. But she felt she could only say it once, and it would have to be passed on from one of them to another after she was gone. It did not occur to her that they might come seeking her together after what had happened in the afternoon.

It made no difference that it was Goss's steps she heard climbing the wooden stairs as he came in. But though she was ready to say her say, she put up her arm to protect and hide her eyes when he turned on a lamp beside his easel. She was not ready yet to look at his face.

After a while she said, "Well, we've done this, too. Now I'll have to go away somewhere on my own. But now I can. You know it's what I always wanted. From that time you came up the stairs in Paris, anyway. But I never wanted you to think I was a frivolous woman."

"You'll stay with Susan and me. We need each other."

She shook her head in wild refusal. "I won't. It was right this afternoon. I knew for once it was right. Because of the rain. I wanted it and I had it. It's what I was born for. There are things like that that happen and nobody has to explain. Jason's right. There are things that are immortal. I couldn't be that close to you and Susan and Jason all the time. Everything was together. It wouldn't be if I stayed. I thought I'd go tonight. After one of you'd given me my lecture."

He said nothing. She felt his patience enclosing her, as if he had sealed up the corridors of her escape. "You can't keep me. I'll jump out the window if I have to."

Again he didn't answer. She panicked, thinking, It's not fair that I have to do the talking. *They're* supposed to be the sensible ones.

"It can't be," she said. "It's too weird. It's farther out than anything Jason and I ever got into."

"It's very simple."

"It comes down like rain!" she scoffed. But she saw that scoffing could not gain her anything, and she meant to get away from here without losing anything either.

"I told you it was what I was born for," she pleaded. "It

couldn't go on being that way. If I don't get away I'll destroy you or Susan. Or both. I killed the baby."

"No."

The old habit of rebellion flared in her. "You don't know everything. I wasn't *frivolous,* but I was worse."

"There's nothing worse."

"Well, not for a woman," she said without exactly knowing what she was agreeing to. "I didn't kill the baby. What I am killed him. What I did to his imagination. Jason's, I mean. I don't know what I mean. Jason thought he'd already given the baby to death when he gave it to me. He thought you wanted him to die when you made him come down here to the farm with me. See how tangled it got? How will you straighten it?"

"Life isn't straight."

"Pour fatherly wisdom on me? You're not my father. *Now.*"

"I'm not your father. Husband," he said gravely.

She tried to laugh that off too. "Some kind of Mormon? Well, I always liked the idea. It won't work."

"Husband," he repeated.

It may have been the word itself that betrayed her. Why couldn't he stick to his painting and leave words to other professionals? The word, all by itself, set off something strange— but all too familiar—in her lower body. "You're trying to trick me by making me hot," she said. "Other people fucked my mind."

Then she said with a wail, "It would be just like Jason to tell me this is *all right.*"

"I think so."

"With the two of you after me. . . . Yeah, but what does Susan say?"

He did not answer her lightly or at once. Finally he said, "Susan's as afraid as you are."

"You're not afraid of the two of us?"

He could answer this more quickly. "No."

"She's afraid . . . but what'd she actually say?"

"She believes I need you."

"For your work, or . . . ?"

"For everything. It all goes together. She wants you for me."

"She's not enough for you?"

"Sometimes too much. Not every day is a feast."

She nodded this away without argument. "If I stayed . . . No. This afternoon'd better be enough for me. If I stayed with you I'd want everything. A child, too. I do. I did want it. Children. As many as came. I'd want to be wild and for you to be wild with me and I'd show you things . . . I can't control myself, so it wouldn't work even if Susan believes it could."

"It will work as long as we want it to," he said. "But if you— or Susan—didn't trust each other and yourselves, you shouldn't trust me. She's ready to gamble, that's all. I don't think the jealousy could start from her. There doesn't have to be any of that if we are true to what we've been shown."

"How can I promise anything right now? I never learned how to share or even keep track. Which of us would you sleep with tonight?"

"You."

"You make me crazier inside than I ever was. What if I said, sometime, 'Send Susan away'?"

"I wouldn't do that."

She nodded with a secretive smile of satisfaction. "But when you . . . we . . . go back to North Atlantic . . . I can't see what we'd do there or under various circumstances. What Fiona thinks of me is very important. I couldn't stand it if she thought I'd done something crooked again. She stood by me once."

"I believe she's already accepted it. She knew Jason wouldn't stay. No doubt I knew it too. Fiona has always—always—kept up appearances so she won't have to set limits on crucial things. There will have to be lies about unimportant things to unimportant people. To keep the way open for what we can make of what we've been given. She knows us better than you suppose."

Again an anguish of uncertainty gripped the girl. "I love you and Susan both. I'll do what you need me to. Why should I be afraid if you're not? But there's Jason to think about." She was struggling hard to adjust desire and responsibility. "I said he might think this was all right. You said once that if Maggie was calling him it wouldn't be to any harm. Do you believe that still?"

"I need your help to believe it."

"I thought I was helping him all last year. If the baby'd lived
. . . But having the baby was just a make-believe for us like so
much else we did. We got all twisted up in our make-believes.
All the time I was with him I never knew what was *so* and what
was only made up and exciting to believe. I don't know if he was
a god or a little boy or a saint or really sick."

Goss took her hand and lifted her to her feet. He led her down
the creaking wooden steps and out of the barn. They went
across the wet lawn toward the house where Susan would be
waiting for them. The smell of the rainy wind blew through the
orchard. It smelled like the flood that had drowned all the past
and where, eventually, they might be drowned with others.

"This is so," he said.